D1555241

Hopeless Magic

The Star-Crossed Series

Volume Two

Rachel Higginson

Hopeless Magic
The Star-Crossed Series
By Rachel Higginson

Editing services provided by Jennifer Nunez.

Printed in paperback May 2012 and available in Kindle and E-book format as of May 2012 through Amazon, Create Space and Barnes & Noble.

To my children who inspire me daily,
You are the reason I write, the reason I publish.

To Zach, the inspiration for every Great Love
I will ever write. Thank you for believing in me.

To my mother, my biggest fan and loving mentor,
Thank you for the babysitting, the advice and the support.

The light of the camp fire burned low, the embers glowing in the utter darkness only found in the secret places far from civilization. The woman let her endless black hair fall over her shoulders and cover her bare arms. She leaned in closer to her husband, braving the cold mountain air, not daring to use magic.

This was the last night they would stay here, and they had made this fire to say goodbye. The conversation had dwindled with the fire. The tone had turned serious and there were important questions that had been put off until now. Questions that needed answering.

"And where will you go next?" the black man asked in his thick Caribbean accent from across the fire. He was an old friend, but even old friends could not be trusted these days.

"We don't know," she answered honestly. She hadn't known the answer to that question in a long time, too long to remember.

"Will you go to them?" the black man pressed, reaching for a long, worn walking stick that he used to stir the small flames of the leftover fire.

"No, not yet," her husband answered. "It's not time for that yet."

"There is word that maybe an alliance will be made, between your people and theirs," the black man stated, his eyes narrowed in suspicion. He had a name, but it was rarely used, only by those that had known him since the beginning and even they used the title in whispered tones.

"They are not our people," the woman whispered fiercely. "Do not make the mistake of linking us with them, for their sakes."

"Yes, yes, I suppose," he replied quickly, moving the black, ashy logs around, staring at the cinders.

"And what will you do?" the husband asked, leaning forward conspiratorially. He was used to secrecy, used to whispering plans and artfully cryptic messages.

"I will do what I always do. Survive." the black man's gray eyes clouded with memories of different times and the woman thought they lost him to the painful past.

"Will you help them, should they ask?" the other man

pressed.

"No," the black man said simply. "I have been drawn in before and my people are the ones who suffer. The old man has done his best, but he is not enough. The magic is too binding, there is no hope. We must do what we can with our freedom here and if they come, rebuild somewhere else. But no, I will not help them. Not again."

"Yes," the woman whispered sympathetically, "Your people have suffered too much. Of course it is better to stay out of it."

The black man grunted an amused, short laugh. He had not expected empathy, but the woman hardly ever did anything people expected. "But you will help this time?" he asked, although it was barely a question. He was accusing them.

"This time is different," the man looked down at his wife and tensed with the foreboding wisdom that a war was imminent. And that this time they would not be capable of escaping the call to fight.

"Yes, yes. I suppose it is," the black man had settled back down into the pensive ancient he was. "I should like to meet them, these children that call you out of anonymity."

"You will not find them hiding here, behind your mountains and isolation," the man put his arm, protectively around his wife; it was dangerous to provoke this man who carried the weight of a hunted people on his shoulders.

"We shall see," he smiled into the face of the fire.

"What do you know?" the woman asked in a panicked voice. "What have you seen?"

"Ah, and now I know the reason for your visit."

"That is not true," she retracted, defensively. "Only you reference the future, and I cannot help but.... You must understand...." she trailed off, hardly able to explain her deep hunger to know how this would end.

"It is dangerous to know the future, is it not? Too many variables, too many moving pieces to know anything for sure," the black man chided.

"If they come, will you welcome them?" the woman changed the subject, her carnal need to protect overwhelming her.

"I will not know until they come," the black man replied cryptically.

"She saved one of your kind," the husband spoke up again.

"Yes, those are the whispers that blow into this camp," the black man looked up from the fire into the eyes of the woman. Her onyx eyes were darker than his and they had a profoundness about them that unsettled the average eye; the eye that didn't understand the depth of her suffering or the completeness of her love.

"Will you help them?" she asked again, in a low voice that was not to be ignored.

"The question is not if I will help them, but if you will," the black man countered, standing up from the fire.

"Thank you for your hospitality," her husband recognized the end of the conversation and stood also, extending his hand across the extinguishing flames. "We will meet again."

"Yes we will," the black man whispered, walking backward into the trees that surrounded their meeting place.

His skin blended with the midnight sky and he was gone, the loud roar of a jungle cat the only sound echoing in the darkness.

The man looked down at his wife, reaching out to her and pulling her to him. "It is time to end this," he whispered into her ear, through her thick, black hair.

"Not yet," she said firmly, calling on those ancient skills that had been passed down to her through the blood of her father.

Chapter One

"Eden, pay attention," Avalon pulled my thoughts out of a daydream and grudgingly brought me back to the Romania debriefing. Thirty pairs of eyes turned to stare in my direction, after my twin brother embarrassingly called my name.

I turned my head sharply in his direction and glared. I felt bad enough the debriefing centered mostly on me, there was no need to bring more negative attention my way. It was not like I wasn't paying attention at all; I mean, the whole weird twin channel that connected my mind with Avalon's was keeping me caught up. I just wasn't giving the meeting my entire interest.

"So, despite some major setbacks," Avalon continued his debriefing with another aggravated glance my way, "we were able to extract the team safely. Please join me in welcoming Jett, Ebanks, Oscar and Ronan."

The entire room turned to smile and clap for the young team that was held captive for almost two months. The men, all in their beginning twenties, smiled and acknowledged their fellow Immortals, but didn't return the same congeniality. They looked exhausted, their eyes were sunken in and their heads hung as if they were too heavy to hold.

Although they could not have been more culturally diverse, they shared the same Immortal magic that ran through the rest of our veins. Only theirs had been drained…. by me.

I sat in the center of a room full of Immortals that referred to themselves as the Resistance. In the middle of Nebraska cornfields, on a classic Midwestern farm, and on a cliché hay bale located in the back of a tractor barn perpendicular to a field of horses; I watched my fellow Immortals, magic coursing through our blood in unison, and felt completely out of place.

I had kept my distance thus far from the rescued team, afraid to even look them in the eye. Since not one of them had even attempted to glance in my direction either, it was pretty safe to say they were not exactly ready to make amends. I had nothing against them personally, but the fact that I was the reason they were locked up in a Romanian prison over the last few months and tortured unscrupulously hadn't exactly broken the ice between us.

Had I known who they actually were last September, I might not have opened my field of magic so drastically on them, but I couldn't actually say that for sure. They did after all make an attempt on Kiran's life.

I would never have been able to sit back and watch another Immortal take the life of the man I loved beyond measure. But as it were, I was still in the dark about the Resistance at that time; I was even clueless that I was fighting against my own twin brother, the only Resistance member able to walk away from that fight.

I stared self-consciously in the direction of Ebanks Camara. He sat tall, above the rest of his team, his midnight skin, once smooth and perfect now etched with scar tissue tracing jagged lines across his body. His eyes never left the barn floor, his expression remained stoic. My heart stung with the pain of guilt and I blamed myself for his obvious lethargy.

I could still feel the current of electricity run through the rescued team's blood, but it was slow and faint, as if struggling to survive. Once, Amory told me I drained them of their magic; I realized now that I didn't know exactly what that meant or if they would ever be restored. A sinking feeling formed in my stomach and I suddenly wanted to help them, I wanted to repair the damage I alone was responsible for.

Amory's strong hand on my shoulder brought me out of my regret and I looked up at him with pain in my eyes. He patted his hand reassuringly on my shoulder, as if he could feel my hurt and the simple gesture accomplished his intention. I felt hope, knowing that Amory was on my side.

Amory, my grandfather…. It sounded weird to say "grandfather." I had only known the truth for a couple of weeks and I found it hard to believe that the last few months had not only revealed my true identity and nature, but brought me both a brother and a grandfather.

For sixteen years I had assumed my only living relative was my Aunt Syl. Little did I know she was not even blood related. Not only was she not really my aunt, but we were not even the same species. She was, of course, human like most others on the planet. I was however something more, something my people called "Immortal." Although as it turned out that didn't actually mean we would live forever. Instead "Immortal" referred more to longevity of life and supernatural abilities.

Immortal wasn't always a watered down word to my people. I had been told that once we did seem as though we would live forever; but when the Immortals elected a King everything changed. But that happened way before I came along, like thousands of years before I came along.

After the first King, Derrick, was crowned, he banned intermarriage between the four species of Immortals and initiated the first deaths by killing Immortals in their sleep through a method called Dream Walking. Since then, only one lineage has ruled, and I have been told they only continue to worsen our existence.

I had yet to determine my stance on that whole issue since I happened to be madly in love with the next King in line for the throne. His father might be a bad guy, but I held hope that Kiran Kendrick would change things for the better.

Until I could prove this however, I would sit and be a party to the Resistance. Especially since my best friend, Lilly, was rescued from imprisonment, just for being a Shape-Shifter. I couldn't, in good conscience, agree with the current policies of the Monarchy.

Although, I believed without a doubt that for now I was on the right side of everything moral; I held doubts if joining the Resistance officially was the right move. Despite pressure from not only Amory, but Avalon and my aunt as well, I still refused to join an organization bent on the destruction of Kiran. So I waited.

"So for right now, we are going to put any assassination attempts on hold," Avalon's subject change drew me back into the meeting. I could hear the disappointment in his voice and I found it sadistically comical that he was frustrated he wouldn't be trying to kill my boyfriend anymore…. only Avalon. "Since the Crown Prince played such a pivotal role in the release of Lilly Mason, and Eden's escape, Amory has decided that we should see how things play out." Again, Avalon said the words with a thick layer of sadness and I shook my head at him angrily. He chose to ignore me.

"That's right, Avalon. For right now we will simply be monitoring him very closely. If circumstances change, or he becomes a threat to this organization, then we will reevaluate; but for right now it appears as though he is smitten with my granddaughter and she appears to feel the same way," Amory's authoritative voice educated the room on what I had hoped to remain a secret from these people. Heat rose to my cheeks instantly when most of the room turned to give me disapproving stares.

"So what is our next move then? The King?" Jericho Bentley asked in a very businesslike tone. I was always surprised at the seeming disregard for human life from members of the Resistance. To some extent I realized that their goal in destroying one life was to save the lives of every other Immortal. But the brutality of murder was something I could not take lightly, no matter who the victim was.

"I've been thinking this over, and although that is an objective I would truly like to achieve, too many have already been captured. I am not willing to wage war yet. If we make an attempt on Lucan's life and fail, the consequences would be dire. If we succeed I am unsure how the son will handle our involvement. For right now we will train, and recruit. Of course we will run surveillance both here and in London constantly, but we need to be smart. The Prince is not naïve to our existence. If he fears we are a threat to his family then it would be the end of everything we have worked for," Amory had a melodic tone to his deep voice, the entire room listened unfailingly to him and I had no doubt that they would also follow through with his commands to the smallest detail.

"Will any of us be going to London?" Jericho asked a follow up question. I found myself staring at him, but he never once looked my way. I thought I could consider him a friend, but he hadn't said one word to me since we returned home from Romania.

His distance had peaked my interest in an irritating way. He stood, leaning against a wall, wearing blue jeans and a gray hooded sweatshirt with a baseball cap sitting low on his forehead. His hair had been long in Romania, but sometime after we returned home, he had cut it very short. He was attractive, like every other Immortal, but something about his quiet demeanor was more mysterious and maybe a little dangerous.

"Titus, Xander and Xavier will be meeting the Morocco, South Africa and India teams in London to run point there," Amory answered Jericho. "Other teams will be joining us here as well, the Brazil team, the Swiss team, and most likely the Czech Republic team if I can convince Ryder he is needed. We are going to up security and surveillance here enormously, while still doing our best to remain discreet."

"Fantastic," Jericho mumbled sarcastically. I realized I was not the only one confused by his frustration. He looked up suddenly, apparently not meaning to have said anything out loud. He glanced in my direction, and although his face was marked by embarrassment I noticed a hardness in his expression when our eyes met and I was only more confused.

"All right, if that is everything, then I suppose we are finished," Avalon clapped his hands together, before stretching his arms wide. Tonight had been very long, I was not the only one exhausted by the amount of information we covered in the last five hours.

"Wait, I have a something to say," Lilly, who had been sitting perfectly still beside me for the entire meeting stood up suddenly, speaking confidently. The room of Immortals paused all activity to hear what this shy, timid girl had to say. "I would like to join you. I mean, become one of you." Lilly continued bravely. My mouth dropped open in surprise.

"Lilly, do you understand what the Resistance asks of you? Do you understand the commitment you are making?" Amory asked Lilly seriously. She nodded animatedly, her vibrant red curls bouncing frantically. "And do you understand the process in which the magic is applied? It is not an easy undertaking."

"Avalon explained everything to me. I still want to join. I have to. He's holding my parents. You don't understand," Lilly's words fell out in a rush of nervous excitement and her voice cracked from emotion.

I found myself holding back tears at the mention of her parents who still sat in a Romanian prison waiting for the day Lilly would graduate from high school. Although Kiran was able to argue Lilly's release from prison, Lucan wouldn't grant any of Kiran's other terms without compromise. Lilly was only allowed to attend Kingsley while Kiran was also there, if her parents were held as collateral. She would have gladly dropped out of school to save her parents the pain, but the bargain had already been made. She was also a prisoner in Omaha.

"Lilly, I understand," Amory replied with equaled sorrow. "We won't wait; you may join tonight as I suspect was your hope. Angelica, please prepare the magic." Amory addressed an elderly

15

woman, with kind, violet eyes. The woman who would appear in her seventies or eighties, although I knew was hundreds of years older than that, quickly stood and left the barn.

I looked at my friend wringing her pale hands in her lap. I could see that she was nervous, but I also saw the fierce determination set in her eyes. Lilly was infinitely braver than me to be so sure this was the step she wanted to take. I envied her for a second, hating my indecision and middle-ground position. As I felt her magic flare with unwavering resolve, I realized that I could not stand in the middle for long. Someday soon I would have to make a final decision, and without a doubt, that decision would set me on a journey of fate shaping, not only mine, but the destiny of the entire Immortal race.

Chapter Two

"You'll come with me, won't you Eden?" Lilly whispered nervously. Her soft voice trembled and I noticed her hands were clenched together so tightly that her knuckles had turned white.

"Of course I will," I tried to sound reassuring, without actually knowing if I could keep my promise.

To be honest I was almost as nervous as she was. The little I had heard about the initiation into the Resistance did not sound easy. Avalon explained some things to Lilly once we returned from Romania. She had a thousand questions, and although he said he couldn't go into too much detail, he did say it was an extremely painful process. He related something about adding to the magic in your body, changing it somehow, and then branding it in a way to bond the initiate specifically with the rest of the Resistance.

I inhaled a big breath to focus my nerves. The rest of the Resistance sat together in anxious clumps. The frenzied energy circling the barn tonight testified they were obviously excited that another Immortal would be joining their ranks.

I glanced at the rescued team members sitting off by themselves in a quiet corner of the metal barn. They maintained their slouched postures and hanging heads. Most of the gathered Immortals had paid their respects, including Lilly, who I was realizing, shared a common thread after living in captivity with them for over two months.

Lilly stared at them as well. Oscar Rodriguez glanced at her with a half-smile on his face. It wasn't much, but it was the most of an expression I had seen from any of them. He gestured at her with his hand to join them, but she hesitated, uncertainty flashing across her face.

"Are you, um, are you going to give them their magic back?" Lilly asked in a shaky voice. I couldn't tell if she was nervous to ask the question or if she was still nervous from her impending induction.

"What do you mean?" I asked mortified. "I didn't realize that was an option!" I continued to shriek dramatically. I had been told that I drained them of their magic, but I hadn't been told I could give it back. Does that mean that I've been holding on to stolen magic this whole time? Or using it? I shuddered at the thought of using someone else's magic; it seemed like a gross invasion of privacy.

"Eden, what is the problem?" Amory joined our circle of two, concern marking his expression. He laid one hand strongly on my shoulder, in a gesture that had become familiar to me whenever Amory wanted me to calm down.

"Amory is it possible for me to give those boys their magic back? Have I been holding on to it this entire time?" I demanded, crossing my arms stubbornly.

"Well, yes you have," Amory laughed genially. I scowled at him, frustrated. I didn't necessarily blame him, but I always felt one step behind…. More than one step. I never knew what was going on. I had never, not once, regretted my human up-bringing, but this was seriously getting out of control.

"Then how do I give it back?" I didn't lose my frustrated tone.

"Eden, if that is what you would like to do, then, of course, you can give them their magic back," Amory replied soothingly.

"Why didn't you tell me sooner?" I whined. "I feel awful for holding on to something that's not mine for so long. Look at them. They look miserable."

"Not miserable," Amory continued softly. "Tired, exhausted, like they've just been through hell, but not miserable. They asked me not to make a big deal about it. I think they hoped you would give it back to them, but they can't force you. You alone have to make the choice." Something about the last thing Amory said struck a chord, and I realized he was not only referring to the rescued team's magic.

"Of course I want to. It's not mine. I shouldn't have taken it in the first place," I hung my head, ashamed. I wished I knew what I was doing more than just some of the time.

"All right, Eden, do you know how to give them their magic back?" Amory began walking in their general direction and I noticed all of them struggle to sit up straighter and put on a smile. They stared at Amory with a sort of hero-worship that made me proud to be his granddaughter.

"How could I possibly know that?" I blurted out, a little over dramatically.

19

"Oh," Amory sighed, sounding a little defeated.

"Oh," Lilly echoed Amory's concerned tone.

"What do you mean.... oh?" I stopped dead in my tracks, afraid I wasn't the only one who was out of their league in this particular situation.

"Well, I'm sure it will be fine," Amory put on a smile again, finally approaching the team. "Boys, once again I would like to say how wonderful it is to have you all back, safe and sound. I would like to introduce you to Eden, my granddaughter; although I'm afraid you've already met. She is here to try and restore your magic if you're up for the challenge." I instantly saw light behind all four boys' eyes; clearly they would be up for any challenge that resulted in returning their magic.

"Ok, so what do I have to do?" I asked Amory, hoping he would have some kind of answer for me.

"That is an excellent question, Eden. Why don't you work with these boys and try to figure the process out while I check with Angelica to see how Lilly's induction ceremony is coming," he smiled sheepishly and turned quickly on his heel to retreat.

"Are you telling me you don't know what I am supposed to do?" I called after him, demanding an answer. It seemed beyond impossible that Amory of all people wouldn't know how to solve this problem.

"I'm sorry, dearest. The process is different for each person. Besides what you did hasn't actually ever been accomplished before, and certainly not by me. So I'm afraid I don't know what to tell you," he explained while walking backwards hands waving apologetically in the air, and then he left the barn in search of Angelica.

"What does he mean it's never been done before?" I turned on the rescued team and Lilly crossing my arms again and stamping my foot frustrated.

"It's been done before, Eden." Lilly tried to reassure me. "Not four Immortals at once, but the Titans used to take people's magic all of the time, back when the Monarchy first began. But then usually those people, just.... died. I think the whole issue is actually returning the magic and, of course, making sure you give the right person the right magic," she smiled again with confidence, but a ball dropped in my stomach and I realized for the first time what was at risk.

"Ok...." I cleared my throat with instinctive nervousness. "So how do you guys suggest I go about this?" I looked pleadingly at the rescued team, open to any and all suggestions.

"We could try one at a time...." Jett Fisher suggested, while subtly nudging Ebanks in the back with his elbow.

"Be my guest," Ebanks responded with his low, melancholy voice.

"I thought you guys wanted your magic back," I was confused. I thought the rescued team would want nothing more than to have their magic restored, but now that the opportunity was in front of them, it would appear none of them was willing to try. Or maybe none of them was willing to try with me. I couldn't really blame them for not trusting me. After all, I was the one who got them in this mess to begin with.

"Well, it's just that," Ronan Hannigan began with a shaky Irish accent, "it's just that, when you took our magic we assumed you were going to kill us, or at least knew how to give it back." He finished his sentence by hanging his head and I watched as my inexperience and lack of knowledge only discouraged them more.

"I wish that were true," I replied, just as distraught as them. "But the truth is, I didn't know what I was doing then and it would appear that I still have no idea what I'm doing now." Once again the four hurting boys could not look me in the eye and I was struck with an overwhelming sense of guilt. "We could always try though, couldn't we?" I fought for optimism, hoping it would spread.

"What if you give us the wrong magic?" Ebanks questioned.

"Yeah, or what if you can't give the magic back at all?" Ronan's fiery Irish accent was less than enthusiastic.

"Or what if you finish the job?" Jett mumbled underneath his breath.

"Ok, I get that we are all scared here. I'm scared of those very same things. Or, um, some of them anyway." Especially now, since I didn't know those were real possibilities, but I didn't say that to the team. "But are you happy with the way things are now?" I looked at the four seemingly strong Immortals, with their heads hung low and their shoulders slumped. They shook their heads wearily. "Then I say we try this, if it doesn't work, it doesn't work, but I can't imagine that you would want to stay the way you are for the rest of eternity. And for God's sakes Jett, I'm not going to kill anybody!" I ended my lecture with a flare of the dramatic. My speech had the desired effect and all four boys struggled to sit up a little straighter.

"Ok, I'll try," Oscar, who was silent through most of the debate, stood up confidently.

Oscar walked out of the tight circle the rescued team had been sitting in and faced me. He stared at me for a few seconds as if trying to read something on my face. Suddenly he held out his hands as if I should take them. Apparently he trusted me. It was time I trusted myself.

I reached out and clenched his hands in mine. I barely felt a magical pulse underneath his sweaty palms and I could only imagine the exhaustion he must have been feeling. Oscar closed his eyes tightly as if afraid of what would come next. I followed suit, but only to achieve better concentration.

Or so I told myself.

The longer I held Oscar's hands, the more my magic surprisingly began to stir. Something deep inside of me, almost as if there was magic in the most secret part of my soul, began to move. The hidden magic as it were, did its best to surface, while my body fought to keep the magic locked away. Unwillingly, my magic struggled to suppress Oscar's and locked it deep inside again. I inhaled sharply, feeling the struggle in every fiber of my being. I pushed the magic with my mind toward the surface of my body and into the palms of my hands. Oscar's magic felt freedom and soared with him so close. My magic continued to bury the stolen energy back into the recesses of my soul. Although I fought with my mind, the magic that filled my blood was too strong and I was unable to release to Oscar what I had stolen from him.

In one last effort to force Oscar's magic out of my skin I thrust my magic and everything I had into my palms. Suddenly we were flying through the air. Our bodies flung forcefully like rag dolls to opposite sides of the barn. We landed in painful clumps on the concrete floor.

I heard Oscar groan and I jumped to my feet in an effort to see if he was all right. My magic had already finished healing my own body, but I could tell from where I stood, just inside the open double doors, that what was left of Oscar's magic had not been able to revive him. The rest of his team and Lilly had flocked to his side and were helping him sit up. He held his head and when he brought his hand away I saw that it was covered in dark, crimson blood.

I turned around, frustrated and unable to look at him. I felt helpless and responsible. Any other Immortal would know what to do; any other Immortal would have had the training necessary to be able to return the magic that didn't belong to them.

I walked out of the barn into the cold night air. A thousand stars shone down on me, stretching on eternally through the wide Nebraska sky. I wrapped my arms around my body, holding in the warmth, refusing to use the magic that had me so frustrated at the moment.

"You'll figure out how to give it back, these things take time," Jericho was suddenly at my side. I turned to stare at him, surprised by his comforting words, but he was looking at the ground, his baseball cap pulled low on his brow.

"I hope you're right," I winced. I couldn't bear to send another one of that poor team flying. "What does it feel like?" he finally glanced at me from underneath his hat.

"Trying to give the magic back?" I asked, unsure if I wanted to share the feeling. Jericho nodded an affirmative. "It feels like I don't want to give it back. I didn't even know I had been holding on to their magic, but now that I've found it, it's like my body will do anything to keep it."

"Will you keep it?" Jericho asked tentatively. He was the third person to ask me this question. What kind of person did these people think I was?

"Of course not," I spat, and then regretted my tone immediately. "I mean, of course I want to give it back to them. It's not mine; I should never have taken it in the first place. I just didn't know what I was doing then. I still don't.... I will find a way though. I will give them back their magic," I said determined, and at that moment I realized just how determined I was.

"Others would not give it back. In fact, if you are successful, you would make history by returning their magic," he smiled softly at me and I noticed the hardness in his eyes slowly dissipating.

"What do you mean?" I asked, impressed by the prospect of making history, but a little more daunted by the task at hand.

"Other Immortals have drained magic before, but usually

23

they do it on purpose," he smirked at me, enjoying his sarcasm. "However, since they accomplish the task on purpose, that has tended to mean they refuse to give it up. I have just always thought they were greedy and power-hungry, but maybe they couldn't have given up the magic if they wanted," he looked back down at the ground and kicked a rock, making it skip along the gravel drive.

"Who?" I asked, but believed I already knew the answer.

"The Monarchy, of course, and their Titan Guard," he smiled sadly at me and I was struck by the perfection of his lips.

"Oh. I can see that though. I mean just now, when I was trying to give Oscar back his magic there was such a hunger inside of me to keep it, I was scared. I don't want their magic; I only want to give it back to them. But I was overcome by this, this overwhelming greed. I know more than ever it does not belong inside of me. I will do whatever it takes to give it back to them," I folded my arms defiantly, as if inwardly challenging myself to finish the task.

"You do deserve to be Queen," Jericho whispered and I was surprised by his words, I turned to say something to him, but could not think of anything appropriate. So instead of speaking I simply stared into his eyes, searching for the reason behind his statement.

"Eden, Angelica says the magic is ready. Will you still come with me?" Lilly's soft voice called to me from the barn doors and I turned without saying anything more to Jericho. I walked to Lilly's side and joined her for the biggest moment of her life thus far.

Chapter Three

I followed Lilly through the other side of the barn and around the large white farmhouse. A small group of other Immortals walked silently with us. All of them were the older generation except Avalon, whom I noticed was allowed more of a leadership role than anyone else our age, including me.

Angelica led our small group behind the farmhouse and down into a storm cellar. Lilly and I followed Conrad, Terrance, Amory and Avalon down a set of worn stone steps. The men all carried fiery torches and as we walked through a surprisingly long tunnel, they stopped and lit suspended torches along the wall.

What I expected to be a typical Nebraska tornado shelter, meant to protect from seasonal storms, had turned into a long, but wide tunnel, leading further and further into the earth. The already cold November night continued to stiffen the frigid air the farther into the passageway we walked.

Lilly's hand in mine, I could feel her tremble with anxiety. The look on her face was sheer determination, etched with near panicked hysteria. Her already pale skin had turned translucent by fear and her vibrant red curls framed her face in a haze of frizz. I squeezed her hand, hoping to comfort, except I couldn't help but empathize her same fears.

Eventually we came to a thick stone door. The small group ahead of us mounted their torches into frames already nailed to the walls. Through the dim firelight I could see small markings bordering the outline of the door and then another large symbol set exactly in the middle at eye level: a snake, wrapped in a circle, swallowing its own tail.

Angelica was the first one through the door. She put her finger, just below her ear, where her jawbone met her neck, and I watched the faint flare of light. I realized she was illuminating the same symbol of the snake eating its own tail, the same symbol Lilly was on her way to receive. Angelica carried the magic in her finger, from her neck to the symbol on the door. She placed her index finger ever so softly on the serpent and I watched with quiet awe as the door glowed in the same color as Angelica's magic before opening into a circular room.

The door closed behind Angelica. Conrad was next in line. He repeated the same procedure as Angelica, only this time the door illuminated in army green, to resemble the type of magic he carried. I realized at that moment that I may not be able to keep my promise to Lilly and stay with her through the whole process, since it seemed to enter the secret room of the Resistance one must already be a member or on their way to become one.

I squeezed Lilly's hand tighter as I watched Terrance and then Avalon both enter the room. Amory turned towards us, his expression one of pure excitement. He held out his hand to Lilly and she accepted the offer silently.

"I'm afraid you won't be able to join us, Eden dear, unless you are also willing to become a part of our humble cause tonight," I saw the hope in his black eyes and felt ashamed when I shook my head no.

"Then you must wait out here," his smile softened into a sadder version of happiness. I was struck with guilt. Some small part of me understood that I could not waver in the middle much longer. Sooner or later I would have to make a choice: I would have to join a cause that would eventually lead to the death of the person I loved with all of my soul, or I would have to turn my back on this cause and alienate myself entirely from the only family I would ever have.

I squeezed Lilly's hand one more time before letting go and gave her an encouraging smile. She returned my smile with renewed confidence and I suddenly felt envious. Her brilliant emerald eyes shone with sheer determination and something more, something much like victory. Then, Amory was lighting the door and I watched them disappear behind the thick wall of stone.

Can I watch? I spoke to my twin brother telepathically, hoping he would understand my need to be involved. Although I could have easily opened our twin sense and made the decision for myself, I felt obligated to ask Avalon for his permission. I had a hard time invading his privacy unannounced. He, on the other hand, had absolutely no problem spying on me.

As long as you don't interrupt. Avalon replied, slightly exasperated. I loved my brother dearly, but when he was in super commando-leader mode, I couldn't help but find him more than a little irritating.

I leaned against the cool stone wall in the wide passageway. On this side of the door the torches flickered, casting long shadows on the rough floor. I closed my eyes and melted my mind with Avalon's, opening my senses with our similar magic. I saw through his eyes, heard through his ears and felt through his senses.

Although my vision was limited to what Avalon was looking at, I could still take in the room. The space behind the thick stone door was smaller than I had imagined it to be. A large, worn wooden chair sat in a circular area, illuminated only by candle light. Hundreds of tiered candles sat on long, low tables circling the rooms. They took up most of the wall space, except where a door was located.

There were four other doors besides the stone one blocking my path. They were wooden, not made from stone; however, the same symbolic snake crested them as well. A deep pot of sorts sat not far from the lone chair that Lilly had now taken. The large cauldron was full of some type of iridescent liquid and although I couldn't see any fire beneath the pot, it seemed to be bubbling as if boiling.

Avalon stared at Lilly intently. I could see the tension in her eyes and she gripped the arm rests of the chair tightly with both hands. Amory was asking her a series of questions and she nodded confidently despite the terror I could tell she was feeling.

Avalon was also tense; I could feel that he was afraid she would back out. I could feel him admire her beauty, which felt a little bizarre coming from Avalon, and that he would desperately like her to join the cause. In part, but not entirely, he felt that way because he thought Lilly would have influence over me. I smiled from outside of the door, wondering if he was right.

"Lillian Elizabetta Mason, you are about to join a cause that stands directly opposed to the Monarchy and King and if you are found out, the price is your life. Are you sure you want to give up your rights as an Immortal, your eternal life as an Immortal and your fate as an Immortal, surrendering them all under the cause of the Resistance?" Amory asked Lilly gravely.

She responded with a strong "Yes."

"Then, Lilly, through any trial, tribulation, torture and trap, the Resistance will always give you aid, always give you support and always give you sacrifice. You are, little sister, one of us, wholly, and forever."

Amory paused to smile benevolently and reassuringly at Lilly before gesturing toward Conrad and Terrance. They moved towards Lilly in slow, but swift movements, and then began to strap her down with restraints attached to the chair I hadn't noticed before.

I stood up straight, overcome with anxiety for my dear friend. Why on earth would they need to strap her down? She looked like she was about to be electrocuted by some old-school torture tool, something straight out of a fifties era death-row chamber. And, although I could see that Lilly was willfully allowing them to tie her to the chair, and through it all seemed to have significantly calmed down, I could not believe she really understood what she was about to go through.

I began to pace the hallway nervously, doing my best to find a way into that room. If things went badly for Lilly, I refused to do nothing. I did not risk my life to save her in Romania from Lucan, only to bring her back to Omaha and watch her die at the hands of my brother and grandfather.

Calm down. You're so dramatic. Avalon sent me a thought and I inwardly cringed, realizing I had promised not to interrupt him.

You better not hurt her. I seethed through my thoughts, finding it slightly ironic he was the one calling me dramatic. He rolled his eyes, not only inwardly but physically as well.

Eden, the whole process is hurt. She's going to be in a lot of pain in just a few seconds and there is absolutely nothing you can do about it. Just remind yourself that she chose this path, and this path comes with a price. Avalon's words hit a nerve and I was suddenly agitated. I knew that he didn't mean to hurt me, but he was right. She chose this path willingly and there was absolutely nothing I could do about it.

When I tuned back in to the events unfolding beyond the stone door, Lilly was completely buckled down, from the top of her head to the soles of her feet. She looked painfully uncomfortable even if this was her choice. Besides the chair restraints, Conrad, Terrance and Amory had also taken hold of her as if adding to the support of the buckles.

Angelica stood in the corner near the bubbling cauldron of

29

shimmering light. She had put on a pair of long, thick work gloves and held a lengthy, cylindrical glass tube with a bulb on one end and a narrowed point on the other. When Amory nodded his head, Angelica dipped the cylinder into the vessel point-side down. She stirred the flickering illumination around until the tube itself seemed to be full of the same mysterious mixture, something not quite liquid, not quite light.

When the glass bulb itself began to glisten, she pulled the cylinder out of the cauldron. Angelica walked carefully, methodically over to Lilly, holding the glass cylinder by the point. Once she reached her, she took a long moment to breathe and meditate before pressing the bulb against Lilly's neck and jawbone just beneath her right earlobe.

Suddenly I understood the restraints. As soon as the glass tube touched Lilly's skin she let out a blood-curdling scream that engulfed the small room. I covered my ears instinctively, although technically no sound reached beyond the stone door.

Lilly began to thrash aggressively, despite the fact that she had three grown men and numerous buckles holding her down. Her eyes rolled into the back of her head and I could see her seize violently. She continued to scream, loud and menacingly, a sound that would haunt me for a very long time.

Despite Lilly's struggle, Angelica continued to hold the glass cylinder to her neck, never faltering, never moving. I noticed the light inside the tube begin to drain, and Lilly's skin begin to turn a shade of shimmering violet. Her entire being was engulfed in the beautiful lilac, shining and glistening.

If my friend wasn't in so much terrifying pain I would have found the effect absolutely captivating. Unfortunately, despite her beauty, Lilly seemed to be in an insurmountable depth of hurt. She continued to scream and shake long past the last drops of light had drained into her skin.

Suddenly the shimmering lavender intensified into a deep and bright purple, painting everything in the small room with its concentrated color. As quickly as the color grew bright, it diminished into a small snake eating its tail just below the earlobe of Lilly's right ear. And finally there was silence. Lilly slumped, unmoving in her chair.

I relaxed, exhaling a breath I had not realized I was holding.

Apparently my relief was premature; however, as only seconds after Lilly calmed down, she began again with another round of screaming and thrashing. I left Avalon's head unable to withstand the sight of my dear friend enduring so much pain. I cowered against the wall and let out a choking sob.

The door opened slightly and Avalon slipped through to my side of the stone. His face was etched with the same pain that I imagined mine was, minus the tears. He stood facing me with a mixture of sorrow and exhaustion that aged him for a moment. For only a moment, I didn't see my sometimes irritating and always over dramatic twin brother. In his place I saw a great leader, and a great man. I shook my head quickly, reminding myself of the here and now.

"Where is she?" I peered around Avalon, expecting the door to open again at any second.

"She has to stay here for a while. She has to recover," Avalon spoke softly and with compassion.

"What do you mean? We have school," I said plainly, as if the choice Lilly just made shouldn't interfere with high school.

"Lilly won't be able to come to school for a while, Eden. You don't need to worry about her though; she's in very capable hands," Avalon began walking towards the exit and I followed, realizing he was right.

"She will be alright?" I asked timidly. I wanted to trust him, I knew I needed to trust him, but the image of Lilly facing so much physical pain would give me nightmares. I could not imagine willingly going through the same torture myself.

"Of course. I'm just fine, aren't I?" Avalon replied. I held back a sarcastic thought. "Just fine," was pretty relative. "Besides don't you have a rendezvous with what's his name? You'd better forget about Lilly for now, until that kid isn't around anymore. Eden, he can't know anything about her induction, got it?" His compassion had turned into hard lecturing, although I did understand his point.

"I got it," I replied, confident that it wouldn't be a problem, but uncertain Lilly's induction wouldn't cloud my thoughts the rest of the evening, all the same. "And you can use Kiran's name. Amory's not going to kick you out or anything."

Avalon only grunted his reply. We both knew Amory was

31

not the problem. Avalon hated Kiran with a passion and never missed an opportunity to remind me.

Despite Avalon, I blushed at the thought of seeing Kiran tonight. I hadn't seen him alone since before we came home, at his hotel suite in Geneva, Switzerland. Our time there was so intimate and special I had been nervous about seeing him again since.

Kiran sent Talbott over late last night to inform me of our date tonight. Well, I didn't really know if you could call it a date, but we would finally get to be together…. away from school, away from Seraphina and away from Talbott. The horror of Lilly's induction faded quickly when replaced with the sweet thoughts of my upcoming moments with Kiran.

"You mean booty call? I'm coming by the way," Avalon interrupted my daydreams and I stopped dead in my tracks.

"What?" I squealed.

"Eden, seriously?" Avalon turned around to give me his best chastising glare. "Prime surveillance opportunity. Wouldn't miss it for the world." He turned quickly on his heel, leaving me gaping after him. A date with Kiran, might be more than a little awkward if Avalon was planning on chaperoning.

Chapter Four

Kiran's car was already waiting in my driveway by the time Avalon's now dirty truck sped into his designated space. I threw the door open and jumped out as quickly as modesty would allow. Avalon's red four door truck was literally a beast and the cab sat ridiculously high off the ground.

Kiran immediately stepped out of the back seat of his classy, black Rolls Royce with an amused look on his face. Talbott was not far behind him and my heart sunk at the possibility of having not one, but two chaperone's on this impromptu date.

I stood there for a moment, unsure whether I was allowed to leap into his arms, or if we had to play casual until we were in a secured location. I inched slowly closer to the most beautiful man I had ever seen, all the while feeling like a small child trying to get close to something she was specifically prohibited from.

Kiran leaned back against his car all the more amused. His tussled, dirty blonde hair was cropped short, although still allowing his wild waves freedom to move. And even though his muscular frame played casual in a relaxed stance, his aqua blue eyes bore into my soul, beckoning me closer.

Kiran tipped his chin in a gesture of calling and I obeyed immediately. I leapt, as gracefully, but as quickly as I could into his open arms and found utter bliss wrapped inside his strong embrace. Our bodies melted together and as he lifted my chin to find my mouth with his, our magic mingled together in a heady and wild sensation.

I was lost in Kiran's sweet kiss, unable to distinguish between his magic and my own. I mentally willed him to never remove his lips from mine. Our love affair may have been forbidden, it may have been dangerous, but Kiran's touch completed my soul. As if my heart had been searching for its other half all of my life, I had found completion in him.

Talbott coughed behind us and I was momentarily forced to leave Kiran's mouth. I did not however have to leave his arms, and so I stayed wrapped inside them, unwilling to leave his touch for even a moment. I laughed a little to myself when I noticed that neither Avalon nor Talbott were able to look directly at us.

Prime surveillance opportunity. This should be fun for you. I sent this thought poignantly to Avalon and watched him return it with a scowl. Our exchange was short however, and I doubted Talbott or Kiran would have understood it even if they saw a look pass between us.

The fact that Avalon and I were twins had to remain a secret from everybody but the Resistance. Although our connection and bond was as natural to me as breathing, if anyone were to find out outside of the Resistance we would be instantly captured or have to go on the run.

Twins had always been somewhat of a phenomenon in Immortal history, but since the ban on interracial marriage, they had been non-existent. The fact that we were twins did not only suggest an amount of power unattainable to the rest of the Immortal population, and possibly the restoration of eternal life, but it identified exactly who our parents were.

In order to be twins, a certain mixture of magic had to occur, including all four Immortal types in recent genealogical history. And since interracial marriage was completely banned in the Kingdom, except for the royal family, a mixture like that was impossible for anyone else. But, Avalon and I contained all four types of magic from either our parents or grandparents. Because of this we were unique among all Immortals and would be hunted because of it.

Not only would the current King, Kiran's father Lucan, desire our literal Immortal potential, he would use us as a trap to bait out our parents. Unfortunately, Lucan fell in love with our mother a long time ago, and instead of marrying him, she ran off with our father, Lucan's personal bodyguard.

Now our parents, Delia and Justice, were out there, somewhere, or they were not out there… they were dead. We didn't really know. All we did know was that my mother was part Witch, part Medium and my father was part Titan, part Shape-Shifter. These powers combined gave birth to Avalon and me and now our true identities were our most dangerous asset.

"Should we go inside?" Talbott cut through my thoughts with an authoritative voice and gestured towards the house. Tonight, Avalon and I were not the only ones who should be paranoid. We followed Avalon into the house and Talbott did a short search of the premises. My Aunt Syl was still at the hospital, there was no sign of life inside the house. Avalon plopped down on one of the oversized couches in the living room of our quaint Tudor style house. He used magic to turn on the lights in both the living room and chef's kitchen through an adjoining doorway.

The rest of us stood there awkwardly staring at one another, no one entirely sure what to do. Kiran had yet to let go of me, and I stood nestled in his embrace wishing everyone else would just disappear.

"Does anybody want something to drink?" I asked, trying to play hostess. I noticed Talbott shake his head negatively and Kiran didn't get a chance to answer before Avalon spoke up.

"Yeah, I'll take a coke," Avalon was clearly not as disturbed by Kiran's presence as he once was. He dropped his feet noisily onto the coffee table and flicked the TV on using magic once again. I rolled my eyes but made my way to the kitchen, while Sports Center came to life on the large flat screen.

Kiran followed me into my aunt's gorgeous chef's kitchen. Although Aunt Syl was a very skilled ER surgeon, her cooking skills lacked finesse to say the least. This didn't stop her from renovating the kitchen a few years back to any chef's dream set up. All of the appliances were state-of-the-art and oversized. And her counter tops and floors were whatever was in at the time.

A giant gas stove sat against one wall with every amenity one could imagine. To one side of the kitchen was a cute little breakfast nook, while the real kitchen table had an even larger space parallel to the middle island. In the middle of it all sat a large island with tall bar chairs, where Aunt Syl and I tended to spend most of our time.

Kiran took a seat at one of the tall chairs as I dug out a coke from the refrigerator for Avalon. I walked through the doorway and tossed it to him, hoping to shake it up violently, before returning to the kitchen and returning to Kiran's arms.

"You were late tonight," he pouted. "I thought you might have found something else to do." His crisp English accent stirred my soul and I fought butterflies from overtaking my stomach.

"I'm sorry," I said sincerely. "I just got.... hung up." I snuggled deeper into his arms and contemplated inviting him upstairs where we would be more comfortable.

"You got hung up, huh? With.... Avalon?" Kiran pulled me closer to him still, resting his chin softly on the top of my head. He was jealous.

"Believe me, all I could think about was you the entire time I was gone," I lifted my head up to kiss the bottom of his chin, hoping to deflect his questions. "And Avalon is actually staying with us for a while," I cringed inwardly, hoping Kiran's jealousies weren't too deeply founded. If only he knew that he had absolutely nothing to fear in that department. "His parents are back in Brazil and so he is staying with us so that he can finish school," I did my best to believe the lie I was telling him.

I hated lying to him, I could barely say the words, but I was trying to understand that everything was not about me. Some things I had to do for the sake of my brother and my grandfather and now the Resistance, especially since Lilly joined. If that meant a few white lies to Kiran, to protect the ones I loved and make things make sense to him, then so be it....for the time being.

"Oh," Kiran said dejectedly.

I didn't let him think about Avalon or anything else, anymore. I pulled his face down to meet mine and our mouths finally found each other again. His magic overwhelmed me, making me dizzy and faint. Our powers swirled together in an almost palpable energy field around us and I lost myself in him. Butterflies mixed with frenetic energy threatened to overcome me but I stayed focused on Kiran's perfect lips, relishing in this stolen moment.

Another cough interrupted us this time, and I was more than embarrassed to find its source Aunt Syl. Holy cow. Well, Kiran had to meet her some time....

"Hi, Aunt Syl," I cringed, turning my reddened face towards her standing in the doorway to the garage, Chinese food in her arms. My face was flooded with heat and I could barely look her in the eyes.

"Hello, Eden," she mumbled, her face turning an equal shade of red.

"This is um, Kiran," I cleared my throat and tried a smile.

"Hi Kiran, I'm Sylvia, Eden's aunt. Well I guess not aunt, since you know that I'm human, but um, Eden's guardian," Aunt Syl was surprisingly nervous to meet him, and severely embarrassed to have walked in on such an intimate moment.

Although Aunt Syl was human, she understood the laws and by-laws that I lived by, perhaps better than me. Kiran's position as Crown Prince did not have less gravity with her just because she was human, if anything it meant more.

"Pleasure to meet you," Kiran was instantly on his feet and ready to shake her hand. He was the perfect picture of English chivalry. Aunt Syl took his hand weakly, stunned for an instant by the oddity of the moment.

"Thank you," she responded, half in a daze.

"This is my b-, this is my friend Talbott," Kiran gestured for Talbott to move from the doorway leading into the living room to also shake Aunt Syl's hand. Talbott obeyed, eyeing her suspiciously.

"Hi Sylvia," Avalon completed the group, bursting noisily through the doorway. "Did you bring food?" he asked excitedly, before taking the brown bags directly from her arms and digging in immediately. "You are the best!" he paused for a moment and grabbed Aunt Syl around the waist, pulling her close to him and kissing her cheek roughly.

Aunt Syl pushed Avalon away, used to his antics, but embarrassed in front of such important company.

"Would you boys like some as well?" Aunt Syl gestured towards the opened cartons of fried rice and Mongolian beef, but I had a hard time picturing Talbott sitting down to stir-fried wontons with Avalon.

"Actually we really must be on our way," Kiran turned to me with true sadness in his eyes. "We have to be going, Love We've been gone long enough," when I mimicked his disappointment, he made his way back to my side and pulled me into his arms.

"That's not fair," I mumbled into his chest.

"I know. I wish you would have gotten home earlier," he said softly. I heard the tiniest bit of reproach in his voice. "No worries, though. Next time we will go to my place. We will hopefully have a little more privacy," he whispered into my hair and I felt another blush creep its way up my neck.

"When?" I demanded, totally willing to leave now.

"Soon," he kissed the top of my head and pulled me close before letting me go completely. I knew that it was silly, but I couldn't help but feel cold and less complete without his arms around me. "Thank you Sylvia for your hospitality. I should hope we meet again soon," he smiled genially, and Syl nodded in return. Avalon rolled his eyes and suddenly started a coughing fit, pretending to choke on Kung-Pow chicken.

"Yes, thank you for your hospitality," Talbott echoed Kiran's sentiment in his own version of an accent, but my aunt had yet to find her words.

The boys turned to leave and I followed them to the door.

"See you at school tomorrow," Kiran said while Talbott opened the door and waited for Kiran to pass.

"I can hardly wait," I groaned sarcastically. The thought of Seraphina's hands all over the man that I loved made me nauseous, but that was the price I paid to stay out of prison.

"You know that I am always thinking of you, Love," he enfolded me in his arms once again and tipped my chin up into the sweetest kiss. I stood there, or rather floated there for several seconds believing that what he said was true.

"And I think only of you," I whispered when his lips finally left mine.

Kiran released his embrace and turned to leave. Talbott said nothing on his way out, but closed the door behind them. I heard the Rolls Royce start and then watched the headlights back out of my drive way.

"He's only using you," Avalon's snide voice came from the kitchen doorway. He was standing their casually, holding a box of lo mien noodles and chopsticks.

"Avalon, please don't start," I walked in his direction, fully intending on finding my own box of noodles, as long as Avalon hadn't eaten everything.

"You can't blame him though. You hold the only hope of true Immortality he'll ever have. If I were him, and destined to die so soon, and you came along believing all of my lies, I would for sure play that out," he handed me his carton of noodles, realizing I was on a quest to look for them. I gave him a sharp look and then took them grudgingly.

"You know you're crazy. You just don't like him. I'm sorry brother; this is something you're going to have to learn to live with." I found my own pair of chopsticks and noticed Aunt Syl duck out of the room, unwilling to listen to the conversation she had heard over and over for the last few weeks.

"Eden, I hope I have to learn to live with it; because the other option is your sacrificial death all in honor of the very boyfriend you seem to love so much," when I put my food down, unable to find my appetite, he continued, "Remember, you may be pretty, but you are much more valuable as a solution to all of their problems. He has more interest in your dead body than your live one." Seeing that he accomplished his goal of getting to me, Avalon left me alone in the kitchen staring at a half-eaten box of lo mien noodles.

I knew with every fiber of my being that Avalon was wrong and that Kiran loved me completely without any thought of what I might mean for him. But even still, Avalon's words were hard to swallow and part of me wondered whose lies I was buying into…. Kiran's or Avalon's.

Chapter Five

"Eden, can I talk to you for a moment?" Talbott confronted me at the entrance to English. I had to force myself to be polite.

"Sure," I responded casually, and assured Avalon that I would be all right via telepathy.

Avalon walked slowly past, not entirely convinced that I would be. I opened my mind, a little reluctantly, but wanting to give Avalon a sense of security. He eventually moved past the classroom door and found his seat near the back and next to mine.

"What's up?" I asked Talbott, searching the halls for the still absent Kiran.

"I understand your feelings for Kiran are deep," he began and then cleared his throat nervously. "I'm just worried that this relationship, or whatever this is, is going to end badly for both of you," he coughed again and I did my best not to groan out loud at what was turning out to be another "You should know better" speech. "What I'm trying to say, is that Kiran will never be able to walk away from you, not willingly; and I'm afraid of what will happen if he is forced to walk away unwillingly. Eden, you are the strong one, you are also the one with more to lose. You have to understand that he cannot hide you forever. What if you have to suddenly go on the run? Or you disappear one day? Think about him and what that would do to Kiran," Talbott pleaded with me and I recognized real pain behind his dark, chocolate brown eyes and thick, matching eye lashes.

"Ms. Matthews, are you going to stand out there all day, or will you allow me to begin class?" I heard Mr. Lambert's nasal reprimand from inside the classroom and stood there stunned for a moment longer. Talbott's words had hit their mark; what about Kiran? What would happen to him if I had to leave? What would happen to me if I had to leave him?

I smiled sadly and apologetically at Talbott before entering English and finding my seat. Talbott followed behind and sat down next to me as well. Avalon in a surprise gesture put a comforting, but strong hand on my shoulder and gave it a squeeze. He, thanks to the twin connection, felt every emotion that I did, whether he agreed with them or not.

"All right, let's resume our discussion on Romeo and Juliet," Mr. Lambert began. "This story as we know is ripe with teenage angst, something I suppose the lot of you would know plenty about. Of course, it is easy to judge young Romeo's folly and fair Juliet's impetuousness. But one day, maybe soon, your innocent hearts will find love. And with love comes all manner of hasty and most often selfish decisions."

The classroom door opened slowly and Mr. Lambert was forced to pause his lecture. Kiran walked slowly into the classroom with a grin on his face, having just finished a conversation before entering English. Amory, or Principal Saint during school hours, was right behind him followed by another boy I had never seen before.

"Pardon us, Charles; I have yet another new student to introduce," Amory smiled in his benevolent way and Mr. Lambert simply shook his head, as if it was no bother at all. "My dear scholars, this is Sebastian Cartier, Mr. Kendrick's' cousin," Amory placed his hand on the back of Sebastian Cartier who grinned widely in reply.

He was taller than Kiran, although they bore a striking resemblance in facial features. Sebastian's hair however was dark brown and kept very short, his eyes were a deep hazel that sparkled when he smiled and his shoulders were just a tad bit wider than Kiran's. Other than that, they had the same distinguished nose and masculine lips. In my opinion he was nothing compared to Kiran, but altogether I was sure other girls found him attractive.

"Sebastian is from Marseilles, his mother, of course, is Princess Bianca. Please welcome him to Kingsley," Amory squeezed his shoulder gently before leaving the classroom.

"Great, more royalty," I heard Avalon mumble underneath his breath and I couldn't help but laugh.

Mr. Lambert directed Sebastian to a seat in the back near Kiran who continued to joke and laugh with his cousin. For some unexplainable reason I found the idea of Kiran's family at school unsettling. The only other family member I'd even heard of was his father, whom I needed to avoid at all costs. So the fact that his cousin was attending the same school as me felt strange.

Kiran, as always, ignored me completely during the remainder of the morning. Our policy was usually to have

43

absolutely nothing to do with each other during school. Kiran had to continue his role as most popular kid in school engaged to the prettiest girl in school act and I had to perpetuate my social outcast act.

Truthfully I enjoyed the whole outcast thing; it was the ignoring Kiran I had a problem with. While I sat alone with Avalon in most social circumstances I was forced to watch Seraphina's ever inappropriate touching. As far as she was concerned she owned Kiran and treated him accordingly.

Today at lunch was especially irritating. Seraphina could not keep her hands to herself and while she enjoyed my boyfriend and her salad, I had lost my appetite completely. Avalon, noticing my nausea, had helped himself to my chicken-salad sandwich and chips. I held my Dr. Pepper protectively, unwilling to give that up.

"What do you make of another Kendrick joining the student body?" Avalon asked softly, before helping himself to a dill pickle off of my tray.

"I don't know. It all seems strange to me. I suppose Amory will know more of the details, but I don't understand why he is joining us now. And who is he really?" I struggled to keep my voice soft while my irritation flared to a new level. Seraphina had draped both arms around Kiran's neck and was whispering, God-knows-what into his ear.

"Yeah, me too. I don't like it, not at all. Amory probably didn't have any warning himself, which makes me nervous. Kiran's already here, why would they keep his cousin coming over a secret? Unless, he is their own version of surveillance, you know what I mean?" Avalon looked around conspiratorially, but was unable to locate Sebastian Cartier. I myself had been wondering where he was during lunch, and why he wasn't devotedly near his cousin's side, like the rest of our class.

"What do you mean surveillance?" I asked, suddenly nervous.

"Well, sure he heard everyone's side of the story, but Lucan himself has not tried to look into exactly who you are. That fact has always made me nervous. You completely disrespected his court and his honor, and on top of that, you're a spitting image of the girl who scorned him. Is he really just going to listen to a bunch of testimonies and then write you off? What if he is trying to be more

44

discreet about finding out your true identity, more discreet than we give him credit for? Maybe he is afraid if he makes too much noise, then you'll disappear and he'll lose her again."

"Our mother?" I whispered, horrified.

Avalon nodded, and looked like he was about to say something else before he was shockingly interrupted.

"May I sit here?" Avalon and I both snapped our heads up to stare, open-mouthed at Sebastian. His accent was unmistakably English, although for some reason I had been expecting it to be more French, since he was apparently from France.

"I think the Prince is over there," Avalon found his voice first and I realized that in his mind his suspicions were confirmed, making me very nervous.

"Yes, thank you, but I was hoping to meet the Shape-shifter, the girl whom Kiran raised such a fuss over," he smiled widely and I could see that although I refused to trust him, he had a certain charisma that would make him easy to like.

"Oh, she's not here today," Avalon continued.

"Not here? After all of the work Kiran went through to make sure she could be here? I hope she's not ungrateful." Sebastian took a seat next to me anyway, despite Avalon's clear rejection. He set his tray down and turned to face me directly. Although his words sent a chill through my spine, his manner was so inviting and warm, that I was able to hold myself together.

"I'm Sebastian by the way," he extended his hand to me, gazing deeply into my eyes. I reached out to take his hand politely, when Avalon clumsily spilled my Dr. Pepper all over the table. I stood up instinctively, hoping to save my uniform from the fizzing soda.

Sebastian however, was quicker than me and stopped the brown liquid with his magic, before it reached the end of the table. He then made the soda disappear completely, leaving only a half-empty, still-foaming can. He looked up at me with a quizzical expression, but I laughed it off nervously and took my seat once again.

"Eden, you forgot again," Avalon teased through gritted teeth. "She was raised human, did you know that?" He addressed Sebastian by giving him far more details than I ever would have, until I realize what Avalon saved me from doing.... If we would have shaken hands he would have gotten to feel my magical imprint. I knew it was impossible for him to recognize a similarity between me and either one of my parents since they had been missing for over one hundred and fifty years. But better to be on the safe side. I quickly took my half eaten-croissant back from Avalon and busied my hands with holding it. "I'm Avalon St. Andrews by the way," Avalon introduced himself to Sebastian, who only stared back suspiciously.

"Avalon, you say 'humans' like it's a bad thing," I laughed casually, trying to hide my nerves.

"Humans? How is that possible?" Sebastian once again searched my eyes deeply in a way that I suddenly found invasive.

"Her parents both died of the King's Curse, or so we assume because she was abandoned in the woods. A hiker found her and then when no one came to claim her, she kept her. Eden didn't even know she was Immortal until she came to this school," Avalon told the story dramatically and I couldn't help but smile at my overly expressive brother.

"That's unfortunate," Sebastian's eyes continued to narrow in suspicion, but he maintained a friendly smile. "So if you didn't know you were an Immortal, how did you end up at Kingsley?" Sebastian specifically addressed me, even turning his body to exclude Avalon.

"A…. Principal Saint found me, I mean he didn't find me of course, but he followed my progression in the papers and had his own suspicions, I mean his own thoughts on me. I kept um…. breaking things before I knew the truth. I guess once he figured it out, he talked my aunt, I mean not my aunt, my guardian, into sending me here. She thinks this is just a school for the gifted," I babbled nervously.

"Lucky for you Principal Saint was there to help you," Sebastian said coldly.

"Yep," is all I managed.

"So your friend, I mean I was told she was your friend, the Shape-Shifter, where is she today?" Sebastian pried, inching closer to me. I dropped my napkin onto the floor casually and bent down to pick it up, while doing my best to move, discreetly away from him.

"Her name is Lilly," I said a little snottier than I intended.

46

"Where is Lilly?" he corrected, with renewed politeness.

I glanced at Avalon who smiled congenially in our direction, but was telling me to be vague inside of my head.

"I wish I knew," I responded, hoping this would be all the answer Sebastian needed.

"What do you mean? Isn't she your friend? Aren't you the one who interrupted her trial claiming she was innocent or something along those lines?" Sebastian looked at me pointedly and I took a big bite of chicken salad to cover my nervousness, nodding my head as if I were embarrassed.

"She heard her mother has come down with the Curse, I think she is hoping to be able to visit them." Avalon spat out suddenly and then shook his head and rolled his eyes. "Stupid right? Girls and their sentiment," he grunted rudely and if I didn't know my brother so intrinsically, I would have believed his arrogance.

"That is stupid," Sebastian agreed, although I was not sure he was entirely convinced. "She'll probably find herself locked back up. Well, that's why they are the ones in hiding, right?" Sebastian looked at me for approval.

"Ha. Damn right," Avalon played patriotic and prejudiced, slamming his fist on the table and revealing one of his many tattoos. I just nodded my head enthusiastically, biting off more than I could chew of what was left of my sandwich.

"Cousin, join us please," Kiran called from across the lunch room. He sounded enthusiastic and looked like he really did want Sebastian to join him. I found that strange because all I wanted was for Sebastian to un-join us. But I supposed they were cousins. Kiran probably really did like him. I smiled through a mouthful of food and kept nodding my head as if to say he should go.

"If you will excuse me then," he smiled apologetically at me. "It was a pleasure to meet you Eden. You are even more exquisite than they say," I realized I had never given him my name, and before I could respond he bent down and kissed my cheek. I sat stunned realizing he had finally accomplished his goal of touching my skin and also embarrassing me. He had been able to memorize my magical imprint. He turned around swiftly and left us staring after as he made his way to Kiran's table.

"Damn it," Avalon said softly, but menacingly, under his breath. "Well, I guess we have our answer."

"I guess so." I replied, while rubbing my cheek roughly where Sebastian's lips had just been. I stared after him as he joined Kiran's table, where he fit in flawlessly.

"We'll have to keep an eye on him," Avalon mumbled, appearing to lose his appetite and simply push the remainder of his lunch around his plate with a half-eaten pickle. I could see the wheels turning in Avalon's head and I heard his thoughts deciding which Resistance members he would send.

"I think he's having those same thoughts, Avalon," I said in a small voice, realizing for the first time that Sebastian's presence at Kingsley made me more than nervous. I was afraid.

Chapter Six

"Eden," a strained whisper beckoned me into the theater the next morning at school. I recognized Kiran's voice and obeyed immediately. Sending a thought to Avalon and instructing him to continue on to class, lest anyone get suspicious. I ducked into the theater and found Kiran just inside the double doors.

First things first, he pulled me into his arms with a passionate kiss. I gave in immediately, letting his mouth press against mine, relishing the stolen moment. I pushed Kiran's back against the clothed wall and tangled my hands in his tussled hair. He pulled me closer with a firm hand on my lower back, his other hand getting lost in the tangles of my own hair.

Eventually he tried to pull back, remembering there was a reason he called me in there, but I refused to relinquish my hold, pulling his neck down once again. He didn't resist and I found his lips strongly against mine once more. My shirt came un-tucked and his fingers found their way underneath the hem and on to my lower back. It was the first time Kiran had been brave enough to touch my usually-hidden skin so boldly and it made me only want him more.

I pressed my body closer to his, kissing him even more fervently than before. My hands tugged at the hem of his shirt, and then slipped underneath, until I felt his skin hot against my hands. Our passion was illuminated in a swirling cloud of mingled magic surrounding us.

Outside the theater doors several girls walked by laughing and talking loudly. We were suddenly several feet away from each other, doing our best to recover our composure. Kiran's hands worked swiftly to re-tuck his shirt and straighten his tie, while mine struggled to regain the length to my skirt and smooth out my own shirt. I saw him smile adoringly at me even in the darkness, and returned it with my own version of a shy smirk.

"You're awfully brave," he teased, but the look in his eyes told me he wouldn't have it any other way.

"There's just something about those lips," I replied coyly, walking over and giving him the smallest, but sweetest kiss I could restrain myself with.

"Stop distracting me," he whispered sweetly, while pulling

me into his arms again. The passion between us threatened to ignite, and I forced myself to remember he probably had a purpose in calling me in here. "I need to know what my cousin wanted at your lunch table yesterday," he was suddenly matter of fact, making the anxiety from yesterday fresh in my mind.

"He was asking about Lilly, but seemed interested in me, Kiran. Why is he here?" I asked, letting the tension slip into my voice, not on purpose, but it was there all the same.

"I am not entirely sure. His interest in Lilly is perfectly natural, especially from someone in my family. I'm sure it's nothing. He is obviously wondering what all the fuss was about I'm sure. And I know his mother was not happy with my father for sending me stateside. So he could be telling the truth about that, too. Where is Lilly, by the way?" he asked, calmly dismissing my fears. "Did you know he was coming?" I returned to the subject carefully, not willing to lie to Kiran so early in the morning.

"No, I didn't, which doesn't exactly mean anything. He says his mother wants him to go to school with me, and I believe him. Like I said, she was more than upset at my father for leaving Sebastian behind." Kiran tried to sound confident, but I could see him thinking deeply about this. "If father sent him, then he is only curious. If he truly suspected your identity, he would have sent more than Sebastian. Believe me, and he would have done it a lot sooner than now. We will just have to be more careful than ever. That includes not getting caught in the theater," he reproached playfully and then kissed my ear sweetly.

"I suppose you're right," I mimicked his accent, before turning to kiss him on the mouth. "Besides," I continued, returning to my deadpan lack of an accent, "we both know that Mr. Lambert is going to welcome your arrival to class no matter how late you are, and I will be blamed entirely for it. He will probably tell you I'm a bad influence on you," I said dramatically as we exited the theater.

"Aren't you though?" Kiran teased and we both laughed or rather giggled at each other until we made it out into the hall and found Sebastian wandering around the lobby. We both stopped dead in our tracks. Neither one of us able to come up with a sound excuse we suddenly felt that we owed Sebastian.

"We were just, um, we were just…." Kiran stammered. I recognized his flare in magic and his instinctive need to protect me.

51

"It's all right, cousin," Sebastian assured us soothingly, "Your secret's safe with me." He smiled, but it didn't reach his eyes and gave him a menacing, evil look.

"No, it's not; I mean there's no secret. Eden sometimes forgets to use her magic and then she lets it build up and then she has to release it and she usually does so in the theater. I was actually looking for Talbott. We just happened to bump into each other," Kiran explained quickly, but with confidence. "Where is he anyway? Have you seen him, Sebastian?" Sebastian shook his head negatively and I watched his smile diminish ever so slightly, but the suspicion in his eyes was unmistakable.

I began walking towards class, leaving Kiran behind me. I didn't acknowledge him anymore, hoping to prove Kiran's excuse.

"Is that true, Eden? Sometimes you forget to use your magic?" Sebastian was by my side in a moment, walking up the marble stairs to English.

"Yes it is true. One of the perks of being raised human," I laughed out loud, hoping to sound casual.

"That sounds dangerous," Sebastian said pointedly. "What's the longest you can go without using your magic?" He questioned further, and a feeling of uneasiness crept up my spine.

"Oh, not very long at all. If I go even thirty minutes without using it, I suddenly cause an explosion or burn down a building or something," I turned to face him and gave him my most charming smile. I pulled my long dark hair out of my face to give him the full effect of what I hoped to be a very captivating gaze. He stared back, deeply into my eyes and I forced myself not to look away. We stood there paused on the marble steps, competing with each other in a silent staring contest.

"Eden Matthews, I need to see you right away," Amory's sharp voice suddenly called from the bottom of the staircase. "There is a mess in the theater and if I find that you have been blowing trash cans apart again without cleaning up your mess, you are going to be in serious trouble, young lady," Amory had taken on the role of principal and the effect was actually terrifying.

I turned immediately back down the stairs, leaving Sebastian to stare after me. Kiran was nowhere to be seen and I was suddenly grateful my grandfather was also the principal of this school. Amory pointed towards the theater and I quickly obeyed his unspoken command.

"Off to class with you, Mr. Cartier. It may only be your second day, but that is no excuse for tardiness," Amory maintained his authoritative tone until after Sebastian had ascended the stairs. He then followed me silently into the theater, lighting the house lights enough so we could see each other.

"This is no good," Amory worried softly once we were behind the double doors of the quiet theater.

"So he is here to spy on me?" I asked, afraid of the answer, but already certain I knew the truth.

"I can't be sure Eden. He seems too curious about you for his sudden arrival to be a coincidence; but then again it was his mother who called and enrolled him, not Lucan. Maybe he was only curious after your interruption at the trial, his presence here might not have anything to do with Lucan," Amory chewed on his thumbnail while pacing nervously. His image was strikingly similar to Avalon's, both men great leaders despite their small habits.

"I don't like him, Amory," I whispered, reminding myself of how disturbing I found his presence.

"No, I would hope not. His personality is much more similar to his Uncle Lucan's than even Kiran's. I think it best if you steer clear of him altogether," Amory turned his gaze on me and smiled sadly.

"I've been trying," I mumbled, grumpily.

"I know," Amory replied sympathetically. "I'm afraid those Kendrick boys don't know how to leave you or your mother alone."

"Great."

"Aw, the price of beauty," Amory pulled me into a side hug and kissed the top of my head.

"Yeah, right," I groaned sarcastically, but blushed from the compliment all the same.

"Ok, here's a pass, off to class with you," he handed me a pink slip of paper, excusing me from being late to class.

"Mr. Lambert's going to be so mad at me," I squeaked, but Amory only laughed at me.

I bounded up the stairs, hoping that Amory was right. Hopefully Sebastian was only curious about my opinion at Lilly's trial over the All Saints Festival. Maybe there was nothing else to his arrival.

53

Let's ditch the rest of the day. *Avalon sent me his thought telepathically in the middle of French.*

I've missed too much already. I'll get behind in chemistry. *I responded glumly.*

Ok, Eden. It's time you come to terms with your magic. What good is it if you don't use it for homework? We're skipping and that's final. *Avalon made a good point.* But I couldn't help but feel guilty for both skipping and cheating on my homework. It's not cheating, for the last time! *Avalon read my thought and I heard him grunt audibly behind me.*

Fine. *I gave in.* It will probably be better to get away from Sebastian for a while anyway. Do you think Amory will excuse us?

This is a legitimate skip, Eden. If there are consequences to pay, we'll pay them. We can't continue to rely on Amory to excuse our behavior. People will get suspicious, especially that new Kendrick. *Avalon's mind voice was full of disgust, and I felt how sick and tired he was of having another member of the Monarchy around and it had only been two days.*

After French, Avalon and I made our way down the marbled staircase on our way out of the building, hoping to remain undetected. We were almost to the back door when a snotty voice rang out from behind us.

"And where do you think you're going?" Seraphina's piercing high-pitched voice demanded of us.

I turned around not entirely sure what to say. Although I would have liked to ignore her completely, I felt guilty for some unexplainable reason and couldn't just dismiss her. Ok, maybe not so unexplainable. I was cheating with her fiancé....

"Avalon forgot something in his truck," I replied sweetly, at the same time riddled with remorse.

"That takes two of you?" She stared at me, long fingers on small hip. Her shiny blonde hair was brushed into perfection and her lips a shiny shade of pink gloss.

"Um, yes," I said simply, and ran my fingers through my wild wavy black hair subconsciously, trying to untangle it.

"Listen Eden, I don't know what you think you're doing, but

you should know that I am not going to sit back while you try to steal my boyfriend." My mouth dropped open from surprise, but she continued, "And listen, you better watch out because I will destroy you. Do you understand me? I will ruin your life and make you wish you never discovered those stupid powers of yours. To think Lucan wanted to know if there was anything special about you! Are you kidding me? You're nothing but an insignificant peasant; you don't even know how to use your magic, let alone what to do with it. You are absolutely nothing to me and you need to learn your place. Stay away from Kiran or I will annihilate you. That is a promise," Seraphina stood there perfectly poised and perfectly put together, her one hand gripping her waist firmly. She was much too pretty to be this mean.

I stood there, cowering. I knew I was in the wrong. And I knew she was fully capable of delivering on her promises.

"Whatever, Seraphina," I mumbled weakly, my voice shaking from fear of her.

She stood there staring after me for a few moments longer, the blue of her eyes turning to ice. I felt myself struggle to swallow, wishing she would just go away. And then finally, with one last look of contempt, she turned on her heel and walked away, her black stilettos making a hard clicking sound against the polished marble floor. One hand never left her hip, while the other hand flipped her glistening hair over her shoulder. This was why she would be Queen one day; she was capable of striking fear into all people.

Avalon burst into a fit of laughter as soon as Seraphina was gone. He was practically rolling on the floor, unable to contain himself.

"You might as well have said, 'Yes, ma'am,'" he wheezed through explosive laughter.

"Shut up," I spat back defensively. "What was I supposed to say?"

"Oh man, that was the funniest thing I have ever seen," his hilarity eventually subsided into a softer version while he wiped tears of laughter from his eyes.

"I will never have a good day at Kingsley, will I?" I turned around and pushed the backdoor of the History and Language Building open, walking out into the fall drizzle that had clouded the early afternoon sky.

Chapter Seven

By the time Avalon and I reached the farmhouse the Nebraska sky was dumping water from above. Despite the torrential downpour, Avalon skidded off the gravel road and onto the drive of the Resistance farmhouse spraying mud and water everywhere.

I let out the breath that Avalon's driving had caused me to hold and cringed at the thought of stepping out of the vehicle. Several young men stood in the doorway of the metal barn watching us. I recognized about half of them and realized there were several new additions.

I noticed Avalon's hand on the door handle, and decided the best way to get through the rain was to face it head on. I flung the door open and did my best to sprint through the mud and gravel towards the barn. My clogs sunk deep into the puddles of grimy wetness and by the time I reached the barn I was soaked to the bone and splattered in mud.

The boys milling around the entrance to the barn scattered out of my way as I tumbled through the barn doors dripping dirty water everywhere. I did a little shake, much like a dog, and double-fisted my hair to force it away from my face.

I flung my head upwards, spraying everything around me with water. I was positive my black eye liner and mascara were running down my face, but I was helpless to stop it. I squinted through the black haze, and stared back at the thirteen or so faces gawking at me. A shiver ran down my spine, and I was frozen to the bone by icy water.

Suddenly, a familiar laugh burst through the silence and I recognized it as Jericho's. I shifted my gaze to his, and watched him bend over, clutching at his stomach. It dawned on me, a little slowly, that he was laughing at me, and I hoped suddenly it was just because of my appearance.

I had hoped, for a moment that Avalon would share my humiliation and we could take on the "wet dog" look together. I was wrong. Avalon strolled casually towards the barn, unconcerned and completely dry. He was surrounded by a cloud of magic that not only kept the rain from touching his clothing, but dried the ground before he even took another step. By the time he entered the barn, he was as hysterical as Jericho and laughing loudly at me.

"Piece of crap," I yelled, irritated and freezing.

"Ok, seriously Eden. What is wrong with you?" Avalon asked sarcastically in all his dry clothes glory.

"Avalon, don't be so hard on her," Jericho recovered from his fits of laughter to come to my aid, albeit a little mockingly. "Eden can't help it if she forgets about her magic."

He smiled mischievously at me and I heard a new guy question, "How is that possible?" The rest of the newcomers eyed me suspiciously as if I was dangerously more than I seemed.

"Hey, hey, hey," Jericho arrived at my side, placing a gentle hand on my shoulder, simultaneously comforting me and drying my icicle of a body with his magic. "Like I said, she can't help it, guys," He smirked playfully, before placing his other hand in front of his mouth to whisper to the group loudly, "She was raised human."

I pushed Jericho away with mock injury and pretended to pout. I heard the group of boys snicker to each other as I pulled myself together. I finished the dry-out job Jericho had begun, by using my own magic, half warming myself, half proving to the bystanders that I did, in fact, know how to use magic.

When I turned around, Avalon had already taken charge of whatever leadership role was available to him and was introducing himself as much more of a legend than I would ever have given him credit for. I contemplated for a second, joining the group again, but remembered Lilly and decided I couldn't do anything else until I had checked on her. I began to walk further into the barn but not before Jericho caught up with me.

"Did I fix my makeup?" I asked him, already forgiving him for any fun he had at my expense.

"I don't know what you mean by that." He smiled, confused, a typical guy response.

"My mascara, is it like running down my face?" I brushed my fingertips underneath my eyes as if demonstrating my question.

"No, your face looks.... fine," Jericho blushed when he finished his sentence and so I was not entirely sure if I could trust him.

I remembered the compact in my brand new back pack and tried to grab it as inconspicuously as possible. Feeling a little bit vain, and even more self-conscious in front of Jericho, I rushed the mirror in front of my face, checked my make up as scrupulously but as quickly as I could. Then I shoved the little compact mirror back into the abyss of the bag that had replaced the backpack Romania destroyed, satisfied with what I had seen.

"What? Don't you trust me?" Jericho nudged my side gently with his elbow.

"Absolutely not," I said playfully, and then gave him my most charming smile. "Hey, do you know where they are keeping Lilly?" I asked, anxiety slipping into my tone but unable to stay silent on the issue.

"Yes," Jericho responded simply.

"Well, can you take me to her?" I countered, feeling as though my request shouldn't be necessary.

"I don't think so," When I turned a scowl on him, he continued quickly, "I don't think they want non-Resistance members up there. I mean, it's like a sacred place. Since you're not an official member, they have kind of forbidden you from going."

"What?" Forbidden?" I half demanded, half shrieked. "Why hasn't anybody told me?" I crossed my arms and stomped my foot defiantly.

"Do you remember the last time you were forbidden to do anything? Yeah, it didn't work out so well for the rest of us," although Jericho was teasing me, he stopped walking and turned to face me. When I followed suit, he put both of his hands on my shoulders, sending his magical imprint racing through my blood. I could tell that he was nervous touching me, but what I didn't expect was to be nervous too. "Eden, trust me," he said smoothly, gazing deep into my eyes. "Lilly is going to be fine; this whole thing is a process. But seriously, look at the rest of us. We all made it through. She has the best care anyone could hope for," he smiled softly and I cleared my throat, bringing my mind into focus.

"You're right. I mean, I should trust you guys. How much longer do you think this will take though? People at school have been asking questions," I casually shrugged Jericho's hands off my shoulders and began walking again; reminding myself of Kiran and the overwhelmingly strong feelings I had for him.

"What people?" Jericho asked suspiciously.

"Well, Sebastian Cartier," I stopped dead in my tracks,

realizing I left Jericho somewhere a few feet behind me. I turned to face him, and saw the wheels in his head spinning.

"Sebastian Cartier is here? In Omaha? At Kingsley?" he whispered harshly.

I nodded my response, a little afraid of what I had let slip. He turned back around in the other direction, leaving me to run after him.

"Avalon!" he hollered at my very loquacious brother, who somehow had managed to maintain the newcomers' attention this entire time. "Avalon!" he hollered again.

"What?" an irritated Avalon swung around to face Jericho straight on.

"Sebastian Cartier is here? In Omaha? Why haven't we been informed?" Jericho demanded.

Damn it Eden, you just had to go and open your big mouth. Avalon sent me a direct and irritated message. I blushed, but turned right around again towards the opposite side of the barn. I had apparently done enough damage; I didn't need to get into the middle of a fight between those two.

I noticed Angelica towards the back of the barn, talking to some girls who looked only a little bit older than me. I considered joining them, but couldn't find the courage. Avalon was usually my social crutch around here, and unfortunately he was currently in the middle of a battle between need-to-know basis and left-in-the-dark. I rolled my eyes; inwardly laughing at the precarious relationship Avalon and Jericho seemed to hold- sometimes best friends, sometimes leadership rivals.

"Eden, won't you join us?" Angelica noticed me wandering around aimlessly. I had hoped to avoid what would assuredly be a socially-awkward situation for me. But apparently I was just not that lucky today.

"Hello, Angelica," I greeted her sweetly, remembering tenderly that she was close to my mother at one point. I had yet to garner any details from her, but I didn't tend to give up easily.

"Hello, dear." She returned my smile and brought me into a warm hug. Her lighter, almost effervescent magic wrapped me in a warm bubble and I felt oddly comforted. "The other teams have arrived. Have you met them?"

"Um, no, I haven't. I mean, Avalon was introducing himself

61

to them, so I just thought I would connect with him later," I blurted out, feeling like I needed to explain what I meant by our twin connection, but I decided not to get into detail. I mentally reminded myself that I was not actually part of the Resistance and therefore not actually obligated to meet anyone.

"Eden, don't rob yourself of the opportunity of getting to know others like you. Remember you are who you surround yourself with," She smiled knowingly, and I shrugged off the feeling of irritation from the clear dig at Kiran. "Anyway, these girls are too sweet to let Avalon do the meeting and greeting for you. Besides I think they already know Avalon," When she looked at them, they nodded in confirmation. "Eden, this is Fiona Thompson and Roxie Powers. They are part of the Czech team, Ryder's team," she patted Roxie, a short, hard-looking Latina, on the arm before leaving us alone. Roxie returned the gesture with a smile and I got the feeling it was almost painful for her to look so nice.

Roxie had long dark hair like mine, but it was in a low pony tail on the back of her neck, falling in smooth, loose curls down to her waist. Her small frame barely cleared five feet, but her stature exuded a strength that intimidated me. Her chocolate brown eyes searched my face as if looking for a reason to punch me in the nose. I flinched self-consciously before turning my attention to Fiona.

Fiona was much nicer looking, in personality I mean. They were both beautiful girls. Fiona had perfect porcelain skin that looked like milk next to her shoulder length auburn hair. Her overly large green eyes, maintained a look of both innocence and shrewdness. She stood tall as if in a position of leadership and her slender fingers were folded together in a proper sort of way.

"I'm Eden," I said obviously after Angelica had walked away…. after Angelica had left me…. after Angelica had abandoned me.

"We know," Roxie sneered and my suspicions about her were confirmed.

"It's a pleasure to meet you," Fiona covered for her friend. She did not attempt to shake my hand, however, and for some reason that bothered me.

"Y-y-you're Fiona?" I addressed the more polite of the two, asking another obvious question.

"Yes, that's right and this is Roxie. We worked with

Avalon's team to extract the Brazil team after Avalon and Jericho were um, called away," I noticed the look in their eyes as accusation, and blushed defensively.

"So, um, your whole team is here?" I looked around, hoping to be able to place the rest of their team, but my nerves were fried and it felt as though my magic was on the fritz.

"Yep," Roxie mumbled through a fake smile.

"Where are you guys staying?" I returned her smile with a fake one of my own.

"Here. We're all staying here," Roxie responded again, with an edge to her already tough demeanor.

"Like your team, or like all of the teams?" I asked, once again looking around the barn at all the new additions.

"Like everyone that's in the Resistance," Roxie answered my question harshly, obviously not concerned with being rude.

"Rox," Fiona chastised gently. "I'm sure she has her reasons." She gave Roxie a meaningful glance and her large green eyes pleaded with Roxie to be polite.

"I'm sure she does Fi. I just hope her reasons aren't costing an entire race of people their future." It was Roxie's turn to give me a meaningful glare, one that pretty much had me shaking in my shoes. "Come on. Let's go find your husband."

Fiona didn't even pretend to be polite anymore but brushed past me after her friend. I watched as they walked towards Avalon and Jericho and other boys I didn't recognize. I realized then that the rest of Avalon's team was missing.

Fiona and Roxie were greeted with enthusiasm and I even noticed Avalon give Roxie a hug. She looked tiny in his arms, hardly dangerous at all.

Looks could be deceiving.

Fiona slipped her slender, ivory arm through another boy's and they took a moment to gaze into each other's eyes. A thousand words passed silently between them and I recognized their unspoken language as unfailing love. A ball dropped in my stomach and I suddenly had a tremendous need to find Kiran.

I noticed Amory pull onto the gravel drive of the farmhouse and park his black Mercedes sedan next to Avalon's. I practically ran towards him, hoping he would understand my need to flee. I couldn't stand around this room while people continued to judge

63

me. I needed to remind myself that there was a very strong, very tangible, very beautiful reason I chose not to join the Resistance and the small politics of simple peer pressure were not enough to force my hand.

"Hey, Eden, come meet Ryder," Avalon called out, already aware of my plans and hoping to dissuade me.

"Maybe later," I called over my shoulder and picked up my pace to meet Amory at his driver's side door.

I enveloped Amory in my magical shield, keeping us dry and warm. He gave me a look of confusion that didn't seem to fit his polished and well-dressed demeanor. He was not the type of man to feel confused.

"Amory, I know this is a big request, but could I borrow your car right now…. Please?" I was near tears and not entirely sure why, but if I could only get back into the city I was sure everything would be fine.

"Why Eden? Is everything Ok?" When I shook my head in a frantic "yes," his eyes deepened with concern. "Are you sure? I was hoping you could get to know everyone tonight. Immortals have come from all over the world to protect you, my dear. I doubt they would find it very polite if you simply took off before being introduced." He smiled, trying to reassure me; but it sounded more like guilting me into staying than anything else.

"It's ok, I'll just take Avalon's," I pushed past him and threw Avalon's truck door open with my magic. "Can you bring him home tonight? Thanks," I spat out before Amory could say anything else.

I threw myself up and into the driver's seat, starting the engine with a simple thought. I could hear Avalon screaming at me inside of my head, but did my best to repress him.

I was tired of being told what to do, or what to say, or what to think. I was sorry that Avalon was so everything they wanted and expected. But I was not Avalon, even if he was in my head, even if he was my twin, even if I'd just stolen his truck. I was my own person and this person did not want to join their freaking Resistance.

I sped down the gravel road, reminding myself more and more of my twin brother, driving haphazardly at an alarming rate. I took a big breath and allowed the magic to take control. I then opened my palm and willed my cell phone into my fingers.

I was tired of the Resistance, and I was tired of people trying to protect me. What better way to spite them all then to find the one person that was against everything they stood for, the one person I was utterly in love with? My mind was wholly focused now; I was nothing but determined to be wrapped in Kiran's arms before I internally imploded from frustration.

Chapter Eight

I skidded parallel into a parking spot across from Kiran's building. On the drive from the farmhouse to downtown Omaha I practically mastered my magical driving ability. There were a few rough patches on the interstate, but no casualties, so I called my drive a success.

Having gotten even more worked up on the forty-five minute drive from the middle of nowhere to the upscale part of downtown Omaha known as the Old Market, I could not wait to see Kiran.

I hesitated a few more seconds before leaping from Avalon's oversized truck. The last of Kiran's Guard disappeared around the corner and subsequently a light was turned off in Kiran's loft apartment and replaced with a candle, a sign that the coast was clear.

I reached for the keys from the ignition and realized too late that I didn't use any, I had used magic. Bracing myself against the whipping wind and icy rain, I opened the door and dashed across the wet and slippery, brick street. There was no using a shield of magic in the middle of a crowded city.

Kiran buzzed me in before I even had a chance to push the button and I magically dried myself and clothes on the way to the elevator. I danced around the lobby anxiously, waiting for the elevator to reach the ground floor. Biting my lip and holding back tears of frustration, the only thought I allowed myself to think was of Kiran and Kiran alone.

The elevator doors opened and to my surprise he was waiting on the other side. I jumped into his arms immediately, not allowing one second of separation between us. My mouth found his instantly and a sense of overwhelming security washed over me. Hot tears finally escaped the tightly closed corners of my eyes, while Kiran's touch melted away my fears and frustrations.

Albeit a little surprised, Kiran reciprocated my passion with his own and soon our magic was mingling together in a swirl of frenetic energy. One of his arms gripped me tightly around my waist, pulling my body close to his in inseparable proximity; his other tangled its way through my hair. My lips refused to leave his.

The elevator came to a stop once again on the top floor and

the doors opened into Kiran's penthouse apartment. I regretfully relinquished my hold on him and quickly turned around to hide my embarrassing display of emotion. I entered the classy, modern apartment that took up the entire top floor of the apartment complex. The exposed brick and cork floors gave the loft space a warm and inviting feeling despite the sparse furniture and manly touches.

The space had several rooms and at least two bathrooms to accommodate not only Kiran and Talbott, but a handful of other Titan Guards. If that weren't bad enough, I'd been informed Sebastian had also joined them until other arrangements could be made. Kiran was close behind me, hands gently on my waist.

"That was quite the greeting," I could hear the smirk through his crisp, English accent, and my own version of his signature expression crept onto my face. This was what home felt like; being with the one I so wholly loved.

"It's been so long since we've been alone, what did you expect?" I sighed deeply and contentedly, turning around in the middle of Kiran's living room to let him envelope me in his embrace again. I couldn't think of any reason to leave his strong arms, ever.

"What's the matter, Love?" Kiran rested his chin on the top of my head and I appreciated his sensitivity but there was no way I could possibly share my issues, it would give way too much away about the Resistance.

"I'm just tired," I faked a yawn before nuzzling myself deeper into his arms. "And hungry," I finished, realizing that was not a lie.

"How about some crisps?" Kiran left my side, leaving me suddenly cold and insecure. I followed him like a puppy dog into the kitchen and took a seat at the high top table just off to the side of the designer kitchen that I was almost positive was never used.

"What are crisps?" I asked amused, watching Kiran rummage around in the walk-in pantry. It was obvious he was not used to fetching his own snacks.

"Oh, right. Um, I think you call them po-ta-to chips," he over-pronounced, as if the words were part of an actual foreign language. Then he turned around with a triumphant smile on his face and arms laden with bags of Doritos.

"Yes, that's what we call them," I smiled back, a little

patronizingly.

"I heard Seraphina gave you quite the mouthful today. Is that why you skipped out on the rest of classes?" Kiran took the seat next to me, intertwining our knees and opening a bag of crisps to munch on. He put an arm around my shoulder, and rubbed my back soothingly.

His small gestures were so charming that I was swept away with adoration. I knew that his extra effort made it difficult for him to eat, but I couldn't help feel a little bit smug that Kiran Kendrick couldn't keep his hands off of me. I looked up into his eyes, a deep ocean of aqua blue, gazing at mine intensely and I had to remind myself to breathe.

"Oh, no, Avalon and I were on our way out already," I explained, realizing too late I should have used the excuse Kiran so perfectly set up for me. I watched his eyes flinch with jealousy and his smirk turn instantly into a frown.

"Why?" he grunted, trying to cover his own reaction.

"Well, I mean, we were on our way to the gas station. I really wanted, um, I really wanted licorice," I fumbled through a ridiculous lie. "I really wanted some junk food, and then yeah, I guess after Seraphina verbally and emotionally abused me; I didn't really feel like returning to be tortured some more. I mean it's complete hell watching her claim you all day!" My voice turned into a whine and although I was using a little bit of misdirection to take the heat off of me, there was complete truth behind my complaint. "She's all, 'Oh, Kiran, I love you,' and touching you and, and I just hate it," I finished gruffly, crossing my arms and looking away from his piercing gaze.

"Come here," he whispered sweetly, and I obeyed without any hesitation. He pulled me into his arms and I inhaled his sweet, herbal scent. "I hate it too. I can't stand pretending this way. And I honestly hate leading Seraphina on like this as well. The poor bird still thinks she'll be Queen one day," he kissed my forehead and an emotion stirred deep inside of me, something like foreboding.

"Won't she?" I asked out of insecurity.

"Absolutely not. Why? Is that what you're worried about? That I'll choose her over you?" Kiran pulled away so that he could look directly in my eyes again.

I nodded, but was unable to give him a verbal response. Hot

tears stung my eyes again and I blinked rapidly to stop them from overflowing down to my cheeks. I bit my bottom lip harder, refusing to give in to such a human emotion.

"Eden, must I remind you that I love you?" I nodded again and a sweeter version of his smirk rose to his lips. "I do love you Eden, with all that I am. I don't believe there has been a more perfect love to ever exist in all of eternity, in fact. And I plan on sharing the rest of that eternity with only you," he leaned in to give me a warm, passionate kiss on the lips. When he sat back again, my fears were somehow lessened. "Right now, might not be the best time to introduce you to the parents, but I will soon, I promise. I will tell my father that I've chosen you and that Seraphina will have to use some other royal family member to get herself a crown. I just think the best thing to do right now is to put some more distance between your scene at the Festival and my change of plans for the Kingdom."

I smiled at him, but it felt weak and unassured. He wiped away a tear that had slipped unforgivably down my cheek. The warmth of his magic left my skin hot underneath his delicate touch. I smiled more sincerely, despite myself and was reminded of why I loved him.

"So you will introduce me to your family?" I asked tentatively. It may have been an impractical request, especially because when Kiran's father, Lucan, discovered my true identity he would either straight up kill me, or use me as bait to kill my parents. But the truth was, I was longing for his parents' approval.... How very normal, yet irritating of me.

"When more time has passed, yes, I would like nothing more than to introduce you to my family as my girlfriend," his smile widened and I lost myself in the perfection of his happy expression.

"Good," I mimicked his smile. "Oh, I've been meaning to ask you...." I paused, realizing the probable outcome of the question I was about to ask, "I've been meaning to ask you what your plans are for Thanksgiving?"

"Thanksgiving? I don't have any plans for Thanksgiving. I don't celebrate Thanksgiving." He said plainly, with a touch of amusement in his voice.

"Oh right, sometimes I forget you're not American," I smiled, embarrassed.

"Eden, obviously that's true. But that's not the reason I don't celebrate it. On my last count, no Immortal celebrates the holiday. Our history with America goes much further back than that bloody Columbus; we don't need to celebrate Thanksgiving, we have more important holidays," Kiran waggled his eyebrows, a smile played at the corner of his lips.

"Oh right," I sighed with exasperation. "Like Fall Equinox and Halloween and what's next, the um, the Winter Solstice? Those aren't real holidays."

I stood up from the table and walked over to the stainless-steel refrigerator. Pulling extra hard on the door handle, I closed my eyes and let the cool air wash over me. The refrigerator was exactly what I expected it to be, empty, save for several different beverage options. I grabbed a Dr. Pepper and tossed another one to Kiran's open hands.

"Eden, Love, you have it all backwards," he laughed loudly at me. I returned his wit with a smile, but a small wave of irritation washed over me. I knew that my annoyance wasn't directed entirely at Kiran, but at the whole species of Immortals. "Our holidays came first, Thanksgiving, Halloween, Mother's Day- they are all rubbish. Sometimes you are still so human."

"I thought you celebrated Halloween?" I leaned against the charcoal granite counter top. I opened my soda, swallowing more irritation before taking a sip of the ice-cold soda.

"We celebrate All Saints Day; Halloween is like a watered-down version of a five-thousand-year-old tradition. Just ask Amory," Kiran stood to join me in the kitchen. Although I was not quite ready to give up my frustration, I realized he was not insulted in the least and couldn't help himself but to close the separation between us. The gesture alone began to melt my stubborn heart.

"Ok, fine. I give up. Thanksgiving is a pointless human holiday. Blah, blah, blah. But I still plan on celebrating my pilgrim predecessors. Besides I think we all have plenty to be thankful for," I folded my arms stubbornly and looked towards a window opposite the approaching Kiran.

"By all means, I would never expect to deprive you of any of your desires, or wishes, Love," he stopped in front of me grinning, both hands on the counter, surrounding me by his overwhelming magical aura. The strength of his magic swirled and floated around

70

me, tempting me to release mine; his soul called to mine in a love song of longing.

"Is that true?" I asked, a blush rising to my cheeks.

"Mmmm.... hmmm...." he pulled me into his arms and whatever irritation I felt before completely vanished inside the palpable energy field our mingled magics created. I felt him nuzzle his face into my hair and I found the courage to ask him the question I set out to in the first place.

"So, if you're obviously not doing anything for Thanksgiving, then will you come to my house? I'm making this huge dinner, with pie and turkey and everything," My voice was muffled because I had buried my face deep into the crook of his neck, but I had no doubt Kiran heard me. I stiffened in nervous anticipation, feeling as if I were requesting the world from him.

"Of course I'll come, I wouldn't miss it for anything," he assured me. I raised my head to confirm his authenticity. Once satisfied, I pulled his neck down so that my lips could meet his.

Once again tonight, I was lost in the wild passion of an intimate kiss with Kiran. Our mouths pressed fervently against one another, with our bodies impossibly melted together. A frenzied cloud of magic spun freely in a tornado-like fashion and I was convinced I would be swept away completely until....

"Well, well, well, what do we have here?" Sebastian's satisfied voice echoed Kiran's English accent from the doorway and I cursed myself for getting so wrapped up inside Kiran's world. Sebastian had us exactly in the worst possible spot, but I was somehow sure this was exactly what he was hoping for.

Chapter Nine

Kiran's arms were wrapped tightly around me, his face a picture of confusion as he stared at the door, open mouthed. My back was to Sebastian who had just exposed our secret affair by rudely walking in on us. My fingers were tangled deeply inside Kiran's wavy locks and I did my best to think fast. I refused to lose Kiran to some creepy little spy, who didn't know how to knock.

I stamped my foot out of frustration and then it came to me. I clenched down on Kiran's ample head of hair and forcefully pulled back. After producing the expected "ow" I knew I could count on Kiran to deliver, I released my hold on his hair and smartly smacked him across the face. He was so stunned and bewildered all he could do was stare at me. I had to let out a small scream of frustration to hold back my laughter.

"How dare you Kiran Kendrick," I blurted out with the best impression of a damsel in distress I could muster. "You may be royalty but you are also engaged. There is no way in hell you can use me as some sort of entitled concubine to fulfill your sick fetishes. Get a life," I spat the words out with such venom, I actually felt guilty, but for the sake of our uninvited audience I pushed Kiran back with a little too much force and fled to Sebastian's side. "If you ever touch me again I will go straight to Seraphina and expose what kind of cheater you really are."

Once next to Sebastian, I intertwined my arm with his and laid my head sweetly on his shoulder. I swallowed the rising vomit and forced myself to forget what kind of person I was touching. Kiran still stood open-mouthed in the kitchen, trying to process my outburst, and rubbing his red cheek with his hand.

"Oh thank goodness you walked in when you did," I turned to give Sebastian a fearful look; remembering my frustrations from earlier to conjure the tears I had fought so hard to banish and forced myself to look into his shallow eyes.

"Thank goodness," he echoed, sounding half confused, half suspicious. "You'll have to forgive my cousin, he's used to getting exactly what he wants," Sebastian's suspicious stare turned from me to Kiran. Kiran looked at the ground, ashamed, or at least a very good impression of ashamed and played idly with the granite counter top. "Whatever you are thinking now Cousin, my intention wasn't to barge so impolitely into you little um, gathering, but to remind you of your commitment to the Club this evening. I'm afraid they have been waiting for half an hour already."

I watched Kiran out of the corner of my eye, realizing I didn't need to pretend to look confused. I decided the best course of action was for me to flee the scene immediately and so I enthusiastically unlinked my arm from Sebastian's and turned towards the door.

"Obviously, you have business. Thank you again Sebastian. I will see you tomorrow," I cleared my throat, hoping to escape without any more suspicion being raised.

"Eden, dear, why don't you accompany us?" Sebastian crushed all hope with one little politely-asked question and I swallowed my paranoia. I wondered what he was up to.

"Thank you, but I'd rather not," I shot Kiran a look of pure hatred; one that I was surprised came so easily. I told myself the hate was aimed at Sebastian, and promised I would make it up later.

"Really, I insist," Sebastian smiled, sending a shiver down my spine. "Kiran will leave you alone, now that he knows how you really feel. Besides, he'll have court all night anyway. I could use the company."

"Well, that sounds exciting; but I think I've actually been banned from Club Kiran," The irritation behind my voice was real after I remembered the embarrassing incident two months ago when my own grandfather had me exiled from the posh Immortal club, Kiran referred to as his American office.

"That's true, Sebastian. Eden was denied access after she broke in, in early September," Kiran joined the conversation, rubbing his head as if he was overly exhausted. He yawned widely and then stretched his arms high overhead, revealing a small amount of abdomen that I would have found completely sexy if it weren't for the third wheel in the room.

"Denied access? That doesn't sound like anything you can't clear up straight away. Unless, of course, you're too tired to go at all? You seem exhausted, Cousin; I could go in your place, if you need me to. If there was anything out of my jurisdiction I'm sure it can wait until you are feeling more up to the task," although Sebastian's words seemed self-serving and greedy, the compassion and concern in his tone was unmistakable. It would seem he actually did care about Kiran's well-being; I was sure however, his inflection was all part of a brilliant plan to manipulate and deceive.

"Thank you, Bastian, but the only thing that truly exhausts me is a prude, self-righteous woman," he grunted pointedly and although I knew it was all part of his act, I couldn't help but feel offended. I wasn't prude. I mean, there was nothing wrong with being prude. "I just need to change. If you'll excuse me."

Kiran left the room quickly, and I noticed him give me a sly sideways glance before disappearing into his room. I stood fidgeting, wishing I was stronger-willed and brave enough to just leave Sebastian staring after a dramatic exit. Sebastian turned to face me, and I realized with dismay that I had already lost this debate.

"Eden, I could really use the company," Sebastian smiled sweetly at me as if he was almost embarrassed to ask me to go with him. "You would be my personal guest," he placed his hand gently on my arm and I shivered from an unexplainable chill.

"Ok, Sebastian, if you insist," I masked my terror with a charming smile and swallowed. I expected an interesting night at least.

"All right, let's go then," Kiran walked out of his bedroom looking incredible. His hair, moments ago, loose and wild, was now slicked back revealing his perfectly formed face. He wore a navy blue sweater with a white dress shirt underneath and a pair of designer, loose fitting jeans. The clean cut preppy look suited him and although I had every detail of his face already memorized, I found myself staring.

I allowed the boys to lead the way and fell in step behind them. I was starting to realize that although at first the whole "star-crossed lovers" thing seemed forbidden and romantic, like an exotic love story or classic tale right out of a page of history, it was a lot more complicated and messy than I had ever wished for.

Talbott was waiting in the Rolls Royce downstairs. I protested riding in it, insisting that I take my own truck, but all three boys demanded that I ride with them, which turned out to be a waste of time anyway, since the club was located only three blocks away.

Once the car was parked, I followed them once again, but this time to the door of the secret Immortal club, located just south of the main downtown area. Kiran stood back and let Talbott open the main entrance door by firmly gripping the unique door knocker. The knocker was in the image of a golden snake wrapped around an apple. When Talbott placed his hand around the knocker, the snake and apple lit up into a strong golden glow, unlocking the door and allowing us passage.

Once behind the door, we walked down a long narrow hallway, surprisingly well-lit, with mahogany tables and black candelabras evenly spaced down the entire length. The carpet was a crimson red and soon my cheeks matched the color as I walked past the place on the wall where Kiran and I had shared our first kiss. After being forcefully asked to leave Kiran's private club, he had walked me to the door and without warning pushed me against the wall. He basically had his way with me, right in front of Amory, my grandfather. And, by have his way, in the total innocent, make out version.

At the second door, Talbott once again placed his hand firmly around another golden snake, this one much skinnier than the first and wrapped around a scroll. The knocker lit and glowed in the same fashion as the first one and we were once again allowed passage through the door. This door opened to a stone staircase, leading deep into the bowels of underground Omaha.

The club, as all of the Immortals referred to it, must have taken up the entire city block. Large, black chandeliers hung from the ceiling with dozens of long, cream candles lit on top of them. A long mahogany bar stood tall and took up the far corner of the large room. Immortals milled about the huge space everywhere, in groups of conversation and drinking all kinds of who-knew-what, in glasses of every shape and size.

As we descended the stairs, Sebastian linked arms with me and slowed our pace a little. I allowed the gesture, for appearances only, although I resented it. Last time I was here, I made a scene with Kiran. As of right now it was more important for me to put distance between us than show my malice towards Sebastian.

The room fell silent when Kiran's presence became known and I watched slightly horrified, but was mainly awed as the entire room bowed in unison when he reached the bottom stair. Kiran paused and allowed the gesture benevolently. He smiled generously and appeared almost humbled by the graciousness of his subjects.

Eventually, he raised his hand and the room regained their upright posture.

A path was formed and Kiran was allowed entry without any physical contact from anyone. He made his way to a sidewall that I had yet to see, due to the masses of people standing in the way. Sebastian and I followed him and once we were through the people I realized there was an immaculate golden throne, sitting on top of a wide crimson riser.

Kiran walked straight to the throne and sat down. Talbott produced a golden crown, bedazzled with all sorts of jewels, from who knew where and placed it respectfully on Kiran's head. I stifled a laugh, before being forcefully pushed closer to Sebastian by the throng of people trying to get as close to the Crown Prince as they were allowed. Since the pushing and shoving was done more in a passive aggressive, more civilized and snooty way, than reminiscent of a mosh pit, I couldn't really complain. But I still did not enjoy the intimacy Sebastian and I were forced to share.

"I'm thirsty," I drummed up an excuse and reclaimed my arm from Sebastian. I turned around without waiting for him to respond. I wiggled my way through the Immortal crowd in a much less sophisticated way than any of them would have, but I was irritable. All of the Immortals were older than me, obviously long out of high school. I wondered what types of complaints and issues they found so important that they needed to bring them before a Prince. Where did they go when he wasn't here?

I still had so much to learn.

I made my way to the bar and stood impatiently, tapping my fingers forcefully on the glossy wooden counter top. When the bartender gave a glance my direction and began to make his way towards me I realized I had no idea what I was going to order. I needed to know how to ask for something brown, disgusting and kind of like liquid smoke without sounding too much like a minor.

"Liam, two Scotch whiskeys, one ice cube each," Sebastian called from behind me. I turned with embarrassment, but grateful for his assertiveness.

The bartender, Liam, poured an ample amount of whiskey into two snifters and I took it pretending I knew what to do with it. Sebastian inhaled the rim of the crystal glass before taking a long swallow. I followed suit, smelling only for a moment the heady,

76

woodsy liquor before taking an equally long drink.

The Scotch made its way slowly, too slowly, down my throat leaving a trail of burning fire. I used my magic quickly to quell the flames and keep myself from choking the dangerous alcohol back into Sebastian's face. I imagined this was what a forest fire would taste like.

"I don't understand this place," I said bravely, allowing the whiskey to dull not only my senses, but my fears too.

"What do you mean?" Sebastian asked, narrowing his eyes with more suspicion.

"I mean, is this a court? Is this a club? What do the Immortals do when there isn't a Prince to solve their problems? Does he come here every night? Is every Immortal allowed in here or is there an age limit? That's what I mean," I set my empty tumbler on the bar, and folded my arms in defiance, daring Sebastian not to answer me.

"Oh," he said simply, a smile creeping into the corners of his mouth.

"Raised human, remember?" I used the excuse I so hated, but I was determined to get answers.

"Well, let's see. It's both a court and a type of social club I suppose. When Kiran isn't present, this is where the elite are welcome, where they come to get away. And there are obviously ways of solving problems when the King or Prince aren't present. Each region of every country is appointed a Regent and under him a team of judges to handle smaller and more menial concerns. If ever a large problem were to arise, then an audience with the King is requested and travel arrangements made. I think King Lucan sees this as an opportunity for Kiran to gain experience and, well, perspective. He is here several nights a week, although not all. He would never allow that. Kiran enjoys his freedom way too much to also enjoy the duties of royalty," Sebastian shook his head as if he was in some way disappointed by this. "And yes, there is an age limit, unless of course you're considered VIP." His smile widened before he drained his snifter as well and then signaled to the bartender for another round.

"I see," I frowned, digesting all of the information that turned out to be far easier to obtain than I had expected. "So who was the Regent of this region before Kiran graced us with his company?"

"Who else? Amory Saint of course," Sebastian's eyes narrowed into a disapproving glare and a sour frown replaced the smile I found so disturbing.

"Why do you say 'of course'?" I asked, honestly out of ignorance.

"Well, he's the only one we can count on not to die," he shook his head as if clearly annoyed before continuing, "You know, because he's the last...."

"Oracle," I finished, proud of myself for finally knowing something.

"Speak of the devil," Sebastian's expression turned even darker and I looked up to see Amory making his way towards us with the same angry expression on his face.

I took my second tumbler of Scotch in one gulp, as if having it taken away from me by force would be the ultimate insult. I still hadn't forgiven the Resistance for their less than welcoming attitude towards me, and grandfather or not, Amory basically summed up the Resistance as a whole. So as he approached, clearly on the warpath, my irritation with the evening only worsened.

"Ms. Matthews, I believe you were asked not to return here not long ago. May I ask what has possessed you to be so bold this evening?" the way that Amory phrased the question left me positive he was not only referring to my presence at the club, but my behavior over the course of the entire evening; starting with my quick getaway off of the farm.

"She is my guest, Sir," Sebastian offered quickly. "I insisted that she accompanied me tonight." He turned to give me an arrogant smirk, as if to say he had this under control.

"I was just leaving," I said dryly before any more fuss could be made. I placed my empty glass on the bar roughly and pushed past Amory and Sebastian. The rest of the Immortals were still deeply involved in Court, whatever that meant, and so there was no audience to witness my exit this time around.

I took the stone stairs two at a time and found myself on the old, brick streets of the Old Market in a huff of displaced anger. In my head, I realized that Amory was not trying to punish me, and Kiran was not trying to abandon me, although Sebastian was probably actually trying to torture me, but I couldn't help it.

I had no control over what I was allowed to do and what I was forbidden to do. I couldn't be with the guy I was in love with, at least not easily or publically. On top of it all, frustrating, irritating and creepy boys had been sent to spy on me, well one boy that fit that description anyway.

Outside, in the cold November night I realized that I no longer had a ride back to my car. I walked, or rather stomped begrudgingly, towards the direction of Kiran's downtown loft, and Avalon's truck. The night just kept getting better.

Chapter Ten

Where are you and where the hell is my truck? Avalon's irritated voice rang in my head as soon as I was headed away from the club.

I'm on my way home now. My response was more irritated than Avalon's if that was even possible and the only response I got back was some kind of mental "Pssshht" sound.

"Excuse me," A man's voice called to me from the shadow of an ally and I was instantly gripped with fear. I reminded myself that I was Immortal and strong enough to take any mugger out.

Despite that, I picked up my pace and kept my head down. I didn't want to take any chances. My magic flared in self-defense and I pulled my tweed coat around me tighter.

"Excuse me, ma'am," The low voice called to me again. This time I heard a faint accent underneath his deep tones reminding me of something familiar. "I'm sorry to bother you, but I seem to be lost."

I squinted into the shadows and vaguely made out the form of a large man leaning against the brick of an office building. He was standing on one leg, while the other was bent and propped against the wall. His hands were pushed deep into the pockets of a coat and he wore a baseball hat low on his forehead.

After noticing my pause, the man pushed off from the wall using his bent leg and walked briskly towards me. Finally his face was illuminated by the soft glow of a streetlight and I was quickly aware of his magical current.

I breathed a sigh of relief, realizing that this man was an Immortal and in all likelihood probably trying to find the very club I just vowed never to return to. He walked purposefully towards me, never slowing his pace and I wondered for a moment if he was in a hurry.

"Are you looking for the club?" I asked, relieved and sure of his intentions.

"Not anymore," He stopped short in front of me and I could feel his hot breath on my face. I had no time to react before he reached out his hands, grabbing me tightly around the neck.

I fell weak instantly, overcome with panic. He was choking

me, trying to kill me and I was too stunned to fight back. I was losing oxygen too quickly to think straight. My magic was lost in a torrent of fear and I fought against myself to move…. to defend myself. Slowly, I began to scratch, claw and kick to get away. Then suddenly I was surged with overwhelming alarm. I would die if I didn't fight back.

The harder I fought however, the quicker I lost what was left of my dwindling supply of oxygen. My strength was waning in the battle and the attacker, whoever he was, seemed undaunted by any of my self-defense attempts all together.

The man gripped my neck tighter, seemingly crushing my throat between his strong and magical fingers. I felt my magic begin to drain into his hands and panic over took me once again. I realized then, that this man wanted my magic; that he was willing to kill me to obtain the eternal life that ran through my veins.

He lifted me effortlessly off the ground, shaking my limp body and pulling my magic out quicker with his own. My eyes began to close without my permission and my breathing had nearly stopped all together. It wouldn't be long until I lost consciousness completely.

I only wished I could have said goodbye to Kiran first, and Amory and my brother.

Thinking their names was all the reason I needed to remember myself. Finally my survival instinct took over. Flight was not an option here, only fight or death. But I would much rather fight.

Though my magic was fleeting, I still had human instincts I could rely on. My body was raised off of the ground, my Immortal attacker holding me victoriously high in the air. With one surprisingly swift and strong kick of my right foot, I found my target squarely between his legs. Even if he was Immortal, he was also still a man.

Unprepared for that strong of an attack from me, he dropped me roughly to the ground and doubled over in pain. Weakened by my depleted magic and lack of oxygen I struggled to my feet, stumbling around as if I were drunk. As quickly as I could and remembering every self-defense move I had ever seen in a movie I used my foot again, kicking upwards into his face and knocking him backwards.

I summoned what magic I had left and inhaled a large amount of air, sending it straight to my brain. My attacker was also recovering quickly, using the magic he stole from me, I guessed. I could feel Avalon pounding at the door to our shared consciousness but I refused to let him in, until I had finished this.

The man turned to face me, and as soon as he did, I shot a strong burst of magic his direction. I was faster than he had given me credit for and I caught him off guard, knocking him once again off his feet. Before he could recover, I pulled the bricks out of the office building he used as cover, down on top of him. My magic willed them easily from the building, leaving a gaping hole into a clean, but dated lobby.

I heard him grunt with the effort of recovery and began to feel hope that I had won this battle. Well, until I was knocked off of my own feet by a large slab of concrete ripped from the sidewalk. Apparently, the man was only feigning weakness. I heard the sickening crunch of bone from the back of my head after I flew twenty feet backwards, landing in a crumpled heap.

The pain was indescribable and I let out a scream of agonizing horror, wheeling in nausea. My magic could not move fast enough to repair my broken cranium and stop my brain from hemorrhaging. When my vision finally returned and my skull became solid once again, it was too late, the attacker was already standing over me, stomping his thick boot down forcefully on my throat, cutting off the oxygen once again.

Forcing my nerves under control and taking one final breath, I sent a rush of all the magic I had left through my veins and shivered under the force of it. And thankfully, when my magic was in full force, I actually didn't need to breathe. I grabbed his foot as strongly as I could, my delicate hands seemed miniscule next to his thick calf and steel toed boot. I pushed with everything I had, pushing him thirty feet the opposite direction and finally giving myself plenty of room to breathe.

With a quick intake of breath, I was on my feet and next to him. I raised my left foot and brought it down heavily onto his face, both feeling and hearing his nose shatter underneath the sole of my navy blue clog. Seemingly immune to pain, however, he reached up and grabbed my arm, pulling me down on top of him. I struggled and flailed my appendages but still he wrestled me underneath him.

82

I let out a scream of frustration, exhausted from the effort and unwilling to lose my life to such a brutal assassin.

"What do you want?" I shouted into his recovered face, fighting to keep his hands away from my exposed throat. Sweat poured down my beaten face, despite the icy rain that began to fall from the sky.

"I know who you are," he growled menacingly.

I didn't doubt that he did. There was pure hate behind his eyes. My magic was dissipating from my veins in a steady stream into his open palms. Wherever his skin touched mine, there was a portal to withdraw my life's blood.

"And you think by killing me, what? You think by draining my magic you'll what? You'll have eternal life?" I mocked harshly, downplaying what was probably the truth.

"I know that I will," he replied with frightening certainty.

As I struggled for breath and consciousness under his iron grip, my short life as an Immortal began to flash before my eyes: my confusion, meeting Kiran, Amory's guidance, Avalon, Lilly, the Resistance, my first fight…. my first fight! I drained those boys of their magic without touching them once. This man, whoever he was, seemed to need physical contact in order to take my magic. I didn't.

I focused what little energy I had left on taking his magic. I concentrated on whatever I could find, pulling magic from remote places I didn't know existed, willing him to give up what was rightfully mine, but it was no use. I was too weak. Whatever advanced skill I used in that first battle had been drained from my blood and the attacker now possessed it.

He was really starting to piss me off.

And then it dawned on me. He could take my magic by touching me, but I was also touching him. I didn't have to take his energy remotely; I could take it back the same way he was.

I sucked in another labored breath and focused this time, not on an idea or concept, but on his actual flesh. I focused on his knees that were digging into my thighs to keep me pinned to the ground. I focused on his hands holding my shoulders tightly to the concrete and I focused on the tips of his boots digging into my ankles. Slowly, almost unnoticeably at first, I began to reclaim my magic.

At first our struggle resembled something like tug-of-war. I pulled a little magic back and he re-took the electricity again. I held

83

my breath, not even allowing the effort of breathing to weaken my attempts. I pulled again, holding the small amount of magic in place for a second, and then a second longer and then two seconds longer.

A drop of sweat from his forehead landed on my nose and I realized, finally, that he was weakening. With renewed vigor I pulled another miniscule amount of energy from his veins into mine, holding onto it until I was sure it belonged to me once again. The next pull was longer still and the amount of magic enough to give me strength to continue.

I pulled and pulled and pulled, until I had drawn what was mine and more out of his pathetic veins. I pushed him off me with minimal effort and stood next to his body. He looked up at me with a primal fear, but even more than fear, with hate. I turned away, fully intending on leaving him just like that.

I walked five feet, but it was not enough. Suddenly I was flying through the air, face first into the building I had half destroyed earlier. I burst through the destroyed brick, sending shrapnel and dirt all over the pristine lobby. I landed in a crumpled heap, thankful he hadn't taken any of my magic yet.

In only a few seconds I stood and crossed the distance between us. Sending a burst of magic at his kneeling figure, I knocked him to the ground with an unadulterated hate I didn't know I was capable of. Before he could even react I began extracting what was left of his magic, and I did not stop until he was completely drained, lying in a crumpled heap at my feet.

I stood above him, greedy with power, letting the new magic join my own, rushing, pumping, and intermixing with my blood. The electricity inside of me was hot with power, jumping and popping like bolts of lightning.

"Kill me," the man whispered hoarsely from his prostrate position on the cold, iced over concrete. "For the love of God, kill me."

I finally looked down at the crippled shell of a man and my heart unwillingly broke. What had I just done? Who was I? I wasn't a murderer. I couldn't take what wasn't mine just because he was willing to. Whoever this man was, I was not like him. I could not return the same hate.

He grabbed my foot weakly with both hands, begging me to end his misery. I closed my eyes, unable to look at him any longer and the tears streamed down my face. A choking sob escaped without permission and I failed to see any other option before me.

But then, to my great relief, a green SUV suddenly came to a screeching halt on the battle-torn street, destruction caused by my own hand. Avalon and Jericho jumped out of the still-running vehicle and were at my side in moments. Avalon, now sharing not only my consciousness, but my emotions as well, opened his arms to me and I fell into them. I wept heavily, unable to calm my broken heart. I couldn't have really been about to kill him.

Jericho shouted orders at Avalon, who shouted back, but refused to let go of me. I held on to him tighter, afraid he would obey Jericho's heartless commands. I was aware of Jericho tying the man up and carrying him to the trunk of his vehicle. I was also aware of Avalon depositing me into his back seat, never once leaving my side.

In minutes Jericho had dropped us back at Avalon's truck and had sped away into the heart of Omaha. I didn't know what Jericho would do with him, and I was not sure I really cared. The only thing that mattered to me now was that whatever happened to that horrible man would no longer be my decision.

In the safety of Avalon's truck, the tears stopped. The horror had lessened and the stolen magic was now as much a part of my blood as my own. I realized then, that particular assassin was not the only one out there with murderous intentions. I was naive to believe my identity was a secret and I was stupid to believe that only Lucan would be interested in the precious magic only Avalon and I carried.

He would not be the last adversary I would have to fight and he would not be the last attacker I drained of all vital Immortality. I was fighting a battle bigger than myself, bigger than a love affair, and much bigger than high school. Lines were being drawn and barriers being crossed. The war had begun and my indecision would no longer stand.

Chapter Eleven

"Morning," Avalon grunted to me on the way back from the bathroom.

"Mmmm-hmmm...." I responded sleepily. I rubbed at my face and walked bleary-eyed towards the direction Avalon was coming from.

I was exhausted from last night. The assassin's dark and ominous face was still burned in my memory and I shivered as I brushed my teeth. I wrapped one arm around myself and stared confused at my ragged reflection in the mirror. Who was the girl staring back at me?

My hair was a tangled mess of impossible curls, extra frizzy from going to bed with them wet. Showering last night was a non-issue after coming home caked in dirt, grime, blood and the filthy feeling of being so near such a possessive evil. My eyes were clear of makeup and my face washed out and paler than normal. I looked ten years older at least; I half checked my head for grays.

I felt worse than even ten years older, more like thirty. I reminded myself I was only sixteen, my birthday was still four months away; but over the last three months I felt as though I had aged well beyond my decade and a half of life.

Shouldn't I be more concerned with shopping and cheer-leading than with civil wars and living for eternity? For someone who was supposed to have Immortal life, I spent most of my time trying not to die.

The thing was, as cool as the whole magic and Immortality life was, I could have been equally as happy living a normal life and dying of old age, or dying really, at any age. When I thought I was human, I accepted that death was a part of life; like Kiran once told me, when there was a cost to living; living became that much more significant.

Now that I seemingly had the rest of eternity to live, my life was threatened at every turn. I didn't know many other high school girls fighting assassins and bounty hunters, and hiding from kings. Even Avalon couldn't relate, although thanks to the connection he could at least empathize, although not by choice. But even still, he chose his path in this life, and not only that, no one had signaled him out so universally.

Maybe I was just being a drama queen, but I didn't ask to carry the weight of an entire race on my shoulders. I didn't ask to be so powerful or so significant. I had always been happy fading into the background. Where was the normality to this life? Where was my security and sense of safety? I was going to give myself a heart attack from paranoia.

I couldn't even stay home from school today. Last night I fought a nasty battle, where my life was practically taken from me. I may have won, but it was at a terrible price. I thought that justified taking a personal day.

Nobody else thought so though. The powers that be, namely, Amory, Jericho and Avalon didn't want to raise suspicion. If I were to stay home, questions would be raised.... People would be sent to look for me.... Actions would be taken.... And so forth and so on.

When Amory came over late last night, he informed me that as of right now, nobody knew what happened to me or the other guy. Whoever sent the attacker could still be hoping for the best, still hoping that I was dead. If I showed up at school today as if nothing happened, and clearly I survived, that would send a message.

I wasn't sure I actually wanted to send a message. Especially not a threatening- "it's you're move, what are you going to do about it now" kind of message. I might as well have worn a t-shirt that said something like, "Hey bad guys, I'm here, I'm fine, no worries. I'll be ready whenever you want to, you know, try to kill me again."

A knock on the door brought me out of my internal rant. I could sense the magic from the other side of the door and realized that it was Jericho. After doing who knew what with the idiot who tried to kill me, he was assigned house duty here with Avalon. It was Amory's idea of upping security.

"I'll be out in a sec," I mumbled gruffly, working on the knots in my hair. And then saying, "Screw it," I threw my hair into a high bun, wrapping it impossibly through a hair tie over and over again until it was secure. I contemplated going sans makeup as well, but decided against it for the sake of all decency.

Smearing on some thick, black eyeliner and charcoal eye shadow, and topping it off with some lash-extending mascara, I looked goth-chic and was kind of digging the style. My onyx eyes gave me a wild, dark appearance and a feral feeling swept over me. Finishing the look with a deep, scarlet lip gloss, I called it good and opened the door for Jericho.

"Sorry," I grunted, taking in his expression while his eyes swept over me. "It's all yours." Jericho stood in the doorway, blocking my path. I could tell he was not quite sure what to make of my gothic appearance.

"No problem," he stood there still, unmoving, staring into my eyes.

"Hey, um, thanks for finding me last night," I put all of my weight onto one leg, fidgeting nervously.

"Avalon's really the one who found you. I just, um, I didn't know what he would find when he found you. You really scared me, um, us. You really scared us," he repeated, his voice breathy. He smiled shyly before taking a step forward, as if he were trying to get into the bathroom but then remembered I was in the way. He stopped suddenly, but didn't attempt to take a step backwards.

"Well, thank you anyway. I wasn't sure what would happen to me either," I said quietly, realizing I didn't mind his closeness.

"It's just, you're really important to me, I mean the Resistance. You're really important to the Resistance," his voice trailed off and I watched him swallow strongly. I stared at him for a moment, recognizing I owed him a lot.

"Eden, we're going to be late," Avalon called too loudly from the top of the stairs. I jerked out of my thoughts and gave Jericho an apologetic smile.

I brushed past him, and when our magic met, his was strong and pulsing. He didn't move back, leaving me little room to move by him. A blush rose to my cheeks and I began to think I didn't understand Jericho any more than I did any other boy. Didn't he want nothing to do with me only a few days ago?

The ride to school with Avalon was quiet, we were both lost in our own thoughts and shared consciousness. Avalon was deeply worried about me, and his anxiety was rubbing off on my already frayed nerves. He pretty much wanted to keep me shut in the house, surrounded by armed guards and all sorts of magical protection charms.

Although I felt he was over-reacting, I realized along with him, that this attack was only the beginning. After last night, I believed Avalon would never leave my side again, but the thought of putting him in danger made me sick to my stomach. My brother, my twin, half of the only family I had, the other half of the future of the Resistance.... I couldn't bare it if something happened to him.

Nothing is going to happen to me. Avalon growled defiantly in my head. "Nothing's going to happen to you either," he finished out loud as he pulled into a parking space at school.

We left the car silently, both purposing in our hearts to make Avalon's statements come true. I would let nothing happen to my brother, of that much I could be sure. And I knew without a doubt that he would let nothing happen to me.

We walked into the English and Drama Building quickly. The November air was frigid and the icy rain from yesterday hadn't let up. I shook the sleet off of my shoulder, not bothering to use magic. Ever since the assassin's magic became part of my own, I could not bring myself to use it. The energy was building up inside of me and making me edgy and irritable, but still I refused to use what was not mine.

"Come here. I need to talk to you," Kiran walked past me, his harsh whisper beckoning me into the theater. At first I rebuffed his direct command, but when I glanced into his eyes, the concern was etched so deep that my heart instantly filled with longing.

I walked over to him and we entered the theater silently. Talbott was already inside the dark room and I would normally be irritated with this, except my own bodyguard in the form of Avalon had followed me as well. Talbott and Avalon stared each other down and despite my melancholy mood, I found their competition and animosity entertaining.

"Are you all right?" Kiran's whisper had softened and he pulled me into his arms. My body willingly molded into his strong embrace and I inhaled his scent. Kiran's closeness instantly calmed my frayed nerves, my head seemed clearer and my muscles began to relax.

The only difficulty in being wrapped in his arms was his frenetic and intrusive magic. Our magics were so used to finding each other, to mingling together, that Kiran's magic was desperately seeking mine. I refused to unleash my own; I refused to taint Kiran's magic with the evil and sinister electricity from last night's attacker.

"No," I mumbled truthfully and a lone tear fell slowly down

my cheek.

"I'm so sorry, Love, I am so sorry," Kiran's voice cracked from emotion as if it were his fault and my shoulders felt the weight once again of the burden I carried.

"Will there be another one?" I asked, lifting my head off his chest and searching his turquoise eyes for truth.

"I don't know," I knew he was answering truthfully, but deep down I knew that there would be one. Voicing the question out loud gave me false hope; the true answer was already ringing loudly in my ears. "He wasn't sent by my father, he acted on his own accord," Kiran looked directly into my eyes and I wanted to believe him. I knew he believed what he was saying, but I couldn't.

"You can't be serious," Avalon blurted out incredulously.

"Don't start," Talbott growled a warning.

"No. You don't start," Avalon replied menacingly. "How can you say that he acted on his own? He is one of Cartier's personal Guard."

"How can you possibly know that?" Talbott was suspicious, making Avalon hesitate speaking again.

"Sebastian explained to me the circumstances and I can find no fault with him," Kiran stood up straighter, inadvertently drawing further away from me. "He asked Beckton to walk you home after you left the club. He didn't want you to walk back to your car alone. His intentions were completely blameless. Beckton must have been at the trial, he must have put the pieces together on his own. Trust me. This was not my father, nor was it Sebastian," Kiran rubbed his hand against my back, but I found no comfort in the gesture. I felt instead, patronized and I was not happy about it.

Avalon began to defend me, but I cut him off. "Kiran, he was waiting for me. He was hiding in the shadows waiting. He knew exactly who I was and that I would be alone. He tried to kill me.... He tried to kill me," I said every word carefully and pointedly.

"It doesn't matter now," Kiran said quickly, pulling me into his arms again. "He is being taken care of, I have seen to that."

"Wait.... Where is he?" I asked, confused. I thought I saw Jericho drive away with him.

"After I picked you up Eden, Amory relayed everything to Kiran and handed Beckton over to Kiran's guard," Avalon explained quickly, so I did not give anything away about Jericho. He made it clear in our shared thoughts to leave as much about any other member of the Resistance out.

"He will never hurt you again," Kiran whispered soothingly, hugging me tighter.

"He can't hurt anyone again; he doesn't have any magic left," I mumbled, outraged by the thought of him and irritated by the others around me. Wasn't I the one who took care of him? Wasn't I the one who had made sure he could never hurt anyone else again?

"I really wish you wouldn't have done that," Kiran's comment surprised me and I drew back, defensive.

"What do you mean?" I narrowed my eyes in suspicion, a feeling of resentment washed over me and I was unsure what to make of my reaction to the love of my life.

"It's just that, when you do things like that, you draw unnecessary attention to the strength of your power. Now we either have to explain why a sixteen year old girl can drain a trained and vetted Titan Guard or we have to hide all of the evidence altogether. Either scenario is extremely difficult and both could result in dire consequences," his eyes pled with me to return to his arms, but his words were spoken so insensitively and matter-of-factly that I had trouble actually comprehending them.

"Kiran, he tried to kill me. He nearly succeeded.... a couple of times actually. What was I supposed to do? Just walk away? He wanted me dead and if I hadn't taken every last ounce of his magic, everything that made that possible, I wouldn't be standing here today," I watched Kiran open his mouth as if to explain himself but I had enough. I was not bait for either side of this damn civil war to take advantage of. I was a person, a person who was just figuring this whole freaking thing out and my magic was ready to explode thanks to those yahoos and their excessively emotional states. I was the one who should be over emotional, I was the one who should have been arguing and demanding explanations. I had had enough.

I turned around, fed up with all of them and stormed through the double doors leading back into the lobby of the building. I could feel all three boys close on my heels and if it weren't for Sebastian standing just a few feet from my point of exit, I would have left them all in my dust on the way to class. As it were however, I had to stop and face the idiot probably responsible for my near death experience last night.

91

"What?" I shouted, not at all surprised to find him spying on us. The boys all skidded to a halt behind me, clearly more unnerved by his presence than I was.

"I'm sorry to interrupt," Sebastian said snidely, obviously proud of himself for catching us in the middle of something. I crossed my arms defiantly and glared at him until he eventually continued. "Eden, it has come to King Lucan's attention that you were raised human, and that you have just recently been introduced into Immortal society."

"And?" I asked rudely, my tone full of venom.

"Well, if that is indeed the case, then it would seem you haven't experienced the Eternal Walk," he continued as if I were lying about being raised by humans. I could assure him that this was one of the only things I had been completely honest about. "Lucan has ordered that you follow through with this rite of passage as soon as possible. Preparations have already begun to be made." Personally I had absolutely no idea what Sebastian was talking about, but the reaction I felt inside of Avalon made every one of my hairs stand on end. Avalon reacted with such fear and apprehension that whatever this Eternal Walk was had Avalon scared out of his mind.

Kiran instinctively put a hand on my shoulder and I felt his fingers shake where they lay. Despite the boys' reaction, I frankly, was over it. I didn't know what the Eternal Walk was and that pissed me off. I was tired of hiding my relationship with Kiran and my identity from the rest of the world and that pissed me off.

I let out a scream of frustration I couldn't control and finally the magic I had been holding on to all morning rushed out of me. I reached a breaking point in sanity; the internalized magic arrived at its full and powerful limits in the glass of all of the doors and windows of the lobby. Glass shattered all around us in one electric pulse of energy.

I didn't bother with feeling guilty or ashamed, but walked straight passed Sebastian and up the stairs towards English, my clogs crunching on broken glass the entire way. Those four boys had made a mess of my life and so they could be the ones to clean up the mess in the lobby, for all I cared. At least Mr. Lambert wouldn't be yelling at me for being late today.

92

Chapter Twelve

"Ms. Matthews, your presence is requested in the Principal's Office," Ms. Woodsen spoke softly and delicately, despite her wild appearance, to me before I could reach the entrance to Drama. I smiled graciously and turned around on my heel.

Fighting through the pressing crowd of my classmates, I came out on the other side relieved. Drama was not my forte, to say the least, and I wasn't exactly emotionally prepared to work on dramatic prose this morning. I'd had enough drama in my life to satisfy the most avid attention seekers, I could easily go without a peer group of judgmental adolescents all bent on my literal destruction.

In the lobby of the English and Drama Building, men had already been called to repair the broken glass. The marbled floor was pristinely clean and the window sills wiped and waiting for new panes to be installed. I smiled to myself, content with the gratifying feeling of destroying something and walked through the crew of men working without a single hint of guilt.

I made my way across campus quickly, the November air was frigid and windy. The Nebraska sky had ceased to send soft, refreshing rain and was now in a steady state of spitting ice. I pulled the hood of my jacket over my head, an accessory that had now become my constant companion.

Mrs. Truance nodded her head in disdained approval on my way to the staircase leading up to Amory's office. I grudgingly used my magic, to dry my clogs and coat before entering "Principal Saint's" office without knocking. Amory would not have been pleased if he knew I was withholding my energy for the simple sake that I could. He would have been even more upset if he knew how I dispelled the built-up electricity this morning.

"Eden," he gasped upon my arrival, standing at his desk shuffling papers. I rushed to his arms and he held me tightly to him.

Suddenly I burst into sobbing tears, soaking his expensive tweed suit jacket. I felt foolish and childlike. I might have been able to hold in my magic, but my emotions had overtaken me.

"There, there," he soothed, rubbing my back. His deep, melodic voice reached to my soul and I had never been more relieved to be in my grandfather's calming presence.

"They're never going to stop are they? They are never going to stop and I'm going to have to keep hurting them!" I wailed, my sweeter emotions overtaking my fear and anger.

"Oh, Eden," I heard Amory's voice break and he hugged me tighter.

My sobbing continued for several more minutes. Amory's magic wrapped around me, doing its best to comfort and calm me. I felt as though I was past the point however. Eventually my tears stopped and my shaking subsided. I stepped back, wiping my face with the sleeve of my pressed white uniform shirt.

Amory coughed forcefully, ridding his voice of any emotion before gesturing with his hand for me to sit. I obeyed, sitting with my legs beneath me in one of Amory's comfortable leather chairs opposite his expansive desk. He also took a seat in his own high-backed leather chair.

"I'm sorry about the windows," I mumbled glumly, sniffing and unable to look Amory in his eyes.

"Oh, it's just glass," he smiled gently, but it didn't reach his eyes. Amory had the same black eyes that I had and they were etched deeply with concern. For a moment he looked ancient, as if he had been alive since the beginning of time. "Eden, earlier this morning, I spoke with Lucan," Amory took a moment to pause and let the gravity of what he was about to say settle over me. "He asked many questions about you, none of which were what I expected. He is playing this game carefully; I believe he knows what is at stake if you suddenly disappear."

"Then why is he trying to kill me!" I demanded rather than questioned.

"I am not entirely sure if he is trying to kill you. I am beginning to believe he is only testing you. He is doing his best to find out what exactly you are capable of," Amory folded his hands on his desk and stared at me intently, waiting for my reaction.

"I'm not a research project," I growled.

"Eden, I am afraid that is exactly what you are," he shook his head slowly while looking down at his hands.

"So what were his questions?" I stifled my urge for nasty sarcasm.

"He was asking about your upbringing, your human

95

upbringing," Amory pressed his fingers together and his gesture displayed the gravity of his words. To me a human upbringing was menial and insignificant. If anything, I was proud to have been raised by a human. From what I could tell, Aunt Syl valued human life significantly more than anyone in this over-privileged, snobby, super-human, fantasy world. But as I became more aware of the culture around me, I found that they saw my guardian as a joke, an unbelievable coincidence or even worse, an insult.

"What about it?" I grunted, finding myself only growing more and more irritated.

"There is a tradition with young Immortals when they reach adolescence. When an Immortal child enters a new period of life, such as young adulthood or marriage, or child birth, tradition dictates that they take a symbolic walk. Each new phase of life signifies an extreme change to one's present condition and a taking on, if you will, of new responsibility. Each Immortal life is unique and highly regarded in that there is a ceremony for every major milestone. Normally, when an Immortal is born in to this world there is a baptism of sorts and a three-day festival. We call it the Eternal Baptism, and we bath each infant in holy water, not in the human sense, but in our own version of holy water. In reality your parents bestowed this honor upon you and your brother in the secrecy of their private lives, but when you turned thirteen, the traditional practice was not observed.

"It is entirely my fault, since I am the one who kept you in hiding and kept our way of life hidden from you. Unfortunately, now that you are known to the King, he expects you to fulfill your rite of passage. He has agreed to forgo the newborn christening, since I assured him, I baptized you upon your realization of self, but he has been stubborn about the Eternal Walk, the ceremony conducted when you reach adolescence."

"Why is that?" I asked, trying to get my head around thousands of years of tradition I had yet to catch up on.

"Because the Eternal Walk is significant to understanding what kind of Immortal you are. Before the separation of races, every Immortal would participate in the ceremony and learn what powers they exhibited most strongly and what kind they took on. It made sense thousands of years ago when a Witch could be born from a Medium and Titan and so forth. Today, the ceremony is done for the sake of the King. You see, Lucan, just like his father, and his father's father, monitor every single Walk, so that they can prove to themselves that every member of our community is adhering to the laws. Since the Monarchy, every Immortal has taken the Eternal Walk to prove their allegiance to the King. Well, until you and your brother."

"I don't understand," I said bluntly. "So I take a walk, Lucan is there, and then I can officially be a teenager? Is this like the Immortal version of a Bar Mitzvah?" I was lost.

Amory chuckled, but shook his head, "You, my dear, will endure an agonizing and strenuous test of both character and skill to determine the type of Immortal you are. Lucan will watch the demonstration with a board of advisors, and when you have reached your limit and are wrapped in the Holy Flame, he will discover your true and hidden identity, I'm afraid. Not only will your secrets be revealed for all, but after the fact, you will be weak and displaced and Lucan will be able to do whatever he wishes with you," Amory's face was suddenly grave and took on his ancient expression again. He rubbed his temples with his fingers as if fighting a migraine. I had the urge to walk over to him, but couldn't make myself move. I was too stunned.

"Is that all?" I finally found my voice. "So what exactly is it?" I courageously asked, not entirely sure I wanted to know the answer. I imagined all kinds of terrible scenarios of torture, but nothing I could come up with would leave me as unprotected as Amory suggested.

"The ceremony is not unlike the Induction Ceremony all new members of the Resistance experience. Since I know you witnessed Lilly's induction through the eyes of your brother, I expect you to have somewhat of an idea," he gave me a characteristic look that let me know nothing I did escaped the watchful eyes of the last remaining Oracle. "The Eternal Walk is sacred and private, and will tell you more about yourself than you knew possible."

"You will take a plane to India alone. You must go alone. Self-reflection is part of the journey. Lucan has generously offered Kiran's private jet, if you can call that generosity," Amory took a moment to pause and looked out the window towards the courtyard of Kingsley. I tried to digest India quickly before he continued, but failed, "Once you arrive in Bangalore, you will be taken to the Kendrick Palace, deep in the jungle. If you make it that far, preparations will begin to be made for your walk."

"What do you mean, if I make it that far?" I swallowed loudly.

"I mean, as long as this isn't all some sort of trick to simply get you on that plane. If you land in India, if you make it to the palace, if the plan really is to have you follow through with the Eternal Walk and not some ploy just to lure you on to that plane only to end up in a Romanian prison, or arrive in India only to be kidnapped and held for ransom until Lucan has all of his answers. I have never operated with so many "ifs" in all my life," he finished gruffly.

"Is that what you think will happen?" I clutched my throat, holding my hand tightly against it as if I was in danger of having it chopped off.

"I don't know what to think," Amory looked me in the eyes and his expression held such sorrow that I felt as if his soul was breaking. "But I do know that I will fight for you until I have breathed my last breath," His voice was quiet and unassuming, but the gravity of his words, the words of a man that had survived thousands of years, reached to my innermost doubts and I trusted him, I could not help but trust him.

"Ok, enough of this doomsday-talk. We will assume you make it to India, once on the plane you are forbidden from speaking. This is very, very important. For an Immortal rite of passage, silence is the ultimate form of respect; especially in India, where your stewards have all taken a vow of silence until your task is complete. So, on the ground in India you will leave the city, and ride deep into the jungle, high in the mountains. The trip will take three more days. Once you have reached the palace, you will be allowed to sleep for twelve hours. The stewards will wake you and immediately begin to bathe you. You will have one final breakfast and then fast from that point on. After your breakfast, you will travel again deeper into the jungle, to the Cave of Forever Winds. Your stewards will leave you there and your Eternal Walk will begin," he paused to gauge my reaction.

"Holy crap," I blurted out. "So, if I don't die before I reach the whatever-caves, I will have to do what? Alone?"

98

"Eden, I have no doubts that you will survive whatever fate lies beyond this continent, but it will be difficult. It is always difficult," he grinned at me.

"I suppose no one has ever died from not talking," I conceded. Amory laughed out loud.

"Not yet anyway," he winked playfully.

"So, what happens inside the cave?" I was afraid of the answer, but needed to be as informed as possible.

"You will have to face your worst fears and the worst version of yourself. What that looks like inside the cave is different for everyone and I can't prepare you anymore for that, regretfully. I can tell you this, though. The magical process that will happen to you is identical to that of the induction ceremony. Only instead of the magic entering in through your bloodstream, like you saw happen to Lilly, this magic will enter through your oxygen and happen more like an internal cleansing than external," Amory placed his hands in his lap again, and looked at me from under thick, dark eye brows.

"Oh," was all I could manage. "Well it was nice knowing you," I mumbled sarcastically.

"My dear, you will survive this, if I have learned anything about you, it is that you and your brother truly are Immortal. Both you and he should have died by now if there was a successful way to kill you. And yet, here you stand. This will be difficult, but you will only be stronger because of it. If anything my biggest concern is what this will reveal to Lucan."

"What do you mean, if there was a way to kill me?" I asked, unbelieving.

"I have always suspected that the twin connection you share with your brother meant something extraordinary. After his attack on you and your friends in the woods during that P.E. camping trip, my suspicions grew stronger. You should have swallowed his magic along with the others that night, but yet he was able to escape. When he returned to the farm, he was weak but already he had reclaimed most of his magic. If I am not mistaken you did not even notice the exchange," wide-eyed, I shook my head, and he continued, "Then again, during the Fall Solstice Dance, you fought, and then fell off a roof top. When Kiran landed he had exerted a tremendous amount of magic and the fall made his recovery process a bit more challenging. You however, hit the ground and already had recovered your magic, not missing a beat."

"But Kiran absorbed the blow, Kiran landed first," I protested.

"Kiran may have landed first, but you were the one who absorbed the blow. The amount of magic Jericho used should have been able to kill Kiran, but you took the brunt of it and stood up and walked away. Finally, there was your battle last night. I spoke with Beckton before I turned him over to Talbott and he was adamant that he drained your magic three separate times, yet you walked away from the fight stronger than ever."

"How?" I asked, bringing my knees to my chest, more afraid of this answer than all the previous ones. What did it mean to be unable to die? I had lived with the knowledge of Immortality for several months now, but I had never once tried to grasp the concept of actually living forever, of being unable to die.

"I believe it is the connection you share with your brother. Your magic is in fact, not your own, but a shared entity. When you are physically drained of your personal magic, you borrow from Avalon to recover, and vice versa. I think this is also the reason you were unable to give Jett, Oscar, Ebanks and Ronan back their magic. If Avalon shares your entire magical entity, then he would also claim all the stolen magic as well. Finally, I believe this is the reason you can survive so long as human. The magic still builds up, but functioning for you is a non-issue because you are still connected to the electricity that keeps you alive."

"Well, there you have it," I mumbled, unable to fully comprehend the depth of what I'd just been told.

"Eden, you are more than special, more than unique, you are the future of our race," Amory smiled at me with hope and ease, and I did my best not to vomit all over his crimson carpet.

"Hooray," I responded dryly.

"Cheer up, my dear. You can rest in the knowledge that you are not alone. You will always have your brother and whomever you choose as your soul mate," Before I could ask any questions he continued, "How are things with Kiran?"

"Fine, I guess," I remembered my irritation with him this morning and a new wave of frustration washed over me.

"Hmmm...." he sighed pensively. "Boy troubles?" I saw

100

mischief behind his onyx eyes and I held back a laugh.

"Yes, Grampa," the term of endearment came naturally off of my tongue and I watched Amory beam in reply. "I don't understand him; I don't understand why everything has to be so difficult!" I whined exasperatedly.

"Ah, the trouble with all youth, I'm afraid. I trust that you will work it out and if not, there are plenty of boys vying to take his place," his expression was one of pride, as if I was the most beautiful creature alive, and he was personally responsible for my beauty. "Speaking of which, please let Jericho know that he will be on the India team."

Choosing to ignore the obvious correlation between Jericho and my grandfather's previous comments, I asked a more important question, "I thought I would be all alone?"

"No, my dearest, you will never be alone. You may travel alone, but we will be there every step of the way. I would never leave my only granddaughter in the hands of the unknown," he stood up to walk over to me and so I followed suit.

Amory wrapped me in a strong hug and I realized that no matter how many assassins found me I would always have support. I had nothing to worry about with Amory on my side. Who knew how many people had tried to kill him, yet here he stood. In my grandfather's strong and loving arms, the fears and uncertainty of the future seemed to melt away and I felt only confidence.

Chapter Thirteen

Where are you? I sent my brother an impatient thought as I waited by his oversized truck after school. It had been a long day and all I wanted to do was go home and curl up in bed.

I'll be there in one minute. He was overly kind in his telepathic tone, feeling my irritation as strongly underneath his own skin as I could mine. His calming thoughts helped ease my frustration, but I tapped my toe quickly and crossed my arms defiantly all the same.

"So how much trouble did you get in?" Sebastian approached me with a sly grin from across the student parking lot. I suddenly regretted my self-absorption and stubborn refusal to wait inside Avalon's truck.

"Tons," I responded dryly. I realized the lie was necessary, but I also couldn't make myself care enough to make it sound believable. What did it matter? I was invincible, right?

"They were really that upset about some windows?" Sebastian surprisingly took my side, but I felt like he was trying to trap me.

"Well, destruction of private property, vandalism and all that," that's probably what it should have been anyway.

"Yikes," Sebastian stood only inches apart from me, his legs wide apart and his hands deep in his pockets. His broad shoulders towered over me, I should have felt intimidated or insecure or something, but I was finally past the point of caring.

"Yep," I over-pronunciated the "p" sound, looking bored and self-important. Maybe it ran in the family, or maybe it was a cultural thing that I didnt' understand, but both Kiran and Sebastian had a terrible time taking a hint.

"Are you upset with me?" Sebastian asked, taking a step closer.

"What?" I shrieked, surprised. I finally turned my full attention on him and I saw a flicker in his eyes, but I couldn't define it.

"I'm sorry; I mean I should have apologized first thing this morning," when I didn't respond he continued, "I should have apologized for last night, I feel responsible. If anything I should

102

have walked you to your car. It was very ungentleman-like, and for that I apologize." Several seconds went by and when I still didn't say anything he continued again, "I have to say, Beckton was part of my Guard. But I assure you, Eden, I had no knowledge of his defection or that he had any intentions to harm anyone. Please, accept my apology and let me know that we can still be friends. I just can't continue living knowing you blame me." Sebastian finished dramatically, reaching out to take my hand. I kept it firmly tucked underneath my arm, not softened at all by his attempts to charm me.

"Sebastian, of course I don't blame you," I masked my venom with a sarcastically sweet tone. "Of course it's not your fault I was attacked and nearly killed. I'm sure you had absolutely nothing to do with any of it," I flashed him a smile and batted my eye lashes. He blinked, unsure of what to make of me.

"Sebastian, please tell me you're not serious," Seraphina flanked Sebastian with Evangeline and Adelaide on either side. They stared me down, eyeing me with utter distaste.

"What do you want?" I snapped at Seraphina. I was too tired for this.

"You know, it's pathetic really," Seraphina addressed her friends as if I hadn't spoken at all. "Eden will do almost anything for attention." After she received the proper amount of laughter she continued, "I heard you had another temper tantrum today, Eden. You really should learn to keep that temper of yours under control. As hard as you're trying to trap a Prince, you might try a little class. Anymore outbursts like that and they won't let you anywhere near a palace," she shook her finger at me like I was a small child and her tone was patronizing to say the least.

Everyone around me broke into laughter, as if on cue, including Sebastian. I had to bite my tongue to keep from saying something I would regret. Seraphina might be a complete bitch, but I was the one cheating with her fiancé. As much as I would like to rub that in her face, it would only end badly for me and she would get what she wanted anyway.

"What's all this?" Confused with concern in his eyes, Kiran joined our circle, or rather my public stoning.

"Nothing," Seraphina spat and the hate I felt was evident in her voice. At least our feelings were mutual. "Let's go K. You promised to take me for coffee," she tugged on his arm and rested her bright blonde head on his shoulder. My stomach turned and I swallowed the vomit rising from repulsion.

"Ade, Eva? Are you birds coming?" Kiran called out, while being dragged away by Seraphina. When they turned and followed he called out to his cousin, "Bastian?"

"I'm coming," Sebastian called back.

"Brilliant," I heard Kiran say happily, but his eyes were still on me and they were etched deeply with worry.

"Well, enjoy your coffee," I mimicked Seraphina's voice, hoping Sebastian would finally leave.

"We're all right though? Aren't we Eden?" he pressed, clearly not giving up.

"Yes, yes, yes," I said in a rush, wanting to physically push him away. "We are fine," I forced the words out.

"Good," Sebastian looked visibly relieved. "Then do you mind if I ask you a question?" when I shook my head, he continued, "How is it, that you a girl, who has only known she has magical powers for a few months, was able to defeat a member of my personal Guard?"

And there it was. At least he was finally being up front about it.

"Do you really want to know?" I actually had this answer planned since last night. I assumed this question would be asked of me at some point and so I decided from the beginning I would tell the truth.

"Yes, of course," Sebastian narrowed his eyes, but I could see the light behind them; he could barely contain his excitement.

"The truth is, all guys are the same, Immortal, human or animal. You are all the same. Even a human girl can figure this much out," I was standing close to Sebastian, so when I told him the truth, it took no effort at all. I thrusted my knee upwards as quickly and forcefully as I could, using only human strength, but hit my target with success. I watched Sebastian drop to the ground, grab his groin and grasp for breath.

"What is that about?" Avalon could barely contain his laughter as he approached his truck.

"Finally," I groaned loudly. I stepped over Sebastian and walked around to the passenger's side door.

Avalon was still snickering while he climbed into the cab and started the engine. As we drove away Sebastian had recovered somewhat and was in an awkward half-standing position. He waved brashly at me and all I could do was shake my head.

"Do you want to go to the farm tonight?" Avalon asked me as we pulled into the driveway, several minutes later, although I was pretty sure he already knew the answer.

"Can I see Lilly?" I also already knew the answer.

"No, not yet," he responded, turning off the engine and jumping down from the driver's seat. Since we were officially at home now, Avalon ripped out his pony tail holder and let his shoulder length black waves free.

"Then, no," I said curtly, doing the same with my impossibly long and tangled midnight black hair.

"Eden, that's not fair," he whined and I got a glimpse into what a childhood would have been like growing up together.

We entered the house and noticed Jericho sitting on the couch looking bored. He was wearing a gray, long sleeved t-shirt and black, athletic shorts, bouncing one of his knees rapidly while chewing anxiously on his finger nails. When we walked in he gave me a half smile, and watched me walk around the room, never taking his eyes off me. His demeanor told me he was nervous about something, but I didn't have time to ask him.

"Eden, focus," Avalon called my attention back to him. "If you don't go, I can't go. And I want to go," Avalon whined some more.

"I don't care if you go," I said simply and it was the truth. Avalon would be safe at the farmhouse.

"I'm not worried about myself," he responded to my thought out loud, although I didn't actually voice my concern to him. "I'm worried about you; I'm not going to leave you alone here."

"I won't be alone, Jericho is here," I plopped down on the oversized couch next to him to accentuate my point, but the soft cushions pulled me closer to him than I intended. Our bodies sat sidled next to each other deep in the expansiveness of the soft couch.

"That's right," Jericho slapped my knee casually, but I felt his magic flare next to me.

"I can't go without you Eden. You don't get it. I have to stay with you at all times," Avalon spoke slower, as if I were having trouble understanding him.

"I don't want to go, Avalon, so deal with it," I spoke even slower, irritated that we even had to have this conversation. He should just be able to know the outcome already thanks to our twin connection.

"I was hoping you wouldn't be so selfish," he once again answered more than my words. I gave him a dirty, but stubborn look in response. "You're such a baby." Avalon huffed before taking the steps two at a time into his bedroom.

"Who's the baby?" I mumbled, and listened to Avalon slam the door shut both to his room and to our telepathic connection.

I reached for my ear instinctively and accidentally clipped Jericho in the nose with my elbow.

"Oh my gosh, I am so sorry!" I gasped as he grabbed for his face. "I am so, so, so sorry!" I laid my palms gently on either side of his face, feeling like the biggest klutz ever.

"It's ok," Jericho grunted through muffled hands. "Really, I'm fine," he pulled his hands away from his face and placed them sweetly on the tops of mine. He held my hands to his face while gazing into my eyes and I stared back mesmerized for a moment. His soft hazel eyes were compelling and he searched mine as if looking for the answer to a question he hadn't asked yet.

"I'm really sorry," I said again quietly.

"Eden, really, I'm fine," he broke into a smile I found absolutely charming, his perfect teeth glistened and I noticed one dimple to the side of his soft lips for the first time. My hands were still placed against his face, with his hands on mine. His magic soared and for the first time I realized that he may have real feelings for me.

I coughed nervously and looked away from his piercing gaze. "I should um, I should change out of my uniform," I mumbled, attempting to pull my hands away from his.

Jericho slid his hands from mine to my face so that we both sat there caressing each other's cheeks. I realized I should stand up, but the couch was deep and I was finding it hard to move. Jericho leaned in slowly and I willed myself to move, but I felt captivated and I hated myself for it. His soft lips brushed mine and a sickening feeling erupted in my stomach. He hadn't kissed me yet, but he was

106

going to.

"I can't," I blurted out, ruining the moment.

Jericho's hands dropped from my face and he was several feet away in milliseconds.

"Oh, I'm so stupid," he sighed, frustrated. He stood near the fireplace and bent over, running his hands through his hair.

"No, it's not you, you're not stupid," I stood up as well, with the desire to go to him, to comfort him, but I knew better and so I stood awkwardly on the other side of the room. "I'm the stupid one. I'm so sorry."

"You know what?" Jericho stood up straight to look me in the eye. "You're right. You are the stupid one," his tone was biting and I took a visible step back, hurt by his words. "Kiran Kendrick? Really? Eden, it's impossible, it doesn't even make sense," I opened my mouth to respond, struck by his honesty, and hurt by his words, but he didn't let me get a word out. "He's going to use you and then kill you. Do you understand that? He doesn't have feelings for you. He's not even capable of having feelings for anyone else but himself. You're so blind. I'm sorry that you're new to this whole Immortal thing, but there is no excuse for your behavior. You're endangering not only yourself, but your brother and the entire Resistance as well."

"Excuse me?" I found my voice and my attitude. "Who are you to judge me? You don't even know Kiran. You don't know anything about him or about us. I can't explain it to you, and you know what, I don't have to explain it to you because it's none of your business. I'm sorry I don't like you Jericho, but Kiran and I are the real deal and it has nothing to do with what I have to offer him," I crossed my arms defiantly. Jericho picked the wrong day to mess with me.

"How can you say that?" he shouted at me. "It's everybody's business! You make it everybody's business. You honestly believe that you can just continue this secret romance and then one day Lucan will be dead and you'll be what? Queen? It's a joke. Kiran doesn't want you anywhere near that throne except to steal your Immortality and leave you to rot in prison. And I know plenty, plenty about that so-called Prince Charming of yours. If he loves you like you claim, then why is he still engaged to Seraphina? Why does he still spend every spare moment with her, buying her things, taking her to dinner, spending the night with her?" when I shook my head in defiant shock he defended himself, "Eden, who do you think runs surveillance on him? Hmmm? I've seen it all. Sure, he has you over when she is busy and he is all alone. What do you think he does when you two are not together?" I took another step back. I felt like puking. "And do not tell me you don't have feelings for me when we both know that is a lie. Fine, I get it, I don't manipulate you and charm you the way he does, but what I have to offer you is the real deal. I'm not making promises I don't intend to keep, or hiding you away from everyone I know. You and me, we could be the real deal. Can't you see us fighting side by side? Starting a new way of life for, not only us, but our people as well?" Jericho's tone finally softened and I saw emotion behind his eyes, but he had hurt me too much for me to feel sorry for him. "Eden, I am offering you everything, not just secret parts of me but everything. I am the real deal," he walked over to me, staring into my eyes and waiting for an answer.

"I'm sorry, Jericho, but you can't argue your way into a relationship with me," I spat out, turning on my heel and running up the stairs.

"You're an idiot!" Avalon yelled through his door as I ran by his room. I felt deeply inside of him that he would like nothing more for me then to leave Kiran and date his best friend, but it was too bad.

I slammed my door shut and instantly burst into tears. Jericho had hurt me more than anyone else today and that was saying a lot. The day might as well go down as the worst day in all history.

I let out a scream of frustration and buried my face in my favorite feather pillow. Where was Lilly when I needed her? I was so sick and tired of boys.

Chapter Fourteen

I woke up in the forest, our forest, on a bed of soft, velvety grass. The moon shone brightly through the trees, illuminating the world around me in an iridescent glow, blurring concrete lines into one cohesive flow of flowers and trees. Lightening bugs flickered on and off as they buzzed around the small grotto I had awakened in. A warm breeze lifted my long hair off my shoulders, and around my face.

I stood up, my bare feet relishing the cool grass and looked around. Kiran hadn't called me here, since before I left for Romania and my memories of the beauty of this place, our secret place, had begun to fade. I reached down and ran my fingers through wildflowers of every shape and color. Even in the moonlight, their vivid colors stood out against the darkness.

I rubbed my bleary eyes, enjoying the peaceful surroundings. In a few seconds Kiran would find me, but until then I would enjoy the calm and quiet of this magnificent place. I sat back down in the middle of the clearing and brushed my fingers through the thick grass. I couldn't remember the last time I was really alone, or the last time I felt so still and serene.

The last few weeks had been so chaotic; my life seemed to have been so completely turned upside down. I might have been able to technically live forever, but I was pretty sure a stress-related heart attack would finish me off at any moment.

There was just so much to think about. Sebastian.... Assassins.... The Eternal Walk.... Living for eternity.... Jericho.... Kiran.... It was too much; it was too much for one person. I understood that I lived with a lot of responsibility, but did it really have to be life or death at every turn?

"There you are," Kiran's soft accented voice called from between two trees and he appeared in front of me looking more god-like than human.

He was in his baggy gray sweat pants that he often wore to this place, and his chest was bare revealing a chiseled and maintained physique. I sighed wistfully, at the sight of him. I had not wanted to be interrupted only moments ago, I had enjoyed the serenity of my solitude; but Kiran's presence brought an all-consuming swell of emotions that I now regretted not finding him sooner.

I stared up at Kiran, unable to move, unable to remember why I was so upset. He was the reason for all my difficulties, but he was worth it. Our magics began to search each other out, to swirl around us in a playful game that mingled and mixed together in a united symphony of electricity.

"What's the matter, Love?" he smirked, his perfect lips twisted in an expression that was both mischievous and caring.

"Nothing's the matter. Not now, anyway," I reached out my arms to him and when he touched my hands with his, I pulled him down to the earth next to me.

He landed beside me in a satisfied heap and his lips found mine immediately. With his hand carefully behind my head and his arm wrapped around my waist he brought me underneath him on the carpeted forest floor. A sigh escaped my mouth and I realized how desperately my soul had missed him.

"Kiran," I sighed again, wrapping my arms around his strong neck and inhaling his scent.

"Mmm.... say it again," he whispered hoarsely into my ear.

"Say what again?" I asked, confused for the moment.

"My name," he pulled away slightly so he could look me in the eyes. "I love your accent; say my name again," then he smirked at me with his signature smile and I fell in love with him all over.

"You love my accent?" I giggled, realizing for the first time that I sounded different to him too. "I love your accent." I stated plainly, as if my point was more valid.

"And I love you," Kiran stared deep into my eyes, allowing me to feel the muddled version of both, relaying to me the intensity behind them.

"I love you, too," I said, out of breath.

Suddenly our mouths connected again, a firework of adoration that exploded into our mingled magic in a light show of frenetic energy. He kissed me fervently as if to take all of my soul in this one embrace. I let him, without hesitation. I couldn't stop him if I wanted to. Our two spirits intertwined like a complex puzzle, forever joined, unable to distinguish the beginning from the end. And at that moment it didn't matter how my life was being torn apart or all of the obstacles we had to face to be together. We had each other. And that was all we needed.

Eventually, the kissing slowed down and I leaned back against the grass to catch my breath. I smiled up at Kiran, believing that everything would work out. It had to.

"Are you all right?" he asked, sliding onto his side next to me. He propped his head up with one hand and rested his other on my stomach. His hand was hot through my tank top; I did my best to focus on everything but that hand.

"Now I am," I said quietly, not wanting to relive the gory details of the day.

"I hate all this," Kiran said sadly, tracing his fingers around the wrinkles of my shirt.

"Ugh. Me too," I admitted. "Can't we just stay here forever?" I looked around at the perfect backdrop of the forest, the sky alight with stars and buzzing with fireflies, and I couldn't imagine leaving this to go back to the awfulness of my everyday life.

"We could," Kiran smirked and then buried his face in my neck. "But that probably wouldn't be very safe for the rest of you. And I like the rest of you," he laughed in the depths of my hair.

"The rest of me?" I asked, missing the joke.

"Yes, you know, your sleeping body, the one in the real world," he lifted his head up to kiss me sweetly on the mouth and then the corner of the mouth and then my neck again. He was very distracting.

"Oh, right. That one," I realized he was right. "Someone would find it, and kill it and all that."

"Yes, I suppose so," Kiran stopped kissing me to give me the intensity of his aqua eyes.

"Like Sebastian's Guards, or your dad or even Seraphina? Actually.... probably Seraphina," I grumbled.

"No. Not like them," Kiran replied sternly, like I offended him. "But somebody."

"You really think Sebastian had nothing to do with that attack?" I couldn't believe he was serious.

"Eden, Sebastian is my cousin, and one of my closest friends since birth; he would not lie to me." Kiran sat up, resting his long arms on his bent knees and looking out into the dense greenery.

"I hope for your sake, you're right," I sat up too, the intimate moment ruined.

112

"My sake? Is that a threat?" he asked mockingly.

"A threat? What? No. I meant.... Never mind what I meant. Why are you fighting with me?" I demanded. There was no salvaging this day.

"You're fighting with me," Kiran looked at me with a serious face, but cracked a smile despite himself. I couldn't help myself but smile back.

He opened his arm for me to snuggle up to him and I obeyed. There wasn't the warmth there was before in his arms. The perfection of his presence had disappeared but this was better than fighting.

"I'm just stressed," I mumbled, trying to excuse my testy behavior.

"Me too," he sighed and then kissed the top of my head, leaving his lips there for a few moments, holding me close to him.

"Well, then let's call it a night. I should probably, like actually sleep anyway," I looked up at him, trying my best to give a reassuring smile, but even I was unconvinced.

He didn't say anything, but he did give me a sweet, short kiss on the lips before our Dream Walk was over, and I was awake in my own bed surrounded by my pillows and buried deep beneath the folds of my thick comforter.

I wanted to just fall back to sleep, to forget the day and forget the way I left things with Kiran. But I couldn't. Even the refuge of sleep, that I usually used to drown out the difficulties of life, escaped me.

I lay there, staring at the ceiling till the birds were awake and the sun was streaming through my window. There was too much on my mind and too much to think about. I didn't know how one person could handle it all. Everything.... School, Immortality, the Resistance, Kiran, everything seemed so.... hopeless.

Chapter Fifteen

"Eden, why don't you put out more of those cucumber sandwich thingies and I'll find a place for the silverware," Aunt Syl instructed carefully, while fretting over her elaborate but catered spread. She pulled a pony tail holder off of her unseasonably tanned wrist and wrapped up her bleached blonde hair on the top of her head, the way she wore it when preparing for surgery.

I obeyed, but thought it unnecessary, unless we were hosting every single Immortal, living and dead.

In an effort to make me feel more comfortable, Aunt Syl suggested to Amory that she host the India logistical meeting at our house. That way I wouldn't be so overwhelmed by everyone at the farm, and things would still get done without my stubborn refusal to participate.

It was a sweet gesture, but part of me still wanted to just live in denial that India wasn't actually going to happen. Even though my departure date had been set for December first and I had been working with Avalon for the past week trying to push most of my magic his way, so I could disguise what would surely give me away to Lucan.

Nothing we were able to come up with so far had really worked. All of the other times our Magical Transference, as Amory called it, worked so seamlessly was when we were under extreme pressure. When it was just the two of us, it felt more like pushing Avalon out than giving him something that was mine. When there was nothing forcing us to work together, our magics were very clearly defined between the two of us.

We had also been working on finding the Brazil Team's magic together, but were having even less luck with that. We could both find the stolen magic, but neither one of us could differentiate between the individual magic that wasn't ours, especially with Beckton's magic now in the mix. And so far, we had been even more unsuccessful at bringing our two stolen entities together.

Everything seemed hopeless. I hadn't been alone with Kiran since our disastrous Dream Walk and the only communication I had with him was to assure me he was still on for Thanksgiving in a few days.

Even my Thanksgiving dinner seemed silly now, with India hanging over my head and my life falling to ruins around me. But I made myself hold on to it. I loved the idea of doing something so completely non-Immortal that other Immortals didn't even understand the idea. And I loved the idea of doing something for just me even more. I wasn't going to give it up no matter how ridiculous the idea was.

The doorbell rang and I heard Avalon's noisy descent down the stairs to open the door. He had been a ball of energy all day in anticipation for his precious Resistance members coming over. Avalon hadn't left my side since the last attack on me and since I barely left the house, we had both pretty much confined ourselves to house arrest. Jericho was around too, but we had separately decided avoiding each other would probably be best.

Well, I decided that. And since he made absolutely no attempts at any kind of interaction with me, I just assumed he decided that as well. It was irritating though. I liked Jericho. I liked talking to him and hanging out with him, and he was always open with me, giving me more answers than anyone else. I was frustrated that he had to let his feelings get in the way of our friendship. He should have known better.

I wandered into the living room, curious to find out who arrived first. Avalon and Jericho were both crowding whoever was here around the door, barely letting them inside. I couldn't make out who it was because the two boys towered over them, but then I saw it. A flash of red, chest high of the guys and I closed the distance to the door in seconds.

I pushed through the boys, not caring if I hurt them, or just irritated them. Lilly was here. Lilly was finally better. I threw my arms around her, hugging her so tightly I nearly knocked us over. My cheeks were wet with tears before I even knew to stop them and I couldn't help but feel like things would get better now. They had to. Lilly was finally better.

Suddenly I had a million questions for her. I released my hold and did my best to brush the tears away quickly, feeling sappy and over emotional. She reached out for my hands, tears staining her porcelain cheeks, her bee-stung lips swelling with emotion as well. I felt joyously vindicated.

"Oh, thank God," I sighed, bringing her into another hug.

"I'm so glad you're here."

"I'm so glad to be here," she said excitedly.

The doorbell rang again and I pulled her into the kitchen, letting the boys answer the door for the remaining guests.

"So you're better?" I looked her over quickly, trying to find signs of distress or pain. She looked beautiful as always, maybe even more so. Her hair was just as red as ever in tight ringlets, framing her face. Her skin was perfect and pale; her manner was just as sweet as I remembered. But there was more to her now, almost like she was glowing; her eyes were brighter and her smile bigger. She was breath-taking and with her beauty came an almost gravitational pull to her and a desire to possess whatever it was that made her shine so.

"Yes, finally, I'm fine," she sighed, taking a seat at a bar stool with shaking hands. I realized she might not be completely healed yet.

"I have missed you so much," I said seriously, taking the seat next to her. "Ok, let's see it." I gestured towards her neck.

She rolled her eyes, embarrassed, but moved her hair out of the way and touched her pointer finger to the spot just below her earlobe. A small serpent glowed a vibrant violet and I watched her cheeks blush with pride.

"Pretty cool," I smiled, just as proud of it as she was. She had gone through something extraordinary and she had the courage to decide what she wanted to do with her life. I knew she had feelings for Talbott at one point and maybe still did, but she didn't let those get in the way of her decision. She was a much better person than I would ever be.

"Eden, I'm so sorry I haven't been here for all of..." she began, and the tears were resurfacing in her eyes.

I cut her off with a rapid shaking of my hands. Tears were stinging my eyes again, too and I couldn't let her feel responsible for the mess my life was. "Don't!" I demanded. "Don't feel bad," I cleared my throat of the emotion threatening to overtake me. She nodded, but the tears were even more prominent in her emerald green eyes.

"Ladies, would you join us in the living room?" Amory was standing in the doorway, separating the two rooms, smiling at us graciously. I looked up at him and noticed even he was emotional. I couldn't be sure how long he was standing there, but all of these crying people were making it impossible for me to find my composure.

We jumped down from our bar stools without another word and followed Amory into the living room. By now, the room was full of Resistance members. They milled about, talking quietly, or sitting packed together on the overstuffed couches. The electricity in the room was palpable with anxiety running high and tension thick.

I followed Lilly as she snaked her way to the back of the room, a place we would both be comfortable. She found Jericho and went to stand next to him, probably thinking nothing of it. I swallowed my hesitation and found the courage to stand next to her, next to him. I leaned forward and offered a wave Jericho's direction, but all I got in return was a curt smile and a nod of the head. "Ok, let's begin," Amory called everyone's attention forward. Those standing in conversations moved into better listening positions and nobody failed to give their immediate attention to Amory. "You've probably heard by now that although Lucan hasn't made any outright threats against Eden, he has recently requested that she go through with the Eternal Walk," There was a low murmuring of disapproval from the crowd gathered and the feeling that washed through the room was one of fear. I should have been more upset at the upcoming task, knowing so many Immortals were worried about the outcome. But I couldn't help but feel a sense of camaraderie knowing so many people cared about what happened to me.

"She is set to leave December first and will be flying there on the Prince's private jet. We don't have much time to plan, and I'm positive that was on purpose. I don't want to be naive about the purpose of Lucan's request. Whatever the real reason, we need to assume the worst."

Amory paused for a moment. Terrence, one of the older members of the group, although I couldn't tell how old, interjected, "And what do you believe the worst to be?"

"That this is a trap to get Eden on her own and away from me, and to expose her vulnerability," Amory said with finality. There were gasps in the crowd and another rumble of low murmuring. I rocked back on my heels, almost knocked over by Amory's truthfulness. "Now, before we panic, even if that happens, I have full confidence in my granddaughter to be able to handle herself." He smiled at me, and there was a light behind his eyes, a desire to fight, like I had not seen before.

"I won't be alone though, right?" I interjected frantically. A strong hand was on my shoulder, and I looked over, knowing it couldn't be Lilly's. I was surprised to see it belong to Jericho whose expression had changed from one of indifference to carefully masked concern.

"No, and that is my next point," Amory smiled graciously at me. "We are going to be running teams the entire way from here to India. This will be one of the most difficult and tricky missions to date and I am going to need everyone's full support. Unfortunately for Eden, we cannot even leave her alone while she is in Omaha. So along with Avalon and Jericho, Lilly and Roxie will also be moving into this house."

I looked down at Lilly beaming with excitement. I was thrilled to have another girl in the house, even if that meant Roxie would be here as well.

Amory continued. "Back to the Eternal Walk. The flight over will leave us pretty vulnerable. We will have to rely on faith and Eden's ability, trusting she will land in Bangalore unharmed. That being said, Ryder's team, plus Avalon and Jericho, will take the same trip, at the exact same time, landing hopefully only minutes behind the Prince's jet. Terrence will be running point to ensure a smooth takeoff and landing from here. Ryder's team, you will take Conrad's aircraft, because I think it's the most inconspicuous. Avalon will be running point, Jericho, you will be second in command." Amory paused for a second to look at Ryder, "I'm sorry to put you in an awkward situation, Son, but I need those who care about Eden the most looking after her. Do you understand?"

Ryder nodded, a steely look in his crystal clear blue eyes. He looked like a leader, tall and thin, with every muscle etched to perfection from head to toe. His head was shaved and his skin tanned. Everything about him screamed discipline and commitment. I realized Amory had to make it very clear to him how to take a back seat because it would not be something he could do easily.

I noticed Jericho's hand leave my shoulder and I glanced over at him, missing his touch. His cheeks were flamed red and there was a spot on the floor that suddenly needed his undivided attention.

I knew he had feelings for me, but I supposed he didn't want the rest of our community informed. A pang of guilt punched me in the stomach, as I realized how much I was hurting him. I decided we needed to have a talk. I liked him too much to let our friendship die because I was in love with somebody else, and he was embarrassed.

"Titus Kelly, Xander and Xavier Langley and the Australia team will join you once on the ground in Bangalore from their positions in London," Amory continued addressing the six members of Ryder's team and Avalon and Jericho. "If all goes as planned, Caden's team from Morocco and Alina's team from Switzerland will already be in place in Ooty and the surrounding jungle. Avalon, Jericho and Ryder, you will follow Eden's progress from the airport to the Ooty Palace at a distance, at a very long distance."

What's Ooty? I sent a quick thought to Avalon, feeling lost.

It's the name of the town nearest to the Kendrick Palace. It's a touristy area of India in the mountains. Avalon answered my question quickly and robotically before tuning back in to Amory.

"Eden and Avalon's twin connection should enable the teams to keep a safe, undetected distance while still maintaining contact. We have yet to test the boundaries of their connection, but in Romania they seemed to have no trouble despite the distance of the Citadel and Sighisoara. They will not be that far apart in India," Amory was answering a question when I jumped back in. "Once she enters the Cave of the Winds, she will have to sever that connection, however, and Eden," he turned his attention on me, "you will be the most alone inside there."

Everyone in the room turned to look at me, and I felt as if they could all hear me swallow. I tried to put on a brave face, but I could internally feel the crazy look in my eyes.

"Once the Eternal Walk begins, all we will be able to do is wait. Lucan and his advisors will be in the Watching Place to observe, and I expect the full traveling Titan Guard will be there as well. There will be nothing we can do until her Walk is completed and she exits the cave. During this period I will not have any teams nearby. Avalon alone will run surveillance without magic." When the entire room began to protest he continued quickly, "With the quantity of Titan Guard available for Lucan and the uselessness of standing in a humid jungle just waiting, I find it unnecessary to alert Lucan of a magical presence outside of the Caves and risk any of your lives when Avalon can do the job by himself. I have faith in my grandchildren. Eden will leave the cave and Avalon will not be found, but what happens after Eden has left the cave is more important than what happens while she is in it."

The crowd seemed pacified, or at least calmed for the moment. I glanced over at Avalon bouncing energetically on his toes like usual. He gave me a confident smile. I smiled back, despite my growing anxiety. My brother was a bad ass. Amory was right; nobody needed to worry. Avalon was not going to let anything happen to me.

"What do you expect to happen after the Walk?" Fiona Thompson asked.

"I am not sure what to expect. Eden and Avalon have been working on a few different techniques, but we are not sure what will happen once Eden is alone in the cave. Either Eden will leave the cave by herself and be taken back to the palace, or she will leave with the Titan Guard in handcuffs. Obviously, the latter scenario will not do, and at that point Avalon will reconnect with Jericho and the other teams to extract Eden. If she is taken back to the palace, that still does not mean she will be safe. Lucan might be biding his time, or deciding what to do. Either way, reconnaissance will continue until she is back home in Omaha, safe in her own house."

"What about the Stewards?" Conrad called out, his hand on his chin; he was clearly deep in thought.

"I have thought through our options with them," Amory responded. "They, on one hand, have taken a vow of silence that cannot be broken; on the other hand, their allegiance lies with the general Monarchy and not with the Immortal population. My instinct tells me to leave them out of it all together. They are after all humans and I cannot in good conscience risk any of their lives for a fight that is not their own."

Conrad, as well as several others nodded in agreement, satisfied with Amory's wisdom.

"I think that is everything for now," Amory continued. "There are smaller details that need to be ironed out, but the most important thing to remember is that until Eden is physically harmed or threatened, we are simply running a surveillance mission. The last thing I want to do is send red flags Lucan's direction. We have to proceed with the utmost caution and vigilance. For this mission we must assume at the very least Lucan recognizes Eden and has put the puzzle together. We must also assume that if any Resistance member is caught, after our success at the trial in October, that there will no longer be trials held for traitors. We must assume that Lucan will have anyone opposed to the Monarchy murdered on the spot, that his end game is Justice and Delia, and that he will do whatever it takes to get them. In that respect, even though I say this is a surveillance mission, Eden has never been in more danger."

Amory's black eyes settled on me, his expression set in pure determination. In that moment I understood Amory more than I ever had. Lucan had taken his only daughter from him; because of Lucan she was forced to leave and no one knew what had happened to her. Avalon and I were the only family he had left and the future for his beloved people. He would not let Lucan take the ones he loved from him again. I felt his resolve in my very soul and a soaring feeling of confidence came over me. India was uncertain, the Eternal Walk was uncertain, the future was uncertain. But I knew with all that I was, Amory would die before anything happened to me or my brother. And so far, that had been proven to be impossible.

My grandfather, the last Oracle, who was thousands of years old, who had walked this earth longer than any other living being, was my protector. And I found that was all the encouragement I needed to brave India. Come what may, I had the most powerful man alive on my side and the hounds of hell would not be enough to stop him, let alone Lucan.

Chapter Sixteen

"Eden, I know you are going to feel a little crowded with everyone here, but I really think it's for the best," Amory pulled me into a hug by the front door on his way out.

"I trust you," I smiled up at him. He was right. Things would be overly full with everyone staying here and I couldn't say I was happy he picked Roxie to join the rest of us, but I did trust him. That much I knew for sure.

"Well, good," he stumbled through an easy response, no doubt expecting he was going to have to fight with me. He kissed the top of my head and walked out the front door to his black sedan.

I closed the door behind him and leaned back heavily against it. The India meeting had gone much longer than I expected it to. Everyone seemed to want to hang around and offer words of encouragement to me.

I appreciated the warm words and pleasantries, especially since during my last visit to the farm I had felt sorely out of place. Really, I felt out of place, not just on the farm, but in the entire Immortal world. I didn't fit in at school. I didn't fit in on the farm. The majority of Immortals would gladly give me up to Lucan if they knew my true identity. The other part, the Resistance, wasn't happy with who I really was either. They wanted me to be someone else entirely, someone I could never be.

I was out of place, with nowhere to belong. Eternity felt much longer than forever, thinking about it like that. I sighed, exhausted from a future that hadn't even happened yet.

Stop feeling sorry for yourself and help us clean up. Avalon scolded me telepathically from across the room.

I thought he was in deep conversation with Roxie but when I looked up at him, he rolled his eyes. I couldn't tell if it was for me or for Roxie, but I didn't feel like getting to the bottom of it right then.

I grabbed a few plates of leftover food on my way into the kitchen to find Lilly and Aunt Syl. They were talking and laughing over the dishes while Jericho was tasked with putting the food away. I dropped my plates off with Lilly before grabbing the broom and making my way around the kitchen floor.

"So where is everyone going to sleep?" Jericho asked when

122

there was a break in conversation.

"Lilly can move in with me," I said excitedly before Roxie got any ideas, "and I suppose Avalon will have to move down with you so Roxie can have her own room."

At the mention of their names, Roxie and Avalon entered the kitchen carrying the last of the littered trash from the living room.

"Avalon doesn't need to move downstairs; we can share a room," Roxie offered, sounding more casual than I believed her.

She's just being nice, knock it off. Avalon interjected my thought train.

Nice is not the right word.... Ho-bag. That's the right word. I replied sarcastically, narrowing my eyes suspiciously at the tiny Latina I was deathly afraid of.

"Eden's right," Avalon blurted out, embarrassed by my remarks and forgetting we were having a conversation no one else could hear. When everyone turned to look at him with confused expressions he fumbled for a better response, "I mean, what she said before; I mean, about me moving down with Jericho," his cheeks were bright red and Roxie was giving him a coy look that I did not like.

"My house has never felt so small!" exclaimed Aunt Syl, turning around from the sink and drying her hands on a dish towel. She looked extra tan in comparison to the porcelain Lilly, standing next to her. "This is what's going to happen, Eden is going to move in with me and Lilly and Roxie can share her room. Avalon, you can stay where you're at and Jericho, I'm sorry, you can still stay where you're at," Aunt Syl gave Jericho an apologetic look, having felt bad for him for having to stay in the living room since the beginning.

"No!" I shrieked, "Aunt Syl, you have given up enough of your life for me already, there is no way I am going to make you give up your bedroom too!"

"Eden, don't be ridiculous," Aunt Syl said quietly. "I want to help in any way that I can."

"No. I'm serious Aunt Syl, I have totally taken over your life. You can't give up your sanctuary too," I said firmly, reminding Aunt Syl that her bedroom was the only place she had to get away; even before the whole Immortal and Resistance thing, Aunt Syl had always treasured the peacefulness of the master suite.

"Oh Eden, stop it!" Aunt Syl turned her eyes intensely on me in a look I knew all too well. She was serious and it was time to pay attention. "When Amory brought you to me, when you were a baby, I knew full well what I was getting into. I knew just exactly what I was giving up and believe me; I knew what would happen to my life. Eden, it's worth it. And if all that's being asked of me right now is to give up my bedroom, I will gladly do it. Besides, I'm never here to sleep in it anyway." She paused for a moment, waiting for me to respond, but I was too choked up to fight back. She was right and knowing so, she continued, "So, it's settled. Eden will move in with me, Lilly and Roxie can have Eden's room and Avalon and Jericho can stay where they are at."

"Wow, Sylvia, taking charge! That is so hot." Avalon declared.

"Gross, Avalon!" I turned around and hit him in the leg with the broom I was still holding.

"What?" he threw his hands up in self-defense, laughing at all of the girls standing around him appalled.

"And on that note, I think it's time for bed," Aunt Syl turned the intensity of her look on Avalon and sent him retreating up the stairs and into his room.

I led the way up the stairs after him, with Lilly and Roxie following behind. They carried suitcases of their belongings and I grabbed an empty laundry basket to haul the most important of my things into the master suite.

More than taking Aunt Syl's bedroom away from her, I was disappointed at not getting to share the room with Lilly. I had been looking forward to catching up with her and having time to ourselves. And besides that, I felt bad leaving her alone with Roxie.

"Thanks girls, for staying here," I said while grabbing clothes and underwear and my favorite pillow. I was more thanking Roxie than Lilly, I had been planning on making Lilly move in with us for a long time now.

"Of course," Lilly said in her bubbly way.

"Sure," Roxie mumbled. "Hey Eden, listen." I turned around to face her. She had taken her silky black hair out of her usual pony tail holder and it overwhelmed her tiny frame, hanging down to her waist. "I think we got off on the wrong foot, I can be.... I know I can be a little difficult," she sounded sincere and half smiled at me.

"No, it's not you," I apologized in return, understanding that

124

it wasn't all her. "I get that I don't make a whole lot of sense to most people," I smiled, trying to lighten the mood. "So let's just start over, yeah?"

"Yeah," Roxie smiled wider and forcefully reached out her hand in a businesslike fashion.

I shook it, still confused trying to figure out exactly who Roxie Powers was, but thankful we were starting over.

I finished gathering my things quickly so the other girls could settle in and get to bed. Lilly looked exhausted and I still wasn't completely comfortable around Roxie.

I dropped my things off on Aunt Syl's giant king-sized bed, and sat on the plush ottoman sitting in the corner for a minute. The huge flat screen TV was playing the news on mute and Aunt Syl was in her closet on a phone call with the hospital. I snuck out in search of another relationship that needed fixing.

I walked slowly down the hallway, trying to think of the right thing to say, or how to even approach Jericho. But I was nervous. I didn't even know if he would sit down with me, but I had to try. I wanted to fix our broken relationship and get all of the weirdness out of the way.

"Pssst," I turned to see Avalon calling me from his doorway. I walked back up the three stairs to listen to what he had to say in a very conspiratorial way. "Hey, you need to be nice to him."

"What?" I whispered loudly, very offended. "I am always nice to him."

"No. You're not," Avalon said with finality and continued before I could protest, "Just, listen, he is probably the best guy I know and you need to not be so, you know, you around him."

"What does that even mean?" I crossed my arms, and softly stamped my foot.

"It means," he paused to roll his eyes dramatically, "that if he doesn't want to be friends with you, just let him go. He should get to find someone else. And you shouldn't drag him along."

My mouth dropped open in surprise and I didn't know how to respond to those accusations. I wanted to believe that Avalon was just being over-dramatic like usual. But suddenly I felt unexplainably guilty, like Jericho's feelings for me were my fault.

"I'm serious Eden," Avalon continued, "Be gentle with him. He's a good guy."

"I know he's a good guy," I whispered, frustrated with Avalon for making me even more nervous. "Hey, what's the deal with you and Roxie?" I deflected and waggled my eyebrows.

"Shhh...." he hushed me loudly, looking around the hallway nervously. "I just.... we're just.... she's just a friend," he stumbled through an explanation while pumping his hands to tell me to lower my voice.

"Right...." I laughed before walking down the stairs. I heard Avalon's door close and wished that was all it took to keep him out of the impending conversation.

I found Jericho on the couch. His bed was made but he was still awake messing around with his cell phone. He was in gym shorts but that was it. His tanned, muscular chest was just sitting there, without a shirt, in the dark, just there.

"Hey," I said carefully, before making it all the way down the stairs. I cleared my throat nervously when he glanced up at me. His angular face glowed in the light of his cell phone and I didn't know what to make of his expression.

"Hey," he replied, just as carefully.

"Listen, can we talk for a second?" I tried with more courage.

"Sure," he sat up straighter and put his cell phone down, turning on a lamp with his magic.

"Ok, great," I breathed a sigh of relief and walked the distance to him, sitting on the love seat across from his couch. "So, did you want to put a shirt on?" I asked, finding his toplessness distracting.

"I'm fine...." he half smiled at me and my stomach jumped without my permission. "Right," I cleared my throat again and continued, willing myself to focus. "So, here's the thing. I just hate how weird it is between you and me. I hate that we fought and yelled at each other and I hate that...." I stopped realizing my apology was about to get away from me.

"You hate that I ever tried to kiss you," he finished for me and I couldn't deny that he was right. "I hate that too. Believe me," he looked down at the floor and then back up into my eyes like he was determined to keep eye contact. His hazel eyes burned in the soft lamp light and I realized, probably for the first time, how easy it would have been to fall for Jericho had I never met Kiran.

126

"I just want us to go back to being friends. We were pretty good at that," I smiled, hoping it would be that simple.

"We were good at being friends. I don't think we were reaching our full potential though. But we were good at friends...." he glanced back down at his phone and smiled smugly. I didn't know how to continue at that point, so I just sat there stunned.

After a few moments of my prolonged silence Jericho looked up at me from underneath his thick eye lashes and gazed at me intently. I couldn't bring myself to look away so I just sat there staring back at him, half wondering if he was right.

"Ok. Let's go back to being friends," Jericho said slowly, never taking his eyes off of me. "I mean you were right, I'm never going to argue my way in to a relationship with you. Right?" His eyes never lost their intensity or their focus and suddenly I was squirming.

"Right," I cleared my throat, "I mean, you're right. You can't," I half smiled, lost in his eyes and doing my best to convince myself and him that I was serious.

"So then, friends again," he smiled back, and reached out his hand as if to shake mine.

"Oh, is this what friends do?" I laughed, extending my own to his.

"Yes, it is," he said slowly, our fingers touching and then our palms. The magic between us ignited in a violent spark, shocking us both, but still Jericho connected his hand with mine and shook it back and forth as if what was transpiring between us was completely casual and not a poorly masked strong physical attraction.

My cheeks burned with heat, not only from embarrassment, but from shame too. I shouldn't be this attracted to Jericho. I shouldn't be second guessing my relationship with Kiran. I was in love with Kiran. He was my soul mate. There shouldn't be thoughts of other guys swimming around in my fuzzy head.

I cleared my throat again and retracted my hand, rubbing it against my jeans, "Well, I'm glad we got that settled."

"Me too," Jericho smiled mischievously at me, and I was bombarded with butterflies. "And as friends, we should probably hang out. Don't you think? I mean, that's what friends do...."

I was about to object, but he flicked on the TV before I

could make an escape and the late night talk show host was interviewing one of my favorite celebrities. I started laughing with the TV before I thought twice about leaving.

Jericho seemed to relax a little more, if that was even possible, and lay back further in the couch, lifting his feet up and sprawling out. I noticed his feet, long and boney, his arches were high for a guy and his toes made a perfect arch. I couldn't even begin to understand what I found attractive about them, but for some reason, his bare feet on my couch was absolutely endearing.

"Popcorn?" I blurted out, jumping up before I could concentrate on his feet anymore.

"Sure," he mumbled as I retreated into the kitchen.

I breathed in deeply as I rummaged around the kitchen looking for the box of microwavable popcorn. I was too frazzled to really look for it, so I found myself just slamming cupboards and periodically opening the refrigerator for no apparent reason.

I stopped for a moment, and placed both hands on the cool granite of the kitchen island. I had to get it together or retreat completely up to the safety of Aunt Syl's bedroom. But either way I needed to decide fast.

My magic was pinpricks of excited energy and I closed my eyes searching for the zen I knew was buried deep beneath my firm resolve to love Kiran. I did love Kiran, with everything that I was. I knew that feelings for Jericho did not mean my feelings for Kiran were in jeopardy.

It was just that my relationship with Kiran was in jeopardy and also difficult and also lonely. For such intense feelings, we had seen so little of each other on an intimate level. The entire world was litcrally against us being together, and meeting each other in our subconscious sleep state hardly counted as significant alone time.

Jericho was easy. A relationship with him would be easy. He was laid back and didn't have to worry about running an entire race of people at the brink of a civil war. And on top of it all, he was a good guy, a really good guy, a guy that under normal circumstances would have been an obvious choice for me to fall for.

That was it.

That was all.

I opened my eyes slowly, taking another big breath and

deciding that I would conquer this and enjoy the friendship with Jericho that I so desperately wanted.

However, when my eyes were finally opened there he was, standing in the doorway to the kitchen just watching me. Shirtless, tanned, muscular and amused.

"How's that popcorn coming?" he wasn't really smiling but his eyes were deeply amused.

"It's fine. I mean, it's coming fine," I spun around and began opening the white cabinets again determining to focus. "I just um, have to find it first and then, you know.... make it...." I trailed off, feeling foolish and frustrated. Where was the damn popcorn?

"Oh, good," Jericho, patronized me before walking over to the pantry, opening the door and then pulling out a red box of microwavable popcorn.

"There it is," I smiled sheepishly.

He continued the making process, pulling it out of the plastic and sticking it inside the microwave before pushing the correct buttons to get it going. I jumped up on the kitchen island, swinging my legs and doing my best to distract myself. He stood next to me, leaning against the island and watching the glowing microwave turn the popping bag around and around.

"So what's the deal with Roxie and Avalon?" I asked, hoping to get to the bottom of my growing suspicions.

"Roxie and Avalon? What do you mean?" Jericho turned around to face me. We were too close for my magic not to react. I hoped he didn't notice the elevated level my electricity suddenly surged to, I pretended not to anyway.

"You know, is there anything there? Like between them?" I put my two pointer fingers together in a childish way, indicating that I thought they were kissing. I laughed out loud as I did it, not even able to hide my embarrassment.

"What?" Jericho laughed too, "I don't know. Can't you just do, like your weird twin thing, and figure it out for yourself?" he reached out to stop my fingers that had continued in an absent minded way. His hand was only there for a moment, but I knew my magical reaction was too much to ignore.

I cleared my throat, pulling my hands back behind me quickly and leaning back on them. "I mean, yes I could. But I don't know, it feels like a gross invasion of Avalon's privacy. I have this

129

rule about not digging deeper than what Avalon would just up front tell me. There are some places that are just.... sacred. You know?"

"That's awfully cavalier of you. Does Avalon give you the same respect?" Jericho turned around to grab the now frantically popping popcorn before it burnt.

I burst into laughter at his question. We both knew better. "Yeah, right," I exclaimed, reaching into the now opened bag of steaming popcorn. "There is nothing sacred to Avalon. Trust me!"

"Oh, I know," Jericho looked down at the late night snack, but at least he agreed with me. "I don't think there's anything though.... between them. Avalon is pretty much married to the cause. You and he are so different in that."

"What do you mean?" I asked, reaching for more popcorn.

"I don't know, you're all, relationship first, Resistance second, maybe, second, maybe not even at all. And he's all, tunnel vision and can't even see all the girls just drooling over him. He has a one-track mind and it is definitely not where most guys his age are," he laughed a little rougher, but I realized he was right.

"Why do you suppose that is? Do you think he's a better person than me?" My mood changed and it dawned on me that Avalon was a better person than me; I didn't need Jericho to confirm or deny the question.

"No, not at all," Jericho replied with intensity. "It's just that, I don't know, Avalon was raised for this role. I mean, Angelica never kept anything from him, he knew from day one what his purpose in life was, and he has always been determined to fulfill destiny and all that. You just kind of fell into this life and still can't seem to catch up," he paused to smile at me shyly. "I don't think it's a matter of who's the better person; I think it's just a difference in personality."

"Thank you for that," I said genuinely, while still believing that Avalon was in fact, just a better person than me. "Well, if there was anyone to live up to his dedication though, I'm pretty sure it would be Roxie. Sister is a bad ass." I shivered, remembering how terrified I was of her.

Jericho burst into laughter, "You're right about that. I think she even intimidates Avalon a little bit." I joined him in laughter, finding it hard not to believe.

"Oh, my gosh, is that the time?" I shrieked after glancing at the clock on the microwave. "It is so late, I really should get to bed," I said, truly apologetic.

"Yeah it is getting late," Jericho said, sounding disappointed. "I've got a huge day tomorrow waiting for you to get home from school so I can actually protect something." He smiled at me and I realized how awful his days here must be. He couldn't really be a bodyguard if I was at school for eight hours of the day, and even when I was home, there wasn't a whole lot going on.

I moved my hands forward to jump down from the counter, but Jericho was there. He put his hands on either side of my waist, his palms hot, even through my clothes. Before I could react, he had pulled me forward, gently helping me down from the island. His hands didn't linger, but my magic was erratic from the small contact.

"Oh, that must be terrible for you," I empathized, apologetically.

"Yep, it's pretty rough," he said sarcastically. "I have Rox now though; we'll figure out how to make the most out of our days."

A pang of jealousy rippled down my spine and I felt my magic flare in an unforgivable display of emotion. I coughed loudly to try and hide the outward reaction of unexplainable envy and turned to smile at Jericho, hoping to come off more charming rather than the green-eyed jealousy monster who was supposed to only like Jericho as a friend.

"Yeah, that's true. Well, that will be fun," I couldn't pretend any longer, I had to suddenly get away from Jericho before I sent him anymore mixed signals. "Goodnight, Jericho, I'm glad we worked all of this out."

"Me too, Eden," he paused in front of his couch, and smiled what I imagined was his most charming smile as well. "Goodnight then."

I turned around and ran up the stairs, anxious to have some breathing room and clear my head. But once on the stairs Avalon's thoughts and feelings suddenly came flooding into my mind. It was like he had been holding his breath and trying to make himself as small as possible inside my head. Then all of a sudden he let his breath out and was overwhelming me.

Are you happy? I groaned in my head, feeling Avalon's elation with how things had gone between Jericho and me.

You have no idea. He responded smugly back.

I rolled my eyes at my brother. I knew he felt the gesture, and I hoped he knew he deserved it. I was confused enough as it was; I didn't need Avalon picking a side and then mixing up all his one-sided feelings with mine.

I did a good enough job mixing things up all on my own.

Chapter Seventeen

"Damn it!" I cursed loudly, burning my forearm again on the oven rack trying to balance the heavy turkey roaster. That was the third time I had checked the turkey and it still wasn't done. I cursed again at the famous recipe I stole off the Internet, and turned my attention back to mashing the potatoes.

Aunt Syl would be back any minute with the wine; she had disappeared an hour earlier, afraid of both me and the kitchen. I couldn't blame her. Thanksgiving dinner had been a lot harder than anything I imagined. Between the turkey and the casseroles and the stuffing and the mashed potatoes and the pies, I was at my wits end, and had apparently turned into a sailor with a sudden and deep knowledge of all curse words. Not to mention the fact that I had been up since five this morning baking.

I didn't know who I thought I was, but it felt like one of those irreversible nightmares that once I had stepped inside, I couldn't escape. So I just went on baking and baking and baking and now I was almost finished with the meal portion of cooking. If I could just get that damned red button to pop.

Lilly graciously helped me for the majority of the day and we had fun rolling out pie dough and doing our best to distinguish baking powder from baking soda and what exactly a pastry blender was. But I sent her upstairs forty-five minutes ago so she could wash the flour out of her hair.

I was going to have to rely on magic to pull my look together. Kiran and Talbott were due in half an hour and I was in some serious need of makeup. Amory would be here soon, too. He was Aunt Syl's invited guest; she hadn't wanted to be the only adult.

I was glad she had thought of him, it would be nice to have an actual family Thanksgiving meal. I hadn't meant to exclude him at all, but my mind was swimming with simply trying to figure out how to make Avalon and Kiran co-exist at dinner; that I had forgotten all about my grandfather, who should have been first on my guest list.

Avalon was adamant that Jericho would be joining us as well. I was not exactly excited to share the table with both Jericho and Kiran. I knew without a doubt that I could never leave Kiran, especially for another guy; but that didn't stop the unwanted butterflies every time Jericho and I made contact. Besides, he could be distracting. With Avalon, Amory, Kiran and Talbott all at the same table, I needed my A-game.

Avalon claimed Jericho had to come for my protection and all that, but I knew better. My brother had a very, not-so-secret agenda and he was trying to torture me to prove his point, whatever that point might be.

Roxie was the only one of my bodyguards that would not be joining us. She highly disagreed with having Kiran anywhere near me, especially inside my house and at my table. She refused to share a meal with the "Prince," as she called him in a very degrading tone. But most of all, she didn't understand the tradition of Thanksgiving. Not only Immortal, but born in Peru, she had no desire to sit in on a purely human-American event. And there was something else about not liking turkey.

Roxie's absence was fine with me; it was one less thing to have to explain to Kiran and Talbott. Besides, she still intimidated me and I knew I wouldn't be able to trust her to be polite.

"Do you need any help?" Jericho was leaning on the kitchen counter, three feet from me and I hadn't even noticed him come in.

I looked up surprised, and wiped my forehead with the back of my hand. I couldn't help but smile at him. He looked very handsome in black dress pants and a pressed white dress shirt with a skinny black tie, his sleeves rolled up to the middle of his tanned forearms as if he was ready to work. His hair was styled back from his face; I could smell cologne, something I had never noticed he wore before.

"No, thank you, though. But you look way too nice to get your hands dirty," I thrust my potato masher back into the deep pot. He walked around the island, and stood next to me, taking the masher out of my hands and moving the pot in front of him.

"Please, go get ready. I can handle mashing a few potatoes," he smiled down at me reassuringly.

"I guess, I um, I guess I should go get ready," I looked down at my sweatpants and flour stained t-shirt, agreeing silently that I couldn't very well meet Kiran like that. "Are you sure you're going to be Ok?" I glanced nervously at my precious potatoes not wanting to leave them alone.

"Trust me, I can handle myself in the kitchen," he smiled with confidence and I couldn't help but believe him. He looked down at the pot and left it for a moment, opening the refrigerator and pulling out some milk and butter. I stayed watching while he expertly poured the milk and sliced some butter, making the potatoes creamy and rich. Why hadn't I thought of that?

"Oh hey, can you keep an eye on the turkey then, if you're such an expert chef?" I smiled playfully, still in awe of his kitchen skills.

"No problem, but seriously go get ready, you're running out of time," he turned around, flicking the oven light on and inspecting the turkey.

I, too, turned around, unable to wipe the smile off my face and bounded up the stairs and into Aunt Syl's room. The best thing about sharing a room with her was getting unlimited access to her fabulous closet.

I jumped in the shower, washing the food and flour out of my hair as thoroughly as possible and gave my legs a quick shave. I dried off and then let the magic dry my hair. I noticed over the last few months that it was not only efficient to do it that way, but magic was far more gentle on my hair than a blow dryer. My long, thick black hair was still as impossible as ever, but at least I wasn't struggling with split ends.

I glanced at the clock and panicked, racing into Aunt Syl's closet, going straight for the good stuff in the back. I ran my fingers through her fancy dresses, trying to decide which designer would be appropriate for the occasion.

I stopped on a midnight blue strapless number with a sweetheart neckline. The skirt ballooned out into a fun poof, so even though the top was a little racy and a little low cut, at least the skirt was fun. I zipped the back up with magic and then grabbed a black cardigan for good measure.

Finishing my makeup in record time and spraying some of Aunt Syl's top shelf perfume, I heard the doorbell ring. I rushed back into the closet for a pair of stilettos, beaming with excitement as my eyes rested on a pair of plain black pumps with red soles. They would be perfect.

I heard Aunt Syl welcome somebody but I wasn't quite ready to make my grand entrance just yet. Knocking on my own bedroom door, I let myself in, finding Lilly putting her own finishing touches on and Roxie asleep on the bed. Lilly looked ravishing in a short black skirt and blousy pink top. The pink set off her porcelain skin and fiery red hair and her short legs looked extra-long with that much skin showing.

"Nice shoes," she laughed, gesturing at her own that were still sitting on the bed, but identical to mine.

"That's funny. You must have good taste," I smiled, realizing she did have good taste and I relied on Aunt Syl for my fashion identity.

I walked over to my dresser, pulling out my jewelry box. I needed some accessories. I chose some big silver hoops for my ears and the necklace that Kiran gave me in Geneva. The stone was black inside my jewelry box, but the second it touched my skin, the jewel turned a shining blue, matching the color of my dress exactly.

"How do I look?" I turned to Lilly, hoping for a good result.

"Gorgeous as always!" she replied exactly how I hoped, I chose to believe her.

"So do you. You look stunning!" I gushed, meaning every word.

She slipped on her shoes and we linked arms, moving out of my bedroom towards the staircase. I sighed contentedly, it was so nice to have Lilly healthy and in my home.

"That's a pretty necklace," she said, remarking at the sparkling stone glistening off my neck. "Thank you," I replied without offering any details.

I heard Amory and Aunt Syl in the kitchen and as we made our way down the stairs both Avalon and Jericho appeared in the living room. I was pleasantly surprised to see Avalon dressed up for the occasion. I half expected him to wear gym shorts and a t-shirt. But he looked very dapper in designer jeans, a dress shirt and sports coat, all of his tattoos carefully concealed. His hair was pulled back into his school-style pony tail, but instead of looking rebellious like at school, he looked actually put together.

The boys stopped to watch us come down the stairs, sending heat to my cheeks and Lilly tensing up with anxiety. Avalon couldn't keep his eyes off Lilly and he made no attempt at being shy about it. Jericho stood there, too, mid-step just watching me and doing absolutely nothing about hiding his stare either.

The room was completely silent, except for our heels clicking their way down the wooden staircase. Jericho's eyes burned with intensity, his hazel eyes a smoldering brown with flecks of green shining through. He smiled at me, his dimple pronouncing itself and I didn't know what to do.

I wanted to say something, to break the deafening silence, to make the room feel less like it was just he and I, but I couldn't think of anything to say. I couldn't think of anything but those golden brown eyes and the way they looked at me.

The doorbell rang, cutting the silence with harsh reality and I exhaled, realizing I had been holding my breath.

"Oh, thank God," I mumbled underneath my breath, reaching the bottom step just in time and letting go of Lilly's arm.

I turned my back on Jericho and felt him leave the room. Lilly and Avalon followed, leaving me alone with greeting the company. I hadn't thought about how awkward things would be between Lilly and Talbott until just that moment and suddenly regretted the whole evening. What had I been thinking? This could have been a colossal mistake.

"Hello," I smiled, opening the door and welcoming Kiran and Talbott, both dressed in black suits and ties, into the house.

"Eden, you look too beautiful," Kiran sighed, stepping inside first, and pulling me to him. His mouth found mine, kissing me before I could even say thank you.

My magic surged, finding his and popping frenetically. I let his magic wash over me, reminding me of the love we shared. I had been away from him for too long; I let myself forget what it was like when we were together. The house suddenly felt stifling and too small. I found myself regretting the elegant dinner I prepared, wanting to just run away with Kiran and leave this all behind.

"I'm so glad you're here," I sighed, slowing his kisses and finding oxygen again. "I've missed you." I mumbled with more emotion than I wanted to admit.

"I've missed you too," he said, a hint of curiosity in his voice.

"Well, come in, dinner's all ready," I moved out of the way so Talbott could come inside as well. He had been waiting patiently on the front stoop until we were finished and I was suddenly embarrassed that Talbott had to witness our friendly "hellos." "Hi,

Talbott," I said politely, clearing my throat.

"Hello, Eden," he said curtly, eyeing my necklace suspiciously. I put my hand over it, subconsciously, wondering if it was a mistake to wear it.

"This way," I grabbed Kiran's hand and led the boys into the kitchen where I set the table earlier in the day. I had used Aunt Syl's lace table cloth and her grandmother's china and silver. There were crystal goblets from her father's side and ivory candle settings from an uncle that had lived in Africa for a while. The candles were lit and all of the food moved from the stove and island. The table looked like a magazine spread and I was beaming with pride.

"Jericho, did you do all of this?" I asked, gesturing towards the food and lit candles.

"Well, somebody had to," he smiled playfully and my hand started to sweat inside of Kiran's.

"And my turkey? Is it Ok?" I let go of Kiran's hand to lean over the table and inspect my handiwork.

"Well, Ok. Don't get mad at me," Jericho began nervously. I snapped my head up, afraid of what he had done. "No, see don't get mad...." Jericho backed away from the table with his hands in the air.

"What did you do?" I gasped, inspecting the twenty pound bird once again.

"It was nothing really. It's just that.... Ok, when I pulled it out to look at it, it was kind of.... Ok, completely raw in the middle." He couldn't stop himself from laughing and I took a sharp inhale of breath, knowing it looked too good to be true. "So, I just gave it a little boost of magic and voila, it turned out perfect." He grinned his charming smile at me and I had already forgiven him.

"Oh, is that all," I laughed, reaching over and pushing him gently in the arm. "I thought you were going to say you dropped it or something. It looks amazing, thank you. I forgot I could use...." I trailed off; realizing that finishing my sentence would probably cause the entire room to roll their eyes in unison, even though I had truly forgotten I could use magic on the food. Maybe today wouldn't have been so stressful if I had just magically made everything.

"Eden," Amory scolded, realizing where I had been going, "although we all appreciate the extra effort you put in to the meal, dearest, you need to remember your magic." His black eyes were turned on me and I couldn't help but shrink back from the reprimand.

"Amory's right, Eden," Kiran's hand was on my back, firm with worry. "You cannot let your guard down, even for a moment."

"I know. I'm sorry, I just...." I started to stumble through an apology, completely embarrassed in front of everyone.

"It probably felt like cheating, right Ede?" Jericho came to my defense and I was grateful for the reprieve. "I mean, the Thanksgiving meal is a labor of love." He gestured with his hands and then took a seat at the table. I relaxed, thankful Jericho was on my side. He wouldn't look me in the eye, but I was radiating appreciation.

The rest of us followed Jericho's example and sat down. Amory and Avalon flanked Jericho, while Lilly sat down next to Avalon at the head of the table. I sat down on the other side of her and Kiran took his place next to me. Talbott, unable to ever leave Kiran's side was next to him and Aunt Syl sat in between him and Amory at the other end of the table. At least the seating arrangement went as I had hoped.

"I don't believe we've been properly introduced," Kiran declared bluntly, staring directly across the table at Jericho.

Kiran's eyes were narrowed in suspicion and his hand had yet to leave its protective position on my back. I reached for my glass of wine, nearly knocking it over, before willing myself to calm down and drink it slowly. I really wanted to just down the whole glass, and maybe even the bottle, I had not expected the direction the dinner was suddenly going.

"Jericho Bentley," Jericho said curtly, his permanent smile more calculated. Even his eyes had taken a narrowed position on his face. "Forgive my manners, your Highness; I should have bowed."

Avalon cleared his throat suddenly and I could feel the nauseous feeling sweep over his body at the mere mention of bowing to Kiran. I shot him a hard look, and telepathically asked him to calm down.

"No, not necessary, Jericho. We're all friends here, of course," Kiran smiled graciously at him.

"Of course," Jericho replied, his eyes never losing the hard look in them.

"I hadn't realized Eden had met other Immortals outside of

Kingsley," Kiran turned to face me, eying me just as suspiciously. But I was suddenly interested in passing the stuffing, which in turn prompted everyone else to dish up whatever was in front of them and pass it.

"Jericho is an old friend of mine," Avalon interjected, almost asking to be contradicted. "Our parents work together in Brazil."

"Oh right, your parents are down in Brazil. I forget that about you Avalon," Kiran turned his attention to Avalon with a look of authority and suspicion that I had never seen before.

"We forgot to say grace," I exclaimed, jumping out of my seat and grabbing both Kiran and Lilly's hands. I had had this dinner planned in my head for weeks and so far we were off to a very bad start. I would be damned before I let jealousies and paranoia ruin my Thanksgiving dinner. I started in on a well-rehearsed prayer, pretending not to notice that I was the only one with my eyes closed while everyone else stared each other down from across the table.

Chapter Eighteen

"Everything is delicious Eden, really, I am quite impressed," Kiran complimented me during a lull in what was so far a very forced dinner conversation.

"Thank you," I gushed, satisfied that everything turned out, even with a little help from Jericho. "I have never even attempted a turkey before, so even with Jericho's help, I'm still happy it turned out." I continued, regretting the words as soon as they left my mouth.

"No really, stop," Jericho jumped in, and I couldn't tell if he was happy to be included in the conversation or upset. "I did nothing more than heat the bird, all of the flavor is yours."

"Did you baste the turkey?" Kiran asked, turning his body to face me as if to exclude Jericho all together.

"I did," I smiled sweetly, gazing into his eyes and hoping to relay that there was absolutely nothing to be jealous about.

"I should like to learn how to baste a turkey," Kiran smiled back and I reached for my wine glass.

He's talking about sex. He wants to have sex with you. Avalon sent me the message telepathically and I choked on my wine, spitting it back into my glass and continuing to cough.

"Eden.... Magic...." Avalon mumbled from across the table and I took his advice, but that didn't stop the heat from rising to my cheeks.

"Lilly helped too," I blurted out, trying to erase Avalon's opinion from my mind. Everyone at the table was just staring at me, I had to say something. "Lilly helped me all morning; really everything here is from both of us." I smiled at her, trying to regain my focus.

"Is that true, Lilly?" Talbott addressed her for the first time all evening, his accent thick. His face was bright red and I watched as he struggled to look her in the eye. She just nodded, turning an even brighter shade of red and shrinking back farther into her chair.

This evening was going worse than I expected. I needed to change the subject to something everyone could discuss and not offend anyone at the same time. I had to think of something neutral and safe and the only thing that came to mind was myself.

142

"So. Ok," I began, pushing the corn casserole around on my plate, afraid to look anyone in the eye, lest anyone else get upset or jealous, "I don't get why I have to go to India for this whole Eternal Walk thing. Why can't I just do it here?" I finally glanced up at Amory, hoping he would engage me in some kind of lengthy discussion and save my failed dinner.

"That is a good question, Eden, but unfortunately it is impossible to do the Eternal Walk here, the Cave of the Winds is the most significant part of the entire tradition and it is located in India," Amory smiled at me, encouraging me to ask more questions with his eyes.

"Ok, so what exactly are the Cave of the Winds?" I asked, hoping to stay on this topic for a while.

"They are a sort of Immortal epicenter that reacts more strongly with our magic than any other place on earth. You will feel your magic more intensely there than here, and what is even more of a phenomenon is that the cave actually reacts with you. The Eternal Walk is more of a physical reaction from nature than an Immortal induced event," Amory smiled benevolently and gestured to Kiran as if he wanted to explain more.

"That's right, when you enter the caves an actual reaction from the caves themselves begin to occur and that's why we call it the "Walk," because you have to physically walk through it in order to be released," Kiran took my hand in his underneath the table, but this time not from jealousy or over-protectiveness, this time it was to reassure me.

"How is that possible?" I asked, not believing that nature would actually react to our magic in a conscious way.

"We are not exactly sure," Amory continued, "but over time we have come to notice certain places on the earth are more prone to recognizing our magic than other places. In fact, even the native humans in those places seem to have an awareness of our Immortality, more so, than in other places."

"So more than just India?" I asked, wondering if Romania was one of those places.

"Yes, more than India," Kiran answered, "Romania is of course one, Peru is another, London, Morocco.... another and the entire continent of Africa," he laughed a little when he mentioned Africa and the rest of the table joined him. I didn't get the joke.

143

"So is that why that whole Citadel is in Romania?" I started to put the pieces together.

"Yes," It was Talbott's turn to talk, "over time, these epicenters, to use Amory's term, have presented themselves as the logical places to build our palaces. The citadel was built in Romania with the prisons because it became the most effective way of housing Immortal criminals."

"Oh," I grunted, rather disgusted. "Oh. I guess that makes sense from a ruling standpoint," I tried to cover my negative reaction quickly, but I saw Avalon laughing out of the corner of my eye. "Oh," I said again only this time realizing the answer to something that had been nagging me for a while. "That's why that old lady, on the train.... Well that makes sense," I trailed off, remembering nobody had been with me while on the train to the Sibiu.

"What makes sense?" Kiran looked at me quizzically, calculating my expression.

Wait. Avalon demanded before I could answer what I assumed to be an innocent question from Kiran. I obeyed my brother grudgingly, and forced another bite off of my plate, chewing it slowly. Once the food was in my mouth, I wasn't exactly stalling but rather just trying to force another ounce of food into my already overly-full stomach.

Avalon sifted through my memories rather intrusively, so I threw the memory at him, glancing irritatedly out of the corner of my eye. He replayed the memory and then I watched him shake his head and frown from my peripheral, just the slightest jut of a chin to signal not to say anything. I swallowed the bite of food on cue and took Avalon's advice.

"I don't know, just some old gypsy lady on the train I took from Timisoara to Sibiu. She was scared of me. Like absolutely terrified," I took another sip of wine, shaking my head like I couldn't believe it.

"Really?" Kiran asked sweetly, I turned to smile at him and watched his eyes just barely narrow in suspicion.

"Oh," I blurted suddenly, "and then my cab driver too. He was so freaked out; he wouldn't even take me all the way to the Citadel. I had to walk up, like mountains," I grew dramatic hoping to cover my mistake earlier, although I didn't really understand what

144

the big deal was.

"Do you remember what you looked like?" Lilly laughed in a laid-back way that told me she was working hard at looking more laid-back than actually feeling so. "Eden, you looked crazy!"

"That's very true," Amory agreed, taking his turn at reminding us all how the journey to the Citadel had affected my external appearance.

"Oh my word," I dropped my face into my hands, trying to picture what I would have looked like to everyone else. "How embarrassing," I sighed.

"Yes, I much prefer this look to the one you were trying to pull off in Romania," Kiran teased, leaning over and kissing me gently on the cheek. Hopefully his fears had been erased, whatever the reason was for them to begin with.

"So, Ok, back to the point, these epicenters," I gestured at Amory, making sure I was using the word correctly, "they not only make our magic stronger, but nature will actually react back at us?" I clarified my question, genuinely wanting to get to the bottom of this.

"Yes, so to speak," Talbott jumped back in, "like in India, the people themselves recognize our magic immediately. You will see when you arrive, they show us absolute respect and honor our ways. The palace itself houses almost an insurmountable amount of magical energy and for a long time was the city center of our people. The caves as well, have a unique way of revealing our specific magic on an individual level. After time however, we have found India to be especially draining and so the palace is mainly used now for the adolescent Eternal Walk."

"And summer holiday," Kiran added, seriously.

"Yes, and summer holiday," Talbott agreed, rolling his eyes.

It was the first time I had seen Talbott be so openly insubordinate and I couldn't help but laugh at his good humor. Maybe he wasn't as uptight as he came off.... all the time....

"Ok, what about Peru?" I asked, ticking off the epicenters in my head.

"Both Peru and England seem to boost magic in a way that prolongs our lives now that we are concerned about the King's Curse," Amory explained. "There is not so much a feeling of strengthened energy, but more a calming of the frenetic aspects of

145

the magic. I believe Kiran would agree that there is a more solidified feeling in London than over here." When Kiran nodded, Amory continued, "We heal faster in those parts of the world and we frankly live longer."

"Romania?" I asked, but feeling like maybe I should have felt something while I was there.

"Romania is a lot like India in that the Gypsies have an almost insight into our people that other humans lack." Jericho began to explain and I was surprised to hear him talk, he had been silent for so long. "Like you said, the Gypsies you encountered were scared of you and I think that is the general rule across the country. For the most part they leave us completely alone, which is why we are able to have our Citadel there with active prisons." Jericho spit the last sentence out and I cringed hoping it wouldn't ignite something between Kiran and him.

"Yes, but more than that, the prisons in Romania are specially fortified," Talbott took the floor again, but this time I could sense a little bit of pride in his tone and I felt physically ill thinking about Lilly inside of one. "No Immortal has ever escaped one; there is something in the core of the earth there that is capable of trapping and keeping Immortals."

"Amory escaped," Avalon said plainly; there was not sarcasm, or anger or malice in his voice, it was a statement of pure fact.

"Not from the prison," Talbott rebutted and I felt the tension in the room rise immediately.

"Talbott's right," Amory cut in, giving Avalon the "eye."

"Amory, what does that mean?" I asked in awe. This was a story I had not heard before.

"I will tell you sometime, Eden, but your elegant Thanksgiving dinner is neither the time, nor the place," he smiled at me patiently and I knew he was right.

"Who's ready for some pie?" Aunt Syl changed the subject and spoke for the first time all evening.

I was thankful for Aunt Syl's intuition and stood up to help her clear the table. But a chill ran up my spine, I realized I sorely underestimated the danger Talbott and Kiran still were to my precious family and what kind of danger my family was to Kiran. A sickening feeling of dread formed in the pit of my stomach. I was

146

naive to believe these two worlds could coexist. I was naive to believe a relationship between Kiran and I would solve this world's problems. I placed the china gently next to the sink fearing this was all going to come to a head sooner than I wanted to believe it would.

Chapter Nineteen

I stepped on to Kiran's posh private jet on a secluded airstrip north of Omaha late Thursday evening, with my new backpack and a small carry-on suitcase. I was a ball of nerves already and the plane hadn't even taken off yet.

I willed myself forward, forcing myself to take step after step until I was able to sit down in a luxurious leather chair. I threw my carry-on and backpack on an identical seat across the aisle and used my foot to propel my swiveling chair around and around.

An iced bucket, holding an expensive bottle of champagne sat uncorked on the console to my right and the flat-screen TV took up the majority of the front wall, playing an old movie I would have loved to pay attention to under different circumstances.

I stopped turning when the seat belt sign flashed on and obeyed the safety command. Once in the air I would change clothes, out of my jeans and sweater and into cooler clothing, ready for the heat of India.

I wasn't in any hurry, though, Amory prepped me beforehand on the lengthy journey ahead of me. The plane ride alone would take over a full day and then the trip into the mountains another three days. I would be in India approximately ten days if everything went well and add in the four days total of traveling, I would be gone for two whole weeks.

Thankfully, the trip took place over the first part of December when the rest of my class was on the rock- climbing trip I had been thrilled to be dismissed from. I didn't have to worry about missing school, but I still wasn't happy about spending half of the trip overseas alone and traveling for the majority of it.

The worst part was the no talking. I exhaled loudly, hoping sounds were still permitted, just not the actual formation of words.

Once the plane was in the air, an attractive flight attendant appeared, from what seemed like out of nowhere, offering me a bottle of water and showing me without words how to lean my chair back into a sleeping position. She gestured towards the lights. I assumed she was asking me if I wanted them dimmed and so I just nodded my head to see where it would take me.

I was right and once the lights were softened and the

stewardess left me alone again I leaned my chair back and hoped to find the sleep that had been eluding me since Thanksgiving.

I stared up at the ceiling of the jet and let myself think about all those I left behind. There hadn't been any danger yet and I wasn't really expecting anything at all until after the Walk. I wanted to believe that Lucan was interested in seeing what I was capable of before he made any decisions about what to do with me.

Amory gave me a more detailed description and blueprint set of the Romanian Citadel in order for me to study the escape route we took a few months earlier. I memorized every detail of the plans I kept tucked safely in Aunt Syl's closet, but hoped I would never need to call up the information.

The key was, as Amory explained, to escape before they moved me down into the prisons themselves. Once down there it would be impossible to escape. Well, it had been impossible for everyone else, including him, but he liked to believe I was capable of anything.

I wasn't so optimistic.

Amory, I found out, had at one time or another, been imprisoned by almost every King from Derrick to Lucan. None of them trusted him; since he was the only Immortal that had thus far claimed actual Immortality. Some had just kept him down there, some had tried to kill him, and some, like Lucan, had tortured him in hopes of finding his daughter, or wife, or Shape-Shifters, or whoever they thought Amory could help them find.

I grieved for my grandfather after hearing of his painful life, and how much he suffered, not only in physical pain, but in loved ones lost. From his perspective, there was nothing more evil on earth than the Monarchy, and his beloved people, whom he very much felt responsible for, would never have freedom or peace until he abolished the last living member of the regime.

Amory's prep for this trip was more emotional for me than I thought possible. Hearing stories of thousands of years of oppression and mistreatment, most of them aimed either at my grandfather or the ones he loved, was heartbreaking.

I still couldn't believe Kiran was capable of the same kind of malice though. From his every interaction with Amory I had witnessed, Kiran respected and admired Amory, or at least showed him graciousness. Kiran was not the same man that his father was, nor his grandfather. He was a new breed, a new ruler. He would not treat his Kingdom with the same misplaced jealousy that all of his ancestors had. I had to believe that.

Besides, Amory wasn't in a Romanian prison anymore; he was Regent of North America and Principal of Kingsley, which was the premier Immortal prep school in the Americas. When I asked Amory how he went from escaping Lucan's imprisonment to being judge over this side of the world, Amory explained that Lucan had learned what all of his predecessors had; when you can't kill your adversary you follow the old adage: keep your friends close and your enemies closer. And so Amory had been appointed to leadership in an attempt to keep a closer eye on him. But according to Amory, it was just a different form of imprisonment. He was at the beck and call of the Monarchy and a puppet in their endless stream of tyranny.

Going to India, I was more confused than ever. The Monarchy was, of course, the bad guy. But how could Kiran be? And the Resistance was the obvious answer to the oppression of the Immortal race, but what was their plan of restructuring government? If the Resistance eventually did take over, what would happen to Kiran?

I had even less of an idea of what side of the argument I wanted to be on. I couldn't keep putting my feelings aside, hoping that the love I felt for Kiran would be enough to bandage any situation. The fight wasn't about me. It wasn't about a relationship or soul mates or real love. This fight was about overcoming injustice and saving innocent lives, of freeing the Shape-Shifters so they could become an active part of their world again, and of releasing the ban on interracial marriage so that the magic could be free also. This war was about reinstating the meaning of Immortality to the Immortal race and offering life in a world where it would soon be sorely lacking.

You need your rest. Give it up for tonight and just relax. Avalon's soft, reassuring voice was in my head. I found his presence comforting, despite the distance we were from each other.

You're right. I sighed; wishing he were here with me. I'm just lonely. I complained, thankful for the reprieve and ability to talk. This was probably the longest I had ever gone without voicing my opinions.

Jericho says hi. Avalon responded and I didn't even need to be his twin to feel the double meaning behind his statement.

Well, tell Jericho hi back. I rolled my eyes and snuggled in deeper to the chair. I didn't know what Avalon was thinking, I was not about to flirt with Jericho telepathically through my brother. It was weird.

You're right, it's weird. Avalon, who had been listening in, agreed.

Thank you. I sighed, glad he wouldn't be putting up too much of a fight.

Just remember, we will be on the ground before you even land and with you every step of the way. Eden, you will never be out of my sight. Avalon reminded me and I was surprised to feel the emotion behind his promise.

Ok, but maybe let Jericho take point during the ceremonial bath. I joked, trying to lighten the mood at the same time reminding my brother that the ceremonial bath might not be his ideal surveillance opportunity.

Will do. Avalon said smugly, focusing more on my desire to have Jericho take point while I was in the bath than the gross factor of Avalon doing it instead.

See you on the ground, weirdo. I ended our conversation but didn't leave Avalon's head. I wasn't usually the one to spy, but Avalon transitioned so quickly into a conversation with Jericho about me that I couldn't resist.

"She says she wants you to be the one watching her in the bath, Dude," Avalon was saying.

"I'm pretty sure she just didn't want it to be you," Jericho rolled his eyes at Avalon and I felt the light bulb go off in Avalon's head.

"Huh," Avalon grunted, "you're probably right."

"Yeah," Jericho agreed, and tried to turn back to his book.

"So you're just over her then? That's it?" Avalon was never one to give up easily.

"What do you mean, that's it? She is in love with Kiran; there's nothing else to it. What do you want me to do?" Jericho looked up from his reading material clearly irritated. There was something intense in his hazel eyes making them darker than usual.

"Well whatever you were doing last week seemed to be

working," Avalon said bluntly.

"Ok, listen, she chose the Prince; there is nothing I can do about it. She has made that pretty clear," Jericho shrugged his shoulder and I felt a surprising pang of sympathy from Avalon for his friend.

"That's not all she's made clear, though," Avalon was referencing my magical reaction to Jericho, I felt what he meant, but I wasn't sure Jericho understood. At least I hoped he didn't understand.

"Avalon, seriously. Let's move on. One day, when Eden is ready, I will be ready too. But until then, I'm not going to get in her way. She can make her own decisions and choose her own path. I'm not going to even try to change her mind. Have you seen her listen to anyone else? Ever? Or let things like rules and decrees get in her way? She is the most self-determined, amazing woman I have ever met and if I have to wait for her, I will. So let's just drop it," Jericho picked his book up and held it in front of his face, blocking Avalon and proving that the conversation was over.

"Jericho, that is seriously pathetic," Avalon laughed, satisfied with where Jericho stood even if he wasn't going to share that opinion with him.

Jericho ignored Avalon completely and I felt like I had seen more than enough. I shouldn't have been eavesdropping, it was wrong. It was very wrong, I felt awful. Suddenly I was more than a ball of nerves, I was a ticking time bomb of explosive energy and I felt terrible.

It didn't seem fair that Jericho would be such an amazing guy. He deserved someone truly incredible. I certainly wasn't a good enough girl for him and he shouldn't be spending his time standing around waiting for me. I was taken. And I was in love. It wasn't fair that he was just waiting for me. I was never going to be there for him.

A sinking feeling washed over me and I decided I had enough of thinking. I closed my eyes and turned off my brain. I couldn't think about unchangeable things right now, I had to focus on India. I would be landing in a matter of hours and I still needed to figure out how to disguise my magic in a place God, Himself, apparently designed in order to reveal the most secret parts of our magic.

152

My relationship with Kiran seemed impossible. A relationship with Jericho was actually impossible, but I had more important things to worry about. I had an actual impossible task facing me and if I let these boys cloud my mind any further I wouldn't have to think about any of them anymore, I would be in the bottom of a Romanian prison pit, spending the rest of my life, which apparently would be the rest of forever, wishing I had never met those two.

Chapter Twenty

I stepped off the plane in Bangalore to a wave of humid heat, the feeling I needed to shower and five women in elaborate scarlet saris with gold stitching pressing their palms together in a sort of half bow. None of them looked me in the eye, but I could not take my eyes off them.

They were all different ages, from mid-twenties to middle age. They had long dark hair wrapped in elegant braids or hanging waist-length with golden thread tied through them. They had beautiful tanned Indian skin and between their eyes was the customary red dot, most Hindu women wore.

Elegant floral designs made out of an orange flower paste, called henna, wrapped their right arms from finger tips to shoulder blades. The pretty flowers intertwined each other in delicate brush strokes and mimicked the exotic beauty of the five women that would be my stewards.

I stood at the bottom of the moving stairwell feeling grossly under-dressed and more unprepared for the task ahead of me than I ever had. I mirrored their bow, palms pressed tightly together and nose resting on my middle fingers and if I would have been allowed to talk I would have gladly called on my yoga knowledge and said, "Namaste."

The vow of silence held my tongue and when the women dropped their hands, I followed suit, brushing my plain, unpainted fingers against the tan cargo pants I felt appropriate for the trip. I shouldered my back pack, still trying to get used to its stiffness. A pang of regret washed over me as I remembered my beloved old bag and how it had gotten me through my last overseas trip.

The five women turned around silently in unison and began walking towards a black limousine that could have been plucked from the early to mid-nineteen hundreds. They stopped at the door, opening it for me and allowing me to get in first.

I crawled in the hot back seat and sunk down on the scorching leather. I was already sweating and all I had done was walk from the plane to the car. The women piled in after me and the driver placed my carry-on suitcase and backpack in the trunk before sitting back down into the driver's seat and taking off.

The windows were rolled down and the hot, humid breeze blew through them in a barely satisfying way. The Kendrick airstrip was located outside of the actual city of Bangalore, so I regretfully never saw anything but the outline of the city. We drove through winding, pot-hole stricken roads, passing small farms with nothing more than shanty's for dwelling places and starving children waving us by.

Every once in a while we would pass a temple, either a closed structure, that housed the statues of exotic gods, or outdoor pavilions with tall monuments to Buddha in the middle. Red flags waved from the Buddhist temples and at all the religious sites were thousands of candles lit in prayer to a deity created from stone.

The road was relatively empty and the driver made good time. The women next to me remained silent, their expressions not even changing. I continued to sweat well into the twilight of evening and eventually gave up on consciousness all together. The trip to the palace would take two days of driving and one full day of riding on an elephant, whatever that meant. I was exhausted and sorely jet-lagged; if I couldn't talk, I decided I'd better just go to sleep.

I drifted off with the jungle growing denser around me. The call of wild birds and laughter of monkeys was my sound track to the exotic Indian world I had entered. Even in darkness, the colors of India seemed more vibrant than those at home. The red of the saris seemed brighter than usual, the green of the thick, long-branched trees of the jungle seemed more vivid and the sun that grew lower in the western horizon seemed to glow in unusual hues of pink, orange and yellow. India was enchanting and the mystical feeling of a greater magic waiting for me was pulling at my blood, sending pinpricks of feral electricity rushing through me, draining me from any energy I had remaining.

When I woke, the sun was streaming in through the opened limousine windows and the car was pulled over to the side of the road. I felt disoriented and had no idea where we were. The trees around the car had thick trunks and were dense with leaves. Colorful birds and small, gangly monkeys hopped from tree branch

155

to tree branch in a ballet of jungle life.

I sat up, realizing I was alone in the car. I was drenched in sweat, my shirt soaked through and my hair felt like I had just gotten out of the shower. I wanted to call out to the women, but stopped myself, remembering the vow of silence.

I crawled out of the back seat, thankful for the humid breeze that drifted through my clothes. The car had been stifling and the cooler mountain morning air felt like heaven.

The women were surrounding a small roadside stand eating something out of homemade newspaper packets. I approached them carefully, not sure if I was allowed to. They smiled graciously at me, and a middle aged woman with long braids and a gold head scarf held up her finger to me.

She turned to the vendor, an impossibly skinny elderly man with snow-white hair and a stooped back, and gave him the same gesture. He produced another newspaper packet that the woman then held out to me.

I took it from her, pressing my palms together and offering another small bow, frustrated that even my manners were commanded silent under the traditional vow. She smiled at me and bobbed her head back and forth as if to say it was no problem.

I un-wrapped the newspaper, while the driver and the vendor talked animatedly in a language I couldn't even begin to understand. Their sentences seemed to move impossibly fast and I was relieved that not everyone around me was under the constrictions of silence. Inside the newspaper was a doughy bread, I had to assume was made without yeast. I was pleasantly surprised after biting into it that there was a fried egg inside sprinkled with a mild curry. Whatever the name of the native food, it was the perfect breakfast and I devoured the delicacy in seconds.

After everyone else finished their breakfast and the driver and vendor shook hands, we all piled back into the limousine for the continuation of our journey. The roads seemed to worsen as we drove higher in altitude and deeper into the jungle, the driver had to significantly slow his pace and become increasingly creative.

The jungle grew more exotic the further in we drove. The vegetation was like nothing I had left behind in Omaha, and the animals were wild and feral. The sounds were the most frightening part, loud moans or high pitched screeching sounds made terrifying

156

interruptions to our otherwise silent drive. I wanted desperately to be reassured that they belonged only to large birds or friendly mammals, but with everyone restricted to their own thoughts, mine grew increasingly more fearful.

We drove through the heat of the day; the women eventually produced small hand held fans and offered me one. I fanned myself frantically, hoping I wouldn't be judged on appearance any time soon.

We stopped another time during the day for lunch. This time the roadside vendor produced newspaper packets of rice and a curry sauce. There were no utensils provided so I had to watch until the women dug in with one cupped hand, bringing the food to their mouths between their fingers.

I followed suit, but felt more like a barbarian than the custom dictated. Somehow the stewards were perfectly capable of getting the food from hand to mouth without smearing it all over their faces and dropping it clumsily at their feet. I could not figure it out though and so by the end of the meal, more rice had landed on the ground than in my mouth. The floor was a feast for all sorts of large insects that I would have been perfectly happy to never have met in my life.

Since no napkin was provided either, my black fitted t-shirt had to play the role of paper towel and give me back some of my dignity the delicious, spicy curry sauce had taken from me. My fingers were stained in an orange reminder that I would be making Indian food a permanent addition to my diet when I returned to Omaha.

At the end of the day, nightfall fell fast in the thick jungle. There was no room to see a sunset and with the canopy of trees blocking the full shine of the sun, one minute there was day light and the next we were enveloped in darkness.

Eventually the driver pulled off of the main highway and onto an extremely bumpy dirt road. I bounced along in the backseat feeling like an earthquake victim, and sorely apologetic to the women next to me that I kept jabbing with my boney elbows. I was certain the old limousine was ready to just fall apart at any minute.

At the end of the dirt road was a small wooden building with open windows and a light on. The driver stopped the car in front of what I could tell was a sort of house. My increasingly exhausted looking stewards piled out of the vehicle; I followed suit. The driver left us to drive around to the back of the house.

I stopped before entering, half wondering if this was a trap. If I was going to lure someone away from everyone protecting them and either kidnap them or kill them, this creepy shack would definitely be the place to do it.

The house was surrounded by a small clearing but the jungle wasn't far away and the deafening night sounds coming from every direction were the ultimate decision; I would rather face whatever was in that kidnapper's haven than the army of wild animals seemingly surrounding me on every side.

I swallowed my fear and entered the run-down house with my magic ready to react. It all turned into nothing; however, when I nearly released the electricity on the five women sitting down to a meal on an old door propped up on two buckets sitting unsteadily and awkwardly low to the floor.

There was an empty chair I wasn't quite sure would hold my weight, but I took it anyway looking forward to the meal I just now began to smell. White rice and a chipped porcelain dish containing an amazing curry sauce made with pumpkin and lentils began to be passed around and I heaped the native food onto an identical porcelain plate that had seen years of abuse.

A bread, similar to the one filled with egg, was also passed around and I was delighted to find this one filled with potatoes and onions. I followed the example the ladies set by tearing pieces of the bread apart and using it to pick up the rice and sauce together.

The meal was completely satisfying and despite the silence of the room, I began to relax. The stewards were comfortable to be around and completely gracious. Even the driver, who I could see through one of the open windows, making his bed in a shed where the car was parked, was easy to be around. One other person was out there with him; an elderly woman with floor length, graying, black hair and a delicate yellow sari, dishing up a plate of food for him from a heavy iron pot. I recognized her as the cook of this magnificent meal and if I weren't worried about breaking tradition I would have demanded that she write down the recipe so I could replicate it at home.

After dinner, the youngest of the stewards began to clear our plates. I stood up, joining her. There was a small basin of water off

158

to one-side of the one room shanty and I knew it would take no time at all if we tackled the dishes together.

I began to move the plates to the counter the basin was sitting on; when I heard the first sound any of the women had made the entire trip. The oldest of the stewards gasped in horror at my attempts at helping and reached out to grab my arm and stop me.

I anticipated some resistance and so I looked down at her with the sweetest smile I could and bobbed my head in the back and forth motion that I had seen countless times in the last few days. I knew I didn't pull it off correctly. The Indian people were born with a sort of rubber neck that let them display their indifference at any given moment. I just hoped to replicate the idea in a stiff and awkward movement.

The second sound of the evening came from all five of them breaking into laughter at my attempts at cultural relevance; I had to laugh, too. The laughter, like dainty wind chimes, floated into the cool evening in a refreshing sound of relaxation. I was allowed to help with the dishes, and like I predicted, we were finished in fifteen minutes.

After dinner, mats were rolled out across the floor and mosquito nets hung from hooks in the ceiling. I crawled under my tent-like netting ready for sleep. I hadn't done much the last few days but the hours of traveling had completely exhausted me. I decided to check in with Avalon who had been silent in my head since the jet.

Where are you? I asked, hoping he was close.

I am close. He replied answering my emotions. And then I felt that he was close, out in the jungle, but with several other Immortals. They had set up camp and were eating a dinner not all that different from mine. I have never heard of the stewards laughing, Eden. Not ever.

Oh really? I was happy with myself, feeling like I had the right to be proud of a unique accomplishment.

Actually, I think you are a completely new kind of Immortal for them. He said passively. Avalon was relaxed and enjoying the wilderness. The jungle was completely his domain and I could feel in every fiber of his being how relieved he was that the trip had been uneventful so far. When I reported back to Amory, he said that most of the younger Immortals use their magic the whole trip. You know you don't have to be so hot, and you don't have to be so uncomfortable on the floor, right?

Damn it. I always forget about the magic. I laughed, realizing Avalon was right, I was positive no other Immortal would let themselves get that sweaty or that hungry. I rolled my eyes at myself, but not really regretting feeling India at the human core of what it really was.

You know what, that is exactly how it would go. Avalon reflected, amused. Of course, the most powerful Immortal of probably all-time would struggle to even remember she has any magic at all. He rolled his eyes, laughing good naturedly at me.

Shut up. I grumbled back. You're just as powerful and you never forget. So that makes up for it.

Well, probably more powerful. So I guess you're right. I'll give it to you. I felt him smile and noticed from his point of view Jericho give him a curious glance from across the fire.

So, are we good? I mean nothing out of the normal as far as this whole Walk thing goes? I asked, remembering my journey was far from over.

It would appear that way, so far at least. By tomorrow night you will be at the palace and we should know more. He said with his characteristic tone of authority he used every time he was in a leadership position.

"Avalon," I heard Jericho call from across the fire. "What are you doing? Thinking about a girl?" he laughed and others joined him.

I found myself smiling at Jericho, and not just from his sense of humor.

"Something like that," Avalon called back. Ok, well, get some rest; you've got a big day tomorrow. Let me know how much fun riding an elephant for ten hours is. He finished with dark amusement.

That sounds awesome. I sighed and rolled over, leaving Avalon's head and entering mine. The elephant ride was just the beginning of a seemingly impossible few days ahead of me.

I closed my eyes remembering a trip to the zoo with Aunt Syl when I was little. They had elephant rides for zoo members and Aunt Syl was so excited to let me experience something so exotic. I bounced around on top of the ginormous, leather mammal as it walked slowly in a circle, thinking that would probably be the last time I would get so close to such an enormous creature.

I had been wrong. I fell asleep with the memory of Aunt Syl smiling excitedly and waving while taking pictures from the ground. I had been too afraid to let go and wave back, but the smile had never left my face. When had elephants become an actual mode of transportation for me and not just a kiddie ride at the zoo? This was not at all how I envisioned my life turning out, and I wasn't exactly sure what to do with that.

Chapter Twenty-One

A knock on the door to my palace room pulled me from my musing. I did not bother to answer and the source of the knock did not bother to wait for a response. The five stewards entered my room in differing but equally exquisite purple saris. Their hair was all styled with matching purple ribbons, except for the eldest woman who wore a purple head scarf with gold stitching.

I had been awake for at least an hour, but I wasn't allowed to leave the overly-soft king-sized bed for twelve hours, so I laid there, staring out the latticed window at the glory of the Indian palace.

My room was tiled with marble from floor to ceiling and tall white pillars seemed to hold up the expansiveness of the private bedroom. I was wrapped in silk sheets and blankets, lying on silk pillows and the softest down mattresses, I had no idea even existed. My bed was surrounded by billowy, sheer curtains in a shiny white, matching the purity of the room.

Through my window I witnessed the layout of a palace I did not know reality was capable of creating. Golden rooftops glistened in the sun, tumbling down the mountainside in a glamorous layout of opulence. Between the rooftops, displaying the expansiveness of the palace, were exotic gardens housing every type of blooming flower imaginable. Monkeys climbed mischievously from garden wall to golden rooftop with a nonstop chattering that had become India's music to me.

One of the stewards turned the water on to an elegant ivory bathtub in the corner of my room and another one brought in flower petals of every color and smell. The fragrant perfume from the vibrant petals filled my nostrils and I was suddenly very excited about the ceremonial bath portion of today's festivities.

I struggled to stand up out of the pillow soft bed. I stretched my sore muscles and released some magic on my frayed bones. Yesterday's elephant ride proved to be torturous by the end of the day. As accommodating as the basket sitting on top of the giant animal had been, filled with colorful pillows and a tent overhead to block the sun, the continual bouncing and fear of falling two stories to my death kept me tense and uncomfortable for the entire ten hours.

By the time we reached the palace, the day had turned to night and I knew why they required twelve hours of sleep. I had been completely exhausted and hadn't noticed an ounce of detail before collapsing in the bed and passing out.

This morning with luxury surrounding me, I had to wonder why the trip thus far had seemed to mirror poverty.

The youngest of the stewards walked over and took my hand, with a gentle smile, but not a hint of shyness, pulling me towards the bath and gesturing that I needed to undress. I stood there awkwardly, trying to figure out how to get in the bathtub without exposing my nakedness to all of the women and scarring them for the rest of their steward lives.

I cleared my throat, hoping that wasn't against the rules and when I began tugging at my sticky, filthy shirt; the women graciously turned their backs to me. With the little privacy I was allotted, I finished peeling my cargo pants off and practically belly flopped into the bathtub.

I had expected regular water, hot or cold; I had expected to land in water, but upon entering the bathtub I realized it was anything but. Treated with something much like menthol, the liquid was hot and cold at the same time, both relaxing and refreshing. It smelled sweet but minty at the same time and the liquid was thicker than usual, more caressing than regular water. It clung to my skin, wrapping me gently in the circling current of the tub.

I sunk deeper in the tub, letting the unique liquid wash over me. The steward with the flower petals began sprinkling them across the expanse of the ivory bathtub. The fragrance continued to perfume the air in a sweet, exotic way and the petals floated around me with the swirling water. The eldest steward took my hair in her hands and worked at getting the hair tie out of it. I reached up to help her, knowing I could rip it out much faster, but she gently pushed my hands down, conveying in a gentle way, that this was her job.

I closed my eyes, allowing myself to be pampered. Eventually, my hair was free and the elderly woman took a silver pitcher, filling it with water and pouring it gently over my head. I could almost guarantee they had never had to work with a mess of hair as bad as mine, especially after three days of not washing it in the most humid of conditions; but they worked silently, massaging

163

another heavily perfumed oil through it and rinsing thoroughly when they were satisfied.

I was disappointed when the drain was pulled and a big white cotton towel was held up for me. I stood up, embarrassed by my nakedness, but not knowing how else to escape the bath and let the steward wrap me in the plush towel.

The women directed me to a vanity with a cushioned bench and when I sat down, they began to work on my hair again, brushing it gently out and braiding it with silken, cream colored ribbons and matching fresh flowers. Some of my curls were left out to frame my face and the braid wrapped intricately down my back.

Once my hair was finished, I was directed to stand again and they removed the towel. My face flushed red, standing completely naked in front of open windows while the women worked quickly to dress me. I was wrapped in a sheer ivory sari that wrapped around and around so that it would not be see-through. I marveled at myself in the vanity mirror, imagining myself to wear something this exquisite on my wedding day.

The silky skirt flowed around me, while my midriff was bear, but for the elegant sash that crossed from shoulder to waist and was intricately woven with golden thread. I was stunned at the richness of the fabric and had never felt more beautiful.

Once I was completely dressed, I was taken back to the bench and was motioned to sit down. One of the stewards produced an orange paste and four brushes. Every steward, except the eldest, took a brush and chose an appendage, working to create pretty floral designs intertwining from both sets of fingertips to shoulder blades, or from toes up my feet and stopping somewhere along my calf.

I was worried the clay like henna would stain the ivory sari but through a series of gestures the eldest steward relayed to me that I needed to dry it quickly with magic. And so I did, protecting the beautiful garment and my arms and legs from smudging.

Once the henna art was finished, the eldest steward approached me with make-up. I closed my eyes and let her go to work, painting my face, applying thick eye liner and shimmering eye shadow and finally when she was finished the customary red dot in the middle of my forehead.

I was allowed to stand and admire their handiwork in the mirror of the vanity and I almost didn't recognize myself. I stood in awe at the beauty they created and half wondered if I could take them home with me. I turned around, pressing my palms together and offering the half bow that was the only way I had to display my appreciation. When I looked up, back at the eldest woman there were tears in her eyes and her head was bobbing back and forth. She smiled at me graciously and I returned the expression, truly thankful for the steward's service.

The women turned around in unison and the youngest steward beckoned me to follow them. The halls of the palace wing I experienced so far had been empty; outside of my room the splendor of the palace did not cease. We walked through hallways with vaulted golden ceilings and all kinds of intricately designed wooden pieces of art, displaying statues of Hindu gods, or wildlife native to the jungle, paintings that seemed to be thousands of years old and colorful, fragile vases that I was afraid my footsteps would knock over.

I was led into a dining room adorned in the same beautiful motif. There was an incredibly long table placed in the center that stretched from one side of the room to the other. At one end of the table, a spread capable of feeding twenty people waited for me.

I walked over to the table, gesturing for my stewards to sit down and join me, but they just smiled at me and bobbled their heads while walking away. Apparently I was to eat alone.

The exotic smell from spices I had never experienced before drifted my way and my stomach rumbled. I was suddenly famished and so I sat down, consuming as much as I could. Fresh, local fruits and delicious Indian breads, eggs with curry and turmeric, fresh soft cheeses and homemade yogurt surrounded me, and I was determined to try some of everything.

The stewards returned somewhere between deciding I should stop eating and my sari suddenly feeling too tight. I was nervous about leaving the dining room, but I also knew that I wouldn't be eating again until after I completed my walk and that was only if Lucan decided not to kidnap and imprison me directly following. This could potentially be my last meal, I decided to enjoy it.

I gave up trying to finish the meal made for twenty and the stewards led the way out to the elephants, a staircase waiting for me to climb aboard. I dreaded the idea of another bumpy ride, and decided to be more liberal with my magic and get to the Cave of the

Forever Winds in one piece.

Once, carefully aboard my living transportation, I held on tightly, until the stewards had boarded their own massive mammals. Today our elephants were decorated in colorful paints and head pieces matching either the stewards purple saris or my ivory one. We looked like an elegant parade, marching forward through the jungle and into what felt like very uncharted territory.

The day was not as hot or as humid as it had been before and I was thankful I didn't have to be concerned about sweating through my ceremonial sari. We continued deeper into the jungle, the canopy above blocking out direct sunlight and curious monkeys keeping us company, swinging through the dense vegetation right along with us. The journey was slow and treacherous, but the elephants navigated a make shift trail expertly. My seat swayed back and forth with every step the elephant took and I released more magic forcing myself to trust the gigantic creature.

After what seemed like hours of steady travel the elephants came to a halt, without command, in front of the ruins of a stone temple. Vines and greenery had nearly blanketed the old crumbling stone, but the original foundation stuck stubbornly out. The stewards swung expertly down from their high seats and then led my elephant over to a worn, stone platform so I would not have the fall that the native women had to take.

I did my best to mimic their smooth decent, but landed rather awkwardly on the hard ground. The five women surrounded me closely and moved me in front of the darkened expansive doorway to what at one time had been the entrance to a temple.

The stone ruins were not a full structure like I had originally thought, but instead the front of the entrance to a wide-mouthed cave. Inside the cave, there was no light and I couldn't make out much past a few feet in.

Once in front of the door the earth shuttered beneath my feet, and afraid of an earthquake, I reached out to the women. They steadied me carefully before bobbing their heads with gentle smiles. A surge of magic rushed through my blood, an answer to the tremor and I realized the earth itself was reacting to my magic.

Pinpricks stabbed at my skin and the hairs on the back of my neck stood straight. I was afraid. I had no idea what to expect inside, but the calling of magic was not going to let me leave.

166

The women began to turn away from me and I prepared myself mentally to take the brave step forward and inside the cave. The eldest woman was the last steward blocking my way and before she moved she reached out to cup my face in her hands. I was surprised by her gesture so I paused, giving her my full attention.

Once my eyes locked hers, she seemed to say something without saying it at all. Her eyes screamed at me to be careful, to be smart, but most of all to be strong. She did not speak any words out loud, but I felt her heart crying out to me. I shuddered feeling suddenly emotional and not knowing how to express my gratitude.

She let go of my face, pressing her palms together in the bow that had become our sign of gratitude. I mimicked her, trying to relay the utter respect I felt for her. My palms pressed tightly together, my nose touching my middle fingers, I looked down at the ground for longer than necessary, until I knew that she was gone and that I would have to face the caves alone.

I was ready, completely ready, or as ready as I would ever be, but then Avalon's words rang out clearly in my head, in a voice that betrayed fearful concern and I had to muster all of the courage I had to continue.

Eden, no steward has ever behaved that way before. Not ever. Be careful.

Chapter Twenty-Two

I didn't know much about what would happen during the Eternal Walk, but I did know that it would take a while. I also knew that for the most part I would do the Walk alone. There was no way for the King or his advisors to observe the majority of the Walk. But towards the end, when every Immortal would be at their most vulnerable, each Walk was watched from an observation deck that sat high up in the caves.

I knew that I couldn't let Lucan see the truest part of me, but I still didn't know how I was planning on masking that, if this Walk was really as treacherous as I had been led to believe. I did know that I had a little bit of time to figure it out, though, once I experienced what the Walk would actually be like.

I stepped one unsure bare foot inside of the cave and then the other. A gust of colored wind blew past me in a violent way, blowing my hair and shaking me to the core. The cave was actually reacting to me, and that, in itself, was an unbelievable phenomenon.

I took another step forward, willing myself to be confident. Another colored gust of wind whipped past me, only this time wrapping me up inside of it. I was picked up for only a second, but it was enough to want to turn around and leave. The wind that appeared in an iridescent rainbow of glossy colors was more than strong, it was hot.

I swallowed my fear and took two steps forward. This time the painted wind blew past me as if angry, wrapping me up in a whirlwind of fire and burning my skin before setting me down five more feet inside of the cave.

This was not what I expected. I didn't know what to do. The wind whistled through the cavernous ceiling as if getting angrier and angrier at my presence. Another gust of wind and this time when I was set forcefully down it was in a heap on the dirt floor, there were blisters on my forearms and I could smell burning hair.

Avalon is this normal? I demanded, wanting desperately to run back through the mouth of the cave and give up.

No. It's not. He said with dread weighing on him heavily. I could sense he was on the phone with Amory and I could feel his near-hysteric panic. He was not as close by as he had originally planned; I felt him jump down from somewhere high and begin to move towards me.

The wind was there again, a tornado of angry violence, picking me up in its swirling rainbow current and thrashing me about before throwing me down to the ground. My sari was stained with dirt and the skirt was ripping every time I landed hard against the floor.

Avalon. I cried, terrified that Lucan wouldn't have to bother killing me because this cave had a serious issue and would claim me first; but there was nothing. For the first time since I had discovered our connection, Avalon was not on the other side.

I was now fifty feet inside the cave and whatever magical powers the stone walls held, one of them was to cut off the telepathic connection I had with my brother. I looked back at the peaceful jungle out of reach and remembered the elderly steward.

The wind whistled loudly again, angry and vengeful; I knew this was what she meant. I had to be strong. I was strong. I was the most powerful Immortal to ever enter this damned cave and I would be the most powerful Immortal to walk away.

I stood up confidently, mustering all of my strength, staring defiantly forward and daring the wind to fight. And fight it did. The gust of air came at me again, picking me high up into the air and tossing me about. The whirlwind held on to me tightly, burning everywhere it touched, scorching my hair and melting my clothes.

I lashed out in panicked electricity, sending magic from every direction. The colorful wind clashed with the lightning bolts of energy in a resounding sound and brilliant light show. Individual colors seemed to fight my magical force in a torrent of heat and wind.

I struggled to hold on to sanity as my skin burned and my equilibrium was tested, flying wildly about in midair. The tornado took me deeper into the cave, flashing in every color from royal blue, to iridescent purple, to neon green, and canary yellow. The light was blinding and the flashing colors happened in such rapid succession that I had to hold my eyes closed for fear I would lose my vision.

The whistling wind and roar of the circling cyclone grew to an unbearable pitch and I felt like I would go crazy if it didn't stop soon. I sent out more magic, fighting against the destructive current threatening to destroy me.

The heat grew impossibly hotter and I felt as if I was being burned alive. I screamed for help but knew even if Avalon was out there he wouldn't be able to hear me over the roaring winds tossing my body in midair like a rag doll.

What was most disheartening was that I knew even Avalon wouldn't be able to stop this force of nature from tearing me apart and incinerating every last piece of me into nothing.

I focused again on my waning magic, forcing my mind away from the pain and agony, away from the violent thrashing and away from the deafening scream of the wind. I let the electricity surge through me completely, calling on the very depth of my magic, letting it loose on the tornado without apology.

The colors flashed brighter and faster, working their way through the color wheel in rapid succession. Again, I forced my magic out of me, sending the energy outside the eye of the storm and to the very recesses of the source of the wind.

The flashing colors began to take a more distinctive hue and the royal blue I had come to associate with my shade of magic became more prominent. I let out more magic, wondering when I would run out completely and the glossy blue stayed longer.

As the blue hues increased in the color cycle, the heat lessened and the sound diminished. The winds continued to speed up, however, and I knew I wouldn't be able to hang on much longer before I lost all control completely.

With the release of more magic and a longer stay of blue, the winds did what I considered playing dirty, they took my weakened, helpless body and threw me into a crumbling pillar, finishing the job time had started. Rocks and rubble fell all around and on top of me as I was thrown through the center of the pillar and forced out the other side. I laid there with a broken body wishing the wind would finish me; this was too much.

There was silence for a moment before the cyclone reached through the wreckage, pulling me and the broken stone into its spiraling circle of hell again. This time the rocks trapped in the tornado continued to batter my broken body and I did not have the magic to fight the hateful wind and heal my body at the same time.

I released more magic believing I could win, believing I would be the victor. I had nothing else to hold on to. I centered myself, pulling the electricity with all of the force I had left and letting go, unleashing every last ounce of energy. The air was stained in my royal blue, the wind no longer a rainbow but a solid force of my signature color. All at once, in one final effort to slay me, the cyclone threw me violently into the stone wall and I slid down to the cool cave floor, the blue light glistening off of every single thing in the cave, washing over me, reaching to my soul and infecting me with the color.

I lifted my head, afraid of what I had done and the color itself robbed me of breath. I had hit my head hard against the rock wall of the cave and as I laid there unable to breath, blood pooling around me, I slipped into unconsciousness believing I had breathed my last breath.

Eden. Eden!

I woke slowly, my head throbbing and a mouth that felt like sandpaper. A gentle, soft breeze lifted my hair around me in a careful way as if it was the one trying to wake me.

Oh God. Eden! Please, I can't get in. Please tell me you're still alive. I recognized Avalon's voice in that it sounded like him but I had never heard him so afraid.

I opened my eyes, and reality started to make its way back. I was lying on the cave floor, broken, in pain, and filthy, but I was alive. I was somehow alive.

The once-dangerous, spiteful wind was gentle and soft now, moving around me in a careful way as if apologizing. I sat up slowly, very slowly, working on finding my equilibrium and touching my fingers to my bloodied head. They came away sticky and stained crimson and I sent my magic quickly to heal the painful gash that went from my temple to back of the head.

Eden! Avalon screamed inside my head and I sent the magic quickly there too, to save my pounding head from splitting open again.

I'm here. I'm fine. Avalon, I'm ok. I breathed a sigh of relief, exhaling slowly and letting tears fall down my dirt stained cheeks.

Oh, thank God. Oh, thank God. Avalon repeated and I had never been more thankful to have him back inside my head.

The cool breeze played with the bottom of my torn and bloodied sari, lifting it off the ground and back down again. The colored air was now permanently blue and held a connection with me that I felt deep inside my soul.

I tested my intuition, willing the wind to go where I wanted it to; it obeyed, floating around the destroyed pillar before picking up some rubble and tossing it to the side like I commanded. I stood in awe for a few seconds before trying it again with bigger rocks. I controlled this wind. Whatever happened before I lost consciousness or after, I now was connected to this act of nature on a magical level.

Are you getting this? I asked, disbelieving to Avalon, who grunted in response. Is this normal? I questioned, wondering if this was what the Eternal Walk was like for everybody.

Avalon was on his cell phone in seconds before answering my question, going back and forth with Amory in a series of questions and answers, retelling the details of what had happened as soon as I had entered the cave and eventually what color my magic turned the breeze.

Amory wants to see if you can change the color of the wind. Avalon relayed to me and I tested the boundaries of my control.

At first I just thought about a different color but when nothing happened I released my magic into the wind and that worked. The blue turned from royal to navy to black and then to a vibrant yellow just to test what I was capable of.

Avalon, having full access to what I was doing now, was back on the phone with Amory giving him every detail and answering what little questions the now speechless Amory had.

He wants you to change the color to orange, like Angelica's and turn up the velocity of the wind a little bit and finish your walk. Amory says now that you can control the color you can prove to Lucan that you're nobody special. Do not let him see the blue, keep it orange and only a little violent. He says it shouldn't be able to pick you up off the floor, but it should be difficult to walk and you should be sweating. It should be a little bit hot, too. Avalon instructed word for word what I already heard Amory say to Avalon the first time. But I listened anyway, making sure I didn't miss anything.

I did as I was told; increasing the speed and strength of the

172

wind, turning the blue to orange and making myself sweat with the help of magic. I had really had enough of the licking flames; I didn't need to recreate that sensation when magic would still produce the desired effect.

The rest of the walk through the cave felt relatively short after the mayhem from the first part and when natural light finally filled another cave mouth I practically ran to it, forgetting that Lucan was watching somewhere.

Once back in the humid jungle and the breeze floating in a waning pool at my feet I fell to the ground and began to cry. I wasn't really emotional about almost dying. That had felt like sweet release at the time, but I was traumatized. I had never been physically assaulted on purpose from nature and I hoped to never be again.

"Eden, are you all right?" Kiran was there, kneeling next to me and pulling me to him. I let him hold me, the tears continuing to fall with no end in sight. "What happened in there?" he asked, brushing my matted and bloodied hair out of my face. "Where did all of this blood come from?"

He pulled his hand up to his face before turning his attention fully on me. I didn't know what to say or what to tell him. I couldn't be honest with him here and his father close by, but I had no strength to lie, to make something up. I just wanted to go home.

"It's Ok," he held me closely to him after realizing I was not going to explain the chain of events inside the cave. "It's going to be ok. Let's get you back to the palace and clean you up. All right?"

I nodded my head and let him help me stand up. The gentle breeze was still at my feet, wrapping the orange air around my legs and breathing on me in a sweet, refreshing way.

Kiran looked down, noticing the strange phenomenon and gave me an alarmed expression. I sent the command with magic that the wind should return to the cave, but before obeying, the breeze left my feet in a gentle whirlwind encompassing me entirely, The feeling was far from unpleasant and I stood their wrapped in colorful air, breathing in the wind that I was apparently on good terms with now.

After a few moments the wind was back inside the cave with a gush of power and a whooshing sound. I stared after it, not entirely sure I understood anything that just happened or if I really wanted to. All I could think about now was that ivory bathtub and menthol water. The rest would come later, the ability to understand. Until then I just needed a bath.

Chapter Twenty-Three

I stepped out of the tub feeling infinitely better. I soaked long enough that my fingers and toes were wrinkled but I didn't care. The thick water had been the perfect remedy to my frazzled nerves and beaten body.

Magic healed the burns and bruises covering my body and the gash in my head. My hair was definitely singed but not beyond repair. I fixed the frayed ends with magic and hoped I could cover the rest of the damage with what was left of the healthy hair. Standing in front of the vanity mirror in my white cotton towel I looked back to normal, like I hadn't just walked out of the seventh circle of hell.

My inside was a different matter. I communicated with Avalon on the way back to the palace assuring him I was all right. He, of course, knew better, but it was enough that I was healthy and that Kiran was there.

As much as he hated Kiran, having him around was a hopeful sign Lucan wouldn't be trying to abduct me yet. And Avalon was thankful for that.

I was thankful for Kiran too. I hadn't expected to see him in India or until I got home. He held me the whole way back to the palace, the elephant ride feeling much safer wrapped in his arms and he was very unwilling to leave me alone, even to get bathed and dressed. However, I was very unwilling to let him witness all of that.

I walked over to the carry-on suitcase I had yet to open on this trip and pulled out a floor length, white skirt and black tank top, that I thought could pass off as appropriate in the palace; although it wasn't nearly as elegant as the embellished saris I noticed all of the palace servants wore.

I dressed quickly and put product in my hair without bothering to blow dry it. The cool, wetness of my long hair felt good against my hot skin, and I knew that the humidity of the jungle would destroy any chance of relaxed curls anyway. A little bit of eyeliner and mascara and then I decided to leave the room in search of Kiran. I didn't want to be alone anymore.

I didn't have to search far; he was waiting in the hallway

when I exited the bedroom. He smiled at me, an expression of relief flooding his face and leaned back against the cold marble wall as if finally allowing himself to breath.

"I'm fine. Really," I assured him, answering his unspoken questions.

"I can see that," he smiled, a twinkle in his eyes and his signature smirk rising to the surface. "We can't be.... I mean, here.... Eden, what I'm trying to say is that here I am very much betrothed...." he looked down at the floor, not able to keep eye contact with me.

"I understand," I replied plainly and understood the warning not to touch him familiarly or speak to him possessively.

"All right. Ok," he ran his fingers through his tussled blonde waves, smiling at me again. "I have business in the village, would you like to come?"

"Is it Ok if I come?" I asked, leaning back against the opposite side of the hallway, hands firmly behind my back as if they would betray me and reach out for Kiran without permission.

"Yes, yes of course," he said quickly. "This is the best kind of business," he turned on his heel and started walking quickly with purpose.

I moved after him, struggling to keep up. We walked through more hallways I hadn't seen yet and into a corridor leading outside. I guessed that this was the main entrance to the palace because a covered drive wrapped in a circle down to a broken road and a running funny-looking opened-sided car with a middle-aged driver, sat waiting for us.

The car was more of a three-wheeled motorcycle with one seat for the driver and a back seat wide enough to hold at least two people, maybe three. The vehicle was covered, except for the sides, which made it easy to get in and out of. But I was a little nervous the scooter would be able to do its job efficiently.

I followed Kiran, climbing into the back seat and searching for a seat belt but finding nothing. Kiran smiled down at me, mischief in his eyes, and tapped the driver on the shoulder letting him know we were ready to go.

The small vehicle took off with a jolt and I grabbed onto the seat, trying to decide which mode of transportation I found safer, this or the elephant. We drove faster than I thought possible with the little engine that could, down the winding mountain highway. The driver expertly swerved across the road, avoiding deep pot holes and tears in the pavement.

Twenty minutes later, the driver slowed down as we approached the touristy town of Ooty. Elegant hotels, tea shops, and clean native retailers lined the main roads. The driver continued on, past the more modern buildings I expected would house Kiran's business.

We drove past the Westernized portion of town and out of the city into a village beyond where the tourists would go. The roads were dirt and the houses four walls of rotting wood with a rough piece of tin or plastic, providing a roof. Barely dressed children played with flat soccer balls in the middle of roads, lined with open sewage systems. The smell from the disgusting, green waste filled the air, and I used magic to keep from gagging.

Kiran stepped out of the vehicle, pulling a few large bags from a trunk I would have assumed was too small for them. I followed him, wondering what kind of business waited for him in a place like this.

The children stopped playing their game as soon as Kiran was out of the car and turned on him, yelling loudly and running wildly in his direction. I didn't know what to make of the children and was worried Kiran would not appreciate the excited attention, but to my surprise he set his bags down and reached out his arms, embracing as many children as he could fit. The ones who didn't fit jumped around with a wild energy, yelling his name in their sweet native tongue.

"Just a minute, just a minute," Kiran stood up, laughing while they clambered around him. "How are you all? Yes, good?" He continued to laugh with them, bobbing his head like an expert, picking them up and pretending to inspect them or tussling their hair good-naturedly.

"Can you play with us?" one little boy asked, holding up the flat soccer ball with a twinkle in his eyes.

"Yes, yes of course, but let me speak with your parents first," Kiran smiled in a way I had never seen before, his whole face was lit up and his smirk gone, replaced with genuine happiness.

I hung back, unsure what to do or how to even begin to interact with the children that loved Kiran so much. Tears stung my eyes when I noticed how dirty the children were and how their tattered clothes hung from their tiny bodies. They were barefoot and scrawny, not with bloated stomachs like the starving children I had seen on TV, but with bare ribs and exposed spines.

A little girl with long, tangled black hair, tugged at Kiran's black linen pants; he kneeled down to look her in the eye. She whispered something shyly in his ear, glancing my way with overly large deep brown eyes.

"Well, this is Eden. Children, this is Eden," he reached out to me and took my hand, pulling me into the throng of little ones pressing themselves against Kiran.

"Is she your wife?" a tough little boy asked, putting his hands on his hips and sizing me up.

"No, no she's not," Kiran laughed, putting his arm around my waist and pulling me close to him. "But she would like to be," he laughed harder and I just stared at him, not believing his audacity.

"Why?" the same child asked, narrowing his eyes suspiciously.

"Well, because she loves me," he smiled at the children and then at me. I had never seen Kiran so happy before; I was too swept away in his emotion to reply.

"How awful," The little boy holding the soccer ball groaned.

"I know, isn't it?" Kiran rolled his eyes dramatically.

"Would you like to play with us?" the little girl with big eyes was tugging on my skirt. I knew this was one of those defining moments when I just needed to jump in and, with her sweet expression looking so hopeful, I could hardly say no.

"I would love to," I kneeled down like Kiran had, to her level. "But you'll have to teach me, I don't know how to play," I glanced back at Kiran, asking with my eyes if it was Ok and got a happy nod in return.

"Oh Mr. Kiran, she is American," another boy with a long scar running the length of his arm, dramatically covered his face with his hands and shook his head as if to say he was disappointed.

"Ritesh, I know my boy," he empathized the child's disappointment. "Do you think I still have time to get away?" he grinned down at me, while I tried to hold back my laughter.

"Of course not," the boy answered, pulling his hands away

179

and looking at Kiran seriously, "It's too late for you."

"I'm afraid you are right," Kiran agreed seriously. "Now, I have a job for you. Would you like a job?" The boy nodded excitedly and pushed his way to the front of the children. "I need you to make sure all of your friends get a pair of these."

Kiran opened one of the black duffle bags revealing enough pairs of shoes for all of the children in every size of flip flops. Ritesh began pulling pairs of shoes out and tossing them into the excited crowd of children. They all reached for them, no matter what color they were and then passed them around until they found a child they would fit. Kiran laughed at them, trying to restore order. When every child was finally outfitted with a pair of shoes, Kiran reached into another bag producing a brand new soccer ball which elevated their elation to even higher levels. The children screamed their appreciation and then took off after Kiran tossed the ball further, down the road beginning a new game.

The little girl with the big brown eyes stood tugging on my skirt, silently asking me to join her. I looked at Kiran, not sure if he had other plans for me, but desperately wanting to be a part of the unconditional love these children showered on him without hesitation. He smiled at me admiringly, his eyes shining.

"Yes, of course, go," he commanded, laughing. I walked over; quickly kissing him on the cheek before running after the little girl, hoping the children would be as forgiving as they were accepting, when they learned I had no soccer skills whatsoever.

I ran around with the children, letting each one teach me a little something about the game. The little boy who had been suspicious of me taught me how to stop the ball with the inside of my foot. Ritesh, the boy who didn't like Americans, taught me how to kick the ball, despite his prejudice; my favorite, though, was the shy little girl who had invited me to play in the first place. She taught me how to run around on the outside of the circle without really getting involved at all.

While I played with the children, I watched Kiran walk to each door and knock gently, interacting with the owner of every house. He seemed to be speaking kind words, or he would listen intently to whatever the homeowner had to say. At the end of each visit he would reach into his bag and produce an envelope that looked to be full of money, some bread and a bag of rice before moving on to the next house. Kiran was hugged, bowed to, or said a tearful "thank you" to, but always he waved it off as being nothing and would graciously return the handshake or hug with equal emotion.

This was a side of him I had never seen before, a side I didn't even know existed. I was blown away by his desire to help these people and my heart longed to be a part of the same act of heroism. I felt moved by the simplicity of the village and the genuine authenticity of each individual. But more than that, Kiran moved me. Kiran, in his deep desire to help these people and their love for him, stirred my soul, connecting me more to him than I thought possible. He was a good man.

He would be a great leader.

Eventually he reached the last house; the other occupants left their houses after Kiran visited them to watch the game happening in the middle of the street. The children continued to laugh at me and my poor attempts at getting involved. I was pathetic and they had too much fun reminding me.

Kiran finished with the last house and walked over to the children, conceding that he would play with them now.

"Let's give Eden a break, shall we?" he turned to wink at me, the mischief back in his happy expression.

"Yes!" the boys in the group cheered loudly and I couldn't even feel insulted, they were too funny.

I walked over to the edge of the crowd of parents, the little girl with big eyes following me closely, holding on to my skirt and never taking her overly-large brown eyes off me.

The parents gathered around me, too, engaging me in small talk and voicing their appreciation for Kiran and all the work he had done for them. I listened to story after story of how he had saved one family or the other over time and how the children loved him for an hour, watching him play tirelessly, laughing more than I had ever seen him.

The sun began to set in the sky, making the canopied village grow dark. The parents started to call their children in for the night and the game ended. Kiran put Ritesh in charge of the new soccer ball but made him promise to share the ball equally with all the other children. We said our goodbyes and then climbed back into the waiting three-wheeler, driving noisily away from the village.

My heart hurt to leave the beauty of those families behind. I knew I wanted to help them in more ways, offer them everything I had. I smiled peacefully, knowing that a good thing had been done today and that I had been a part of it.

I looked over at Kiran, wanting him to explain today to me. I wanted to know every detail, of how he came to find the village and grow so attached; I wanted to know how often he went there and get even more details out of him than the village parents had offered. But I couldn't break the perfection of the day by questioning it to death. I just stared at him, an amused smile my permanent companion.

"What?" He grinned, reaching his arm across my shoulder and pulling me close.

"I just.... I had no idea," I smiled back, unable to put into words the feeling that was inside my heart.

"That is what life is about, isn't it? Not different races or magic or kingdoms or life and death. That. People. Giving yourself wholly to someone else and making their life better," he kissed the top of my head, sighing sweetly.

"I agree," I mumbled, finding myself choked up and emotional.

"Thank you for coming with me," he whispered into my hair.

"Thank you for taking me," I looked up into his eyes with all the sincerity I felt. He didn't move to kiss me and I knew that a kiss would ruin the moment; it was about something more than physical attraction. This feeling, this connection was defining our relationship.

"Eden, they knew you," Kiran broke the silent moment, his voice more serious than he had been all afternoon.

"What do you mean?" I asked lightly, wondering how any of them could possibly have known me.

"They said, I mean, each one of them told me that you were part of India.... part of their earth." He gazed at me intently, asking me to explain.

"What do you mean?" I scooted backwards, not understanding either.

"I thought you would know what they meant," he said, letting me go.

"I don't," I said simply, innocently.

"Me either," he mused.

"Maybe because of the Walk?" I guessed, wondering if I should take their words literally, and believe that I had become a part of India's earth or at least the wind.

"Yes, the Walk," Kiran mumbled, pulling me to him again and turning silent for the rest of the ride to the palace.

It was in those moments of silence that I knew I couldn't share the extent of my experience with him…. with anyone. Something about the wind spoke to me, telling me that it was mine alone, that not even Avalon would understand the entirety of what happened. The wind was mine and mine alone and I would bear the secret the same way.

Chapter Twenty-Four

I had one more day left at the palace. I was frustrated and just wanted to go home. After Kiran and I arrived back from the village yesterday we parted ways, he on some important Kingdom business, me to roam the empty corridors alone.

I had a new servant, an Immortal servant. She was Indian, in her mid-twenties, with silky black hair pulled tightly into a bun, and a British accent. Ricasah, was proper and polite but had a strong air of dignity about her that made it hard to believe she was a servant. I liked her, but I didn't really need her around. I wasn't used to a servant; I could do things on my own.

She had brought dinner to my room last night and then told me about a private movie theater inside the west wing of the palace. Ricasah explained that since none of the royal family would be using the room, I was more than welcome to.

I swallowed my irritation with her phrasing, knowing she had nothing to do with the laws and by-laws of the Monarchy. In the end, I opted for the movie out of sheer boredom and fell asleep in the plush reclining stadium style chairs.

I woke sometime early in the morning and zombie-walked my way back to my room, where breakfast had been waiting for me at the vanity. After I sufficiently stuffed myself from the same delicacies I enjoyed the day before, I decided to explore the gardens.

I got lost, both literally and figuratively, wandering around the palace grounds discovering walled gardens with beautiful climbing flowers and ancient shade trees. I found a stone pathway that led to a crystal clear brook that reminded me exactly of the one in Kiran and my Dream Walk world, complete with far off mountains sitting as a backdrop. I stayed there a while, with my feet in the soft current wondering if this was where Kiran had drawn inspiration from.

On my way back from the brook, I stumbled upon the stables for the elephants and had fun walking through, and interacting with the trained beasts from the ground. They were massive, I had never felt so small or delicate standing next to their leathery tree sized legs.

In the center of the palace were more gardens and a huge

atrium with elegant stone statues and fountains. The atrium housed all manner of wild and exotic birds, including colorful but very territorial peacocks that chased me out of their home with haughty indignation.

When I finally found my room again I was exhausted and starving. I missed lunch and was in desperate need of a nap. But only seconds after collapsing face forward on the pillow-top king-sized bed, Ricasah knocked softly at my door.

"Come in," I hollered through a muffled voice, face down in my pillow.

"Pardon me. Your presence has been requested for dinner with the King and Queen this evening," Ricasah announced politely.

That got my attention. I rolled over to make sure she was serious and when I realized she had no reason not to be, I threw my arms across my face with exasperation.

"Why?" I sighed.

"Excuse me?" Ricasah asked, assuming my question was directed at her.

"Why me?" I clarified, still not really talking to her, but too frustrated to care. I didn't want to eat dinner with Lucan and pretend I was someone I wasn't and worry about my food being poisoned or passing some secret test proving I was completely average. I didn't want to have to be polite and call upon the table manners Aunt Syl had drilled into my head as a child; I really just wanted to sleep.

"Why you?" Ricasah asked very perplexed. "Well, because of the Eternal Walk. There is always a dinner in the King's honor after the Walks are completed," she walked further into the room carrying a long white box that I noticed for the first time. "Granted, there are usually hundreds of candidates attending and the dinner is more of a ball than a private setting, but I suppose your circumstances are unique." She finished with an air of dignity.

"Oh, of course. I'm sorry, I'm new to all of this," I sat up, forcing myself to smile even though I truly hated using that excuse.

"I am aware," she smiled forcefully back. "The Crown Prince sent this over, suggesting that you might not have anything appropriate to wear this evening." She set the box down on the bed and opened it, revealing a silk sari in soft pink, the same color of the dress he sent me for the Fall Equinox Dance. I rubbed the luxurious material between my fingers, feeling differently about this gift than

185

I had the last.

"He was right about that." I eyed my carry-on suitcase with a little bit of contempt, wishing I would have been prepared for meeting Kiran's parents at least emotionally. Although, I realized that since neither Amory nor Kiran had warned me before now, the dinner might actually be a surprise to everybody.

"I will be back in an hour to help you dress," Ricasah finished and then left me alone in the room with my thoughts and new sari.

I stood outside the dining room doors not ready to go in yet. I was told dinner would be served promptly at six and I had a few minutes before I would be late. I swayed back and forth feeling like I would be sick, watching my reflection in one of the few glassed windows around the palace.

The pink sari was exquisite, with silver stitching outlining delicate flowers and loopy designs. I opted for minimal makeup, not wanting to draw attention to myself; so other than mascara and a little lip gloss, my face was plain. I was afraid that my hair would draw unnecessary attention, so I had pulled it into a side braid; but now I wondered if I should have gone Ricasah's route and chosen the low bun.

"Did they not tell you we eat supper in the dining room?" Kiran's amused voice came from behind me; I turned to meet him. He looked especially handsome in a white seer sucker suit and soft blue dress shirt underneath, that was unbuttoned at the top in lieu of a tie. His hair was tousled underneath his crooked crown and he fidgeted with it, trying to get the elaborate piece of heavy gold to stay on correctly.

"Oh, and not out in the hallway?" I tried to make a joke, but still couldn't get my nerves under control. I had been having visions of Lucan slamming his fist down on the table screaming, "Off with her head," all afternoon. If I could get through this dinner without being arrested, I would probably be in the clear. I would be able to make it out of India alive and still a free girl.

"Come along, it shan't be all bad," he smiled and held out his bent elbow to me, gesturing with a nod of the head.

186

I linked my hand daintily through his arm, trying to recall my fairy tale knowledge and how exactly a guest of the King should behave.

We walked through the doors of the dining room and I was a little surprised to see the long table I had eaten breakfast at the day before gone, and a smaller, more intimate table set for five. I wondered absently how they managed to move the larger table; it seemed like a permanent and very heavy fixture.

The small table, in its place, made the room seem extra-large. Underneath the table was a wide rug with a colorful mosaic pattern covering the cold, stone floor. The fireplace on the east wall had been lit, but even though the room needed the opposite of heating, I couldn't feel any warmth across the expanse of the room. The chandelier hanging from the ceiling had been dimmed to provide a more intimate dinner setting. An exotic floral arrangement adorned the middle of the table.

Kiran walked over to the table and pulled out a chair for me. We were alone so far in the room and I was thankful for that.

"You look exquisite by the way," Kiran said softly to me, sitting down to my right.

"Thank you," I smiled, but rushed on. "Ok, what are some rules I need to know? Like guidelines? Um, do I need to bow or whatever when your father comes in?" My face flushed red, I felt sick again.

"Relax, you'll do fine," he smiled patiently at me. "When Father enters, you need to stand; a small curtsy will do fine. Make sure you keep your eyes down until Father has been seated and then you are allowed to sit and lift your head. Do not eat anything or even drink anything until Father has taken his first bite. And, don't speak unless spoken to, that is very important, Eden." Kiran finished quickly, giving me a worried glance before standing at the opening of the doors.

Lucan and Kiran's mother, Analisa, entered the room with all of the demeanor I would expect from a King and Queen. Lucan was dressed in a cream colored suit with a white dress shirt underneath and was the perfect older version of Kiran. He had the same tousled blonde hair sitting underneath his crooked but larger crown, only he didn't mess with it the way Kiran did. He had strong blue eyes that swept over the room in an irritated, disapproving manner that made

187

me nervous.

Analisa, Kiran's mother, was breathtaking. She was dressed in a turquoise sari that had silver stitching like mine, but was so superior in beauty she made mine look plain. Her long dark hair flowed about her as she walked. She had turquoise eyes that matched her sari; they were kind and not nearly as unpleasant as her husband's. Her dainty golden crown was the only one that seemed to fit exactly on the top of her head.

Behind them, followed a young girl, probably no more than eleven or twelve. She was also dressed in a sari; hers was in a fun magenta, and had gold beading all over the front sash. Her eyes were a golden brown that reminded me of someone but I couldn't put my finger on who it was. She was wearing a thin band of gold with a large diamond in the center, around her head; her crown was very age-appropriate.

I moved to the front of my chair and curtsied awkwardly, wishing I would have anticipated this moment and practiced the movement earlier this afternoon. I stared at the ground afraid of lifting my head and even more afraid of doing something wrong.

"All right, that's enough of that," Lucan declared gruffly, "Eden, as I remember, you don't have much regard for the Monarchy at all," he took his seat and everyone else followed, Kiran laughing to the right of me.

"No, please forgive me, I have the utmost respect for the Monarchy," I sat down and cleared my throat, defending myself and afraid my previous beheading fears would actually come true. "I was um, I was just raised...."

"Human," Lucan finished for me, his frown turning briefly into a reassuring smile. "We are aware."

"Yes, that's right," I confirmed softly.

"Father, don't be so hard on our guest," Kiran said in good humor.

The servants brought out the first course, a green salad with a citrus dressing, and the delicious Indian bread I had come to love.

After we were alone again, Lucan spoke directly to me, "My son is quite taken with you Eden. I'm quite certain you have bewitched him." He stared at me, his deep blue eyes searching mine; I didn't know what to say. He didn't seem angry, but I felt like he was still accusing me of something that should be wrong.

"No, no, not at all," I glanced at Kiran, hoping he would help defend me, but he was suddenly very interested in his wine. "Kiran is betrothed," I finished weakly.

"I know," Lucan snapped, but not unkindly.

"Of course. Forgive me. What I mean to say is that, Kiran is too respectable of a man to mistreat Seraphina," A deep blush crawled up my neck and onto my cheeks.

"Is that so? Well, my dear," Lucan continued, turning to Kiran's mother, "at least their feelings for each other are mutual," he smiled at his beautiful wife who nodded her agreement eyeing me over with her turquoise eyes.

"I am Amelie," the younger girl introduced herself. "It is very nice to meet you." She smiled genuinely at me, her golden brown eyes sparkling from even across the table.

"Oh yes, Eden, this is Amelia, Sebastian's younger sister," Kiran smiled between the two of us.

I recognized the difference between how she introduced herself and how Kiran had said her name as the difference between the French and English pronunciations; at least French class had taught me something.

"Do you know my brother?" she asked excitedly, a look of pure pride in her eyes.

"Yes, I attend Kingsley with him," I smiled back at her, not wanting to go into too much detail on exactly how well we knew each other. Her excitement was catching, though, and I mused at how sweet and enchanting she was, especially for being Sebastian's sister.

"How wonderful!" she gasped, reaching out for Kiran's hand. "I wanted to join the boys so badly, but mother said I am too young to be that far from home." She pouted, looking up at Kiran with a mixture of hero worship and pleading.

"That you are, Amelia," Lucan scolded from behind his wine goblet.

She was instantly silent; her eyes falling desperately back to her salad. My heart went out to her; she had that kind of contagious personality that demanded empathy with every emotion.

"It won't be long, dearest," Kiran reached out for her hand again, and she looked up at him, her large golden brown eyes flickering with hope. "You'll be with us again soon enough," he smiled down at her and I saw that she believed him; there was complete trust between the two.

The servants appeared to clear the first course and then a second group of servants brought out a delicious-smelling soup. I was pleasantly surprised to find it sweet and a little sour, with apples, potatoes and raisins.

"Eden, I would love to hear more about how your Walk went," Amelia said happily. "I have to do mine this summer and I am so terribly nervous," She glanced at Lucan making sure she wasn't saying anything she shouldn't, before turning her bright eyes back to me. "Were you terrified?"

I cleared my throat, desperately wishing she wouldn't have even broached the subject. I didn't know how to fumble my way through a lie in front of Lucan because I didn't know how a normal Walk was supposed to go.

"Yes, yes I was absolutely terrified," I smiled gently, with honesty.

"Oh, me too," Amelia gushed, offering me the same trust that she had given Kiran.

"Whatever for?" Kiran asked, perplexed. "There's nothing to be afraid of," he said confidently to Amelia.

"Well, Kiran's right," I cleared my throat again, hoping to sound convincing. "There isn't anything to be afraid of really, but it's hard to know that before you've done it." I took a quick sip of my soup, hoping the conversation would end there.

"That's what I keep telling Uncle Lucan," Amelia glanced over at the King who had seemed to grow disinterested in our conversation. "I was hoping he would let me watch your Walk Eden, just so I could get a glimpse of what exactly happens."

"Eden's Walk wouldn't have revealed very much Amelia. I don't believe I've ever witnessed a Walk end so abruptly in my life," Lucan looked down at me from over his glass, I was suddenly very nervous, realizing how erratic I must have come across yesterday.

I blushed and stared down at my now empty bowl. I didn't know if Lucan was expecting an explanation or if he already knew I couldn't give him one.

The servants came in again, providing a much needed interruption to the awkward silence. They cleared our bowls and replaced them with a lamb sauce over long-grain white rice with more bread to eat with, instead of silverware. I watched Kiran expertly tear a piece of bread apart and fold it into a kind of scoop, bringing the rice mixed with sauce proficiently to his lips. I inwardly sighed, knowing this was not the place to attempt a finger food learning experience.

"Thank you for inviting me to dinner, everything is wonderful," I changed the subject, calling on propriety to cover my awkward silence. "I understand this usually only happens once a year," I tried smiling in the general direction of Lucan without actually looking at him.

"Yes. It does," he replied curtly. "But as you know your circumstances are.... unique."

"You have no idea how often I'm told that," I attempted a joke, but only Kiran laughed.

"Well, we are just happy you were so willing to cooperate," Lucan smiled at me politely, but his deep blue eyes were searching my face, waiting for me to react.

"No, please," I smiled, genuinely. "You are the ones who have been so accommodating. I apologize for my negligence in the matter." I did my best to sound grown-up and sincere; I hadn't had a choice in the matter, or even been asked to cooperate.

"In the summer we hold a ball," Kiran spoke up with anxious enthusiasm. "The palace is really quite lovely in the summer, Eden," he smiled at me with more affection than I thought was appropriate in front of his parents, but some instinct deep in the pit of my stomach told me to play the secret lover a little more obviously.

"I would have loved a ball," I cooed at Kiran, swirling the wine around in my glass idly.

"Then maybe next time around, your parents shouldn't die and leave you in the care of a-" Lucan spit out suddenly with cool-toned hatred that sent chills down my spine. He paused only for a second on the vowel and I was certain he was going to say Amory before he continued, "a, a human," he set his glass down a little violently, spilling the crimson liquid on the table.

I didn't know what to say or how to respond, but luckily Analisa, Kiran's mother, reacted before I was given the chance. Very calmly and collectedly, she set her own goblet down, dabbed at her face with her cloth napkin and stood. She smiled at Kiran and Amelia and then at me, before leaving the table and walking out of

191

the dining room without another word.

"If you'll excuse me," Lucan mimicked Analisa's every move minus the smiles and left the dining room before I could analyze the rhyme or reason for any of it.

Chapter Twenty-Five

"Welcome home," Aunt Syl opened the door for me before I could even walk up the driveway.

The December night was frigidly cold, I could see my breath and I was standing ankle deep in snow. The dark winter night was a painful reminder of the warmth and sunshine I left in India. The black sedan that had been my transportation from the private air strip drove away into the night and I let out a sigh of exhaustion that felt like a long time coming.

I dropped my carry-on and new backpack in the middle of the snowy drive and ran the rest of the way to Aunt Syl. I threw my arms around her and she reciprocated in the motherly hug I had always known.

Choked up with emotion, she whispered into my hair, "It's good to have you home."

"It's good to be home," I sighed with my own emotion. I hadn't realized until that moment how afraid I had been of not making it back to this house, and of never seeing Aunt Syl again. Pending revolution aside, this was where I belonged; this home held my heart.

"Well, look who's back," Avalon masked the relief I felt washing over him with mild sarcasm.

Jericho popped his head out of the door too, smiling at me with a wide grin, and waving silently in an adorable gesture.

"When did you guys get back?" I asked, hardly believing they beat me home. Weren't they supposed to be following me?

"Like seconds ago," Avalon replied, while Jericho maneuvered past the rest of us, picking up my discarded luggage and carrying it inside the house. "Once we were sure your taxi would be dropping you at home, we decided to race you here. We won by the way," he smiled at me, tugging at my arm, pulling me away from Aunt Syl and into a bear hug of his own. "We made it," he whispered and that close to Avalon, I couldn't distinguish his emotion from mine; but, either way, relief washed over both of us and we realized that a more strategic game was being played than we had wanted to believe. But for the moment, we were safe.

"Well, come inside you two and let's hear all about it," Aunt

Syl ushered us inside and everyone took their boots off at the door. Avalon and I collapsed side by side on the overstuffed couch, his arm around me. We weren't usually so touchy-feely but the separation over the past few weeks had been rough; our twin connection needed some serious care.

"Is Amory coming over?" I asked, not really wanting to recount the story twice, even though I was dying to talk over the girly details of the trip with Aunt Syl. I knew Amory would hardly care about the color of my saris and all the different foods I got to try.

"Yes, he should be here soon," Aunt Syl smiled, intuition written all over her face. "How about I make some hot chocolate?"

"Sounds wonderful," I mumbled, closing my eyes and wishing I could just sleep for the next several months.

"I'll help you," Avalon stood up, patting me on the head a little roughly and following Aunt Syl into the kitchen.

The doorbell rang and I reluctantly made myself get up off the couch and answer it. I expected to see Amory, so when I flung the door open I was more than a little surprised to see Sebastian standing on the other side, shivering.

"Hello?" I greeted with a question, more confused than I felt emotionally prepared to deal with.

"Hello," he said confidently, smiling back at me. His golden brown eyes were sparkling; I remembered his sister with reluctant admiration.

"What are you doing here, Sebastian?" I asked bluntly, too tired to play games.

"Can I come in?" he dodged my question, fidgeting a little, but unable to stop shivering.

"Fine," I walked away from the door and let him enter. I stood, leaning against the staircase, not willing to let him further into my home, my sanctuary. I heard Jericho moving around upstairs and I was suddenly nervous and wondering where Roxie and Lilly were.

"Don't be so terse, Eden," he smiled mischievously at me, unbuttoning his black pea coat at the collar and loosening his scarf. "Am I supposed to remind you to use your magic for the jet lag?" he asked sincerely.

"No," I rolled my eyes as if he was completely out of line,

195

but secretly used my magic to fix the exhaustion. I couldn't believe I had forgotten again.

"So listen, I know that it's late," he continued. I felt Avalon start to walk into the living room carrying two cups of hot chocolate but sent him a warning thought to turn around and wait. "I just wanted to get a moment alone with you before the dance."

"The dance?" I demanded. "What dance?"

I suddenly felt sick. This was going to be a repeat of the Fall Equinox Dance all over again. Kiran had sent him, wanting me to go to the dance with him, but he was already obligated to Seraphina. A sudden glimpse into a dismal future with Kiran flashed before me and I wanted to vomit.

"The Winter Solstice Dance, at the end of semester," Sebastian replied patiently. "This Friday. I know it's last minute, and I'm sorry for that, but you have been out of town for the past two weeks," he smiled at me with what I was sure was a charming smile, but one that I couldn't process.

"I'm confused," I said plainly, still trying to figure out why Sebastian was standing in my entry way. "Did Kiran send you?" "Kiran? No," Something flashed across Sebastian's face but I was too flustered to decipher it. "No, it's just that, well, after you left for India, I, actually, I haven't been able to stop thinking about you," Sebastian's cheeks flooded with a deep blush and suddenly I was flustered for a different reason.

I stood there dumbly, staring after Sebastian and trying not to believe him. This was just too complicated to comprehend. At the same moment, Jericho walked noisily down the stairs, stopping at the bottom step, next to me.

"Sebastian, that is very sweet of you, but, but, but I already have a date," I grabbed Jericho's arm, clutching to it firmly and pulling him down the last step and next to me. "This is Jericho, my.... boyfriend," I smiled forcefully at Jericho and linked my arm with his.

"Your boyfriend?" Sebastian asked, unbelieving.

"Yes. My boyfriend," I repeated with more confidence. "Sebastian this is Jericho Bentley, Jer," I cleared my throat, trying to make my nickname for him sound natural, "this is Sebastian Cartier."

They reached across what felt like an infinite divide and shook hands, neither boy knowing what to say. After letting go, Jericho put a protective, but awkward arm around me.

"I absolutely apologize," Sebastian retreated a few steps back, clearly unnerved by the idea of my boyfriend, albeit my fake boyfriend. "Forgive me Eden, I had no idea."

"Please, don't feel bad. Jericho and I, um, we just started dating, so we haven't been very, um, public about it," I looked up at Jericho trying to gaze into his eyes, but he was enthusiastically agreeing with me by nodding his head; I could barely hold back my laughter.

"Really, man," Jericho turned his attention to the embarrassed Sebastian, "don't feel bad. I get it. I just got lucky and asked her first," he smiled at Sebastian, extending his hand again. I heard the hard edge in Jericho's voice though, it was faint, but I noticed.

"Again, I am sorry," Sebastian said, shaking Jericho's hand more firmly this time. "I guess I'll be seeing you Friday, then."

"Absolutely," Jericho said, walking Sebastian out. "See you Friday."

Jericho closed the door behind Sebastian and leaned back against it. A smug smile played at the corner of his lips and he looked me over with a look that said, "I told you so."

"Eden," he said sarcastically, "will you go to the high school dance with me?"

"Shut up! I am so sorry!" I wanted to be mad at him, but I felt too bad for dragging him further into the mess my life was.

"Avalon!" he yelled, walking past me into the kitchen.

I followed quickly behind, afraid of the story he would spin to Aunt Syl and Avalon. Roxie and Lilly were just walking in through the garage door carrying several boxes of pizza. Everyone stopped to listen to Jericho's announcement.

"Your sister just asked me to go out with her," he grinned playfully.

"I did not!" I defended myself animatedly. "Well, Ok. I kind of did."

"Yes. You did," Jericho continued to taunt me. "And," he continued with more drama, "She is making me go to the dance with her this Friday."

"Yes!" Avalon laughed. "Lilly, it looks like we're going to

197

the dance too!"

    Lilly blushed a deep crimson red, hating the attention and not sure what to make of Avalon's declaration. I watched Roxie flinch from jealousy and that was enough for me to get over my embarrassment and laugh with the boys. Maybe this dance wouldn't be as bad as the last one.

Chapter Twenty-Six

I smoothed out the black silk of my evening dress while staring at myself in Aunt Syl's full length mirror. My hair had been straightened and styled by a professional hair stylist and my make-up done to perfection by another professional. I hardly recognized myself.

The dress Aunt Syl and I picked out had been an extravagant price, but as I moved the full mermaid-style skirt, swishing the beautiful fabric about, I knew it was worth it. The gown clung to my body, the halter straps tying around my neck and dipping into a deep V. My back was exposed and I turned around self-consciously making sure the delicate silk covered all of the appropriate areas.

A knock at the door drew my attention away from myself and I looked over to see Jericho standing in the doorway. I hardly recognized him either. He was dressed to the nines in a tuxedo with tails. His hair had just been trimmed; it made his crooked nose stand out against his angular face. His hazel eyes twinkled greener tonight, while his fingers tugged at his tight collar.

He was paused in the doorway just looking at me, and I at him. I was more nervous for this dance than I should be. Without any threat of attack, since the Resistance would actually be attending the dance this time, there would come a point in the evening when I would have to dance. My stomach did a flip. I looked at Jericho frantically.

"It's too much, isn't it?" I whispered and when he didn't answer I continued, "The dress, I mean. I can't pull it off." I looked back to the mirror trying to find myself in it.

Jericho cleared his throat and I feared that he would confirm my doubts, "No, Eden," he paused again and I looked back over to him, the panic nearly drowning me. "That dress was made specifically for you," his eyes swept over me in obvious appreciation and I could breathe again.

I walked carefully over to him, in my tall silver stilettos and kissed him on the cheek. "Thank you," I whispered, "I couldn't do this without you."

"Are you ready then?" Jericho cleared his throat again before extending his elbow. "They're waiting for us."

I nodded my head and we walked down the stairs and into the living room where Avalon was, very nervously, talking with Lilly. Roxie sat on the fireplace, playing idly with the brick. She looked very defeated and I felt sorry for her for a second. For an unexplainable moment I wanted to explain to her that Avalon's feelings for Lilly didn't run that deep. He was more attracted to her beauty than the idea of a relationship and he would probably never pursue her. Although after seeing her in that dress, he might change her mind.

Lilly was dressed in a striking emerald gown that covered her feet despite the gold heels that were probably six inches off the ground. I couldn't see them now; she had shown them to me earlier, worried that she wouldn't be able to reach Avalon's arms while they danced, without them. The gown was a full skirt starting at her hips and the bodice tight against her tiny frame. Gold beading made straight lines of flickering light, extending from the boat neck top to the very bottom of the impossible amounts of fabric in her skirt. She looked up at me and the green from her dress set off the green in her eyes in a flash of color that betrayed her timid personality.

Avalon too was dressed in a tux with tails, his hair pulled back tightly in the little messy bun at the nape of his neck that usually only girls wore. He was too confident however for the pony tail to be effeminate and it somehow created more of a masculine impression than diminishing one. He tore his eyes from Lilly a little reluctantly when we entered and the look that crossed his face was anything but flattering.

"You can't wear that," he demanded of me.

"Calm down," I said quietly, feeling embarrassed and suddenly inappropriate.

"Oh stop, Avalon," Aunt Syl swept into the room and this time Avalon conceded to her authority. "Eden looks ravishing. Now, get together for a picture." She held up her camera and we all obeyed.

I was almost too nervous to smile but somehow we all managed the appropriate poses and faces Aunt Syl was hoping for. When she was satisfied with the photo shoot, I gave her a kiss and we headed to the dance in Jericho's Jeep, after stuffing both Lilly's and my dress into the backseat, careful not to harm either by shutting them in the door.

Jericho pulled up to the valet after a long line of limousines; I had to laugh at both boys' sense of entitlement and the feeling of pride they carried at being the only non-luxury vehicle in the lot.

I walked arm in arm with Jericho into the gym. I inhaled a sharp breath; they had somehow out done even the Fall Equinox Dance. Everything was white and sparkling. The chandeliers that hung from the ceiling were crystal and lighted the expansive room in a soft, warm glow. The table cloths were white, with low bouquets of white roses tumbling across the tables and down the sides to the floor, leaving only room for place settings. The dance floor, too, had been made into pure white with millions of white rose petals covering every inch, so when the people would dance, the petals would float up and around them. Tall silver stands were placed around the room with the same style of bouquets flowing down their elegant sides and onto the floor in pools of delicate flowers, painting the room with purity.

I looked up at Jericho with pure delight. I had no idea something this fanciful could exist. I truly felt like a princess at a ball.

"It's just so beautiful," I sighed, losing my anxiety and feeling swept up by the very night.

Jericho smiled down at me, his eyes intense. I could tell he wanted to say something but he didn't. He just looked at me until the moment passed and he was tugging at my elbow, "Shall we find our seats?"

"Yes," I agreed and my eyes floated over the room again searching out Avalon and Lilly who had been ahead of us.

In a moment, the sick feeling was back and the room began to swim. My eyes fell on Kiran's table, and there he sat in all of his handsome glory, Seraphina at his side, having a fabulous time. He was surrounded by the usual group and they sat in an elite circle, laughing and carrying on. I was nearly swallowed whole by jealousy. For the first time that Kiran and I had been secretly together, I felt foolish and naive.

There he was, with the right woman. The woman his father had handpicked for him. The woman he would marry. I was the girl that no one could know about. The secret mistress. The girl who would always love him and never get to be with him. And as he enjoyed his public life with those people a Prince should surround himself with, I had come with a pretend boyfriend and was not even allowed to speak to the love of my life.

"Are you all right?" Jericho whispered in my ear, tensing his grip on my elbow.

"Yes, no, I'm sorry, I'm fine," I felt the color drain from my face and I thought for sure I would vomit. Kiran momentarily glanced our way and I had to escape before I was sick all over Jericho. "Excuse me," I said over my shoulder, nearly running in the direction of the bathroom.

I nearly fell into the plush sitting room, adjacent to the women's restroom, reaching the doors in what felt like just in time. I took long breaths trying to calm my nerves and walked around the center divan waving my arms and willing myself not to start sweating.

In India, things had felt different. I had Kiran to myself and even a dinner with his parents. There were no other, beautiful, more qualified girls to contend with. Seraphina was not there flashing her engagement ring and laying her filthy hands all over him. Kiran had been mine. I had been a part of his home. I had seen a part of him that I had not known existed and had fallen impossibly deeper in love.

India had made me hope, like I hadn't before. The secret part of our relationship had been momentarily forgotten and I had glimpsed a future for us. Now, back in the same halls that had tormented me for months I was painfully reminded that I was no closer to normalcy than before. I was still inhibited from loving Kiran, and still prohibited from having an open relationship. I was a prisoner, a prisoner to my feelings and a prisoner to secrecy.

I stopped when I felt the beginning of blisters on the soles of my feet and leaned heavily against the counter. I talked to myself, making my brain understand that this was no different than school. I had a part to play and so did Kiran. This was no different than school.

Are you ok? What are you doing in there? Avalon sent with a sense of urgency and irritation. Use your f-ing magic and get out here.

With the reminder of magic, I knew Avalon was right. I was being over-dramatic and needed to find my center. I released the magic I had been holding, realizing this was becoming a bad habit every time I started to panic.

With the magic loosed on my frayed nerves, I could breathe again. I fidgeted with my hair in the mirror, applied some more lip gloss and decided to brave the rest of the night. Things were not going to change any time soon and I needed to find a way to cope, and at least enjoy what was left of the beautiful evening. I left the bathroom, ready to find Jericho and maybe even dance.

"What is this about a boyfriend?" Kiran surprised me from the darkened hallway housing the bathrooms.

"I'm sorry?" I asked still trying to shake the startled feeling. Kiran's eyes were a cloudy mixture of all the different blues of his eyes. He was scowling at me in a way he never had before, and I felt his jealousy radiating off him in waves.

"Sebastian came home Tuesday night, informing me that you and Jericho were dating," Kiran accused.

"That's because Sebastian showed up at my house all wanting me to come to the dance with him," I whispered defensively.

"Well, Sebastian would have been better than that bloody bloke!" he scoffed, eyeing me over in disgust.

"Really? You really would have preferred I danced the night away with your nosey
cousin?" I asked, sarcastically.

"At least I know he is a man with honorable intentions," he replied smugly.

"Oh, I'm sure. He's not trying to sleep with me. Just kill me," I rolled my eyes and started to turn around.

"So, he is trying to sleep with you!"

"No. No one is trying to sleep with me!" I whispered harshly at him, doing my best to keep my temper in check. "Not even you," I leveled my eyes with him, willing him to fight me. "And why would you, when you have someone else so easily accessible?"

"Eden, are you coming? The first course has been served," Jericho turned the corner to the bathrooms, not even a little bit surprised at the scene he found. I wondered if he was that good of an actor or if Avalon had given him the heads up.

"No," Kiran spoke up before I could even make a sound. "She is not going anywhere with you," his tone held such hatred that I had to look back just to make sure it was really Kiran talking.

"Excuse me," I turned on him.

"It's all right, Eden, the Prince hasn't realized yet, that he doesn't hold any authority over

you," Jericho didn't even look at Kiran, holding out his arm to me and I took it gratefully.

"That is where you are wrong," Kiran growled. "Eden, go out to my car, we're leaving."

"She is capable of making her own decisions," Jericho said evenly. "And I believe she would like to stay."

"I would like to stay," I smiled at Jericho, ignoring the brooding Kiran. I tugged on Jericho's arm and he escorted me to our table.

Avalon and Lilly were glancing at me nervously from across the table, and I didn't know what to say. I couldn't explain what just happened to me while they were surrounded by a room full of loyal, royal subjects.

"I have never understood the first course," Jericho announced loudly, drawing the attention of our table to him. "What is the point of plating something this small?" he gestured down at the bite-sized hors d'oeuvre and laughed.

"Don't be such a fatty," Avalon mocked him. "This is plenty for me," he took a small bite and then set it down, rubbing his tummy like it had been too much.

The table broke out into laughter and cut the tension and awkwardness I dragged back from the bathroom. Jericho stretched his arm around me, rubbing my back in a protective way that also let me know things would be Ok. I trusted Jericho, even if that meant pissing Kiran off. I couldn't help it.

Kiran had treated me unfairly. I lived my life in jealousy, watching him enjoy his public life. Even Jericho lived with the jealousy that came with the girl he liked choosing someone else. When I fell in love with Kiran I knew that he was used to getting what he wanted and more than a little spoiled, but I would be damned before I let his jealous feelings ruin my night. If I could put up with Seraphina on a daily basis, he sure as hell could put with Jericho for a few hours.

Chapter Twenty-Seven

"Stop it!" I laughed, watching Jericho and Avalon dance together in the middle of a crowded dance floor. Lilly and I had followed the two of them out there after they threatened to slow dance the night away together.

"Oh, does that mean you want me to dance with you?" Jericho asked suavely, slipping his hand around my exposed back and pulling me towards him.

"I guess it does," I blushed, letting him lead me around the floral floor, the petals floating up and tickling the tops of my feet.

"Good," Jericho sighed exasperatedly. "Avalon never lets me lead," He gave me a roughish smile and then twirled me around, before pulling me even closer to him.

"I don't usually know how to dance," I admitted, feeling somehow like an expert in his arms.

"Usually?" He asked, questioning my phrasing.

"Well, you make it very easy," I blushed a deeper red.

"I do what I can." he smiled again, pretending arrogance.

The music, played by a live band, slowed down even more and Jericho followed suit. He stopped moving me about the floor and simply swayed as I clung to him, letting him lead our every move.

Lilly and Avalon were across the floor, dancing in the same slow flowing way, only Avalon was not nearly as smooth as Jericho. Lilly was crying with laughter at some joke Avalon had made in order to cover his lack of debonair.

"So is this what dances were like when you were at Kingsley? Or are these new since royalty is involved now?" I asked, trying to break the silence and not get too comfortable in Jericho's arms.

"I didn't graduate from Kingsley," he replied before spinning me around again and then bringing me back to him.

"You didn't? Then how did you get here?" My hand was cupped in his and I felt delicate and ladylike, exactly the way a girl should feel dancing in a man's arms.

"I grew up in Brazil and went to Canesbury Prep, which is basically just like Kingsley only in South America. That's where I met Avalon."

"Really?" I gasped with a little shock. "I'd like to hear that story."

"Angelica had him go there after the rest of his class completed their Walks, since she obviously skipped his. He was a terror there, always causing trouble. And he was a couple years younger than me, so I really didn't have much to do with him until he got to high school and started excelling in everything magic. I was a residential advisor down there for the boys dorms, since my parents work for the King; it was my job to, how do I say this.... tame the beast." We both laughed and he continued. "So, Avalon and I started to spend a lot of time together; I figured, I don't know, maybe he just needed a male role model," he smiled again and I smiled back, totally absorbed in his story. "But really, in the end, he was the one who sort of mentored me."

"How so?" I didn't want him to stop talking; there was so much about the people I was always around that I did not know and Jericho's history was meaningful to me.

"Well, I don't know. Before Avalon, I never questioned anything," he lowered his voice and brought me closer so he could whisper the rest of his story. I leaned in, tilting my head so that my ear was nearer his mouth and my cheek rested gently against his chest. "I mean, my parents have worked for the palace since before your parents disappeared. My dad at one point was in line to be Regent of North America, but when Amory escaped from Romania and a truce was made between Lucan and him, the job went to Amory. So, my dad instead was given the Regency of South America."

"So your dad's a big deal?" I teased, but Jericho just shook his head and cleared his throat.

"My dad is loyal to Lucan," he whispered hoarsely. "I had been raised to be the same until suddenly I was spending all my time with this punk kid who defied everything I was taught to believe. And then, I don't know, something clicked for me. I started questioning the Monarchy and the exile of the Shape-shifters and the racism that runs deep in every Immortals blood and Avalon started to make sense. Then one day, Avalon was gone. He and Angelica just disappeared. The school was told that Angelica was hoping to get a palace position in London; that was accepted for the most part, because Angelica had been a personal attendant of Queen Karina, Lucan's mother. Anyway, Avalon had planted the seed and my mistrust and rebellion started to grow. After high school graduation, I planned to stay in Brazil and go to a human college before deciding how to spend my future. My dad was determined I would follow him into the service of the Monarchy and had set up a position for me in Morocco as underwriter to the Regent there. I had all of these thoughts and frustrations and didn't want to work for the Monarchy until I figured them out, but at the time I had no other appealing options. Until one day, Avalon showed up, alone. He was three feet taller and had long hair and was covered in tattoos and he sought me out in the middle of Rio de Janeiro, and told me there was a Rebellion that needed me and we were coming to Omaha. And I said, Ok, let's go," he laughed, remembering the moment.

"That's how it happened?" I asked, unbelieving.

"Oh yes, I showed up at the airport where Titus, Ebanks, Ronan and Jett were waiting, we met up with Oscar, Xander, Xavier and Roxie in Mexico City. When we got to the farm all of the other teams had been assembled, including a ton of older generation Immortals and we were given the history of you and Avalon and told that once we got you involved, we would be unstoppable," he winked at me, and because of his over-dramatic tone I hoped he was joking. "Three weeks later, I was given a team and sent to Sierra Leone, while Avalon and his team ran surveillance on the now-heightened situation of the Prince arriving. A month after that, I was brought back here when an assassination mission failed and Avalon's entire team had been captured and sent to prison." "So, there wasn't a Resistance before Avalon?" I asked, almost not believing it.

"Well, not exactly. Amory has had a very loyal following since Derrick. I mean, he was the one who was voted King in the first place," Jericho said matter of factly.

"What?" My voice rose louder than appropriate for the dance floor.

"Oh, yeah," Jericho smirked, enjoying being the one to reveal all of the history I had never heard. "It was Amory the people wanted. But Amory refused because he didn't believe our people should be ruled by one man. From what I understand, he hoped that when he said no, the people would drop the issue; but instead they picked Derrick and from there you know the rest, the blood oath with the Titans, the banishment of Shape-Shifters, and the division of all the races."

"So, wait. I bet Amory is kicking himself now," I mumbled, almost unable to believe it.

"Well, legend says that because Amory is the rightful King, the King every Immortal chose, the Guard is actually loyal to him and your family, and not, in fact, the Kendricks. That's why your dad might still be alive and that's why you and Avalon are fine. You don't hold an allegiance to the Kendricks after all," my eyes grew big and I saw the large loophole that would save an entire race of people, should the Resistance succeed. "Yes, but you know him; he would never risk the lives of so many people on a hunch."

"So is that why all of those Kings have hated him for all this time?" I asked, hardly able to digest any of it.

"Well, yeah, that and because they have always known he is more powerful than them. Believe me, they have all tried to kill him, but they can't. And they're jealous, he has the one thing they've all wanted and can't have."

"Immortality," I found my whisper again, gazing into Jericho's eyes and finally understanding the intricacies of my grandfather's past.

Jericho looked down at me, his eyes twinkling. His hand was hot against my bare back and he held my hand in his gently. For a moment, I forgot his story and forgot there were other people around us, we were floating on a cloud of white rose petals and there was only me and there was only him.

"Seriously, Eden," Seraphina's high-pitched, snide voice cut through our perfect moment, grounding our cloud and piercing my ears. "You're not at a funeral."

Kiran was holding her tightly to him, her lavender gown glistening against his crisp tuxedo. Seraphina was gorgeous in a strapless a-line gown with bustled back and diamond detailing. Her hair was in an elegant up do, soft tendrils tumbling down her neck. As usual she looked too beautiful to be so mean, but that never stopped her before.

"Maybe I am," I sighed, not having the will to fight or the stamina to watch Kiran dance with her.

"At least you tried this time around. You failed, but at least

209

there was some effort," she finished, looking down at me over her nose. I so wanted to punch that nose, but I held back, wanting this dance to end better than the last one.

"Sera...." Kiran chided, but not in a way that said he meant it.

"I don't think you get it," Jericho spoke up, surprising all of us. "Some women don't need to be so obvious." He looked over her dress with the ultimate detest and I couldn't hold back my laugh, it rung out high and clear above the sound of the soft music. "How dare you," Kiran let go of Seraphina to face him directly. "You cannot speak to my fiancée like that."

Jericho let go of me as well, stepping forward as if to protect me, "You know what, you're right. It's just that sometimes I forget that she's your fiancée," Jericho took another step forward, daring Kiran to retaliate.

"I think you are the one who has forgotten his place," Kiran took the challenge and another step forward, both boys eyeing each other with menace.

Talbott and Avalon appeared from out of nowhere, taking their places on either side of the argument. They stood there staring at each other with just as much malice, having had a bone to pick with one another for quite some time.

"And what place would that be?" Jericho dared him.

"Beneath me," Kiran growled.

"Not when it comes to Eden," Jericho said plainly. Then the unthinkable happened.

Kiran punched Jericho in the face with fury, sending him flying backwards into the crowd of people that had gathered around to watch. His nose erupted in blood before he fixed it quickly with magic and pushed off the people he had fallen into. He was across the floor in seconds returning Kiran's blow with one of his own.

Avalon wasn't one to wait around and decked Talbott while he tried to pull Jericho off of Kiran. The boys wrestled around on the floor, the sick sound of bones being cracked and fists finding flesh, echoing in the otherwise silent gymnasium. Blood was sprayed on the floor and tuxedos before magic could be used to stop it. And girls screamed at the display of violence, not understanding the reason for the quarrel.

I stood there feeling helpless, not knowing whose side I was on. Although, it felt like Kiran's side wasn't even an option. Seraphina and her holy trinity stood across the fight staring daggers into me as if the whole ordeal was my fault.

"That is enough," Amory appeared, fighting through the crowd, shouting at the wrestling match staining the white floor with sticky blood.

When none of the boys appeared to listen or even hear, I looked on as Amory Time-Slowed the fight down, using his own magical powers, interrupting the fight, separating all four boys with a simple use of forceful electricity.

"Enough," Amory said more quietly, with more authority than I think I had ever heard him use. "Avalon and Jericho, find your dates and leave the premises immediately. You are no longer welcome here. Kiran and Talbott, I suggest you clean yourselves up and enjoy what is left of the night. If I see any more outbursts like this, I will be on the phone with your father before you can fix your broken nose. How dare any of you interrupt a night like this and behave like animals. Now, go," he demanded. Everyone scattered.

Jericho put his arm around me, ushering me out the doors and I let him. Looking back at Kiran I saw a hateful look in his eyes. His gaze flickered to me and suddenly there was a desperate look of defeat in them. He stood there watching me like he had lost me; I couldn't bear to see him hurt like that, to see the pain of losing me, even for a moment, gave him.

Chapter Twenty-Eight

I awoke in our dream world, but it felt empty. Kiran wasn't there yet because I was the one who would be calling him. I decided that as soon as I witnessed the look in his eyes at the dance.

I couldn't leave him feeling like he had lost me; he hadn't. And he needed to at the very least be reassured.

I had no other way of contacting him, so I decided to take action almost immediately. I had never initiated a Dream Walk before, but I knew, from what everyone had told me and because I had the four different types of magic, that I was capable of doing it.

As soon as we arrived home, I left the rest of the group and went to bed. I didn't know what to say to them, or how to express the sympathy that I wasn't sure I felt anymore.

I was grateful that Jericho stuck up for me, and I let him know that several times, but I couldn't just take his side completely. He didn't understand Kiran or our relationship.

I wasn't even sure that I did.

So I decided to Dream Walk, which in the end would take a considerable amount of magic and brainpower I hadn't even realized I possessed. And now that I was in the middle of our perfect world, I wasn't exactly sure how to get Kiran to join me.

Unlike the Witch side of me that used magic through my blood, the electrical feeling of physical magic didn't apply to the Psychic parts. The Medium side to magic was more like an electrical storm in my brain.

I had never really used the Medium side of my magic before. The Witch part came so naturally, I never really even knew it existed, which in the end made sense. Amory was the most powerful Witch of his generation and that was why he had been the Oracle in the first place.

The idea of all four types of magic used in a different way had never even really occurred to me. I knew the Titan part came out in battle, but only because I had relied on it so many times before. Trying to figure out the Psychic part had been almost an unnerving experience and I didn't even want to think about trying to Shape-Shift. The idea of becoming something entirely different was terrifying.

I had to work up to the magic in my mind slowly. The first time I felt the current run through my brain I had been pretty sure I was about to die of a brain aneurism and I sat there for several minutes saying normal stuff to myself in a harsh whisper testing my memory, like the A, B, C's and counting to ten.

Eventually the feeling became as normal as it could be, for that sort of thing and I was able to concentrate on using it. I tried to Time-Slow which slowed the world around me into whatever pace I desired, not that an empty room was easy to practice with, but I got creative. I tossed pillows across the room, in order to slow them down and move myself into position in order to catch them. When I got good at that, I tested dropping Aunt Syl's jewelry box on the floor, and catching it while replacing all of the spilling jewelry.

I had practiced mind reading with Amory before, but tested it inside the house on Roxie, since the other three were, I felt, off limits. I already had unlimited access to Avalon's mind. It wasn't easy, but eventually I had broken in.

And finally I worked on Dream Walking. But now that I was in our world, I had to figure out how to call Kiran to join me.

I sat down in the velvety grass, the soft moonlight pooling around me. I ran my fingers through the darkened wildflowers, their color not nearly so vibrant in the darkness. I whispered Kiran's name softly into the night, calling him from the recesses of my soul.

I felt the surge of electricity in the Psychic-sphere of my mind and in the stillness of this world felt him arrive. I was pleased it had been so easy. It wasn't like he had appeared magically before me, but there was the distinct knowledge that I was no longer alone.

I stood up, suddenly nervous. I walked through the forest, the moonlight all but gone with the canopy of trees overhead. I stumbled around in the dark searching him out, but also afraid of finding him.

"Sometimes I forget you can do anything," Kiran called out to me in a low melancholy voice.

I turned around and there he was, his back to a tree. He was wearing silky pajama pants and no shirt. His face was obscured from the lack of light and I couldn't read his expression. I didn't know whether to run in to his arms or leave the dream all together.

"I can't do anything," I whispered, standing still, afraid to approach.

213

"I thought that might be true once, but now I'm not so sure," he did not move, he stayed still against the tree, his face completely unreadable.

"Are you angry?" I asked, finding the courage to take one step forward.

"No," was his only reply.

"Are you upset?" I guessed again, wishing I could pinpoint his emotion.

"Why don't you stop trying to guess how I'm feeling and explain to me what happened tonight." He was still, his face still a black canvas of obscurity.

"I don't know what happened tonight," I began, trying to put in to words what seemed like just a terrible memory. "Kiran, I didn't want to go to the dance with Sebastian. I don't trust him. I know that you do, and that's fine. But I can't trust him. And when he showed up at my house, claiming that he couldn't stop thinking about me, and wanted to go to the dance with me and all of that, I panicked. Jericho was there.... because of Avalon.... and I just grabbed him, lying that he was my boyfriend to get Sebastian out of my house and put any thoughts of me to rest; Jericho, thankfully, just went along with it."

"Well, that's no surprise there," he mumbled, but his tone sounded better, just barely.

"Kiran, if I had any idea of how much I would upset you, I wouldn't have even gone to the dance. I, I.... I just thought it would be a harmless night, and since I had used Jericho as an excuse with Sebastian, I wanted to cover all of my bases. That's all. There is nothing between Jericho and me. There is absolutely nothing to worry about."

"So you say," he stepped away from the tree and the little light that made its way through the canopy of darkened greenery illuminated his face. His expression was softened, but the sadness etched across his forehead and deep in his eyes was unmistakable. He reached out to me and I ran to him, letting him envelope me in his arms. "Eden, you don't see how he looks at you. You don't have to watch some other guy fall in love with you and sit there helpless."

"Yes, I do," I said plainly. "Seraphina has her dirty little hands all over you, all the time. She's the one who gets to go to dances with you and eat lunch with you and be taken on dates. All I

214

get are secret rendezvous' and midnight, subconscious sleep worlds."

"Oh, Love," he hugged me tighter, "We have got to figure something else out. It doesn't do any good for us to fight over these stupid jealousies," he tipped my chin up to him, gazing into my eyes. "Seraphina means nothing to me. And I'm fairly certain all I mean to her is a crown. You have nothing to worry about."

"Nothing? Yeah, right. Except that you're supposed to be getting married to her," my bottom lip jutted out in an uncontrollable pout.

"That will never happen," he smiled reassuringly.

"How can you be so sure?" but the hope was already there, unwillingly and without permission, the small flicker of hope had begun to grow.

"India," Kiran replied with confidence. "Father wanted to meet you, get to know you better. He knows I have no real feelings for Seraphina, which has never bothered him before; but if he does suspect you are who you really are, then he might hope the feelings between us are real. A marriage between the two of us would be.... beneficial.... for all parties involved." There was hope in Kiran's eyes, too; he was beginning to believe there was a future for us.

"Marriage?" I gulped. I was not even seventeen yet and already I had to be thinking about marriage. There was not a doubt in my mind that Kiran would be the only man I would ever want to marry, but did we have to start talking about it already?

"Don't tell me you have cold feet already? We don't even know what my father is really thinking," he smirked at me.

"No, I know, I mean, I was just surprised that we could even use that word," I stumbled through what I hoped to be a convincing argument.

"I'm just teasing, Love," he leaned in to me and finally our lips connected. Our magics slammed into each other in a raw connection reminding us that it had been too long since we were alone. Kiran kissed me passionately, dipping me back and holding me tighter. I was overwhelmed by him, feeling heady and lost. He kissed my mouth and my neck, making his way across my shoulder blades and then back to my mouth again. One of his hands was tangled in my hair and the other pressed tightly against my lower back. He was fierce against my mouth and when he left it, finding

215

my ear and neck again I had to gasp for breath.

Gently he picked me up and laid me on the ground, his mouth against mine again. Our magics swirled around us in the palpable magic that had become a connection of our auras. Except this time, I found them distracting. Usually they were alight with an iridescent glow, changing colors too fast to ever make one out clearly. This time however, the deep blue from my magic was overwhelming any other color in smoky wisps of air. The blue from my magic forced Kiran's to be black and the two colors seemed to be fighting in the night instead of wrapping themselves in each other like they usually did.

I panicked for a moment, afraid the wind from the caves in India had followed me home, but then the blue was gone and the magics were back to the fast changing colors they had always been. Kiran was kissing my mouth again. I tore my eyes away from the magic trying to give him my attention, but I was too distracted. I slowed down his kisses and eventually ended them, trying not to give the wrong impression.

"So, marriage, huh?" I cleared my throat

"Yes, marriage," he whispered, full of affection. "If that's all right with you." He lay next to me on the soft forest floor, still kissing me sweetly.

"Will that make me a Princess then?" I asked dreamily, still trying to forget the magic.

"And one day, Queen," he whispered.

"But more importantly, I will get you." I forced myself to look into his eyes. They were turquoise; a reflection of his mother's and full of love for me. In that moment nothing else mattered, I didn't really care about being a Princess or even Queen; but if I were, if that dream came true, I would be able to make everyone happy. I could set the Shape-Shifters free, the Titan Guard as well, my family would be safe, and I could give the Kingdom freedom to marry whomever they chose. If I were Queen, I could solve everyone's problems without anyone I loved being in danger. And I would be with the man I loved, without secrecy or threat of danger. We could be together forever.

"And I get you," he finished, confirming my future plans.

"And of course, live happily ever after," I sighed, finding the perfect nook of his arm and cuddling closer.

"Well, of course," Kiran said happily. "We will know more in a week or so when father comes to visit," he finished off-handedly.

"Wait, I'm sorry, what did you say?" I sat half way up. Lucan? In Omaha?

"Yes," he laughed at me. "He wants to visit for the Christmas holiday and stay through January for my birthday."

"He has time to stay for a whole month?" Lucan in Omaha for an entire month could not be a good thing, no matter how much closer to progress Kiran and I were.

"Eden, he is the King, he can do whatever he wants." Kiran sat up with me and laughed again. "It will be all right dearest. I said it before; he would very much like to see us together. It's a strategic move for the Kingdom and of course he wants me happy."

"No, I know that's what you said. I just didn't think he needed to come here, to, you know, make up his mind," I smiled weakly, trying to reassure myself that this was a good thing. If Lucan wanted us together then it didn't hurt to speed things along. Still, Avalon and Jericho's faces flashed before me and I couldn't drown the sick feeling that they and everyone on the farm would be in danger. How could I protect them before I was Queen, before I really had any power at all?

Chapter Twenty-Nine

"Avalon, seriously, I can't shop for your Christmas present if you are with me. I'll be fine," I pushed Avalon away, laughing at him. We had been at the mall for hours, Lilly and Jericho had gone off to find something special for Aunt Syl as not only a Christmas present, but a thank you for her hospitality; and I was finally down to just Avalon's gift, but I couldn't get him to leave.

"I can't leave you. Amory's orders," he said stubbornly, crossing his arms and giving me the defiant look I had started to believe was genetic.

"Listen, I've got Roxie, there is nothing to worry about," I tried again. "Besides, don't you need to get me a present?" I asked with all sincerity.

"No, you don't deserve a present," he rolled his eyes and then turned around, scanning the mall in every direction.

"It's all right Avalon," Roxie came to my defense. "Listen, if I see anything suspicious, anything at all, I will call you, or make Eden call you with the twin connection thing."

"Yes!" I agreed. "I will totally just let you know if anything seems out of the ordinary!" I exclaimed, excited to have someone on my side.

"Besides, Eden already knows exactly what she's going to get you, right Eden?" Roxie asked and I nodded my head furiously. "Can we get it in less than twenty minutes?" I nodded again.

"See Avalon? You have nothing to worry about. You can even sit right here and we will come find you as soon as we pick it up," she looked at me again and I nodded for the third time.

"I don't like it," Avalon grumbled, but we both knew he had conceded.

"And no cheating," I demanded, tapping my temple with my finger.

"Yeah, yeah. Ok, then get going, I've already started timing you," he held up his wrist watch, waving it at us, and Roxie and I scattered off in a different direction, walking fast and laughing.

"Oh, he can be such a drama queen!" I sighed, exasperatedly.

"No, I don't think so," Roxie defended him, but in a nicer

way than usual. "No, I think he just cares about you."

I looked over at Roxie, surprised by her. She just smiled and I didn't know what to say. We walked into the electronic store and my eyes floated over the big TVs and fancy cameras and camcorder displays, looking for the game console I wanted to buy Avalon.

I wandered around the store with not much direction and Roxie gave me a little space, making her way over to the new movie releases. Eventually, I found what I was looking for and I stared at the two options I had researched, still not really sure which one to choose.

I had no clue which one Avalon would prefer; I just knew that he wanted one. He owned every kind of electronic anything back at the farm, but he had left them all for the visitors staying there. I knew he wanted something for our house, but felt that to go buy something would be negligence of his duties.

I couldn't make up my mind and none of their descriptions were helping me choose which one was better. I felt like everything was written in a different language, a techie language that was as good as French to me. I was contemplating buying them both and just explaining the extra charges on my credit card later to Aunt Syl, hoping she wouldn't care.

"Can I help you find anything Miss?" I barely glanced up at the sales associate trying to make a commission.

"No thanks, I've found what I'm looking for," I smiled politely, while turning my attention back to the two items in question.

"I'm very happy to hear that," he said snidely, but didn't move anywhere.

"Really, I've got it," I snapped my head up, not even pretending to be polite anymore. I was irritated.

Irritation quickly changed to fear when I realized the man bothering me was not a sales associate at all. He was dressed in a nicely tailored black suit and had the distinct military look of a Titan. I felt his magical current, faint beneath his blood and chastised myself for not finding it earlier.

"I think we have more of what you're looking for, back this way," he gestured his hand towards the back of the store. I looked frantically around for Roxie but couldn't see her anywhere. The man put a firm grip on my arm, pulling me away from the people milling around the different displays.

Avalon, find me. I opened our twin connection while stumbling through an employee door that led to the concrete hallways out of sight to the average mall-shopper. Once on the other side, I gasped; there were six more Titans waiting and one of them was holding a flailing Roxie, his hand over her mouth.

I felt Avalon tense up, and knew he was watching what was happening. Get Jericho first. I demanded. I didn't care how powerful I was supposed to be, I wasn't going to win this fight without some back up.

"What do you want?" I growled, irritated more than scared at having to be put in this position.... again.

"Want? Why, will you give it to us if I say pretty please?" The man who brought me back asked sarcastically and a few of the other men just laughed.

I couldn't help but feel intimidated by the seven grown men standing in a circle around me. Fighting one grown man had been hard enough, and this wasn't a bunch of kids in a forest. These were trained Guard with a purpose.

"Listen," I cleared my throat, and forced courage into my voice, "if you let us go, I promise not to take every single one of your magics. I'll let you keep it, k? And we can walk away and just forget this ever happened."

A chorus of harsh laughter mocked me.

"Yeah, poor Becks," one man offered, clearly not taking me seriously.

"You don't really expect to be able to take all of our magic, do you?" the first man asked, stepping closer to me.

"Well, obviously that's why Lucan sent you. He's testing me. He doesn't actually expect you to succeed," I decided to stop playing games and just get to the bottom of this.

"Don't get ahead of yourself," another man spoke up. "We're just curious. We want to see what Becks was actually up against. That's all."

More evil laughter.

"Fine, but don't say I didn't warn you," I mumbled before throwing Roxie's captor back against a wall, cracking the concrete blocks in the shape of his body, but releasing his grip on Roxie. He didn't have time to stand up before she had thrown him down the hallway making him pay for ever touching her.

The rest of the men closed in on me fast, one grabbing my arms behind my back, while the others tried to pick me up. I used my magic quickly with the guy holding my arms and threw him against the ceiling before letting him drop painfully to the ground. There were too many of them for me to focus on every one. While I was fighting off one of them, another would sneak up on me. I did my best, sending random blasts of magic behind me, trying to keep the others at bay while dealing with them one on one.

Unlike the team of four I drained of magic in the forest, these men were not leaving me alone to focus that much energy. Quick bursts were all I could work up and they were anything but debilitating.

Roxie was at the other end of the hallway, kicking some serious ass, but that was all she could handle at once. I was amazed, though, at how much power came out of such a little body; I gave her due credit for the attitude she carried. She was pretty much a bad ass.

The hallway was crumbling around our fight. Huge splits in the concrete floor and cracks up the walls would leave dangerous evidence of a super human fight. At the moment though, I didn't have a choice.

I was determined to drain someone's magic, hoping that if the rest of them witnessed the devastation, I could get my message through. But six against one was frustrating and exhausting and for some reason felt like I needed martial arts training.

I was losing ground and the six men were getting closer to stopping me. My magic needed more strength to get through. They seemed unstoppable; nothing was slowing them down.

I sent another man down the hallway, crashing into a clothes rack on wheels, sending metal hangers flying, but not phasing the man at all. He stood up and snarled, a sick smile twisting his lips. A look of pure enjoyment filled his eyes. I shuddered, while trying to dodge another Titan, this one diving at my feet and pulling me to the ground with a tight grip on my ankle.

I lay on the ground, with the six men, murderous intent written on their faces, above me. I took the moment of silence to gather my energy. Even if this was it, I would take the down time to gather my strength and bring as many with me as I could.

The door behind the men slowly opened and Jericho, Avalon and Lilly came walking nonchalantly through it, until the door closed behind them. They stood facing the men, ready to fight back. I couldn't help but smile. The cavalry had arrived.

"I told you it was a bad idea, Eden," Avalon announced, good naturedly. He hadn't been in a fight in a while; he was morbidly looking forward to this. "You should have listened to me."

"Avalon, Merry Christmas," I joked back, out of breath. "This is your Christmas present."

"Aw, you have such good taste," he joked before sending three of the Titan Guards flying in every direction and reaching over to help me stand up.

The real battle began at that point, Witches against Titans, everyone, except Lilly, who was pacing the hallway wanting desperately to change into her tigress form. The hallways of the mall, however, were not a place for a jungle animal.

Avalon and Jericho were nearly unstoppable. The Titans did not stand a chance against them. Roxie too, was finishing her fight off and I had finally gathered enough magic to do some serious damage.

The men wouldn't quit, they were weakening but were not going to stop. I wanted to finish this thing and go home.

Drain them. I sent to Avalon, who nodded in silent agreement.

We stood back to back against the four men we were fighting and started, drawing power off each other. The electricity moved freely back and forth between our blood and was quick to draw the magic out from the angry Titans.

The pull was easy. They continued to fight, but did not even try to keep their magic. Avalon and I drained them in seconds and they fell in crumpled heaps to the floor, gasping for breath, the twisted smiles still mocking me.

The other three Immortals, backed away slowly from Roxie and Jericho before taking off down the hallway in full sprint. Jericho started after them, but Avalon stopped him with a hand on his shoulder.

"Let them go, we're safe for n-" Avalon stopped short before finishing his sentence and then doubled over, grabbing at his side.

I let out a scream of pain, feeling the same agonizing stab in my stomach. Before I could recover, another searing stab seized my leg and I reached down further, crying out again.

"What the hell?" Avalon yelled at the men still lying defeated on the floor.

One of them let out the cruel sound of malicious laughter. He could barely keep his head up, but the hatred in his eyes never softened. "The King's Curse!" he panted, struggling to breath. "We all have it."

Jericho let a string of curse words fly, kicking the man in the face and knocking him out. I screamed again, not believing that pain this severe existed. I fell to the floor in agony, wishing for death or at the very least unconsciousness. Avalon crumpled next to me, gritting his teeth, sweat pouring from his face.

"Lilly get on the phone with Amory, now!" Jericho yelled at her as she fumbled around for her cell phone.

The stabbing was back, burning my insides and terrorizing every molecule inside of me. I couldn't breathe, I couldn't think, all that existed was pain. The darkness started to close in and I welcomed it, whether this was death or sleep it did not matter. I had to escape the pain.

Chapter Thirty

The pain didn't stop. I was in and out of consciousness for what felt like eternity. I had no concept of time or location; everything around me was a blur of agony. I could feel myself scream, but couldn't hear anything in return. I couldn't move, I couldn't breathe I was wrapped in searing pain. My body felt like I was being ripped apart and I decided that was what hell would feel like.

The worst part was the connection I shared with Avalon. Everything felt amplified, our shared misery echoing off each other's consciousness. I felt his misery and wished for death.

In the depths of despair and the blackness of pain I had nightmares of all the people I loved being trapped in the same disease. Amory, Kiran, Jericho, Lilly.... all chained to the unrelenting torture that was the King's Curse. I couldn't help them, I couldn't save them, there was only death waiting, but unreachable.

I knew we would die. I knew there was no coming out of the curse. Everyone had died from it. And Avalon and I would be next. The hopes of the Resistance would rot with us. Kiran's love would fade away. I would become a whispered rumor of what once could have been. My brother, the great leader that died too young.

It didn't seem fair for Avalon. Someone born with his potential should be given the greatness in life he demanded. I was the lost girl, the girl who dragged my brother away from his destiny and into a meaningless duty that would, in the end, be his demise.

I was at fault. Avalon was an innocent victim of the crimes I had accumulated. If I had made up my mind.... If I had said "yes" to the Resistance.... If I would have stayed away from Kiran.... If I wouldn't have wandered off alone.... If I would have left Avalon out of the fight and let the Titans take me away.

I was to blame. And I would die because of my sins. I wanted to die, rather than face Avalon again. I would never be able to make this up to him if we survived and the alternative was too much.

Hold on. Avalon demanded, through unquenchable pain. You cannot give up. It's not over yet.

I couldn't respond; I couldn't use the energy to talk back. But

I held on to Avalon. I refused with what little willpower I still held on to, to fade away. I found hope where there had been none and pushed it forward, making the smallest flicker of light in the dark abyss of agony.

But the darkness still came. The blackness found me and swept me away to unconsciousness. I tried to hold on, but in the end, the pain was stronger than what was left of me and I let go.

"Eden, Love," the whisper of a familiar voice called me from the nothing. "Come on, I know you're still there."

I felt the pain again; the hot rippling of tendons and fibers, of blood cells and enzymes, but it was lessened. This was not the seventh circle of hell, this was less, something had happened.

"Eden...." the accented whisper called to me again and this time I felt a gentle hand against mine.

I felt a warm hand against my hand; I felt something other than pain. I came further out of darkness, aware that I was better. I could feel the bed and the pillow my head rested on. I felt the blanket that covered me and wanted to throw it off; I was on fire and didn't need any extra warmth.

I could feel Avalon too, awake and in less pain. He was breathing regularly and not screaming anymore. He was alive and in less pain and that was all I needed for the rest of my life; I just needed to know that he would be all right.

I opened my eyes, shutting them quickly again against the dim candlelight that felt brighter than the sun. Slowly, I opened them, realizing how desperate for water I was. I tried to lift my sweat-soaked head off the pillow, but wasn't strong enough yet.

The whisper was there then, in front of my face and smiling. Kiran looked down at me like an angel, an exhausted and gaunt angel, but an angel all the same.

"Oh, thank God," he whispered again, and let out a long sigh, giving me the impression it had been a long time since he had breathed. "Amory," he called, "Amory, she's awake."

My grandfather ran into the room, pausing in the doorway as if to make sure, before walking carefully over to me. Kiran let go of my hand and allowed Amory to sit down next to me. He brushed the

225

hair off my forehead and looked at me in the ancient way he sometimes had, reminding me exactly who he was.

He reached over to the nightstand and picked up a glass of water with a straw. He held the water with one hand, while lifting me off of the pillow with the other so that I could drink.

"Slowly," he said in a low voice, but he didn't need to warn me. I was barely able to take one drink before the violent nausea washed over me.

"I'm alive?" I whispered, in a barely audible voice.

"Yes, my dear, you're alive," he smiled at me, looking very much like a grandfather. "I don't think it's wise to use your magic just yet, but you seem to be making a turn around."

"Avalon too?" I knew the answer, but I needed to hear it from Amory's mouth.

"Yes, Avalon too," he held me up again for another drink.

"How long?" was all I could ask with my dry and scratchy voice.

"Two weeks, Love," Kiran offered from the back of the room and I realized for the first time that this was not my bedroom.

"But how?" I wished they would just explain everything to me, I didn't want to talk right now, or maybe even ever again.

"At the mall you met some Titans?" Amory asked, gauging how much I remembered. I nodded, clearly remembering the fight and the first feeling of stabbing pain. He continued, "When you and Avalon took their magic, it was already infected with late stage King's Curse. The whole event was set up for you to take their magic. From what Jericho says, I understand that you took two and Avalon took two and, Kiran?" He turned around before continuing, "I'm sorry to inconvenience you, but would you mind running down the hall and finding some cool cloths for Eden," Kiran nodded and turned to walk out the door, "Oh and also.... Would you mind finding Lilly and Sylvia? I'm sure they would be happy to know Eden is awake." When Kiran left the room, Amory continued, "The two of you had a combined four different magics infected with the King's Curse inside of you. I thought," Amory cleared his throat and shook his head as if to gain composure, "I didn't know how you would survive. Your own magic was infected with the awful disease and so when your bodies would try to heal themselves there would only be more pain. Your magic is still recovering. Avalon woke up

226

yesterday, and is doing better today, but you both need to be careful. I don't know what saved you or how you were able to both come out alive, I'm just thankful you did." He hung his head without looking at me.

"Just as long as he's Ok," I whispered, closing my eyes again and wanting sleep.

"He said the same about you," Amory replied, the pride clear in his tone.

"Where am I?" I asked, remembering I wasn't in my house.

"The farm. We thought we could give you better care here, but nothing we did seemed to make any difference.

"What about.... Kiran?" I asked, dropping my whisper down even lower.

"We brought him in, hoping he could help you. In the end, I'm afraid we only shocked him, but I think he was glad to be here. The boy cannot lose you, Eden, I am afraid of what will happen to him if he does," Amory patted my hand, before kissing my forehead and standing up.

Lilly and Aunt Syl were through the doorway seconds later, hovering around me in the gentlest of ways. I smiled at them both, the best I could; and accepted their offer to help me with drinks of water.

I was exhausted and still miserable from the leftover pain, but would never complain about anything less than the King's Curse agony again. That was real pain. That had been true misery.

Kiran stood in the back of the room while they talked softly about nothing things that I found interesting. He just stared at me, an unreadable expression on his face, while Aunt Syl told me how they celebrated Christmas and Lilly talked about the Christmas ball I had missed, but Amory had made her go with him. He had to chaperone and she just sat at the table wishing she was back here.

Eventually, when I couldn't keep my eyes open any longer, even through their sweet chatter, they got up to leave. They said goodbye to Kiran at the door and he took the chair next to me after they left. He held my hand, bringing it to his lips and kissing me sweetly.

"I cannot lose you," he whispered hoarsely into the quiet room. My eyes were closed but his lovely words felt like medicine.

"You won't," I whispered back before finding the sweet

surrender of sleep again.

"I just want to see that she's all right," an angry voice woke me later. Sleep was still heavy on my eyes and I could barely move. The pain had lessened even more, but exhaustion would be the next battle to fight.

"There she is. She is all right. If you really cared about her, you never would have let her out of your sight to begin with. Now please, leave," a second voice tried to stay calm, while clearly upset with the first voice.

"I want to see her," the first voice growled.

"Not while I'm here," the second voice sounded even more dangerous than the first and I heard the door close forcefully and then nothing else.

"Who was that?" I asked, my eyes still closed.

"No one, Love," Kiran sat back down next to me, reaching for my hands and holding them tightly.

"Don't you need to go home and sleep?" I asked, struggling to open my eyes. The candle had been blown out and the room was completely dark.

I couldn't tell if it was the same day or a different one from the first time I had awoken, but Kiran was still in the same clothes, looking worse than ever.

"No," he said simply but kindly.

"Kiran, I'm better now," I had more of a voice this time, but my throat still burned and my eyelids were still heavy.

"I know," his voice broke with emotion before he continued, "I just have to know.... I just have to know that you'll stay better."

"Believe me, I will never get that sick again," I tried to smile. "And if I do, I'm just going to die. I can't do that again." I sighed, not joking at all.

"No, don't say that," Kiran knelt down next to me, his face close to mine. "When I said I couldn't lose you before, I meant it. I cannot live without you. You hold too much of me. I would never survive it," he was desperate and I believed him, I had no choice but to believe him, the same would have been true had the tables been turned. "Besides," his voice lightened, "I need at least one male son

228

before I can go off and die. I can't leave a Kingdom in chaos." He smiled at me and I smiled back.

"Well," I cleared my throat, trying to cough away the fire, "then we better not plan on dying for a long time. I am just not ready for the responsibility of parenting," I smiled bigger, finding my sense of humor and a little more of my health. I had no idea how I came out on the other side of the King's Curse, but I did. And Avalon did. And Kiran was by my side. All was right in the world again.

At least for now.

I worked at listening to Ms. Devereux. I had the book opened to the right page, my brain thinking magically in French, and the right answer already in mind should she ask me a question, but I couldn't focus. I couldn't even pretend to look in her direction.

I couldn't even blame my still weak body. I wasn't completely recovered yet from the King's Curse, and I was still afraid to use my magic fully. But I was at school and doing my best to not get behind, although I got tired quickly. Avalon was the same way and together our shared fatigue seemed to double our symptoms, though none of that had anything to do with my inability to focus on French.

I wasn't alone in distraction. The entire class, even Ms. Devereux, was craning necks as best as we could to catch a glimpse of the King. Lucan had arrived in Omaha with as much pomp and circumstance as is expected from royalty.

The school had been in a frenzy for a week. As soon as Christmas break was over and we returned to regular classes, the announcement had been made. Lucan would be visiting Omaha and sequentially Kingsley.

Today was the day he toured the great halls of the exclusive Immortal prep school and everything was to go perfectly. Or so the teachers, staff and students had been told. But from conversations with Amory at home, I really had a hard time believing he cared at all.

Kiran hadn't been in school since his father arrived, although he was allegedly here today, guiding Lucan across campus. Talbott, the ever faithful bodyguard, had been away too and I was surprised at how relaxing the week had felt without the two of them around.

Lilly had also been missing for the week, but not by choice. Although it was Ok for her to be at school while Kiran was there, it was definitely not Ok for her to be there while Lucan was around. He demanded that Amory keep her home for the week and she had gladly complied.

I was actually jealous of her. Days at home were sounding more and more fun with Jericho, Lilly and Roxie. Avalon and I were usually in terrible moods at school, wishing we could be away from the Kingsley crowd and home with our real friends.

At least something was happening at school today. We could all hear Lucan and Amory out in the hallway, but not make out what they were saying. Avalon was the only student not interested in the activity, I could feel the irritation and resentment radiating off of him, but I dismissed it. Good or bad, Lucan was still King, and still at our school.

The door opened slowly; Amory and Lucan stepped inside the classroom. There was no need for the noise to stop, the entire class was already silent and offering their attention. Someone in the front stood up first and the rest of the class followed suit, paying Lucan their respect.

Avalon was quick to stand up and I was surprised at his reverent bow. I had expected him to be the last out of his seat and barely show any sign of respect.

I don't want to draw unnecessary attention to myself. He sent me, answering my question.

"Jacqueline, pardon the interruption." Amory addressed a fidgeting Ms. Devereux; I had to laugh at her nervous behavior. Finally, she seemed human. "Do you mind if I introduce our King?" he continued politely.

"Not at all," Ms. Devereux mumbled, her icy demeanor melted for the moment.

"This is our Freshman French Honors, your Highness. Jacqueline Devereux teaches all of the secondary students and this would be her youngest class. As you know, most students arrive with a basic working knowledge of the language, but Jacqueline makes sure they know how to both read and write fluently before the year is over," Amory smiled reassuringly at Ms. Devereux whose mouth dropped open just slightly and offered no reply.

The door behind Lucan and Amory opened; Kiran and Talbott slipped in quietly. Both boys looked oddly casual in respective jeans and sweaters. Kiran was wearing a cream cable-knit bulky sweater that looked especially warm and Talbott, a black, more-fitted, wool sweater that showed off his thick arms and muscular chest. Out of the school uniform Talbott looked years older, but Kiran only looked more handsome.

"Kiran, are you in this class?" Lucan asked his son without turning around.

"Yes, I am Father," Kiran replied and then cleared his throat.

"But this is a beginner's class," Lucan continued, the disdain obvious in his tone.

"By the time Kiran arrived, language classes that may have suited him more favorably were already full," Amory interrupted, his tone firm. Ms. Devereux looked like she would throw up. "I was given instructions not to treat him differently than I would other students," he finished, looking straight ahead and out the second story window.

"Surely, an exception could have been made," Lucan turned on Amory, who nodded his head without giving an answer. I didn't know what to make of his head nod. Was he agreeing with Lucan but refusing to do anything about it, or was he defying him completely, or was he complying with his not-so-straightforward command? I really did not understand the dynamic between the King and my grandfather.

"Father, please. This class is perfectly fine," Kiran laughed lightly, shaking his head and dismissing the entire discussion.

"Is it?" Lucan asked, his eyes flitting over me. I quickly looked down at my desk, afraid that my very presence would create an outburst or argument between father and son.

"Eden, you are also in this class?" Lucan asked directly.

"Yes," I nodded.

Your majesty. Say "Your majesty." Avalon pushed the command at me and I realized my mistake.

"Yes, your majesty," I clarified quickly.

"Did you speak French growing up?" Lucan continued to ask me questions and I hated answering them while all of the eyes of the class were on me.

"No, I did not sir," I didn't know if "sir" was appropriate, but I thought I would give it a go. "Your majesty" and "your highness" felt way too make believe for me to say them without wanting to giggle.

"In your human home, they did not speak French to you?" he asked more pointedly, his face etched with disbelief.

"No, sir," I replied humbly, but my rebellious nature was growing frustrated.

"It hasn't been a struggle to learn I'm sure, now that you have magic at your disposal." He said with finality and no evidence of a question.

"Actually, sir," I spoke up, and I saw Kiran flinch behind him, but it was too late, I had already gone down the rabbit hole, "I prefer to learn the language the old-fashioned way," I smiled, in an attempt to be charming.

"The old-fashioned way? And pray tell, my dear child, what way is that?" Lucan's blue eyes turned to stone; he stared at me, daring me to defy him.

"You know," suddenly I had lost my courage, "without magic."

He stood there staring at me, his eyes never leaving mine and I wanted to squirm but I had too much pride. Avalon coughed behind me and I hurried to finish the part I had forgotten.

"Your Highness," I said quickly, relying on the reverence of the title to pull me out of trouble.

"That is the old-fashioned way?" he asked calmly. I knew I had gone too far and I wasn't exactly sure how to remedy the situation.

"No, it's not. Forgive me. I was just trying to...." I couldn't even explain my behavior. The room was deathly silent; no one was even moving. I had no idea how to recover.

"Ms. Matthews why don't you finish your thought out in the hallway," Amory spoke up before I dug myself into a deeper hole. I gathered my things quickly and with head down bolted into the sanctuary of the empty halls.

"Are you crazy?" Kiran was fast behind me, but his eyes were amused and his tone barely serious.

"Everyone was so serious in there; I was just trying to lighten the mood," I grumbled, knowing that wasn't the real reason. But since I didn't even know the real reason, it was a better excuse than anything else I had.

"Fantastic job of it, Love," Kiran rolled his eyes, but the smirk was there.

"I miss you," I changed the subject, my voice barely audible. "Do you?" He smiled, taking a step closer to me. "Then let's do something about it, shall we?"

"Yes, please," I agreed.

"How about I take you to dinner tonight? Are you free?" I nodded, excitedly, hardly believing a real date could be my future plans for the evening. "Good. Then, I will pick you up around seven and make it just the two of us." He took another step closer to me, the smile growing and his eyes twinkling.

"How are you going to manage that?" I asked, disbelieving he could possibly get away from Talbott.

"Don't you worry your pretty little head, I'll figure it out," he looked like he was about to say more, but the door opened and out walked Lucan, Amory and Talbott.

I curtsied politely and kept my eyes on the floor, hoping to recover any ground lost before.

"Don't be too hard on her Amory, Eden and I became very special friends in India," Lucan smiled down at me, the same wicked expression found in Kiran's smirk, present in his eyes.

"Of course," Amory replied gruffly and put a firm hand on my shoulder.

"Well then, Amory, thank you for the tour and I shall see you at dinner this evening," Lucan smiled benevolently at Amory who nodded a sort of short bow in return.

Lucan placed a hand on Kiran's back and ushered him down the hallway. Talbott followed a few steps behind and I wondered for a moment where Lucan's bodyguard was.

"Am I in trouble?" I looked up at Amory, not really afraid of him, but still worried he might have to punish me for appearances sake.

"Eden, my dear, you are always in trouble," he patted the shoulder his hand was resting on and followed in the direction Lucan had gone.

"Does that mean I have to go back to class?" I whispered loudly, hoping the outcome would be in my favor.

"Of course it does," Amory replied without turning around. "And Eden, if you wouldn't mind, try not to offend your entire race of people by the end of the school day."

"No promises," I called after him.

I slipped back into class, trying my best to make it to my seat without being noticed. It was no use. The entire class stared. Even Ms. Devereux stopped lecturing, and stood in silent distaste.

That was really nice Eden. You have more balls than I give you credit for. Avalon laughed at me inside our shared consciousness.

"Ok, being human is not that bad," I put my hands out and defended the unspoken accusations; but it was no use, the class remained silent and once I reached my desk and opened my book, Ms. Devereux continued with her lecture, ignoring me all together.

Chapter Thirty-Two

"I'm going alone Avalon, don't even try to come along," I paced back and forth in the entry way, arms folded and defiant. Kiran would be picking me up soon and the last thing I wanted was an entourage.

"Eden, you can't be serious," Jericho stood up from the overstuffed couch and crossed his arms, equally stubborn.

"Jericho, stay out of this," I turned on him and stomped my foot.

"You know what?" he started, louder than he had been before. "Fine, do what you want; there is apparently no stopping you." he put his hands up in mock surrender and left the room.

"Great, Eden. That's real great," Avalon growled from his place by the fire place. "Listen, I'm tired of dealing with this. I don't think it's a good idea, but do what you want. I have bigger things to worry about."

"Thank you," I sighed, exasperated and feeling a little hurt.

Avalon walked into the kitchen and joined Jericho. They were quiet in there and I had the urge to eavesdrop on them from the safety of Avalon's mind, but I resisted. It wasn't fair to them. And I had the feeling I didn't really want to know what they were whispering about.

"On the bright side," Lilly smiled at me from the couch, in between Aunt Syl and Roxie. "You look amazing!"

"Yes you do, Eden," Aunt Syl agreed. "But are you sure you don't want a warmer coat?"

I shook my head. I knew the icy January evening would not be kind to the black and baggy, sheer top I was wearing and short jean skirt. But in my defense I was wearing thick black tights and furry boots to protect my feet against the three feet of snow outside. I looked down at my bare shoulder and shuddered. Maybe Aunt Syl was right.

I opened the coat closet and glanced over my winter coats, none of them feeling very date-like. Instead of practicality, I opted for a bright pink pashmina scarf that had been a Christmas present last year.

"Is this better?" I turned around and smiled. Aunt Syl rolled her eyes and sat back in the couch laughing at me. "I'm magic, remember?" I said with finality.

"Oh yes, you're magic," Roxie mumbled, only half amused.

There was a knock at the door and I jumped, my heart beating wildly; I prayed silently that only Kiran was standing on the other side. I counted to ten, not wanting to open the door too quickly, took a couple of deep breaths for good measure and let Kiran inside.

"Hello, Lovely," Kiran said softly, his turquoise eyes smoldering and his trademark smirk turning up one corner of his mouth.

"Hello," I giggled, stepping forward and kissing him on the cheek.

He looked more handsome than ever in a crisp white dress shirt, open at the neck, a sharp black suit coat and designer jeans. His hair was slicked back in a movie star way that signified a dress-up event; he had a black scarf wrapped several times around his neck to pull the whole look together.

"Hello ladies," he took his eyes off me, almost regretfully, and waved at Aunt Syl, Roxie and Lilly watching us from the couch.

"Hello," they replied back in unison.

"Lilly, I hope this week hasn't been too terribly awful for you. I hate that Father is so stuck in his ways," he smiled carefully at her and heat flushed her porcelain cheeks before she could even open her mouth.

"No, it's fine," she quickly replied. "I don't mind missing school at all."

"Of course," Kiran laughed. "Well, then, are you ready Love?" he held out his bent arm for me and we walked carefully over the ice-covered sidewalk to his car; a black sports car with no back seat that screamed fast before he even started it.

The deep, soft snow blanketed the city, creating a quiet not present during the rest of the year. Kiran kept the radio off while we drove downtown, the crunch of packed snow or splashing slush was our only sound track in the silence of night.

"So how did you get away all by yourself?" I asked, truly curious.

"Oh, I have my ways," he smirked, glancing over at me in an

overtly appreciative way. I tugged at the hem of my skirt, suddenly self-conscious. "How did you get away?"

"I, too, have ways," I played his game, pretending to be mysterious.

"Oh, do you now?" he pulled into a parking spot off the street of one of Omaha's expensive downtown bistros.

"Yes, of course. All kinds of ways. Ways you've never even seen," I continued, allowing him to walk around and open the door for me.

"You'll have to demonstrate those later for me," he mumbled, and I couldn't stop the blush from painting my cheeks.

We walked into the restaurant with candle-lit center pieces on small tables only meant for two. Kiran spoke to the hostess, who immediately walked us to a table in the far corner of the bustling bistro. She offered us menus, explained the specials for the evening and then gestured to the bartender who immediately brought over a bottle of wine.

Kiran's pocket began vibrating while the hostess poured two glasses of crimson red wine and I watched him reach irritatedly into his pocket, silencing his phone.

"This is nice," I said quietly, reaching for my glass of wine and taking a small drink.

"Yes it is. We haven't been alone in a while," Kiran stated, reaching for his pocket again, stopping the vibrating.

"Do you need to get that?" I asked, realizing a night alone might actually be impossible.

"No. I do not," he stated clearly, reaching for my hand and holding it on top of the white table cloth.

"So your birthday is coming up, yeah?" I watched him grow just a little bit uncomfortable.

"Yes," he mumbled.

"Come on, it's exciting!" I gushed, having always loved my own birthday.

"I suppose," he took a sip of his wine and looked at me intently. "I just wish.... I just wish that it didn't have to be such a big deal. You know? Father is planning this god-awful party in which he is inviting half of the Kingdom and I will have to sit there and pretend to like everyone and dance with hundreds of snotty and single girls, while their parents plot and plan how to break off my engagement and get their daughter a crown instead of Seraphina."

"Oh," I stared at him, a little shocked. That wasn't really what I had expected from a royal birthday party.

"Don't they believe you love Seraphina?" I asked.

"Nobody believes that," he laughed bitterly. "Everyone understands Father's agenda." When I gave him a curious look he continued, "There hasn't ever been a royal wedding where the couple married for love. It's all about power and longevity. My engagement is no different and most of the Kingdom understands that. So, they hope that they can find a way to convince Father their daughter, or niece, or granddaughter, or whoever is more suited for Queen."

"Would he ever change his mind?" I gasped, finding it hard to believe marriage was thought of as nothing more than a business transaction.

"Well, I don't know. Seraphina was very carefully chosen, and her father played his cards right. A very compelling case would have to be made. And I am pretty sure Father would lose a lot of money, should the betrothal be called off."

"What does that mean?" I asked in shock.

"George, Seraphina's father, negotiated very shrewdly. I don't know all of the details but I do know that there was a lot of money involved, and whatever deal was struck meant enough for me to leave England and end up here." Kiran looked around the restaurant with the tiniest hint of disgust.

"So your birthday party is just one big dating show?"

"Most likely," he mumbled, taking another drink of wine and silencing his pocket once more.

"Well, that sounds.... awful." I looked down at our clasped hands, not excited about the prospect of all those girls oogling Kiran at all.

"Are you jealous already?" he smirked at me. The amusement in his eyes was unmistakable.

"What? No," I replied, not convincing either one of us.

"You've nothing to worry about, Eden," his eyes grew serious, their light turquoise turning to a dark blue in the span of a thought, that seemed to reveal the depth of his soul, "I am nothing less than bound to you." He smiled shyly and my heart was suddenly beating as if it would escape from the confines of my chest. "I cannot escape you."

"Kiran, I...." I didn't know how to reply, I couldn't define the feelings that echoed his out loud, they seemed too much.

"Eden," he cut me off, hitting his jeans pocket and forcefully quieting his buzzing cell phone. "when you were dy-, when you were infected with the King's Curse, I knew that would be the end for me. If you wouldn't have made it, if you wouldn't have.... survived, I don't know how I could have...." His voice dropped and he looked away, ashamed of the nearly overflowing emotion."I didn't though. I mean, I don't think there was really any threat of me dying," I said casually, hoping to erase his fears, but remembering how I had longed for death in those torturous moments.

"Yes, that's right, the invincible Eden," he smiled again, but his eyes remained serious. "When I said before that I couldn't lose you, I meant it. Losing you would be the end of me."

"I love you," I whispered,

"I love you, too," he leaned in and kissed me gently on the lips, my magic found his, tangling the two together in a rapturous web and I felt his words to the very core of my being.

"So, is there any chance that I can convince your father-"

"Bloody hell!" he exclaimed suddenly, pulling his phone out of his pocket and answering it roughly, "What?"

He had withdrawn his hand and I reached for my wine, watching him grow more and more frustrated with the caller. He argued for several minutes before growing completely quiet, and that's when I assumed his father got on the phone. He listened for a few more minutes and then hung up without saying another word.

"Would you mind terribly if we finished dinner with my parents?" he asked quietly, clearly annoyed.

"Thank you for the offer, but really, it's fine. You can just drop me off at home." I shuddered at the thought of having to sit around another family dinner pretending not to be in love with Kiran and hoping it wasn't the night Lucan decided to throw me in prison.

"I would love to under different circumstances, believe me. But your presence has been specifically requested." Kiran's scowl said all that it needed to; my heart dropped into my stomach and I took a big drink of wine, trying to drown my nerves.

"Why?" I asked, when I could find my voice again.

"I don't know what my father is playing at." Kiran replied, gesturing to the waitress and handing her a black plastic card from his wallet to pay for the wine.

I poured myself another glass of wine, rather unladylike, and forced myself not to just down the whole glass in one sip. I didn't understand the dinner invitation or the mystery behind Lucan's obvious interest in me. If he was going to use me against my parents, I wished he would just get it over with. He wasn't the only one interested in whether they were alive or not.

The waitress came back with Kiran's card and I finished my wine while Kiran signed the receipt. My magic was still recovering from the last remnants of the King's Curse, so if I was in real danger I might also be in actual trouble. I didn't have much of a choice, though, and surely Kiran wouldn't let anything happen to me. I didn't know much about the relationship between father and son, but I believed he meant what he said and that he wouldn't let anything come between us.

Chapter Thirty-Three

Kiran drove the sports car abruptly up to the valet. I braced myself with one hand on the arm rest and the other gripping my seat belt, and watched the poor attendant jump out of the way. Kiran was at my door before the valet could recover. I was charmed by his chivalry, but the Titan in me fought against the idea that this was a trap and screamed at me to be careful. Despite the dull but still painful stabbing feelings I felt every time I used magic, I released as much as I could to keep my instincts sharp and warm up my intuition. Hopefully, dinner in the penthouse suite of Omaha's Magnolia Hotel would be exactly that, just dinner.

Kiran led me through a narrow but stylish lobby, trimmed with gold and accented with red velvet furnishings, past the front desk and elevators. We walked through a marbled hallway out into a courtyard filled with snow and up salted stone steps into the presidential suite. He was silent the entire way and did not attempt to touch me or even offer me his elbow. I was thankful he had decided on caution as well.

The suite was magnificent, two stories with a full kitchen and dining room. I was assaulted by delicious smells before any of my other senses could react. The Magnolia Hotel had been remodeled out of one of the older buildings in Omaha. The taste wasn't modern and definitely not as high tech as some of the newer hotels downtown, but the old world feel was comfortable, and the luxury and class still obvious.

"Ah, there he is," Lucan stood from a rich, dark wooden round table that sat nine other guests, including Kiran's mother.

"Yes, Father. Here I am," Kiran said good-naturedly, as if a switch had been turned and Kiran was suddenly happy to be there. "Hello, Mother." he said more quietly, bending over to kiss her on the cheek, while I hung awkwardly back, afraid to leave any proximity to the door.

"And you've brought a guest, I see," Lucan announced happily, as if I was a surprise, and not there because of his specific command, "Please, join us Eden."

I curtsied clumsily, before removing my hot pink scarf and handing it to a maid that appeared out of nowhere. I looked down at my disheveled clothes. I had wanted to look edgy, feeling more rock and roll than royalty; cringing at my furry boots and wishing someone had run this turn of events by me as an option for the evening before I left the house.

"I believe you know Amory, your Headmaster." Lucan gestured two seats to his left, on the other side of his wife; I nodded solemnly. I was thankful Amory was there, but still afraid to look him in the eyes. "Next to him we have Victor and Thora Dane, Victor is the Minister of Foreign Relations for the Kingdom. And then, of course, is my darling sister, Princess Bianca and her husband, Jean Cartier, the Grand Duke of Canesbury; they are in town for Kiran's birthday. You have already met Amelia; next to her is the Advisor to Military Affairs, Petru Beklea. Next to him is the Counselor for Military Maneuvers, Constantine Tirlia. For everyone else, this is Eden Matthews, a friend and schoolmate of Kiran's. Thank you, Eden, for joining us."

"No, thank you, your Highness. The pleasure is mine," I replied, shakily, taking my seat in between Kiran, who was sitting at his father's right hand and the gray haired, bull-dog looking man, Constantine Tirlia, who was apparently the go-to man on all things military in action. I swallowed the lump in my throat and pulled my shirt over the exposed shoulder I had thought was so sexy just a couple hours ago.

The first course was brought out by an overwhelming number of servants, I would have thought impossible to fit in the posh but small kitchen. I waited like everyone else until Lucan took the first bite of his fish drenched in some fragrant white sauce and everyone else followed his example. I had never been one to appreciate the taste or texture of seafood but I found the courage and forgot about being finicky for now.

The adults eased into grown-up conversations about different high ranking officials that were either doing phenomenal jobs or awful jobs and should be imprisoned. I didn't recognize any of the names and got lost quickly between the extensive fancy titles and hard to pronounce names, representing every region of the world.

I focused on my fish, looking forward to the next course. Kiran was an ice sculpture next to me, frozen in place, except to move his fork to his mouth. He joined in the discussion, giving those that might have been in trouble hope, by testifying of some obscure great thing they did for him. I kept my eyes on Amelia, who despite the glossed over expression dimming the usual brightness of her deep chocolate eyes, still exuded the warmth and gravitational pull I noticed in India. She was still the magnet all eyes turned to and the spark of life in an otherwise dreary dinner conversation.

"I know now how I recognize you," the Minister of Foreign Affairs stared me down from across the table during a lull in the conversation and middle of the third course. I cleared my throat, afraid of where this was going. "You're the girl from the trial last October."

Every head snapped to attention, facing me directly. Eyes made of stone, accusing me silently, stared me down, daring me to deny it. I couldn't deny anything; it was the truth and I could hardly convince anyone here otherwise.

"Yes," I cleared my throat. "That was me," I glanced at Amelia hoping to find solace in her warm eyes, and she did not disappoint. At the mention of the trial, her glossy eyes flickered to life and she stared at me as if encouraging me to speak my mind.

"The girl that tried to save the Shape -Shifter?" Princess Bianca asked in a delicate English accent. She had long golden blonde hair, the same color as Lucan and Kiran's. It fell in endearing waves down her back, a little messy but glorifying her porcelain skin and perfect bone structure. She had the deep blue eyes that Lucan had and was his perfect mirror in female form. She seemed to be older than Lucan, the creases in her smile more pronounced and the corners of her eyes turned up in the smallest of wrinkles. But the signs of age did not diminish her beauty in any way, they only enhanced her elegance.

"Yes, that's right," the military man to my right agreed.

"I wasn't there darling, but I heard you caused quite the uproar," Bianca addressed me straight on, her deep blue eyes as unsettling as Lucan's, when holding my full attention.

"Well, I, um, she was my friend," I tore my eyes away from the Princesses and turned them to the basket of bread, untouched but sitting in the middle of the table.

"Your friend?" scoffed Victor the minister. "That is blasphemy child."

"You'll have to excuse Eden," Lucan spoke up, clearly

amused by the change in subjects. "She was abandoned as a child and a human raised her. She is still learning all of the different customs of our people," his smile turned wicked, and I knew he was enjoying watching me squirm. "How can that be?" gasped the Minister of Foreign Affair's wife Thora.

"I've asked the same question myself," Lucan answered, not giving me a chance to speak. "Really though, Amory should be the one to tell the story. After all, he is the one who found the poor thing, causing quite the trouble in the human world as well. Or so I'm told."

The attention of the table moved from me to Amory who took over the story telling with the melodic, deep tone of his voice and I exhaled. Amory would know what to say, how to walk carefully through the mine field Lucan was engineering for us.

"Kiran," Lucan turned to his son, with a quiet voice. "See if you can track down Talbott and find out what's keeping Sebastian."

Kiran nodded to his father and stood up without acknowledging me or the rest of the table. I suddenly felt very exposed without Kiran blocking Lucan's direct view of me and wanted to run after Kiran and beg him to take me home.

"You are like the wind." Lucan said quietly and I half turned to him, not understanding who he was talking to. The rest of the table stayed engrossed in Amory's retelling of my ignorance of magic and the schools I closed down before Kingsley came into my life. "The wicked and wild wind, Eden. You are sweeping through my Kingdom in a melee of destruction, aren't you?"

I snapped my head up when he used my name and sat speechless. His eyes remained amused and the wicked smile still turned his mouth up. I did not know whether to drop down to my knees and beg for forgiveness or pretend like I still had no idea what he was talking about.

I shook my head in quiet desperation, not knowing what to say or how to respond. Lucan's eyes grew more serious, but the mysterious smile did not leave his lips. He turned more towards me, the smallest flash of frustration marring his amusement for only a second.

"The wind, Eden," His voice was quieter still and I leaned in just slightly to make sure I caught every single word. "It can be a deadly force, can it not?" I shook my head, agreeing with him. "So soft at times, the gentle breeze, the refreshing puff of air; one might almost forget the baleful power it's capable of. Isn't that you? So innocent, so naive? And yet you are a tornado of destruction, uprooting thousands of years of tradition with just your simple questions and ignorant interruptions."

My mouth dropped open; I didn't know what to say, or how to react. My mind was reeling, trying to wrap my head around the accusation. I had no excuse or speech planned to walk out of this trap. I searched for Kiran from my peripheral, but he was nowhere in sight, so I scanned my consciousness for Avalon but he too was involved and unreachable.

"I'm so sorry...." I began, swallowing my panic and digging deep for courage. "It was never my intention.... Please, forgive me if I've ever acted...." I whispered frantically, the fierce regret completely genuine.

Lucan held up one hand and silenced me immediately. "Relax child. You have won the favor of my son and that is enough for me. But something will have to be done, of course. This will simply not do." He looked me over, amusement replaced momentarily with disgust. I didn't know what to make of it.

"And so here we are," Lucan turned his attention back to his guests without missing a beat. "I could hardly have treated her with the full letter of the law after finding out her unfortunate circumstances." Lucan looked at me with pity while the other guests nodded solemnly as if I truly were the poor orphan. "Thankfully for us, Eden is very talented magically, and so along those lines we have nothing to be afraid of. She won't be burning down Kingsley any time soon. I'm afraid it's just her way of thinking that gets in the way. She has that stubborn American independent spirit I find so annoying."

The guests laughed politely at Lucan, eying me over with renewed suspicion. I searched again for Kiran, not even able to imagine what could be keeping him.

"So then, you have befriended a Shape-Shifter?" Thora asked me directly, the disgust thickening her tone.

"Well, yes. I mean, I didn't know she was a Shape-Shifter when I befriended her," I started and then rushed on, frustrated with how I fumbled my explanation. "I mean, I am still friends with her, she is really the sweetest girl. She's probably my-"

246

"Actually it was Kiran who saved her in the end, wasn't it Lucan?" Amory interrupted, asking the King a pointed question.

"It was," he replied curtly. "I'm surprised to hear you ask though. You ran off so quickly, I thought you had lost interest in the trial," Lucan did not even pretend to hide his irritation with Amory and I couldn't help but feel like the dinner party was taking a turn for the worse, and that is was my fault.

"I had," Amory sighed, taking a long sip from a tumbler full of scotch.

"Forgive me for boring you with the formalities of our justice system," Lucan snapped. "Next time one of your students is found to be a malicious traitor; I won't bother you with the smaller details of their execution."

I gasped involuntarily and the eyes of the table turned sharply on me. It wasn't a sound that my consciousness would have allowed me to make in such an intense moment, if not for the concrete tone in Lucan's voice, reminding me of why I went to Romania in the first place.

"You wouldn't have really executed Lilly, right?" The words tumbled out of my mouth before I could stop them. I felt the panic flood Amory's expression and the wise warrior inside of me scream for caution. I felt Avalon suddenly join my thoughts, the warning bell alerting him to my recklessness, but I couldn't stop it. The words were there and they wanted out. "She wasn't a malicious traitor. You cannot say that." I demanded, full of righteous rage.

"Can't I?" Lucan narrowed his eyes at me, while the rest of the table sat in stunned silence.

"It's not true," I dared to continue; "She fought to save Kiran's life, not harm him. She would never hurt anyone. She's not capable of hurting anyone. She is too good of a person."

"And how would you know what she is capable of? Were you present during all that went on? Perhaps you were an eye witness?" Lucan spoke evenly and with controlled anger. I was too far in to give up now, but I remembered my cover story too late.

"No, I wasn't," I shook my head, but my argument had already started to weaken. "But I know her. I know how good her intentions always are and the purity of her heart. She is a good person," I finished with emotion.

"But that is the thing, isn't it?" Jean Cartier, the Grand Duke of Canesbury and Sebastian's father spoke for the first time all evening in a thick French accent, "She is not a person, she is not human and she is not Immortal, she is a Shape-Shifter. And we know that they are all evil. Pure evil." There wasn't accusation in his voice or even a hint of conjecture, Jean Cartier was stating a fact.

"Here, here," mumbled Victor, tapping his stein of beer heavily on the table surface.

I caught Amory's eye for just a moment, but it was enough to tell me to shut up. The argument was finished and I had lost. To these people I made no rational sense and to fight the King on such a concrete issue would certainly be a prison sentence, if not more.

"Forgive me, Your Highness. I forgot my place," I bowed my head in humility, hoping to at least see the end of this terrible dinner party without a death sentence being signed.

"That seems to be the root of the problem, doesn't it?" Lucan asked facetiously and without emotion, raising his glass and tipping it towards me before drinking. The rest of the table also took a drink and I had the oddest feeling the toast was to me, but couldn't understand why.

"Excuse me, Father?" Kiran entered the room again, his hair more disheveled than when he had left and Sebastian at his right arm. "Talbott is ready to take Eden home."

My heart leaped with joy, even if going home meant a car ride alone with Talbott. The only thing left for me at the dinner party was the wrong side of a guillotine. I looked to Lucan for permission to leave the table, while trying to remain poised. He gave me a nod of the head. I thanked him again for the lovely meal and all but ran from the room, ignoring both Kiran and Sebastian.

I had said too much and defended a group of people the general population of Immortals accused of being malicious, untrustworthy liars and universal outcasts. Lucan was playing a careful game of cat and mouse, trapping me into situations where I was either vulnerable for attacks or shooting myself in the foot.

My beliefs still held true and I didn't even think I was capable of not treating people as equals; but instead of feeling encouraged that I wasn't losing myself, I felt overwhelmingly lost. I had dreamed, not that long ago, of a scenario where I united the Kingdom and set the Shape-Shifters free.

I was finally understanding what a monumental task that was

going to be and coming to the realization that while there was a Monarchy in charge, no matter who was the ruler; the goal for elitism would never die. Someone would always have to live on the bottom. I wasn't prepared to completely reeducate an entire society deeply rooted in racism and lust for power.

Suddenly I didn't know Kiran at all. What if he had these feelings? How would I convince a King to give up the racism? How would I convince a people that we were all created equally and with just as much worth. I would have to figure it out. I would have to set those people free or my aspirations to be Queen would be worthless.

Chapter Thirty-Four

"When is Amory going to be here?" I plopped down on the couch next to Jericho, my feet landing on his lap.

"Any minute," he pushed my feet without removing them from his legs and scowled at me. "What makes you think this is Ok?"

"Of course, it's Ok!" I grinned, "You've forgiven me by now, plus, I think you secretly like how my feet smell." I accused him playfully, doing my best to get him to stop being mad at me without actually having to apologize to him. He had been furious with me when the events of my date night with Kiran had come out a week ago.

It wasn't just Jericho, though. Everyone had been mad at me. I was, like usual, saying things that were getting me into trouble. Amory scolded me severely for not being more careful and Avalon had been yelling at me both verbally and mentally for days. Roxie had not stopped mumbling things under her breath whenever she was in close proximity to me; even Lilly had been caught sending disapproving glares. Jericho, at least, had stuck with the noninvasive, silent treatment; but I was getting bored.... and lonely.

Aunt Syl had been busy at the hospital, barely home and when she was home, she was doing her best to catch up on sleep. Other than a concerned look and a request to be more careful, she was the only one not blaming me entirely for the preemptive destruction of the Resistance. But there were too many people in her house, and too many sick people at the hospital for her to want to stick around just to mildly defend me.

I needed an ally, and I knew Jericho couldn't really stay mad at me. Or at least I hoped he couldn't.

"I love how your feet smell," Jericho replied dryly, and reached for a maroon throw to cover his legs and my feet with.

"I knew you couldn't stay mad at me," I smiled at him again, but he wouldn't look at me. "Oh, stop being such a baby," I grew frustrated quickly, I was tired of this. "You can all stop being babies," I said louder as Roxie, Lilly and Avalon filed into the living room. "I get it, I messed up. Are you really going to keep punishing me like this?"

"Was that an.... apology?" Jericho asked with just the slightest sarcasm and smallest turn of the mouth.

"Fine. Is that what you want?" I rolled my eyes, "Fine, fine, fine. I'm sorry," I mumbled, finding the words hard to get out.

"Um, what was that? I couldn't hear you," Avalon put his hand to his ear. I swallowed my irritation.

"I'm sorry," I said louder and the rest of the group mimicked Avalon. "I said I'm sorry." And finally sincerity found my tone, "I shouldn't have gone out with Kiran alone and I especially shouldn't have gone back to the hotel with him."

"Thank you," Avalon replied firmly, but finally the faces of everyone in the room softened. "We're not unreasonable Eden, we just expect common courtesy," Avalon continued, taking sarcasm to the next level, "Oh, and we expect you to admit when you're wrong. That's all. It's just unfortunate for you, that you're wrong all of the time."

"Oh brother," I rolled my eyes. "You know, under normal circumstances my apology would have meant something completely different...." I said, finding my point hilarious. The girls laughed with me, softening the vibe in the room.

"Well, I don't like that joke," Jericho grumbled seriously and the rest of us broke into laughter at his expense.

Amory walked into the house through the front door pleased to see us getting along. He removed his over coat and bowler hat and then sat in an overstuffed chair across the room from the two couches the rest of us were occupying. Our laughter subsided as we settled down with respect, giving Amory our undivided attention.

"I'm glad to see everyone getting along again," he smiled at me, the warmth in his eyes encouraging, reminding me he was always on my side. "And I hope everyone has learned a valuable lesson about not putting yourself in unnecessary danger." Amory turned serious, while we nodded our heads in unified agreement.

"Some of us didn't have to learn that lesson," Avalon mumbled and I pulled a throw pillow from behind my back chucking it maliciously at him.

"Oh well, good," Amory responded, a little distracted. "Because, you will all be attending Kiran's birthday celebration and I just wanted to be clear on where we stood." Amory's black eyes turned steely and a wave of nausea swept over me.

251

"His birthday party?" Avalon jumped from his place on the couch, shouting. "I thought we agreed surveillance, nothing else! How is that staying out of unnecessary danger?"

"Yes, that is what we agreed," Amory stayed calm, but his eyes were dark and his tone icy. "It would appear we are no longer masters of our own agenda." He cleared his throat, taking a moment to turn towards the window.

"Amory, forgive me, but the entire Guard will be there, not to mention Lucan, Bianca, Cartier and the rest of them," Jericho argued, moving to the edge of the couch and knocking my feet to the ground, forgetting they were on his lap.

"I am aware," Amory replied quietly.

"So why on earth would you ever send us in there?" Avalon asked, completely incredulous.

"Why would you send Eden in there?" Lilly's voice was etched with deep concern and I was surprised to hear her speak up at all.

"You're exactly right, Lilly," Amory turned to her, clearly appreciating her wisdom. "It is not my decision, but Lucan's. You are all on Kiran's guest list. Well, except for Lilly, I'm sorry child. But, even Roxie has been invited, although your name isn't listed exactly, but he has you down as, Eden's other friend."

"So is it Kiran or Lucan that wants us there?" Jericho asked, narrowing his eyes.

"I can't be sure; but if I had to make an educated guess I would say that it was Kiran's idea to invite all of you at Lucan's suggestion to invite Eden. Lucan is well aware now of Kiran's feelings for her, but Kiran would never have had the audacity to invite Eden if it had not first been suggested by his father. With what I've learned of Kiran over the past few months, I don't believe he wants Eden at the party any more than we do."

I smiled warmly at Amory; I was happy to hear his good opinion of Kiran, it made a future with him somehow feel that much more possible.

"What do you think Lucan's end goal is here Amory? Do you think he's still playing a careful game, or do you think he really is putting Kiran first?" Jericho asked shrewdly, sitting back in the couch and putting an absent hand on the top of my knee.

"I don't believe for a moment that Lucan does anything but

play careful games; whatever he is working towards is for his interest. But that doesn't mean he wouldn't also be looking out for Kiran. I had been afraid that Lucan would be blinded by rage at meeting Eden, that he would have a one track mind in terms of how to act," Amory paused for a moment.

"Like, you mean, he would just want to kill me?" I asked meekly.

"Well.... yes," Amory relented. "But maybe he is not beyond reason after all."

"What do you mean?" Avalon asked quietly.

"If Eden and Kiran were to marry, he wouldn't be able to save himself, but he could preserve his line. Eden is the key to guaranteeing the Monarchy eternal life," Amory replied pensively.

"Do you really believe he's that selfless?" Avalon scoffed.

"No, I don't. But I've been wrong before," Amory responded.

"When?" Avalon asked, unbelieving.

"Avalon...." Amory scolded, his humility shining through. "Well, for starters, I was wrong about Kiran."

"So far," Avalon clarified. "You've been wrong so far. That story has yet to play out."

"Avalon!" I gasped, irritated with his stubborn hate for Kiran. "I have a question," I stated, moving on. "What do you mean; a marriage with me would preserve the line? How?"

"Sex," Avalon grumbled, crossing his arms and staring at the floor.

"Excuse me?" I stared at Avalon, wondering what in the world he was talking about.

"Sex, Eden," He sighed, exasperated with me. "You give it up to Kiran, and he gets all the benefits of that precious eternal life of yours."

"Is that true?" My cheeks were bright red and my forehead started sweating; I looked at Jericho, hoping he would give me answers quickly before Amory said something. I really did not want to talk about the birds and the bees with my grandfather right now. Or.... ever....

"Afraid so, Doll," Jericho replied, without actually looking at me.

"Wait, so I don't understand," I held my hands up, trying to figure this out. "So, every person I have sex with gets eternal life too, like I share my magic with them?"

"First of all," Avalon spoke up quickly, "how many people are you planning on having sex with?"

"Ok, that is not what I meant...." I blushed deeper, trying to figure out how to not come off like a hooker.

"It's all right, Eden," Amory cleared his throat and took over the conversation. "Let me explain and then if you have more questions you can ask them at the end." I nodded and Avalon sat back into the couch, relaxing a little. "Sex," he cleared his throat again, a little nervously, "sex, is a very sacred act with our people. It is a reserved right, saved for the privilege of marriage. When a man and a woman," another throat clear, "celebrate that right, they not only become one, but their magics also become one. They are then, every moment forward, one entity, wholly bound for eternity. Even if one of them were to die, the others magic would stay with them forever. In Immortal society there are no divorces, there are no separations, because once a couple has come together, in terms of marriage, they cannot leave each other, they cannot separate the magic."

"So, like, how it is when I take someone else's magic?" I asked, trying to understand.

"Well, not exactly, no," Amory continued, "That is not permanent; I believe there is a way to separate your magic from stolen magic. On the other hand, the connection between two lovers is unbreakable."

"Ok, like when you guys kiss," Avalon spoke up, although he was having a hard time looking at me. "You and Kiran, don't you feel how your magics like find each other?"

"Yes," I said, understanding dawning on me. "So it's more external than internal."

"Only you would know," Roxie mumbled.

"Exactly," Amory replied. "But it is also completely life-changing, a couple truly becomes one flesh and the magic is shared between the two."

"But not like Avalon and me?" I asked, trying to understand everything exactly.

"No, not at all like you two. The magic doesn't move back and forth from one person to the other, it has been changed. And Avalon still has his magic and you have yours, you can share between the two of you and you can choose to withhold. In marriage, that is not possible, the magic is indivisible," Amory finished, and I finally understood.

"And that all happens when you have.... sex?" I cringed, using the word in front of my grandfather.

"Yes. The same connection happens with your soul, even in humans, when two people have.... sex," Amory struggled saying the same word. "The difference is a soul is not a binding contract, humanity has the option to split their souls; however detrimental, once the connection has been made. Magic on the other hand, does not allow for separation."

"Marriage is super serious for us, Eden. We don't just have tons of boyfriends and make out with tons of different people." Roxie explained further, in the rough manner I was struggling to get used to. "You have to be very careful to whom you give your magic."

"Well," I began, feeling like I was being judged for being a floozy. "I was always planning on.... you know.... saving myself." I finished humbly, and hating the awkwardness of the conversation. "Listen, Aunt Syl did her job as a parent."

"Eden, no one here is accusing you of anything," Amory said sternly, eying Avalon and Roxie, "You just need to be aware of the heightened consequences for your actions. If you and Kiran did walk down the path to marriage, then your magic would save his. He would benefit from your.... indestructibility." Amory smiled and softened the building tension in the room.

"Oh," Was all I could say though. I had never really had serious thoughts about having sex before marriage. Aunt Syl had ingrained in me the sanctity of waiting until after the vows, but things between Kiran and I had been heated before. Suddenly there was a lot of pressure to not only wait for marriage, but to make sure I was marrying the right person.

"At any rate," Amory continued, "Kiran's birthday celebration is in a few hours, so I assume you will all need to get ready."

"Aw, shoot," Jericho grumbled. "My tux is still at the cleaners, I'll have to run back to the farm."

"Tux?" I sat up straight. "What is the dress code for this shindig?"

"Black tie, of course," Amory replied patiently.

"Black tie?" I whined, sinking back into the recesses of the couch. "What is it with you people? I'm running out of dresses."

"Eden, class and sophistication are to be honored," Amory scolded.

"That's all fine Amory, but you try wearing a silk evening dress in the middle of winter," I wasn't going to give this up easily.

"That is why you have magic, my dear," Amory stood up and walked into the kitchen, ignoring my complaints and reminding me I really didn't have anything to complain about.

"Hey, Jer, can I go back to the farm with you?" Roxie asked familiarly, "I don't have anything nice here."

"You can borrow one of Aunt Syl's dresses." I offered, not liking the idea of Jericho and Roxie riding to the farm together.

"No thanks, I think it would all be too big. I brought my own stuff."

"Ok...." I didn't really know how to reply to her, granted she was the tiniest thing I had ever seen, but I still felt like she was insulting Aunt Syl who had the perfect waist, in my opinion. "Lilly, I'm sorry you don't get to go." I turned to my dear friend, truly upset that she had to be left behind.

"Don't worry about it!" she gushed, "I hate those kinds of things."

"Really? I just don't want you to feel left out," I said sincerely.

"Eden, seriously," she smiled, talking in her shy, whispery way. "I would rather go back to prison, than an elegant affair with Lucan there. But can I help you get ready?"

"Actually, yes!" I replied, loving her laid back attitude. She had changed since joining the Resistance. She was more relaxed, but more confident too. "Will you help me straighten my hair? I don't want to stand out."

"Straightening your hair is not going to help you blend into the crowd." Jericho announced from across the room where he was putting on a coat and scarf.

"What is that supposed to mean?" I asked, not sure if I should be offended or not.

"It just means that.... It just means that I don't think you're capable of blending in." He smiled roguishly at me, his bright hazel eyes smoldering.

"Get out of here," I grumbled, and then followed Lilly up the stairs, still set on camouflaging myself as best as I could.

I had mixed feelings about going tonight. On the one hand I was excited to be part of Kiran's birthday and celebrate with him; but on the other, bringing all of my friends felt like a set up. I wanted to believe Kiran was just being thoughtful and didn't want me to feel awkward or alone, but there was a part of me screaming that Lucan was running his own surveillance. I thought of Avalon and Jericho and even Roxie, knowing that I would protect them first under any circumstance. Lucan would never touch them as long as I was around to save them.

Chapter Thirty-Five

"Which one do you think?" I held up the two dresses I was deciding between, asking Lilly for advice. One of the dresses was the soft pink gown Kiran had sent as a gift for the Fall Equinox dance in October, which I still hadn't worn. And the other one was a refugee from Aunt Syl's closet, a short black pin-striped number that was strapless and on the provocative side.

"Um, probably the pink one," Lilly said with finality. "Is that the one Kiran gave you?" She walked over, picking up the soft hem and fingering it delicately.

"Yes," I sighed. "And I don't want to be too obvious, especially after that whole.... sex education class down there." I sighed again, and plopped down on Aunt Syl's king-sized bed. "Apparently, I need to do some serious shopping and stock up on ball gowns." I sighed wondering if this was what royal life, one tiring formal event after another, would be like, should I someday be Queen.

"The pink one will be fine. More than fine," Lilly sat down next me, putting a gentle hand on my back. "He's probably the only one who knows about the dress, so if anything it will be.... romantic," she smiled encouragingly and I started to feel a little bit of hope.

"You think?" I asked and she nodded.

I stood up with more confidence and decided she was right. I walked into the bathroom and undressed, changing into the appropriate undergarments and pulling the dress carefully over my head. I stood staring at myself in the mirror.

It felt like I was here a lot lately, in front of the mirror and in some fancy dress. Elegant affairs were beginning to lose their appeal; still, I couldn't help but admire the delicate workmanship of the couture gown.

The soft pink silk shimmered iridescently when the light hit the fabric just so. The skirt was full and long, but pleated, a stark contrast to the softer lines of the top. The designer of this dress was very bold, creating a concept I had never seen before. The neck line plunged to the waist, away from the delicate cap sleeves and covering just enough to maintain the preface of modesty. The back plunged in the same v, meeting the narrow waistline in symmetrical uniformity. The stitching was gold, glinting against the pastel silk, and matched the strappy stilettos Kiran had sent along to complete the look.

Either Kiran had perfect taste, or someone who worked for him did. The dress flattered me in all the right places and met my measurements exactly. My skin tone had faded over the winter months and behind the beauty of the gown I looked more like a porcelain doll, than a rebellious teenager.

Lilly had straightened my long hair and then wrapped it in elaborate lines, folding it over and over again into an artistic and secured up-do. I finished my make up with simple and soft pinks and a little eye liner and mascara. I stared again at myself, feeling self-conscious and unsure.

Walking over to my jewelry box, I pulled out the pendant Kiran had given me in Geneva, deciding that I would truly look like a gift just for him. The black stone was dull, sitting inside the silver setting. I looked at it closely for a minute, trying to find the magic behind the plain rock.

I put the silver chain around my neck and watched the stone flash a myriad of colors before settling on royal blue. The necklace, hanging down on the bare part of my chest, did not match my dress and I found that frustrating. Using a burst of magic and igniting my blood, I changed the stone from royal blue to the pastel pink of the gown.

As soon as the necklace settled on the color I had chosen, the bathroom door slammed shut and a gust of royal blue air whooshed past me, blowing my skirt violently and ruffling my hair.

I screamed at the top of my lungs, not expecting the wind or the slamming door. It took me a moment to calm down and get a hold of myself. My eyes darted around the bathroom, hoping for a source besides my magic. I didn't understand the burst of wind, or the color painting it.

There was no one else in there, I was all alone. The blue air settled around the hem of my skirt, floating in tiny whirlwind circles and spreading out into a cool mist against the tile floor.

"Eden, are you all right?" Lilly knocked on the bathroom door.

"Yes, I'm fine," I willed the wind behind me, hoping it

259

would disappear into Aunt Syl's closet and then eventually blend in with the rest of the normal air.

Lilly opened the door, her mouth falling open just barely at the sight of me. "You look amazing. Like, the best you've ever looked," she gushed.

"Really?" I asked skeptically, my heart still pounding in my chest. "You're sure this is how everyone else will be dressed? I'm not like, way too overdressed?" I still felt self-conscious and afraid of the evening.

"No, no one else will be dressed like that!" she smiled, "But they will wish they were!"

We laughed our way into the hallway and to the staircase. Lilly went to grab her camera from my room and I started my descent down the stairs. Jericho was standing in the middle of the living room, straightening his tie, when I caught his attention; he turned to look at me. A smile played at the corner of his lips and I drew in a quick breath, caught off guard by how handsome he looked. He was wearing a black, double-breasted, tailored suit and his golden brown hair was slicked back, the product making it darker than usual.

"Don't you ever get tired of watching me walk down the stairs for these things?" I asked, playfully, realizing he was always in the living room whenever it was time to leave for these events.

"It's my cross to bear, I suppose," his eyes twinkled and he held out his elbow for me when I found the bottom step. "I thought you were going to try to blend in?"

I glanced down at my dress and swallowed nervously, "Do I look bad?"

"No, oh, no, that's not what I meant," Jericho stuttered nervously, before swinging me around to face him. "You.... you are.... You are making me nervous," he blushed deeply, never taking his eyes off of mine. "You're stunning, really," he smiled and I smiled back.

"Thank you," I whispered.

"Are we ready?" Avalon walked into the living room from the kitchen with Roxie on his arm. Avalon was wearing a deep blue suit without any tie and an unbuttoned jacket; he looked like he belonged in the rat pack. Roxie was the prettiest I had ever seen her, but she still hadn't lost her hard edge in a black halter top ball gown and her hair pulled back into a severe bun at the nape of her neck.

"Yes," I stated simply, allowing Jericho to lead me outside. Amory was driving separately and wouldn't be acknowledging us anyway, so we took Jericho's Jeep downtown and to the Immortal club, Kiran called his office.

Parking was crazy, black sedans and SUV's lined the streets on either side for blocks. I was more thankful for magic than ever, after walking the entire way from our parking spot to the club front door in tall stilettos and freezing cold, icy temperatures.

There was a doorman at the entrance to the club; it was the first time I had ever seen a Titan policing the doorway. Usually, the golden serpentine knockers were enough to identify magic and keep out those who didn't belong.

Avalon gave the Guard our names and he let us pass, eying us skeptically. We walked through the main corridor; the usual source of lighting had been turned off in the hallway and the candelabra lining the walls had been lit to compensate for light.

I couldn't shake the feeling I was walking through a haunted house. I could hear the music through the floor, it sounded like a full orchestra and hauntingly beautiful. I followed Avalon and Jericho down the hallway to another Titan, guarding the door to the stairwell. Avalon gave him our names again and the door was opened.

Once on the stone stairwell, I marveled at how the underground club had transformed into much more. Candles of every size and shape lined every wall, burning softly and casting long shadows of the dancers moving about the open floor. The furniture had been removed except for one corner and just a dance floor was left in the expansive room with hundreds of people dancing.

I froze on the stairs, not even knowing how I would handle the night. The magic from all of the excitement and revelry was almost overwhelming and I had a hard time believing the humanity living in any proximity to this would not be able to feel it.

"Are you all right?" Jericho asked gently. "Use your magic."

I nodded and let him escort me down the stairs, holding my full skirt carefully, so not to trip on it. I turned on the magic and my nerves disappeared.

At the bottom of the stairs Kiran was waiting with his father and mother. There was more royal court with them as well, but I only recognized the Cartiers, Sebastian's family. All of the men were dressed in expensive tuxedos with tails, and the women in elegant ball gowns that both flattered and boasted of their wealth. Kiran and Lucan had styled their hair back smoothly, away from their faces, and their more elaborate crowns were worn in an identically crooked way. I wondered if they were wearing their party crowns; Kiran's was solid gold with rubies and emeralds glinting in the candlelight. Lucan's was also solid gold but his stones were all diamonds.... huge diamonds.

"Your Highness," I curtsied, extending my hand to Kiran, mimicking Roxie who had been before me.

"Eden," Kiran responded slyly. When I lifted my head I was greeted with an unabashed smirk. His eyes were smoldering and he had yet to let go of my hand.

"Happy birthday," I smiled back, leaning in. Something about Kiran's attitude encouraged me to throw caution to the wind.

"Thank you," his smirk grew and his eyes took a sweeping view of me, returning to mine obviously pleased. "You'll save a dance for me?"

"Of course," I replied coyly, but really hoping he wouldn't ask. If he found me attractive now, dancing later would just ruin that. "It is after all, your birthday."

"Eden, what a pleasure for you to join us," Lucan moved me down the reception line by calling my attention to him. I curtsied politely, extending my hand to him as well. "You look beautiful as always."

"Thank you, Your Highness," I lifted my head and met his careful smile with my own.

"I hope you will save me a dance as well." Lucan let go of my hand and moved me down the line before I could respond. I stumbled to Queen Analisa trying to think of an excuse or exit strategy but I was caught. I curtsied for Analisa and then left the line before meeting any of Sebastian's family.

Jericho was waiting for me at the end of the reception line and I ran to him, trying to keep myself together.

"Lucan wants to dance with me," I whispered frantically, out of breath, my head spinning.

"Now?" Jericho asked, looking around for Lucan.

"No, I mean, I don't think so, later some time," I smoothed out my skirt and checked myself over to make sure everything was where it was supposed to be.

"Oh," Jericho said simply. "Eden, that's normal, I think he's obligated to dance with almost everyone."

"Oh," I echoed. "But I don't know how to dance," I whined, afraid of the scene I would make.

"Then we better practice," Jericho grabbed my hand and pulled me to the floor.

He put a strong hand on my lower back and held my other delicately in his hand, leading me around the dance floor expertly. I laughed at Jericho's serious face and business-like manner, letting him lead and teach me.

"I forgot how good you are at this," I laughed, completely relaxing in his arms.

"Seriously, how could you forget that?" He smiled back at me and slowed down a little bit.

"That is a good question!" I agreed and then screamed a little when he suddenly dipped me low without warning.

"Relax, I got you," he whispered, lifting me back up and bringing me closer to his body. He looked deep into my eyes, the green part of his eyes flashing golden, before returning to a mixture of chocolate brown and emeralds; they were blazing, as if set on fire by the candle light, and I forgot the room around me for a moment.

"Um, should we, should we find Avalon?" I ruined the moment, but I couldn't let Kiran find me like that in Jericho's arms. Their confrontation at the Winter Solstice Dance flashed through my memory and I didn't want to ruin Kiran's party.

"Yes," Jericho narrowed his eyes at me, "that is a good idea."

He took his hand from my lower back, but led me through the crowd of people with his other one. I followed closely at his heels, using magic to keep from tripping on my long train.

"I could get used to this," Avalon grunted, when we finally found them near the bar. He was holding a plate of small appetizers. "Eden, you should get these recipes."

"And do what with them?" I laughed.

"So anything interesting happen?" He ignored me, scanning the room with his well-trained surveillance eye.

"I have to dance with Lucan later," I grumbled, praying I wouldn't make a fool out of myself.

"How awful," Roxie empathized and I was thankful she understood how terrible it would be.

"Thank you!" I exclaimed, "And do I have to talk during it, or can I just I save myself the trouble of putting my foot in my mouth!"

"You don't have to talk if you don't want to, Love. You can just stand there and look pretty, I'm sure my father won't mind." Kiran answered from behind me, clearly amused.

"Well, hello," I turned on my heel to face him. "I didn't expect to see you so soon."

"Didn't you?" he smirked, extending his elbow to me. "You could hardly expect me to stay away for long; look at you." His eyes shimmered in their deep ocean of a way, "Will you dance with me?"

I nodded respectfully and took his arm. Kiran led me to the dance floor, twirled me about the floor, all eyes watching him. I was effortless in his arms, a characteristic I didn't even know that I possessed.

The music changed, slowing down and so did Kiran. Pressing my body to his and resting his cheek against my temple. The moment was enough to easily forget the rest of the room, although in the back of my mind I knew we were never alone.

"You're the envy of every lady in this room tonight," Kiran whispered in my ear.

"I suppose they're all jealous of my dance moves," I joked, sarcastically, assuming he meant because I was the one dancing with him.

"Of course," he agreed, dramatically, pulling away for a moment to gaze into my eyes. "I meant because of your incomparable beauty."

"Oh that. I mean, obviously!" I was still joking, but my cheeks blushed from the compliment. "Well, I can hardly take credit for the dress."

"Nor should you," he kissed me on the cheek and I was shocked at his boldness in front of everyone. "I have excellent taste."

"Yes, you do," I smiled adoringly at him, and his eyes swept over me, taking me in again.

264

"Is that the necklace I gave you?" he stopped moving for a moment and took the soft pink pendant in his hand, fingering the stone as if rubbing the color off of it.

"Yes," I answered. The look in Kiran's eyes changed from obvious love to strange curiosity. I cleared my throat, suddenly nervous I made a mistake.

"How did you do that with the color?" he moved closer, bringing the necklace to his face.

"I don't know," I began, "I just put it on, and that is the color it turned," I was a bad liar. I didn't even know why I was lying, but something in the expression on Kiran's face made the hair on the back of my neck stand up.

"But that is impossible," Kiran looked up at me, a flash of betrayal passed across his face and I opened my mouth to explain the truth, but we were interrupted.

"May I?" Lucan was behind Kiran, extending his hand to me.

"Of course," Kiran replied respectfully, bowing to his father before disappearing into the crowd.

Lucan took another step forward and I placed my hand gently in his. He moved me across the dance floor with grace, while keeping me at a healthy distance. For a while he didn't speak, he looked over my head at the gathered room dancing. I was thankful for that and didn't offer any conversation, doing my best to keep my eyes from staring at my feet.

"Are you having a good evening?" Lucan asked curtly.

"Yes, lovely, thank you, Your Majesty."

"Good. And your friends? Are they also having a good evening?" Lucan looked towards the bar, where Avalon, Jericho and Roxie stood watching us, drinks in hand.

"I believe they are," I smiled politely, but Lucan didn't notice, he was still watching my friends.

"Your friend, what is his name?" Lucan asked, his careful tone never changing.

"Jericho Bentley, Your Highness," I replied, worrying that I was over-doing it with all of the titles.

"Yes, I know Jericho. His father has a position in my court. The other one, what is his name?" Lucan had yet to take his eyes off Avalon.

"His name?" I cleared my throat. "His name is Avalon St. Andrews."

"And he is in your grade?"

"Yes, he is," I said softly, beginning to worry about Avalon.

"And what are his parent's names?" Lucan turned his eyes from Avalon to me, and their steely blue, icy stare sent a shiver down my back.

"I don't know his parents," I offered honestly, "I don't really know any of my friends' parents though.... your Highness."

"Hmph," Lucan grunted and then looked back into the crowd of dancers. "Eden, I would like you to be aware that tomorrow morning I will call off the engagement between Kiran and Seraphina."

I tripped over my long train, catching myself awkwardly on Lucan's shoulder. "Forgive me," I gushed, "I'm so sorry."

"Are you surprised?" Lucan was amused.

"Yes," I answered a little overzealously. "What I mean to say, is that, I didn't know that was.... I thought.... I don't understand."

"It's simple," Lucan explained, the amusement gone. "Kiran is clearly not happy with my choice for him. I would like to prevent any rash or reckless behavior and so I have decided to give him the choice. If he chooses Seraphina, then so be it. If however, he chooses someone else...." His eyes found mine again, "Well, then I trust his wisdom."

"Of course," I mumbled, my thoughts racing. "And when will he have to decide?" I gulped, swallowing my fears about the future.

"Soon," Lucan said simply. "The Kingdom wants stability. They want an heir."

I gulped again.

"And Eden," Lucan continued, "Whomever Kiran chooses, will always have to put the Kingdom before her own interest," he stared at me seriously, dropping my hand and taking a step back as the song ended.

"Naturally," I said with a gravelly voice and curtsied.

Lucan returned a respectful head nod and then walked away, leaving me in the middle of the dance floor. My eyes fell on Kiran and Seraphina, twirling expertly and laughing happily. Seraphina's dreams were about to end, this was her last night as the Crown Prince's betrothed.

I turned on my heel, searching out Avalon. I would let her have this night. I owed Seraphina nothing but revenge, but I knew how terrible the morning would be for her and I had no right to intrude on her last night of entitled happiness. It was time to leave.

Besides, I was suddenly finding it hard to breathe. Everything I had thought so impossible, so unrealistic, might actually be happening. I needed to think. I had to find solitude and silence and prepare myself for change.

And then, I would need to find Amory. I would have to explain.

Chapter Thirty-Six

Avalon pulled into his designated parking spot five minutes early for English. He jumped down from the cab of his monstrous truck and started in for class.

Are you coming? He asked telepathically, without any intention of waiting for me. Ugh. Yes. I grunted and scrambled down from the truck, following Avalon to the English and Arts building.

I dreaded going to class, but I dreaded a lecture from Mr. Lambert about the sins of tardiness even more.

I was tired today. More tired than I should be. But when Amory had come over yesterday announcing that the engagement was actually called off, I had stayed up most of the night, too nervous to sleep.

I hadn't been expecting the proposal to happen instantly, but I knew that it was coming and felt wholly unprepared.

I kept reminding myself that this was the life I wanted. I wanted to marry Kiran. I wanted to be able to change the Kingdom without war. I wanted to be in a position to keep my family safe and stop all of the suffering.

Although I had yet to talk to Kiran about it, I was pretty sure he would be asking me to marry him at any given time. I was the reason that Lucan called off the betrothal, and I was who Lucan was referring to. Wasn't I?

I shuddered, afraid that maybe Kiran wouldn't ask me after all. And then I shuddered again, afraid that he would.

I felt like I was about to be mugged and in the worst way. I knew that it was coming, but had no idea when. The sneak attack element of the whole situation was hard to accept.

"Remember in the human world, when two people liked each other and went out on dates? And it was years before they started talking about marriage and babies?" I mumbled to Lilly, but then realized she was still at home until Lucan left Omaha.

The suspense was turning me into a crazy person.

When Amory arrived yesterday with the news, I dropped and shattered my coffee cup. I had been expecting the announcement for almost twenty-four hours, but the finality of the decision still surprised me.

I winced, remembering Amory's dark eyes and how sad they looked. I asked him if he was disappointed in me. It was obvious that he had been planning something different for my future, but he assured me he was only worried about me.

Still, when he pulled me into a hug, I felt the weight of his sorrow and had to use magic to hold myself together. I felt like a disappointment, even if I wasn't one. I was tormented with the sickening feeling of letting down my brother, grandfather and my closest of friends.

And when I tried to convince myself that not only would I get to be with the one person that my soul belonged to and I loved whole-heartedly, I couldn't help but feel inadequate for the task ahead of me.

I didn't know the first thing about being a Queen. And I certainly didn't know how to reverse thousands of years of racism and prejudice. Or how to protect my family from a King that would still murder them at the first opportunity.

I swallowed hard and leaned against the bathroom door, not ready to face the reality of school or the promise in Kiran's eyes. I had expected a length of years before I would have to deal with any of this and I was now realizing how naive I had been.

The bathroom door suddenly swung opened and I fell through the open space, landing in a heap on the floor.

"Well, look who it is," Seraphina's wind-chimed voice snarled at me from above.

I stood quickly to my feet, the bathroom door slamming behind me once I was out of the way.

"Hello, Seraphina," I said carefully. My heart fell to the pit of my stomach, taking in the sight of her.

Her long blonde hair was limp, tangled and somehow duller. Her eyes were a mess of smudged mascara and swollen, reddened eyes, their once pretty blue, now an unlit cavity of anger. Black streaks stained her pale cheeks and her bee-stung lips were more swollen than usual. Her uniform was wrinkled and untidy, her tights torn and her shirt untucked. She literally looked like the scary movie version of herself and I tried to push down the fear-induced lump in my throat.

"Hello, Eden," she growled, unmoving, and then stood

269

silently staring me down.

"I, um, I.... I should.... Um, I should get to class," I wanted to run from the bathroom screaming, but more than that I wanted to fill the terrifying silence and remove her stare.

"No!" she screamed at me, shaking the glass of the mirrors and rattling the door behind me. "You will leave when I say you can leave." Her voice dropped to a menacing whisper and I let my magic loose in my veins, the electricity igniting my senses.

"What do you want?" I asked with an even tone.

"Don't ask me what I want," she replied, her eyes turning to stone, "You do not want to know what I want."

"That is probably true," I mumbled, finding courage in my magic. The last bell rang in the hallway and I was officially late for English, again. I turned to leave the bathroom, hoping, unreasonably, that she would understand.

"Stop!" she screamed at me and I did. This time the force of her magic shattered all of the glass in the bathroom and I covered my head with my arms to protect myself from flying shards of broken mirror. "You have ruined my life." she accused loudly, "You do not just get to leave. You're going to have to answer for this."

"For what?" I asked innocently, watching her swirl the broken glass around behind her in a dangerous tornado of pointed shrapnel.

"I was supposed to be Queen!" she screamed and a glass dagger broke from her whirlwind and flew at me. I ducked out of the way just in time, and the shard slammed into the brick wall behind me where my head had been, shattering into a million tiny pieces.

"I don't know what you're talking about!" I screamed in fear. I didn't know how to act. I could take her down with my magic, but I also felt that she had a right to be mad. I didn't hate her the way she hated me. Just because she was willing to kill me, didn't mean I could do the same.

"Kiran was mine and you took him from me!" she accused and sent another glass dagger soaring through the air, this time at my leg. I moved out of the way, but not soon enough and the glass sliced my thigh before breaking against the brick wall. Hot, crimson blood soaked through my white tights and plaid skirt in seconds before I could use my magic to stop the bleeding.

"Please, Seraphina," I held up my hands, surrendering. "Kiran is not mine. This was Lucan's decision." I believed my answer, but apparently Seraphina did not, because another glass dagger came flying across the room, narrowly missing my throat.

The spinning cyclone of glass moved faster and with more force. I pressed myself against the brick wall afraid of the dangerous weapon Seraphina was feeding her magic, but more afraid of the hateful look darkening the eyes that controlled it.

"No," she said calmly, but the tempest of shrapnel behind her betrayed her true emotion. "You did this. All of this. And now it's my turn to take back what's mine."

"Seraphina stop!" Avalon burst through the bathroom door, and with one meaningful look and burst of his magic, he dropped the glass pieces to the floor.

Seraphina, too, fell to the floor, sobbing hysterically. Avalon grabbed me by the arm, pulling me from the bathroom roughly.

"Are you crazy?" he half shouted, half whispered at me. "Were you just going to let her kill you?" He spun me around in the hallway, making me face him.

"No, of course not!" I answered back with the same conviction.

"Then what the hell were you doing in there?" he yelled, staring me down. His emerald green eyes demanded answers.

"I.... I don't know...." I stumbled, "I just felt like, I don't know, that.... I just felt bad." I hung my head, realizing I had been punishing myself. I felt responsible for Seraphina. I felt responsible for my family. I had wanted someone to take their hate out on me, because I felt like I deserved it.

"You don't," Avalon answered the thoughts in my head. "You haven't done anything wrong."

He pulled me into a hug, wrapping his huge arms around me and comforting me. My head was pressed against his chest and I could see the faint outlines of his tattoos underneath the long sleeved white uniform shirt.

I started to cry. I didn't deserve Avalon's forgiveness, or his compassion. A marriage to Kiran was not Avalon's answer to the problem with the Monarchy. Avalon wanted the Monarchy destroyed completely and the entire Kendrick line wiped out. I was another roadblock now, another obstacle in the way of Avalon's

271

perfect dream for our society.

"I've ruined everything," I cried into his shirt, my voice muffled against his chest.

"Well, Ok, that's true," I could hear the smile in his voice, "But that doesn't mean you deserve to be punished." He patted me on the head, like I was a small child and I felt comforted.

I'm sorry. I said inside of our heads, hoping he could feel the sincerity behind it.

"All right, that's enough. No more feeling sorry for yourself," Avalon pushed me away playfully, grinning at me. "Go find Amory, he'll let you call someone to come pick you up. I don't think it's a good idea for you to be at school today."

"Ugh. You're probably right," I started walking backwards to the stairwell. "What are you going to go do?" I called out, curious why he wasn't coming with me.

"I'm going to go deal with the train-wreck in the bathroom," he smiled mischievously. "Do you think?" his expression turned serious, "Do you think it's too soon to ask her out?"

"Oh, Avalon," I gasped, appalled at his twisted sense of humor.

"What? It is too soon, isn't it?" he turned to the bathroom, "How long then? A week? Two weeks?"

"There is something wrong with you," I called out before turning around and running down the stairs.

I sprinted out of the English and Arts building and across campus to the Administration building. I flew through the doors and up to the second-floor teacher's lounge before Mrs. Truance could stop me. There were no teachers upstairs, but I could see the light on in Amory's office at the end of the hall. I walked the rest of the way slowly, trying to catch my breath and a little afraid to fill Amory in on Seraphina's nervous breakdown in the bathroom.

I knocked on his door politely, waiting for Amory to invite me in. He looked up at me from an older-looking document on his desk and smiled.

"And what do I owe the pleasure?" he asked from his deep, melodic voice.

"One of your students just took a serious ride on the crazy train," I replied glibly, taking a seat in one of his leather chairs.

"What do you mean?" Concern flickered in his eyes.

"Seraphina just tried to stab me to death in the girl's bathroom," I answered, more put together than my shaking hands believed I was.

"Oh, Eden," Amory gasped. He walked around to the second leather chair, sat down and took my hand. "Are you all right?" he asked, his eyes finding the crimson stain marring my skirt.

"Yes, I'm fine," I said quickly, trying to smooth out my blood-soaked uniform. "I'm just a little, um, shaken up." I blinked several times in a row, trying to hold back the tears.

"Of course, you are." Amory whispered soothingly, patting the hand that he held.

"Can I go home, Amory?" I asked meekly, wanting nothing more.

"Of course, you can," he paused for a moment, "Actually, I have a better idea." Amory sat up straight, letting go of my hand and reaching the cell phone sitting on his desk. "I think it's best if maybe you leave for a little bit. The news of the broken engagement will travel fast and if there are more out there that want you dead, this might quicken their plans." I was speechless. I watched silently as Amory's mind worked quickly, deciding on the course of action he would take. "I think it's best if you get out of town for a while." "Out of town, but what if-" I started, thinking about Lucan's reaction if Kiran wanted to find me and couldn't.

"I'll deal with them, we have to think of your safety first," Amory sat back in the chair and started dialing a number. "I am sending Jericho on a mission. He was going to leave this afternoon." "Jericho?" I asked, putting the pieces together.

"Yes, Jericho. I think it's best if you go with him," Amory didn't wait for my reply; he pushed send on the phone and was explaining the details of the day to Jericho before I could object.

Sure, my safety came first, but I was pretty sure leaving town with a boy that was not Kiran was just as dangerous. I was maybe only days away from becoming engaged to the Crown Prince and Amory wanted to send me away, alone with a boy that not only had feelings for me but was in a Rebellion completely in opposition to the Monarchy.

Oh, boy.

Chapter Thirty-Seven

Jericho pulled up to the school in a black Escalade with severely tinted windows and no license plates, screeching to a stop right in front of me. I jumped into the passenger seat quickly, Jericho barely waiting for my door to be closed before taking off again.

"In a hurry?" I asked sarcastically.

"Obviously," he replied curtly.

"Hey, thanks for picking me up and you know, taking me with you," I tried to break the tension with thankfulness, but Jericho wasn't having it.

"Yep. Didn't really have a choice though," he mumbled, staring straight ahead through dark aviator sunglasses.

"No, really," I wasn't going to give up. "Seraphina was seriously trying to kill me. She had like this spinning weapon thing made out of broken glass. It was crazy."

"Your clothes are in the back seat," he replied, ignoring me. "You should change; I don't want blood on the seats."

"Ok...." I didn't know what to make of Jericho's attitude. He had picked me up, and not even questioned Amory about taking me with; but ever since the news of Kiran's broken engagement had been announced at our house yesterday, he had avoided me at all costs.

I pulled the duffle bag that Lilly had packed for me from the back seat and unzipped it. All of the shirts inside were warm and black and she had packed a couple pairs of dark, washed jeans and some black yoga pants.

I looked over at Jericho, who was wearing a black long sleeve shirt and dark washed jeans and figured out this must be the uniform of the Resistance spy. I laughed out loud; apparently this was my first real mission.

"How long are we going to be driving for?" I asked, realizing it would affect what I would wear.

"A long time," Jericho replied snidely.

"Ok...." I pulled out my yoga pants and an oversized thin black sweatshirt that hung off one shoulder. I usually wore this outfit to workout in, but a long car trip required comfort. I took off my shoes and unbuttoned my skirt, hoping Jericho knew what he was doing by demanding that I change.

"Not up here," he snapped at me. "Seriously, Eden, go to the back."

"Oh, sorry," I mumbled, tossing my duffle bag to the back seat and crawling awkwardly over the center console.

"And do something with your hair," he called from the front seat.

"Why?" I asked innocently, fingering my long, tangled curls.

"Because," he answered crossly.

"Because why?" I pressed, hoping to irritate him. I didn't appreciate his rudeness.

"Because it's...." I watched his aviator sunglasses tilt towards me in the rear view mirror. "Because it's everywhere."

That wasn't really an answer, but I obeyed anyway. I pulled a hair-tie off of my wrist and wrapped my hair into a messy bun on the top of my head. I slipped down to the floor, below the range of the rear view mirror and changed into the comfortable black sportswear that would be road-trip appropriate.

"That's better," I sighed, sliding back into the front passenger seat.

I watched Jericho glance at me for a moment before clenching his jaw and turning his attention back to the road. He let out a snicker that was actually hurtful.

"Is there a problem?" I asked carefully, sounding more sensitive than I would have liked.

"Yes, there's a problem," Jericho snapped at me again, and I flinched. This trip was going to be miserable.

"What did I do to make you so mad?" I whispered, not really expecting him to answer.

He turned to look at me full on for the first time since I had gotten in the car. I couldn't see his eyes behind his dark tinted sunglasses, so I had no idea what to make of him, and that bothered me.

"You didn't do anything," Jericho conceded, and his rigid shoulders slumped. He pressed down on the gas even harder and we accelerated past all acceptable speed limits. "It's just that.... Well, I was looking forward to taking this trip alone."

"And you're mad that I'm tagging along?" I asked

tentatively.

"I don't know. I just felt like I really needed some alone time."

"I can understand that," I said honestly, feeling like I needed the same thing. "I won't say a word. You'll completely forget I'm here." I pretended to zip my lips closed with two fingers pressed together, and turned to face the window.

"You are the one person that I actually don't think I'm capable of forgetting about," I turned my head quickly, watching as heat crept up the back of his neck.

"So, you're Ok with me being here?" I asked hopefully.

"Ugh, yes," he sighed exasperatedly. "Only if you hand me my coke," he held out his hand and I looked around for a soda.

"Sure," I said energetically, "Where is it?"

"It's in the cooler in the trunk, Lilly and Roxie packed us some snacks so we wouldn't have to stop."

I unbuckled and leaned across the back seat, reaching with an extended arm into the trunk, awkwardly pulling a blue cooler across the seats. Jericho jerked the car to the left suddenly and I fell clumsily on top of his shoulder, before righting myself and giving him a disapproving glare.

"Sorry," he offered sheepishly, his face red, matching the tone of his neck.

I opened the cooler and took out two plastic bottles of Coke before turning around and sitting back down in my seat.

"So, where are we going?" I asked, realizing I had agreed to a mission I knew nothing about.

"The Mexican Border," Jericho replied casually.

"Really?" I was surprised, I hadn't been expecting Mexico, but then again, I hadn't really known what to expect. "What's there?"

"I don't know exactly," Jericho said pensively. "Amory just asked me to deliver a letter for him. He said it was of the utmost importance but that I couldn't tell anyone and that my contact would find me and not the other way around."

"Oh, well that sounds.... confusing," I laughed.

"Yes, it does," he agreed with me.

"So, the Mexican Border? All right. When do we have to be there by?" I folded my arms and smiled, this was fun, I was beginning to feel like a real spy.

"We have to be in El Paso by four AM, but I'm hoping to get there a little bit early and stake the place out." he said matter-of-factly.

"Oh, right," I tried not to laugh. "We don't want to be walking into a trap."

"Exactly," he replied seriously and when a laugh escaped me, he turned around, a little offended. "It's called due diligence, Eden, we have to be careful."

"No, I know. I'm sorry," I couldn't stop laughing.

"It's all fun and games until someone gets caught and sent to prison."

"No, you're right. It's just that, this is my first mission, come on, give me a break," I pushed his arm a little and his bicep flexed rigidly beneath my fingers.

"Just this once," he mumbled, turning his full attention back to the road.

"Is this what all the missions are like?" I asked a question I had been wanting to know the answer to for a long time.

"No, not really. Well, sometimes," he answered vaguely.

"What are they like, when they're not like this one?" I dug deeper.

"I don't know. We do all kinds of things."

"Like what?" I pressed, not willing to let him get away with avoiding my questions. "Like what were you doing in London before Amory asked you to come back here?"

"Just a lot of surveillance stuff. I had a list of dignitaries that I was supposed to watch and report back to Amory about. He wanted to know if Lucan was planning on arresting anyone, or if there had been Shape-Shifters turned in. Stuff like that," he admitted.

"That sounds kind of boring, actually," I mumbled, without thinking.

"Yes, boring, but necessary."

"Why?" I had a hunch, but I wanted to hear Jericho say it out loud, for some reason I loved to hear him talk about the Resistance.

"Well, I don't know, depending on the person being arrested, Amory would make a decision whether to rescue them or not. Or like the Shape-Shifters, we always rescued them and depending on the arrest, Amory was always worried Lucan would find the colonies."

"What colonies?" I asked, completely enthralled.

"Over time, most of the Shape-Shifters have moved into secret colonies in remote places of the world. Some of them still live in populated areas, but most of them try to stay completely hidden from all civilization."

"Why?" I couldn't stop my questions.

"Well, for two reasons I suppose. The first being, that Lucan would arrest them if he found them; the second, that since the decline of magic they try to stay away from humanity."

"Why?" I felt like a toddler, but I couldn't help myself.

"Because, Eden, they used to be able to shift into anything they wanted, that's how they got their name. But since the ban of intermarriage, their magic has been diminished and they are only able to shift into one thing, usually an animal. That's why they avoid humans, they want to shift naturally and in a habitat that makes the most sense."

"So like Lilly...." I started to put the pieces together.

"So like if Lilly were to find a colony, she would most likely go to the jungle regions because she is a tiger. I know there are colonies in almost every rain forest. There is a huge colony in the mountains of Peru, and one way in the north part of Russia. But so far, they have remained under the eye of the Monarchy."

"Ah," I finally got it.

"You can't tell anyone about them though," Jericho demanded suddenly.

"I won't," I sighed, defensively.

"Eden, I'm serious. You can't tell anyone," he said slowly and with more force.

"I'm not going to," I answered seriously, although I didn't really feel like I needed to explain that.

"Ok, enough with the twenty questions. Why don't you try to get some sleep, we're going to have a long night ahead of us," Jericho reached for the radio, turning on mellow music, but turning it up loudly so we couldn't talk naturally anymore.

I followed his advice, leaning my head against the cold window and closing my eyes. I was finished talking anyway. I didn't understand Jericho that was for sure. This road trip had been nothing but bizarre so far.

Chapter Thirty-Eight

"Eden, we're here," Jericho put a strong hand on my knee, shaking me awake.

I opened my eyes slowly and stretched. I was tired. More tired than I expected. I had slept the entire way to the border. My muscles were stiff and my neck terribly sore from resting awkwardly. There was a cold spot on my forehead from where it pressed against the window.

I sent a surge of magic through my blood, waking myself up and expelling the stiffness to my muscles.

"That was fast," I turned and smiled at Jericho who had removed his sunglasses.

The sky was overcast and black; I couldn't make out a star in the sky, not even the moon. I couldn't even see far beyond my window. We were in the middle of nowhere, completely alone.

"We are going to have to walk the rest of the way. It's a little bit of a hike," Jericho explained.

"Like, walk the rest of the way out there?" I gulped, taking in the midnight scenery and losing courage.

"Yes, come on. I don't want to be late," Jericho reached for a black messenger bag behind his seat and jumped down from the luxury SUV.

I followed suit, shivering in the cold desert night air. I used my magic to turn on my senses and examine my surroundings. We were in, what felt like, the middle of the desert. There was absolutely nothing around us except sand, rock and cactus.

Jericho took off walking on a dirt path headed south and I followed quickly behind him. Magic or no magic, I wasn't going to be left alone in the middle of nowhere.

We walked silently for an hour or more until Jericho consulted with a hand held GPS system he pulled from his messenger bag. Satisfied with our location, he found a few rocks to sit down on that surrounded a pit, that at one time had held a fire. There were half-burned logs and twigs inside, ashy and charred.

"And now we wait," Jericho answered my question before I got a chance to ask it.

"This is exciting," I exclaimed, rubbing my cold hands

together.

"What is?" Jericho asked, using his magic to start the old logs on fire. The heat from the flames felt good and I held my hands out to them, snuggling closer to Jericho's rock.

"The mission," I replied, obviously. "Aren't you excited?" When he shrugged his shoulders, I continued, "You know, because it's my first mission and I've never been on one before, it's just very exciting! And I think we make an amazing team. They will probably want us to go on like, every mission together. Don't you think?"

"Well, enjoy this one, because there aren't going to be any more missions for you," Jericho threw a rock into the fire.

"What do you mean? Why?" I was hurt by his response. Had I irritated him by sleeping all day? Did he not think I was good enough to be in the field? Or was he still mad that I crashed a trip he was supposed to take alone?

"Future Queens do not go on missions for the Resistance, Eden," he answered, very condescendingly.

"How do you know?" I forced myself to be playful, hiding my hurt.

"Eden, don't play games. This is it for you," Jericho crossed his arms, and stared intently at the fire. "Tomorrow or the next day or whatever day Kiran asks you to marry him and you say yes, that's it. You're done with missions and the Resistance.... And you're done with me."

"Jericho, you don't mean that," I reached out, holding on to his arm.

"Yes, Eden, I do," he wrenched his arm out of my grasp, refusing to look at me.

"Why are you being like this?" I asked, anger and irritation finally catching up with me.

"Why am I being like this? Are you kidding me?" he scoffed at me loudly.

"No, I want to know," I crossed my arms defiantly.

"What do you want to know, Eden? Do you want to know how upset I am that you are not going to be around anymore, that I'm going to have to disappear out of your life completely? Would you like to know how scared I am that I won't be able to protect you anymore? Maybe you want to know how terrifying it is that you are choosing to hand yourself over to the Monarchy; that you are going willingly to be slaughtered and I get absolutely no say in the matter. Or maybe you want to know how hurt I am. Is that what you want to know?"

"Hurt?" I swallowed the nausea I felt rising in my throat. I didn't want to hear Jericho's answer, but I couldn't stop myself from asking the question.

"Yes. Eden, I fell in love with you, I want to spend the rest of my life with you. But you fell in love with somebody else. And he gets to marry you. And then probably murder you. But you'd still rather be with him than with me," he finished quietly, unable to look at me.

"Jericho, that's not fair," my voice was hoarse, and the tears had started to pool behind my eyes. "I didn't know you loved me."

"Would it have made a difference?" he asked, tipping his chin my direction.

"No," I choked, the tears spilling onto my cheeks. I couldn't even bend the truth for Jericho. I knew that.

"Why? Why him? Why not me?" he asked simply and I had to fight the emotion to answer him in a voice he could understand.

"It's not that it is 'not you.' And it's not that I don't love you too, because I do," I answered honestly. "Jericho, I do love you. But, not in the same way that I love Kiran. It's like he holds the missing part of my soul." Jericho shook his head and I rushed forward to explain, "I know that sounds cheesy, but it's the truth. Ever since I met Kiran, it's like my body and mind and soul have been fighting to get to him. And not just when we're apart; when we're together too. It's like this all consuming need; I need him. I need to be with him. What we have is love at the deepest meaning of the word. I didn't choose to love Kiran when I met him; in fact I wanted the exact opposite. But it's like I have always loved him, I just had to find him. He is my soul mate, nothing less. And I can love you or anyone else, but it will never be complete like it is with Kiran. It will never be my calling. With him, there is no one else. There can be no one else. And it's the same for him. Does that make sense?" I placed a gentle hand on his, hoping he would look at me and understand.

"No, it doesn't make sense," he grumbled.

"Jericho please. I don't want you to hate me. I couldn't take it," I begged him.

"Eden, I don't hate you," he turned to face me and the emotion behind his blazing eyes took me aback. "I just, I want you to know that I do love you. It's not something I wanted either, but it happened to me too. As strongly as you feel for Kiran, he isn't your only path; you have options." He was so sincere that I wanted to believe him.

But I couldn't. I had tried to stop loving Kiran. I had tried to stay away from him before. We were drawn together and our destiny was clearly not in my control. I smiled at Jericho wanting to explain that, to make sure he was completely clear that there was no chance for us and that I had chosen Kiran forever, for the rest of eternity. I opened my mouth, but a dark figure moved over the rise behind Jericho and I jumped, startled by a tall black man, dressed in dirty work pants and a worn forest-green sweater.

Jericho turned around and stood up, walking over to the man and reaching out his hand.

"I am Jericho," he said plainly and the other man took his hand warmly.

"I am Silas," the man replied with a thick Jamaican accent. He smiled and perfect, white teeth shined in the firelight. "It is a pleasure to meet you."

"Yes, for me, too," Jericho smiled. "Amory sent this for you," he reached into his messenger bag and pulled out a thin manila envelope.

Silas took the envelope and held on to it tightly. His eyes flickered my way, noticing me for the first time and his smile disappeared. He walked slowly to the fire, staring intently at me, his unsettling gray eyes never leaving mine.

"What is your name?" he demanded.

"Eden," I cleared my throat and glanced nervously at Jericho, who stood cautiously behind the man.

"Eden," Silas repeated out loud, saying the name carefully. "Eden," he said again.

Not sure what to do, I looked at Jericho. Maybe he was only told one person would be at the exchange and I had spooked him. I probably should have waited in truck.

"Amory was the one who asked Eden to come," Jericho offered, having the same thoughts I did.

"I am glad that he did," Silas reached out his hand to me and

I took it, shaking it carefully.

When our palms touched, his magic ignited in a painful spark. I wanted to let go, but I couldn't. My magic was too curious to release.

"You are the one," he said, his gray eyes searching mine again, only this time they were friendlier.

"I don't know what you mean?" I looked to Jericho for help, but he stood there silently watching.

"The one. The next Oracle," he said gravely.

"I've been told that before," I admitted humbly.

"It is true," he affirmed and a shiver slithered down my spine. "It will not be easy. There is only pain ahead for you."

I tried to pull my hand away from him, but I couldn't. I was afraid and gave Jericho a frantic look but he was not moving.

"What do you mean?" I asked nervously, not really wanting to hear the answer.

"Pain and sorrow; that is your calling. You must fight through it, though. You cannot be the next Oracle if you let it swallow you whole. Rise up, great one. Rise up and find your destiny." He was squeezing my hand too tightly, it was starting to hurt.

"I don't know what you mean," I cried out in desperation.

"You must find me when everything has ended," he nodded his head, expecting a reply. "You must find me," he demanded.

"Yes, Ok, I will find you," I agreed.

He let go of my hand and turned around. He leaped into the air, turning into a sleek, black panther. I jumped back, not expecting his transformation. Silas, the panther, ran off into the darkness, not looking back and leaving me sitting dumbfounded behind.

"What was that?" I asked, feeling like I was slipping into shock.

"I have no clue," Jericho admitted, loudly. "That was wild," his mood had clearly changed for the better and I found myself irritated by that.

"He's all doom and gloom and suddenly you're in a good mood?" I demanded, standing up and stomping my foot.

"Oh, relax. He's just an old Shape-Shifter. What does he know?" Jericho laughed and I started to see reason.

"You're right. I'm being ridiculous," I shook my head.

"You know, some of the old generation did have the gift of prophesy," Jericho said off- handedly, putting out the fire with his magic.

"Jericho!" I whined, all of my previous fears ignited.

"Come on, Great One, it's time to go home," he started off down the dark trail and I watched after him, stunned for a moment by his audacity, before the wilderness was too much. I ran after Jericho, unwilling to be alone with Silas the panther running around.

Chapter Thirty-Nine

"It was super-disturbing," I declared, propping my feet up on the bar stool that Lilly was occupying next to me.

"Oh, stop being such a baby," Jericho reprimanded from behind the refrigerator door.

We had just gotten home from Texas. The drive had been long and tiring, and I just wanted to go to bed, but as soon as we walked into the house, Roxie and Avalon demanded a debriefing. I knew Amory would be there any minute. But I couldn't stop myself from relaying the details of our prophetic run-in with Silas.

"You sound like you're enjoying this Jericho," Aunt Syl remarked. She was leaning next to me on the kitchen island and I was glad she had picked up on it as well.

""Yes, thank you!" I exclaimed. "Aunt Syl, he has seriously been giddy ever since we left the desert."

"Jericho!" Lilly gasped.

"What?" he closed the refrigerator, opened the freezer and removed a half gallon of chocolate ice cream. "I just don't think Eden should be so upset about it, that's all." He opened the silverware drawer and removed a spoon, digging into the carton of ice cream hungrily.

"Yeah, right," I rolled my eyes. "He's all, 'there's only pain in your future.' And I should just relax."

"Jericho's right," Avalon agreed, picking out his own spoon from the silverware drawer and sharing the ice cream straight from the carton with Jericho. "At least until we ask Amory," Avalon clarified quickly, noticing I was about to protest.

"You guys are disgusting," Roxie said with disbelief.

"What?" They asked in unison, while we stood there watching them eat.

"Well, hello there," Amory said happily, walking in through the garage door. "I'm glad to see you two home, safe and sound." He looked to Jericho and me. "Successful trip?"

"Yes, I think so," Jericho announced, through bites of ice cream.

"Jericho!" I shouted, offended.

"What?" Jericho asked innocently. "I'm just saying, we got

the job done. Oh, and Eden had her future told, that's all. So, all in all, pretty successful trip."

I gave him a look that had daggers behind it, but he just kept eating his ice cream.

"Uh, oh," Amory walked over to Aunt Syl and pulled her into a side hug, kissing her on the cheek. "Would you mind if I borrowed my grandchildren tonight? I would like to work with them on something."

"By all means," Aunt Syl replied sweetly, standing on her tiptoes to return Amory's kiss with one of her own.

"Gross," I cried out. "That is so gross," I covered my eyes and pretended to be severely offended.

"Come now," Amory looked at me disapprovingly.

"Amory you're old enough to be her grandfather," Avalon reminded him sarcastically.

"I'm a lot older than that, child," he joked and we all laughed. "Jericho, why don't you go pick up some pizzas or something, you look like you're starving," Amory handed Jericho a hundred dollar bill that he stuffed into his jean pocket.

"I am," He agreed.

"Jericho," Aunt Syl chided, "I have never seen a person eat more in my life. Between you and Avalon, I'm surprised the grocery stores are able to stay stocked."

"So true," Roxie agreed, still watching in awe as the two boys devoured the contents of the ice cream carton.

"All right, Eden, Avalon, you're with me tonight, let's go," Amory walked back out through the garage door; I followed Avalon out.

Amory had left his black Mercedes running, so we climbed in quickly. I gave Avalon the front seat because I imagined his legs too long for the back seat of a car.

"What do you have in mind, Amory?" Avalon asked, unable to hide his curiosity.

"I want to follow a hunch. We're going to work on something tonight," Amory replied cryptically.

He drove in silence towards Council Bluffs, a city just on the other side of the Missouri River from Omaha. He followed the same route Avalon had taken before; when we worked on my magic the first time I met him. The car wound around the curvy roads of the

Bluffs until we came to an empty parking lot somewhere high above the river and railroad tracks below.

"All right, use your magic to stay warm, but we are going to need a lot of room to work," Amory instructed before getting out of the car.

Avalon gave me a curious look, before following Amory; I was forced to do the same.

The end of January was absolutely freezing with temperatures well below zero and snow covering every inch of the ground. I used magic immediately to warm my body and keep my nose from falling off. I realized I hadn't even grabbed a coat and I was still in the same outfit from the mission.

"What is this about?" Avalon asked Amory, while we stood in a foot and a half of snow.

It was just early evening, but the sky was already black, only this far out from the city a million stars lit up the night from above. From below, the blanket of snow glowed in the dark, creating light enough for us to see each other without magic.

"I know what happened in the Caves in India, Eden. And I want to test a theory," he smiled at me, and when I looked back confused, he continued. "Those Caves hold a special magic, you know this, an exaggerated magic. The wind inside the Caves can read magic and pull it out of the young Immortals. What I think happened to you, is the exact opposite. You, Eden, pulled the Wind into you. Your magic fused with the Wind in a way that now you are capable of manipulating it."

"What do you mean?" I asked, remembering the blue smoke in the bathroom just a few days ago.

"The Forever Winds have never been violent before. Never," Amory turned grave. "And when you walked into those Caves, it was almost like the Wind wanted to hurt you, from how Avalon described it. Maybe even kill you," We both nodded, and Amory continued. "Well, of course, no one like you, an Immortal that had absorbed multiple magics, had ever entered before. At first I thought, maybe the Winds were just confused and had difficulty finding the real source of magic. But, then I realized that you and Avalon possess a new magic, something completely evolved from what the rest of the population holds. So, naturally the Winds saw you as an enemy."

288

"Naturally," I mumbled.

"And then, Eden, you did what you always do, what you do best, you absorbed the magic. Just like every Immortal that has tried to attack you has lost at your hands, so did the Caves," Amory's black eyes twinkled in the darkness. "And now, I think you can control the Wind."

"Haven't I always been able to control the Wind?" I asked, thinking in terms of the natural wind.

"Yes, yes of course. But I mean, the Wind. The Forever Winds."

"What would that mean?" Avalon asked in awe.

"It would mean, you both would wield a power stronger than anything we have seen before," he said with finality and I swallowed loudly. "Go ahead, give it a go." Amory nodded to me. I didn't know what to do.

I reached out my palms and let my magic go; but it was just magic and the leafless tree twenty yards away took the brunt of it.

"Don't think of it like electricity, Eden; it's not. Think of it like the wind, like the breeze and the air, like the force in that Cave," Amory instructed. Avalon watched on, his mouth slightly opened.

"Ok...." I sighed.

I tried again, remembering the necklace and how I had changed the color. I concentrated on that, wanting to change the snow at my feet. And there it was, the blue gush of Wind, coming from nowhere, but with great force. The blue gust of Wind settled at my feet, pooling around my ankles and whisping around me in gentle whirlwinds.

"Fantastic," Amory exclaimed in awe.

"What is it?" Avalon asked, walking carefully closer.

"I have no idea," I answered honestly. I moved the blue smoke around me, showing off.

"What does it do?" Avalon reached down, moving his hand around inside the smoke. I pushed it up his arm and around him, enveloping him inside the dark air.

"I don't know that either," I replied, while Avalon waved his hands in front of his face, trying to see. "Amory, what does it do?"

"Eden, I have never seen anything like it before in my life," Amory mumbled quietly, walking closer to investigate. "Can you

289

always control it?"

"Yes, I can. I mean, as soon as it's there I can control it, but sometimes it just shows up without me, like, calling it," I stumbled through an explanation, trying to find the right words to describe my connection with the wind.

"How interesting," Amory mumbled again. "Avalon can you control the Wind?"

"I can try," Avalon stood up straight and determined. I felt him struggle with the Wind, demanding what it should do, but nothing happened. It didn't take long for him to grow frustrated; a small burst of his electricity escaped into the snow with an explosive pop, sending snow ten feet in the air.

"Take some of my magic, and then try," I offered, feeling Avalon's irritation and wanting to get our emotions under control.

I noticed the smallest escape of magic, from my blood to Avalon's. The feeling wasn't unpleasant and I barely noticed, but it was the first time I had physically felt Avalon take magic from me. In the past, I had been distracted enough to not notice the exchange.

Once Avalon had borrowed my magic, he could manipulate the blue smoke just as easily as I could. He had fun, sending it high up into the air, rushing it quickly into the forest and then back again and wrapping it around me, mummifying me in thick, blue, magical air. But one thing was clear, my magic was necessary to control the Wind, it belonged to me and not Avalon.

"This is truly fascinating," Amory said in awe.

"But you have never seen this before?" Avalon asked, slightly distracted by the fun he was having with the smoke.

"Never," Amory answered with finality.

"So we have no idea what it does then? Besides this?" Avalon demonstrated by swirling the air around, boomeranging it fifty yards out and then bringing it back to him.

"That is correct," Amory agreed. "I want you two to be working with it though, on a daily basis. If there is more to this.... smoke, than meets the eye, I would like to get to the bottom of it. If it can be used as a weapon, we need to know. Study it, work with it, and find out what it does. This could be a vital tool in the near future, and I want every advantage on our side."

"What do you mean?" I gasped, a haunting feeling of foreshadowing washing over me.

"Kiran has asked for your hand, Eden," Amory cleared off an iron bench with his magic and took a seat. Avalon and I followed him, waiting for more of an explanation. "He approached me yesterday, while you were away and asked permission to marry you."

"Haven't we been expecting that?" Avalon asked.

"Yes, we have," Amory said thoughtfully. "But he wants to take Eden back to London with him at the end of the month, and marry her later this spring."

The weight of Amory's words hit me like a slap in the face. London? This spring? I could barely comprehend marriage in a few short months. And how would I ever be able to leave my family here and move to London? But how could I say no to the man that I loved? My heart felt ripped in two, and my stomach was on the verge of emptying itself. Nothing was easy in this world. Not having a boyfriend. Not having a family. And certainly not having a mind of my own. Whichever way I played out the scenario in my head, the end result felt simply hopeless.

Chapter Forty

"I don't understand, isn't that a good thing?" I asked Amory. I was mulling over the idea of a spring wedding in my head. Even though I felt severely unprepared, I still couldn't help but feel that a wedding to Kiran was a better alternative to civil war. I snuggled closer to Avalon, feeling more unsettled than ever.

"Yes, I think it is," Amory stared at the sparkling snow in the darkness pensively. "I am hoping that it is."

"Then what is it?" Avalon, the strategic part of his mind working hard to catch up to Amory, spoke up.

"I can't put my finger on it exactly," Amory replied carefully, "This is very uncharacteristic of Lucan. He doesn't have a history of working so.... carefully. I have watched him grow into the tyrant he is. Hell, I watched his father, and his father's father become tyrants. Lucan is effective, he is efficient, but he is not careful. And he is definitely not forgiving. Whatever his motives are for allowing this union, are purely selfish."

"But that doesn't mean they are bad for us, does it?" I asked innocently, wanting to hope for the best.

"No, you're right; it doesn't mean they are bad. Or will turn out bad. I just can't seem to shake.... this feeling," Amory lifted his head and looked me directly in the eyes. His black, onyx eyes seemed to be endless, filled with depth and love, and I could hardly look at him without bursting into tears.

"Kiran wouldn't let him do anything bad," I shook my head, wanting to reassure my grandfather. "He will protect me. I trust him," I whispered and then threw my arms around Amory's neck, feeling like a small child that needed comforting.

"I know that, dear," he said quietly. "He will protect you, I know that."

I sat back and wiped my eyes. Everything was going to be Ok. We were just in uncharted territory, and nobody really knew what to do. It was natural to have doubts.

"Besides when I'm Queen I can settle everything diplomatically. There won't be any need for a war or more fighting or whatever," I folded my arms proudly.

"Oh really? You're just going to change all the laws, make

everyone equal, and just order every one not to be racist anymore?" Avalon rolled his eyes at me.

"Yes," I said simply. "What else am I going to do? I can't be Queen of a Kingdom where people are oppressed. This isn't just about me; I get that. I mean, yes, I get what I want too, but the whole position of leadership, place of influence, like that's my calling, and I get that. This is the end of it all, Avalon. You don't have to fight because I'm going to change it all." I finished passionately and leaned my head against his shoulder. I had been holding these feelings in for way too long, it was time I said them out loud and put pressure behind my ideals.

"That sounds wonderful, Sis, but I'm just not sure it's possible," Avalon replied quietly.

"It's possible, Avalon," Amory interrupted. "It has to be. And if not Eden, then you will be the one to save your people. You two are the hope for this Kingdom. The only hope for survival we have left. And if you fail, so will your people."

Avalon and I didn't respond. We couldn't respond. There was nothing to say; we felt the truth of Amory's words as deeply as we felt our magic and had long ago accepted our fate.

"I need you two to listen to me," Amory began again, and I physically felt the gravity of his words grip my heart, "The Crown belongs to you, both of you. You are the rightful heirs to the Monarchy and I believe with all of my heart that you are capable of commanding the Titans. If things with Eden and Kiran fail...." He paused for a moment and I took the opportunity to chime in. "They won't," I interjected.

Amory held his hand up, stopping me, "Eden, until you appeared, continuing the Kendrick line has never been a possibility. You are the only thing stopping me from ending the entire existence of that family; that needs to be clear. We need to have a conversation about every possibility. I am not going to be around forever. You two hold the key to salvation for our people; you will be the ones to carry the torch. Listen to me."

I wanted to argue. I wanted to remind him that he already had been around forever and that he wasn't going anywhere. I wanted to cover my ears and run away, unbelieving there could ever be a different possibility that didn't involve Amory; but I kept my mouth shut. I decided for his sake I would listen, I wouldn't take him seriously, but I would listen.

"Since the Titans signed the blood oath to the Monarchy, the people, including me, have always believed the oath was made to the Kendricks," Amory continued, "But events in recent years have suggested that maybe that isn't the truth."

"Like what?" Avalon asked, anxious for more information.

"Well, starting with your grandfather. Barrick, your grandfather on your father's side was a Titan. What no one knew until your grandmother's famous betrayal was that Celia was not a Titan; she was a Shape-Shifter. They married in secret. This was a direct violation to the Monarchy and Barrick knew that; yet he didn't die until after your parents disappeared. What I'm saying, is that if the oath was made to the Monarchy, then it should have been binding; he should have died immediately. Then, your father Justice also betrayed the Crown and ran away with your mother. He also should have died; yet here you two are. Furthermore, you both possess the Titan bloodline, but especially Avalon, who holds no reverence for the Crown. Finally, and this is the last piece of the puzzle, but also just a theory, the other Titans you two have gone up against, have all fallen at your hands. I believe this has something to do with your twin connection and your solid Immortality; but another hunch I have formed recently is that their allegiance was made to our bloodline, not the Kendricks."

"But what about the three guards that got away, at the mall?" I asked, trying to put all of the pieces together.

"They're dead," Avalon answered coldly. "Their bodies were found while you were in Texas. Titus and Xander discovered them in London."

"But they were already sick with the King's Curse," I reminded them.

"Like I said, it's just a hunch," Amory admitted, "But it's worth looking into, especially since the Titans will be the first of our people to die out if interracial marriage isn't reinstituted soon."

"Why?" I asked, one step behind like usual.

"Because women are scarce in their kind. There aren't enough women as it is; their numbers are dwindling severely with each generation. If Lucan keeps this up, or Kiran, they will die out soon enough," Amory answered. I shuddered remembering the attraction between Lilly and Talbott. It seemed so long ago; now it seemed so impossible, but also soberingly necessary. Amory continued, "The most difficult obstacle you will face, however, is convincing the Titans you deserve their allegiance."

"Most difficult?" Avalon cut in, "Try impossible."

"Yes, I suppose so. You will need to find your father; if they could see Justice then they would know. They would understand then," Amory said with finality.

"Our parents? But how? You don't even know where they are...." I reminded him.

"That's true. If things go south, if things should get bad and I were not here, I believe they will come out of hiding. They would have to," Amory said quietly, as if to himself.

"Where would we start?" Avalon asked, always the strategic thinker.

"South America. Silas was in contact with them not too long ago and I have no reason to believe they would have moved on."

"Like the whole of South America? That's what we have to go on?" I asked in disbelief.

"Yes, it's better than the whole world," Amory replied snidely and I couldn't help but laugh at his sarcastic humor.

"You're right," I had to admit. "Wait. You don't mean Silas as in Black Panther Silas do you?"

"Yes, I suppose, I do. Although, Eden, he is the oldest living Shape-Shifter and I don't think anyone refers to him as Black Panther Silas," Amory scolded with an amused twinkle in his eye.

"Well, I do. He totally creeps me out," I grumbled.

"Whatever for?" Amory asked incredulously.

"He told Eden her life was going to be full of pain and suffering. That made her mad," Avalon tattled on me, so I elbowed him in the rib.

"Is that true?" Amory asked.

"Yes, he was all, your future is full of pain, but don't let it swallow you, and then he called me the next Oracle, and then he told me to find him when it was all over. Oh, and he kept calling me Great One," I explained a little over-dramatically.

"He is the second person to call you the next Oracle, Eden," Avalon pushed my shoulder, making fun of me. He was right though. Silas and the old gypsy lady had both called me the next Oracle.

"What does that mean Amory?" I asked in a quiet voice.

"Hmmm...." Amory's black eyes turned to stone and although his expression was almost unreadable, the fear I felt earlier resurfaced. "I hope that my suspicions are merely being confirmed, that you two are truly Immortal. The woman in Romania, was there any defining feature to her? Something that made her unique from other humans?"

"Well, I don't know. She seemed to know me, like she knew exactly who I was, but she didn't have any magic. Oh, and she had violet eyes. Like Angelica's. Yes, just like Angelica's," I remembered.

"She must have been magic then. Some of the old Shape-Shifters, the very old ones had the power of prophecy, nothing that was completely clear or vivid, but they had visions. There is a Shape-Shifter colony in Romania. Not a big one, in fact, it's very small. I wonder...." Amory trailed off and I didn't know how to prompt him to continue, because I could barely comprehend what he had already told me.

"So what does that mean?" Avalon asked for me. "If she was going to be Queen, they would have said Queen, wouldn't they?" A flicker of panic flashed though Avalon's blood and I felt it as if it were my own.

"That may be true," Amory replied calmly. "But they also wouldn't have called her the next Oracle if she were going to be martyred."

Avalon relaxed and so did I. Amory was right. There wouldn't be prophecies about me if I was going to die before my wedding night.... or the night after, for that matter.

"Whatever happens," Amory started. "Eden, Avalon, look at me." We obeyed immediately, "Whatever happens my dears, know that watching you two become who you are today has been the greatest gift of my life," he paused for a moment as if collecting himself and a hot tear escaped the corner of my eye without permission, wetting my lashes and leaving a trail of emotion down my cheek. "This life, this over-exaggerated life I have lived, was wasted until I found you. You have given me purpose, you have given me hope, and I believe in the core of my being that you are our salvation."

Amory reached over to me, pulling me into a hug, and then

beyond me to Avalon. We were speechless. I stayed close to Amory, relishing the moment and trying to shake off the horrible feeling that this was goodbye. London wasn't the end of the world, and marriage wouldn't mean I would never see my family again. But I didn't dare move from that moment; for fear that I was wrong. For fear that this was goodbye.

Chapter Forty-One

"Eden, there's someone here to see you," Aunt Syl poked her head into my bedroom door where I was in the middle of watching a movie with Lilly and Roxie. We were all lying on my bed quite comfortably and I was reluctant to move from the warmth of the covers.

"Who is it?" I asked sleepily. It was only late afternoon, but the sun was already low on the horizon and I had a terrible time trying to sleep after Amory had dropped Avalon and me off late last night.

"Kiran," My aunt said with a smirk.

I didn't respond, but jumped out of bed, running to the mirror. I rubbed my fingers quickly under my tired eyes, trying to fix my smudged eye liner. I pulled my black, impossible hair out its pony tail and tried to arrange it with my fingers, but it wouldn't lay right; so I threw it back up into a pony tail. I straightened out my hooded sweatshirt and exchanged my sweatpants for a pair of jeans lying on the floor. I was thankful they were Lilly's and not Roxie's and consequently long enough for me. I gave her a thankful smile and then walked casually out of the bedroom and down the stairs.

Kiran was standing in the living room with his back to me, hands deep in his pockets and rocking back and forth on his heels. I looked around for signs of Jericho or Avalon, but remembered they had gone to the farm to work with some younger recruits who had just arrived.

"Hey," I said quietly, reaching the hardwood floor at the bottom of the stairs.

"Hey," Kiran turned around nervously. "Hi," he repeated.

"Hi," I echoed, and realized I was just as nervous.

"I'm sorry to just pop over," he took a step forward and then back as if he wasn't sure he should touch me or not. This was the first time we had seen each other since his engagement had been called off and I didn't think either one of us knew what to do, there was too much pressure.

"No, really, it's fine. I was just watching a movie."

"Oh, right," he ran his hands through his messy hair and looked up at me from under his eye lashes. "Can we go somewhere?"

"Yes," I sighed, relieved. It was still Kiran. There was nothing to be nervous about. We were meant to be together, and it wasn't like we would be getting married tonight. "I would like that," I smiled.

"Good," he smiled back, his soft, genuine smile with mischievous eyes that sent butterflies soaring in my stomach.

"Um, can I change first?" I asked, noticing his designer jeans and navy blue sweater. He looked handsome and dressed up and my old sweatshirt and borrowed jeans wasn't going to cut it.

"Of course," he backed away, taking a seat on the couch.

"I'll just be a second," I promised, turning on my heel and running up the stairs straight into my closet.

"What's going on?" Lilly asked, with the obvious tones of excitement in her voice.

"I don't know," I replied honestly, "he just wants to go somewhere," I turned around for a second and smiled widely.

Lilly let out a quiet squeal and jumped to her knees on the bed, bouncing an irritated Roxie around. "So do you think this is it? Do you think he's going to ask?" She whispered, pointing at her ring finger.

"I have no idea!" I whispered back, throwing clothing item after clothing item on the floor. What did one wear to a possible proposal?

"The purple one," Lilly demanded, pointing to a plum-colored short sweater dress. "With black tights and black high-heeled boots."

"And use magic on your hair," Roxie offered with an obvious lack of interest.

I obeyed, all of their suggestions. I used magic on my hair and on the static from the sweater, turning around for them and gaining nods of approval. I sprinted to Aunt Syl's bathroom where I freshened up my makeup and grabbed the pendant Kiran had given me. I left the stone black, deciding the best way to accessorize, and grabbed some silver hoops that I put on while walking back towards the stairs.

"Hey, Eden," Roxie called from the bedroom. I paused and poked my head back inside the room.

"You look gorgeous!" Lilly squealed again.

299

"Hey," Roxie pulled my attention back to here. "Do you mind if we go to the farm, too? Since you won't even be here?"

"No, I don't mind at all. Have fun!" I said genuinely.

"You, too!" Lilly could barely contain her exhilaration and I found it catching. I walked down the stairs a ball of frenzied energy.

"Wow," Kiran stood up from the couch, pleased with my transformation.

"I have a gift," I joked.

"I don't think I will ever grow tired of how beautiful you are," He smirked at me, and I felt the heat flood my cheeks. "Every time I see you, I am moved by your beauty." He closed the distance between us and pulled me into a kiss. His mouth met mine with the force of his frenetic magic and we collided into bliss.

I let him hold me at the bottom of the steps, reminding me of the depth of my feelings for him and the hope for a future together. His mouth moved against mine with the passion belonging only to a man lost in love; he held me to him, melting his soul into mine.

"Let's get out of here, huh?" He pulled away reluctantly, pressing his forehead against mine and closing his eyes as if parting our lips took sacrifice.

"Yes, please," I whispered and then louder, "Aunt Syl, I'll be back later."

"Ok, dear," she called back from the kitchen.

"Where's Talbott?" I asked, teeth chattering once we were out of the house and into the frozen night.

"He had other plans this evening," Kiran replied without looking at me.

He walked me to a brand-new, black sports car and opened the door for me. I climbed in and buckled up, remembering his need for speed. He joined me and then took off through the twilight streets of the neighborhood and downtown to his loft.

We walked silently through the old building's doors and onto the elevators. He reached for my hand and I let him, swept away with the sweet gesture. The elevator rose slowly to the top floor and when the doors opened I gasped, afraid to move.

Kiran's apartment had been transformed from a manly loft into the most romantic setting I could have ever imagined. The room was lit by skinny, ivory candles sitting in elegant silver candelabras placed all over the room. The high top table had been replaced by a small one that sat lower to the ground and was covered with a black table cloth and silver platters, holding amazing looking appetizers and desserts. Full floral arrangements with the most delicate white flowers on every surface enhanced the room, and instead of the giant couches from before, the floor was covered with a white silk blanket and Middle Eastern style table that sat on the floor surrounded with colorful, embroidered pillows.

Kiran pulled me into his loft still wearing his smirk. We walked silently to the low table. He sat down first, tugging at my hand for me to join him. I couldn't resist and so I sat down too, snuggled in luxuriously soft pillows with the most intricate, exotic designs on them, leaning into Kiran and breathing him in.

"Eden, my love," he said in a low voice, "you are always a surprise to me, never doing what I expect or what you should." He laughed sweetly, clearly not meaning it as an insult. "And because of that, ever since I met you, my life has been unexpected. I could never have predicted we would be sitting here today, free of my betrothal and with the blessings of both my father and your grandfather."

I looked up at him suddenly, realizing for the first time completely where this was going. I swallowed, finding strength in the confidence of Kiran's eyes. My hands started to shake and I was completely at a loss for words.

"Before you," Kiran continued, "I did not know love could exist like this.... So all consuming.... So powerful.... So.... Binding. But that is the thing, Eden, I am bound to you, completely. And now that I have found you, there is only one way for me to live, only one way that I can live and that is with you as my wife."

Tears pooled behind my eyes. Kiran moved from behind me, to on his knee in front of me, taking my trembling hand in his, "Eden, my love, this is only the beginning. We have eternity to walk hand in hand and explore the depths of this love. That is, if you will have me." I sat speechless, as Kiran reached into his pocket and pulled out a small black box. Opening it, he asked, "Eden, will you marry me?"

"Yes! Yes! A thousand times yes!" I found my voice and answered with more confidence than I had felt up until that moment. It wasn't the romantic setting, it wasn't even the gigantic emerald stone Kiran was taking from its place in the box and slipping onto my ring finger. It was him; it was always him. There was no answer; there was no thought, other than yes.

He slipped the ring all the way onto my finger and then found my mouth again, pulling me down with him to the floor. Our magics crashed into each other in an ecstatic collision of euphoria. He wrapped me into himself, his arms holding me tightly to him and his mouth unrelenting against mine. The tears waiting impatiently behind closed eyes finally escaped in hot streams, reminding me how deeply the love we shared was felt.

Happiness was all consuming and hope for the future finally a concrete stamp on my heart. There were no more thoughts about uncertainties or impossibilities. The next Oracle was a fleeting idea. The next Queen was the sure path, the only future for me. I could have it all.

"All right, I'm hungry," Kiran declared, but didn't move from our position on the floor.

We had been laying there for hours, permanent extensions of each other, wrapped in our exclusive magic and dreaming about our future together. I had been holding my ring finger up for the better part of an hour, listening to his soft accent paint pictures of London and a wedding ceremony and children.

The gray sky had turned black and the candles burned low. I turned to face him, unwilling to let him go, not even for a moment.

"Aren't you hungry?" He asked, his smirk in place and his turquoise eyes smoldering.

"Not hungry enough to let you get up," I kissed him, hoping to distract him and it worked.

He kissed me back, each kiss growing more feverish, desperate for more. I reached my hand into his dirty blonde locks, tangling them inside his thick waves and maneuvering him on top of me. He sighed with the sweetness of complete happiness and I couldn't stop my smile, even if it stopped our kiss.

"And what's so funny?" He looked down at me amused.

"Nothing. Absolutely nothing," I smiled wider. "I just didn't know that this kind of happiness existed, that's all," my smile grew even bigger and I thought I would burst from bliss.

302

Kiran's aqua eyes clouded for a moment, changing their color to a deep navy blue. He pulled away, propping himself up on a bent elbow. "Eden, will you remember this? Will you remember how happy you are in this moment?" His forehead wrinkled and the concern on his face was real.

"Of course, I will," I promised. "I don't know how I could forget," I said with finality, lifting my head up to kiss him gently on the lips.

"And is this happiness.... Am I.... Am I worth this?" he asked self-consciously.

"Yes. Yes, you are," I assured him with the deepest sincerity I could convey. "There is no other way for me, Kiran. This happiness only exists with you. It's the only way for me."

"All right. Good," he smirked again. "Then we are going to need some sustenance. Forever doesn't happen without a few supplies," he winked at me, standing up and walking over to the table covered with food.

"I suppose," I sighed, sitting up and arranging pillows behind me, so we could eat comfortably.

The elevator dinged, startling us both. Kiran set down the trays of food he had prepared to bring over and walked to the elevator, a dark look masking his face. I sat still, wondering who could possibly be interrupting our evening.

The doors opened and somehow I wasn't surprised when Sebastian walked out, with wet hair and wearing a thick coat covered in snow. He looked like he had been standing outside for a very long time. I wondered if since Talbott was off doing something else, Sebastian had been tasked with guarding Kiran's building.

"Sebastian?" Kiran asked in an obviously worried tone.

"May I speak with you for a moment?" Sebastian didn't wait for an answer, but walked straight into one of the bedrooms.

"Excuse me for a moment, Love," Kiran turned to apologize to me before following Sebastian.

I sat alone in the living room for a few minutes before standing up and walking over to the food. Now that I was alone, I found that I was hungry. I picked at tiny appetizers that held more flavor than I thought possible and poured a glass of champagne.

"Eden, I'm so sorry," Kiran began immediately after exiting the bedroom a few minutes later. "My father needs me. I am terribly sorry, but I shouldn't be gone long."

Kiran looked at me, and I couldn't help but feel that something was wrong. His eyes were panicked and he had already put a coat on. He walked hurriedly over to me, kissing me on the cheek and turning around before I had a chance to say anything.

"Sebastian will keep you company. I won't be long," he smiled, but it didn't reach his eyes and then he was on the elevator and pushing buttons.

"Ok," was all I could get out before the doors were closed and he was gone.

Sebastian walked out of the bedroom without his coat on but with dry hair. He had changed from jeans into sweatpants and a t-shirt. He smiled at me, but his smile too did not reach his eyes.

"Is there a problem?" I asked tentatively, feeling awkward with only Sebastian there.

"No, not at all," he turned the lights on with his magic, and I was thankful for that. "Congratulations by the way. I am told I will call you my Queen one day," his eyes flickered to my ring finger.

"One day...." I replied awkwardly. I didn't really know how to reply to that. "Would you like some food?" I offered, trying to find normal with Sebastian.

"No, thank you," he walked over to the window, staring out it intensely. I noticed for the first time that it was snowing. Although it was only the first of February, I hoped that we would be done with snow and start getting ready for spring.

"Sebastian, please." I was really starting to worry. "If something is wrong, please tell me."

"Nothing is wrong Eden," he turned around, a smile on his face and I wanted to believe him, but that was when I heard the first terrifying scream.

Eden! I covered my ears and bent my head, trying to protect myself from the agony. But the sound wasn't coming from the room I was in. The sound was coming from inside my head.

It was Avalon. And he was in pain. And in trouble. And I was here, away from it all.

I looked up at Sebastian while my brother screamed for help inside of my head and realized that we had been set up.

I had been set up.

Chapter Forty-Two

"Where's Kiran," I growled at Sebastian, simultaneously comforting Avalon inside of my head, assuring him I would be there soon.

"He went to help his father. He will be back soon," Sebastian answered, in cool, rehearsed tones.

Another ear splitting scream from Avalon and I saw through his eyes for a moment. He was at the farm, surrounded by Titans. They all were. All of the people I loved. And they were being attacked. The Resistance was strong, but there were too many Titans.

"What is happening?" I screamed at Sebastian, coming back into my own vision again. "What are you doing to them?"

Sebastian looked at me curiously for a moment, "What am I doing to whom?"

"My friends! My family!" I shouted, trying to suppress Avalon's screams for help for just a moment just until I could figure this out.

"But how could you possibly know that?" Sebastian asked in disbelief.

"Because I do. Now damn it Sebastian, tell me what is happening," I stomped my foot. When he remained silent, I lashed out in anger, flinging him across the room with a burst of magic. "Tell me!" I screamed.

He recovered; standing up, full of rage. "What do you think is happening, Eden?" he yelled. "Did you really think this would be that easy? Did you really think Lucan would just let you marry his son without an exchange? Without something for himself? There was a trade, Eden."

"What do you mean?" my voice dropped to a whisper, horrified by Sebastian's accusations.

"We've known for a while, about you and your.... brother." Sebastian explained haughtily, the smug look that made my stomach churn plastering his face.

"But how?"

"Truthfully, it was Kiran. He had suspected for a while, the way you two acted around each other, the coincidental family

306

features, his arrogant over-protectiveness. And his last name. 'St. Andrews' isn't really all that hard to figure out. So when Lucan met him at Kiran's birthday party, there was nothing else to uncover. Your traitor parents had twins."

"So?" My voice was gaining volume again, "So what is the trade?"

"Your brother. Kiran can have you, he can marry you, he can do whatever he wants to with you. That is why Lucan called off the engagement with Seraphina, he doesn't need you to get what he wants, he has your brother. Or he will have your brother," I flinched, unbelieving, but that only gave Sebastian the confidence to continue, "Lucan had always planned to use you, no matter what Kiran's sentiments were, Lucan has had bigger plans. But when it came to light that you had a twin brother who would work just as well, he decided to be diplomatic and let his son have you. Either way, the bloodline will be secured and father and son can live out eternity together," a sick smile twisted Sebastian's lips and I turned my head, emptying it of everything I had eaten today.

"And Kiran knew? He knew that he was giving Lucan, Avalon?" I turned my head again, waiting to be sick.

"Of course. Of course he knew. It was his idea. How else was he going to get you? You should really be thanking him, if he hadn't figured out that Avalon was your twin, it would be you up on the chopping block instead of him," he let out a cruel laugh that echoed inside of my head, right next to deafening cries of the brother that had been sacrificed for my happiness.

"He'll never get him. Avalon is untouchable. And Amory is there. Those people will fight to the death to protect him," I stood up again, letting the fear and anger fuel my courage.

"Ha. Those people are nothing but weak throw-aways. They are nothing compared to the full force of the Guard," he scoffed at me.

"Then where did Kiran go?" I asked snidely.

"Well, all right, Amory is somewhat of a problem. But not for long, you can trust me on that. The old man has seen the last of his days, this is the end for him," Sebastian leaned back against the wall, crossing his arms and smiling.

"So what will you do with Avalon once you get him? What will happen to him?" I asked, devising a plan while the battle scene played through my head.

"He will be sacrificed, of course. Lucan will sacrifice him and take his magic. Simple," he said with finality.

"And me?" I asked bravely, not afraid of the answer.

"You get everything you want. You get Kiran and you get a crown. What more is there?" He laughed again, the short, twisted laughter of the very depraved.

"What more is there?" I stomped my foot and the floor shook underneath the force of my magic. "How about my brother? And my grandfather! How about the people I love remaining unharmed?" I screamed.

"Eden, these are the consequences you pay for happiness, don't you get that? Kiran did this for you. This is all being done for you. Just relax, he'll be home soon, and then you can talk to him about it." Sebastian rolled his eyes.

"You know what?" I asked sarcastically. "I don't think I can wait. I think I'm going to go find him right now." I paused for a dramatic moment, "Yep, yes, I'm going to go find him right now."

"Um, no you're not," a flash of worry crossed Sebastian's face and he moved in front of the elevator doors as if that would stop me.

"Get out of my way Sebastian. You do not want to meet my magic," I threatened in a deep, growly voice.

"Eden, I don't want to fight you, but I have been ordered not to let you leave," he crossed his arms and stared me down.

"Oh, really? Then they really should have sent more than just you," I looked at him with pity for the smallest of seconds before sending the force of my magic at him; knocking him back against the elevator doors, bending the metal and opening them several inches.

Sebastian stood up quickly, sending magic my way. The burst hit me in the stomach knocking me back, but not over. I countered with another burst of magic that he dodged by diving behind the kitchen island and my magic hit the range above the stove sending stainless steel flying. I knocked over the refrigerator with my magic before Sebastian could react and he was pinned for a moment before throwing the huge piece of appliance off of him and jumping to his feet again.

"You're going to have to do better than that Eden!" Sebastian screamed at me, sending magic my way in short bursts. Some hit me, some missed, but I dove behind the couch to stay away from the pain.

"Fine, but try to remember you asked for it!" I shouted at him. I stood up quickly to face him and held out my palm, drawing his magic to me. He fought me, sending his magic in painful waves, but they were weakening as I drew out his magic and I was only growing stronger.

I stood up straighter, as he crumpled to the ground in a weakened heap on the floor. I continued to pull and drain every last ounce of magic, leaving him completely weakened and defenseless.

"Like I said, they should have sent more than just you," I wanted to finish him, to use his pathetic magic-less state and destroy him. I had never been more vengeful in my life and I was blind with rage, but I couldn't. I wasn't a murderer. Even when he was an accomplice to the destruction of my family, I couldn't kill him.

He groaned from the floor, reaching a tired, shaking hand out to me. "Don't stop now Eden," he mumbled humorously. "Finish it," he demanded, spitting with the force of his words.

"No," I said, venom dripping in the one syllable. "You deserve a fate worse than death," I lifted him off of the ground with magic, forcing him to look me in the eye, "If something happens to my brother, if one little hair on his head is damaged, I will hunt you down Sebastian."

He smirked at me, hoping for the death he thought I was promising.

"I will hunt you down," I continued, "and make you watch as I do this same little number on Amelia. Then you will know what it's like to be responsible for the death of your sibling," I watched the panicked hysteria flood his face before I threw him against the wall, crashing him into the huge flat-screen TV and rendering him unconscious.

I left him on the floor, in a puddle of blood and raced to the elevators, using magic to accelerate the speed. I was to the bottom floor in a second and out onto the street in two more. It had started to snow heavily by now and the streets were blanketed with fresh, pure snow. I ran across the street to the first fast car I could find and blew open the door with magic.

I started the car the same way and was racing down the

309

streets of Omaha as fast as the car would let me go. I had to get to the farm. I had to help save the Resistance. I was the one who had made them vulnerable. I was the one who had opened them up for attack. And I was even still the one they were fighting to protect.

But I had to be the one to save Avalon. I couldn't let him take my place as sacrifice. He was destined for greatness, not to die meaninglessly at the hands of Lucan. Something had gone terribly wrong. This was not the future I had been promised.

I was what went wrong. I was the problem. If it weren't for me, Avalon wouldn't be in danger, Amory wouldn't have to be fighting to save his grandchild and their group of loyal followers wouldn't be martyring themselves to right my wrong.

But more than me, Kiran was to blame. Kiran, the man I had envisioned a lifetime of perfect happiness with. The man who had just asked me to marry him. The man who had promised such sweet lies. He was to blame.

I leaned over in the car and vomited again. How could I have been so blind? How could I have been so naive?

He was a snake. He promised me happiness in one hand and betrayed me at the deepest level with the other. Happiness was not only impossible for us, it was impossible with this life. This life that suddenly held no meaning without my grandfather. Without my brother. With the blood of hundreds of people on my hands.

I would rectify this. I would make Kiran pay. I had no other choice. I would save Avalon and then I would finish Kiran, for good. And not have another thought about him again.

Chapter Forty-Three

By the time I reached the farmhouse, visibility was near zero. The heavy snow fall had turned into a blizzard and road conditions were dangerous. I threw caution to the wind, however, hitting the gravel road with my foot pressed firmly down on the gas pedal. I used magic to keep the car on the road and took the long drive in seconds.

I slammed on the brakes, jumping out of the car before it had completely stopped. Unnoticed, I stood in mortified awe for a moment watching the battle from afar. The discarded car rolled into a ditch. I could hear the windshield wipers squeak against the glass, as I decided how I would fit myself into the destruction.

The snow blurred the lines between Immortals fighting each other. The metal barn doors had been blown off, and the florescent lights from the structured ceiling bounced an eerie glow onto the wall of snow. Blasts of magic and explosions of electricity were the only other light sources in the gray blizzard of mayhem.

I stumbled forward, not knowing where to start. There were too many people in trouble, too many Guards to fight. A tear slipped from the corner of my eye; in the pit of my stomach grew the hopelessness, a feeling, only hours ago I thought I had banished forever.

Angelica, the wise, old woman lay pinned underneath the magic of a brutish Titan, his lips curled into the satisfaction of dominance. The image of the kind woman with bright violet eyes, twitching in pain, her long gray hair loosed and highlighted with crimson blood, broke something inside of me. In that moment I lost a good piece of me, a piece that stood for justice and virtue.

In its place grew the darkness of hate and righteous anger. A sticky, consuming cloud of malicious vengeance spread through my veins like wild fire and clarity found me. Dangerous, vengeful clarity cleared my mind and I let out a feral battle cry, announcing that I had arrived.

I started with Angelica, blasting the Titan away from her and slamming him against the white porch of the farmhouse. I heard his bones break and the crash of the wood from the porch echoed on the muffled, blizzarded battlefield.

I watched the Titan stand up slowly, healing his body while trying to identify the source who had sent him flying. I pulled the roof above him down before he could heal any further and then reached out my palm, draining his magic faster than I ever had before.

I wanted to run to Angelica, to move her, to help her, but there were others in more peril. Fiona, Ryder's wife was facing two Titans who were laughing back and forth as if her destruction was a joke. I was at her side in seconds, sending the two of them flying and taking their magic before they hit the ground.

There were more, nameless Resistance members, that I hadn't taken the time to meet or hadn't had the chance, but needed my help. The farm was surrounded by the brutal Guard, and the more Titans I destroyed, the more seemed to pop up, greedily taking the lives of the innocent.

I was furious, blinded by rage. I was the collector of Immortal magic, taking from those who killed so easily and saving those helpless souls that I had betrayed. I moved from one fight to the other, knowing the heart wrenching truth, that as soon as I moved on they would be caught in another unwinnable battle. But I had no choice. I had to find Avalon, I had to protect Avalon.

In the back of my mind, I thought fleetingly over what I would do, should I meet Kiran in the middle of this. I wanted revenge. I wanted death. With so many innocent lives staining my hands, what was one more righteous kill?

The Titans just kept coming. They surrounded me time and time again, three or four of their kind tried to stop me, but I couldn't even hesitate before draining them of their life's blood and leaving them weakened and incapacitated on the frozen ground.

The sky continued to wage its own war against the earth. The blizzard intensified, the snow blinding visibility and the wind whipping violently through the open fields of the farm land.

I couldn't see Avalon; I would have to feel where he was. I paused for a moment over my latest victim and turned my attention to him. He was fighting Kiran, a well-matched battle on its own, but Kiran had the help of a dozen Guards. Avalon was losing. These guards were the cream of the crop, their magic not quite so easily accessible. I finally recognized their location through the wall of snow. They were back by the horses, through the metal barn.

I turned, intending to find Avalon but a Titan stood in my way. His arms were crossed with the look of intended evil, a dark mask in the ghostly glow of the snow.

"Are you the one causing so much trouble?" he growled in a dementedly-amused voice.

"You're going to want to get out of my way," I threatened, finding myself severely irritated with the interruption.

Deep, rumbling laughter filled the white void, causing my skin to crawl and my stomach to churn. And before I could react he sent me flying across the driveway and into the frozen garden. I landed deep inside the snow, my muscles and bones jarred from the impact with the arctic ground.

I took a moment to recover and it was a moment too long. The Titan was on top of me again sending the full force of his magic raining down. I screamed out, writhing in agony.

My pain only encouraged the Titan and he pressed his magic down harder. I screamed again, only with magic behind it, and the Titan was pushed back several feet. I stood up, the weight of his electricity still oppressive, but lessened.

I reached my hand out in front of me, and forced my magic to resurface. I sent the man to the ground with a forceful blow, calling upon dozens of stolen magics. Surprised, the man looked up at me, but the advantage was already mine. With one hand pinning him to the ground, I used the other to pull his magic, claiming it as my own.

The process was slow. He was a fighter and had no intention of losing to me. I was growing impatient. The longer I stood there with that man, the longer Avalon had to fight alone. Finally, the last drops of electricity were gone from the arrogant Titan's blood and I moved on, already forgetting about my discarded enemy.

I ran into the barn, my high heel boots skidding across the wet concrete floor. I stopped, afraid to move, afraid to go forward. Amory and Lucan faced off amid the turmoil that was once an organized meeting place. Back and forth went their magic, from King to Oracle, from ancient to tyrant.

I didn't know whether to jump into the fight, or continue on and find Avalon. Amory could surely take care of himself. But Lucan looked determined to do what no other Immortal had yet been able to, to kill him. I couldn't make myself move forward, this

314

fight would decide all of the others.

"Give up, old man!" Lucan shouted from across the barn.

"Will you finally put me out of my misery?" Amory asked, his voice full of dark amusement.

"I'd be glad to," Lucan smirked, a purely evil version of Kiran's. He sent a burst of magic towards Amory that exploded at his feet, a trick I had yet to learn. Amory walked out of the smoke, unharmed, sending one back at Lucan that landed just to the right of him. "Think of it this way; if I get your ancient magic, there will be no need for me to sacrifice your grandson."

"There would be no need, but that won't stop you from murdering him anyway," Amory accused, the humor gone from his voice.

"You're probably right about that," Lucan agreed. "And the rest of your family, for that matter."

"Not Eden," Amory reminded him. "Eden is safe."

Lucan didn't respond verbally, but a flash of hatred turned his expression from carefully entertained to menacingly hostile. In response, Amory stood up taller and took a step forward.

They fired more magic simultaneously, and the electricity met in midair. The two streams of magic became palpable energy fields caught in a road block in the middle of the room. Their energy fields popped and crackled the longer they stood locked together, growing stronger with more force fed to them with each passing moment.

I decided to join the battle. If I knocked Lucan off balance for even a moment Amory would be able take the advantage. I stepped forward, raising my hand strategically and building my magic in order to strike.

A blast to my back destroyed all hope of taking the upper hand, however. I had been paying too close of attention to Lucan and left myself vulnerable from behind. I stumbled forward, catching myself with my hands on the smooth concrete floor.

I rolled over, throwing out my electricity before I could even see who had attacked me. My magic found its mark on a tall, dark-haired Titan who fell to the ground equally as surprised as I was. I was to my feet and over him before he could recover. I didn't even bother with the pretense of extending my hand and just started extracting his magic before he knew what was happening.

315

A man's deep, savage scream from behind me, distracted me and when I whirled around hoping Amory had finally dealt Lucan a death blow, I was devastated to see the scenario I had imagined, reversed.

Lucan stood triumphantly over Amory, a sinister victory grin twisting his lips, his eyes wild and drunk with power. He was draining Amory of his magic. He was taking the original life blood of this race and grafting it to his own corrupt and prejudice bloodline.

"No!" I screamed, forgetting about the half-drained Titan laying on the ground and racing at Lucan, pushing him with my bare hands but finding him unmoving.

I looked down at the anguished, onyx eyes of my grandfather and lost myself in despair.

"Get away from him!" I screamed again, sending my magic full force at Lucan, but not even phasing him.

"He was trying to save you," Lucan laughed out loud; a dark, haunting laugh that would cloud my nightmares for the rest of my life.

"Eden...." Amory whispered through clenched teeth. I knelt at his side, taking his hand in mine, not knowing what else to do.

Suddenly and quite surprisingly, a sharp stream of electricity began flowing through our grasped palms. I tried to jerk away, overcome by the force of magic. Amory gripped my hand tighter, pulling me with unexpected strength back to the floor.

I looked up at him, into his black endless eyes and realized he was giving me his magic. Lucan was taking what he could, but Amory was still in control of his destiny.

I pressed my palm tighter into his and braced myself against the force of Amory's electricity rushing into my blood. His magic was different than mine: lighter, deeper, older. His was the first magic. The ancient magic and it fused with mine in a jolting and exhausting cataclysm.

Sweat poured from my forehead, and my arms and legs began to tremble violently. Amory had more magic than anyone I had ever encountered or taken from. His magic seemed endless, filling my blood for what seemed well beyond the capacity I would be able to hold.

Lucan stood above us in arrogant triumph. Whether he knew

Amory was splitting his magic or not, I didn't know. But either way the evil King was pleased to finally end the long life of the last Oracle.

The flow of magic slowed and Amory leaned his head back against the cold, hard floor with a peaceful sigh. I held tightly to his hand, hoping to give him back his magic, to revive him and help him fight again.

Lucan stumbled backwards, drunk with power and unstable from Amory's magic. I, too, felt wobbly and dazed.

"It is finished, Eden," Amory whispered, closing his eyes when I tried to return his magic and nothing happened. "It's time, my child. It's time for me to go home," he smiled peacefully, and his face relaxed into the ancient man that had lived the kind of life that was happy to end. "Carry on, Eden. Carry on and finish the task." And then he was gone.

Chapter Forty-Four

"No!" I screamed, over and over again, banging my fist against Amory's chest, refusing to give up, refusing to believe that he was dead.

Tears streamed in unrelenting waves of desperate emotion. I laid my head against his chest, hoping for the faint sound of a heart beating for survival but there was nothing, not even the echo of a life once lived. I kept my head against Amory's still warm body, breathing him in one more time.

"Eden, Love, it's time to go," Kiran called to me from above, in his soft, accented voice.

I looked up at him, confused for a moment. The world around me spun and I caught myself against the cold concrete, afraid I would vomit. Kiran held out a hand to me, as if offering help.

"No," I whispered hoarsely back.

"Eden, they are waiting. It's time to go," Kiran was calm and patient, waiting for me to reach for him, waiting for me to let him take me away. Talbott stood by his side protectively, but quietly. He was bruised and unkempt, his clothes torn and hair messy, signs of the fight.

I stood up slowly, without his help. I took in my surroundings painfully. The battle was over and from where I stood inside the barn it looked as if the snow had stopped blowing as well. The Titans, hundreds of them, surrounded what was left of the Resistance, loading them into armored vehicles.

I searched slowly for Avalon, letting my gaze fall on every single member of the Rebellion, on Lilly, on Jericho, on Roxie, promising each one of them silently that I would give them retribution for my betrayal. That I would see them again. And that I would save them.

Finally, my eyes found Avalon. He was beaten and bloodied almost beyond recognition. His face was swollen and one shoulder hung awkwardly lower than his other one. He was surrounded by two dozen guards and isolated from the rest of the captured.

He was watching me, his face expressionless and his eyes cold. I stared at him, wanting something, needing something....

hatred…. hurt…. hope.

Something.

"I am not going anywhere with you," I growled, my tone acid.

"Eden," Kiran's voice broke and he reached out to me again.

Slowly, but steadily more Guards started to surround the two of us. Soon we were standing in the middle of two dozen Guards, watching us carefully.

"You did this," I accused venomously, and Kiran dropped his hand to his side.

"Eden, my love, I had no other choice," his voice was full of emotion and behind his eyes, what I would have once considered tears.

I couldn't trust him now. I couldn't allow myself to believe his lies, or allow him to manipulate me again. Everything had been an evil deception. Every single thing and I had just paid the consequences; I wouldn't suffer any more from naivety. From this moment forward, every breath I took would be dedicated to destroying the Kendrick line. To finding justice for the lives lost here today. I was finished with Kiran, in every sense of the word.

"My grandfather is dead!" I screamed at him, stomping my foot, sending a ripple of magic shuttering across the smooth concrete floor. "My brother is in handcuffs!" I continued to yell, pointing a stiff finger at him. "You had a choice! Damn it, Kiran, you had a choice."

"Not if I wanted to keep you safe, Eden!" he raised his voice at me, frustration reaching a boiling point. His face grew red and he took an angry step forward. "This was all for you! So that you could have a life. So that we could have a life together," he finished quietly.

"So you betrayed my trust and sacrificed the only family I have ever known, just so we could be together?" the pain evident in my voice was unforgivable, but I was desperate for a rational explanation, for a reason for the chaos and shambles my life had been reduced to in a matter of hours.

"I had no other choice," Kiran said again with conviction. "When I realized there was another option, another sacrifice…. When it became clear that I could save you…. I had to," his voice broke again and he took another step forward. "And now we can have the life we dreamed of, we can be together now.... forever."

"You should be thankful, Eden," Lucan chastised me from outside the tightening circle of Guards. "My son paid a price for you, yes, but he saved you, didn't he? And isn't that the most important thing?" Lucan was relishing in Amory's stolen magic and I breathed deeply trying to hold myself together.

"No, it is not the most important thing!" I screamed, my voice echoing emptily in the rafters of the barn, my magic shaking the hard steel violently. "Why Avalon? Take me instead, leave Avalon and take me," I demanded desperately.

"You don't get it child," Lucan broke through the Titans, facing me head on. "Kiran made his deal; he gave me Avalon for you. And as it turns out, because of your brother, I don't need you. So now, I have what I want. And my son has what he wants. And that is how this story ends," he finished coldly.

I swayed back and forth, feeling overwhelmingly sick. The ground was spinning and a high-pitched ringing sound was growing louder in my ears. I reached out; trying to balance myself and Kiran was at my side in a moment, steadying me, holding on to my waist.

"Do not touch me!" I shouted, finding my equilibrium and fleeing from Kiran's arms. I bounced off of a Titan and felt the world closing in around me.

"Eden, stop being ridiculous; it is time to go," Kiran reprimanded me like I was a small child, but his patience was gone. Lucan looked on with unmasked amusement.

"I will never go anywhere with you," I spat back, hatred seeping from the deepest parts of my soul.

"You are being difficult. This is unnecessary," he took another step towards me, and I moved around in the circle, unwilling to ever touch him again. "I will take you with me, whether you want to go or not," he promised in a low, menacing voice.

"No," I said simply. "You have taken everything from me! Everything!" I shouted. "You don't get what you want anymore. You don't get me!"

"Get in the car Eden!" Kiran shouted back, and the floor trembled underneath the force of his magic.

"No," I whispered, my body shaking from rage.

"God, you are stubborn," Kiran collected himself, rolling his head casually, as if his neck was bothering him. He squinted his eyes at me, as if trying to read me, as if I wasn't being clear enough. "Guards," he commanded simply with a nod of his head in the direction of the armored cars.

In that one gesture of possession, I couldn't take it anymore. I rushed at him, intending to rip him apart if I had to. I felt insanity overcome me and I was blind with rage.

I didn't make it to him. The surrounding Guards were on top of me sooner than I had anticipated they would be; Talbott stepped in front of Kiran, blocking my path. Six men grabbed hold of me with iron grips, holding me in the air. I kicked and screamed like a mad woman, shouting incoherently and shaking my hair wildly out of its ponytail holder.

"You betrayed me!" I shouted when I felt myself come back to my senses.

"Betrayed you?" Kiran took a brave step around Talbott towards me, getting close to my face, while the Guards held me still. "I did this for you! I saved you! If it weren't for me, it would be you being loaded on that truck, not him. You would be the sacrifice. You should be thanking me!" he finished loudly.

Anger washed over me in new waves and I spit in his face, staring down at him with more hate than I believed one person could feel.

Kiran wiped at his face, completely disgusted and a Guard lifted his hand against my face, back-handing me in an unspoken demand for respect for my Crown Prince.

"Do not touch her." Kiran turned his wrath on the Guard that slapped me. "Never touch her like that again, or it will be the last thing you do." He growled, but it did nothing to calm the tempest I could feel rising to the surface.

Kiran walked away from me, running his hands through his hair. He turned back and looked at me for a long time while I struggled against the hold of the Guards. "Eden," he continued with more restraint, but his blistering frustration was barely controlled, "I will give you one last chance to stop this foolishness and come with me."

"I will never go anywhere with you!" I shouted again, lashing out against the Guard, but unsuccessfully.

"Fine," Kiran shouted back. "Enjoy your life.... Alone!" he turned around and began to walk away.

"Guards, load her up." Lucan demanded calmly.

"Father, no," Kiran spun around facing his father. "You have what you want, leave her be. If she doesn't want to come with us, that's her own choice."

"I can't allow that," Lucan replied, half laughing. "She is a liability, and clearly mad."

"I said no. She is free to go," Kiran turned his frustration on his father.

"I will decide who is free and who is not," Lucan's voice turned cold.

"We had a deal, Father!" Kiran protested with carefully controlled rage.

"Let me remind you that I am also your King and my word is the law!" Lucan shouted at his son and Kiran flinched in response.

"Your Highness, please. She cannot do anything on her own. You said it yourself, she's mad anyway," Kiran begged softly and with more respect.

Lucan thought over Kiran's words for a moment, looking me over with calculated suspicion. "Fine," he said simply and turned around, walking toward a black sedan, surrounded by Guards.

"This is the second time I have saved your life." Kiran turned his attention back to me. "But I promise you, if we should ever meet again, you will be begging for me to end it."

"The next time I see you, Kiran, or your father for that matter," I replied calmly, I had found sanity again, at least for the moment. "You will be the ones hiding from me. I promise you that."

Kiran laughed in response, "We will see," He sobered up, looking at me one last time, "After this, I will not protect you anymore; you are on your own."

He turned around, following his father. I couldn't take it anymore; I couldn't hold back the rage. With a frustrated shudder of magic, I sent all of the Guard around me, including those holding on so tightly, falling to the floor in helplessness. I righted myself on the concrete and with one last guttural scream, I released another powerful blow of electricity against them, sending the remaining Guard thirty yards back and struggling to get to their feet.

Kiran glanced back at me, hardly paying any attention, before climbing into the sedan behind his father. A Guard shut the door behind him. I watched as the car drove away, through the blood soaked snow, off the farm and out of my life.

I looked back at the last of the Resistance members being loaded into the trucks and panicked, not seeing Avalon anywhere.

Where are you? I demanded telepathically.

It doesn't matter. Do not come after me. He replied sternly.

You know that's not going to happen. I said honestly.

All right, fine. But follow Amory's orders first, find our parents. Like he said, they're going to have to come out of hiding. Avalon instructed me, still the leader of the Resistance. Unwilling to believe it should be any other way a tear escaped my eye, falling hot against my cheek.

South America? But where in South America? I asked, frustrated. I didn't have time to search the entire continent of South America; I had to save Avalon before I lost him for good, too.

Start with Silas; he must have seen this coming. Start with him; he'll have some answers for you. He's in Peru, in the mountains, the colony is not far from Machu Picchu; once there, just follow the magic. Avalon's instructions got faster, the farther from me the armored vehicle drove.

I should be coming after you now, before.... before anything happens to you! I begged desperately.

No. There are too many of them, you'll just end up locked away with me. Avalon was firm, but the emotion behind his command was heart wrenching.

But what if.... what if they sacrifice you before I can get to you? I broke down, tears of rage and heartbreak poured out of my eyes and I fell to my knees, left alone in the wreckage of the farm.

I have a plan. His thoughts turned smug. I am going to give you all of my magic. All of it. Lucan cannot sacrifice a human, now can he? He asked, pleased with himself.

But he can kill a human. Pretty easily.... I replied dryly, realizing it might be our only chance for survival.

Yes, but he won't. He'll save me for collateral. You know that. He reasoned soundly and I couldn't argue with him. We both knew it was our only option. We won't be able to communicate though; if I do this, our connection is cut off completely.

Avalon, I am.... I am so sorry. I begged for forgiveness, using the shared emotional channel we shared, one last time.

I don't blame you, Eden. Avalon answered, forgiveness flooding me. This was a tragedy, but it was not your fault. And now, you are our only hope. You cannot fail. Not for my sake, but for the sake of your people.

I will find you again, Avalon. And I will rectify this. I promised.

I believe you. He said with the utmost confidence in me.

Stay strong, and Avalon.... carry on. I echoed Amory's last command to me and I felt Avalon close his eyes in a silent agreement.

Then I will see you soon. Avalon whispered inside of our heads, preparing to release his magic completely.

Yes, you will. I swore and then felt my blood flood with my brother's identical magic and our minds close for good. We were completely separate, in both mind and magic and it dawned on me how very alone I was now.

I had a mission, an impossible task ahead of me and there was not a moment to spare. But before I could continue on the epic journey ahead of me, there was one last thing I needed to do. One final end to tie up.

Chapter Forty-Five

I watched as the last of the prisoners were driven away, before turning sharply on my heel and running from the barn. The farm was eerily quiet, covered in fresh snow and not occupied by a single soul other than myself. I shuddered, but not from the cold, from the dark realization that I was entirely alone in this world. I was completely alone.

I trudged through the deep snow around the vandalized farmhouse, passed the torn apart porch, and explosions still burning their magical flames. The sky was a haunting gray in the middle of the night and light bounced off the blanket of snow illuminating my path to the back of the house.

The backyard had been untouched and was a stark contrast to the destruction of the house, barn and everywhere in between. The snow was completely pure, not a foot print, or animal trail in the miles of snow that lay like a fresh sheet across an empty bed.

Somewhere buried beneath the virgin snow was the cellar and I was determined to get to it. I built the magic in my blood, slowly bringing the electricity to a boil and unleashed it against the iced-over back yard.

My magic was foreign to me, a melting pot of dozens of energies that didn't belong to me. The most alien of all, though, was Amory's ancient electricity. I could still feel his distinct identity running through my veins and it was enough that I had to turn my head and be sick.

I recovered and forced myself to focus; pushing the iced-over snow away from the place I remembered the cellar being. When I didn't find it right away, I let more magic out, creating a small blizzard of my own design, moving the snow out of the way. The barren, frozen ground below the surface of the snow felt symbolic to me, empty and arctic, descriptions that were synonymous with my own heart now.

The cellar door was there then, underneath the mountains of snow and frozen to the ground. I blasted the cellar door off and was suddenly hit with a fierce urgency. I ran down the stairs, the temperature dropping severely the deeper into the earth I ran, but I hardly noticed.

I didn't bother with the torches, or even my magic. I ran blindly through the underground tunnel, completely focused. I ran straight into the heavy stone door that separated the secret initiation room from the narrow tunnel, banging my head.

I stumbled backwards, frustrated. I stared at the door in the darkness for a moment, trying to decide whether to respect what it stood for or if it even mattered anymore.

I couldn't make myself believe that it mattered at all, so I raised my hand and exploded the door off of its hinges and crumbled the heavy stone into long, jagged pieces.

I walked over the rubble; into the room I had never been allowed in, never belonged in. The space felt smaller now than it had through Avalon's eyes. I spun around slowly, trying to decide where to start, my fingers drifting gently over the chair used for restraint.

I turned my magic on the candles, hundreds of flames bursting to life in unison. The cauldron in the far corner of the room bubbled with iridescent foam and the tube used to extract whatever was inside, sat on the workspace next to it, protected in a glass case.

I walked over to the luminous liquid with careful steps and trembling fingers. I had seen Lilly go through this; I knew the recovery period was extensive. I was worried the process wouldn't even be possible without help. But I had to try.

I had finally made my decision. I would join the Resistance.

It seemed silly now, maybe even unnecessary. I couldn't move forward though, until I had righted this wrong.

These people hadn't asked more of me than joining their cause, a cause I had looked down on in judgment of its motives. And in the end, I betrayed that cause.

I had blood on my hands. Lives had ended because of me. And the rest, loaded up in what felt like cattle cars, probably being driven to their death. I had lost those I loved most.

There was no more indecision clouding my mind. No more hopeful scenarios to dream about. Happiness had died, and it was time to fight for retribution.

I pulled the cylindrical tube from its glass case, marveling at the weight of the glass. I plunged it into the lighted liquid, the bubbles burning my hands, leaving blisters. I gripped tighter to the cylinder, afraid I would drop it into the depth of the unknown, and unwilling to stop until I had filled the tube.

The liquid was scorching hot, and the glass became almost impossible to hold, the more light entered the cylinder. I tried protecting my hands with magic, but either the luminous solution was immune to my magic or it was too strong for it.

The tube was nearly filled and my hands felt like the skin was being melted from them. I took several quick, deep breaths preparing me for the worst and then courageously lifted the cylinder from the liquid and pressed it firmly to my neck, just below my earlobe.

A horrifying scream echoed in my ears and it was several moments before I realized that it was coming from me. My blood grew hot, beyond boiling and I fell to the floor in agonizing pain.

The liquid continued to drain into my blood from its point of contact with my skin and I forced myself to remain conscious, to hold the glass. I couldn't see how much light had drained from the tube, but my body and consequently the room around me began to glow in the royal blue that defined my magic.

Tears of pain streamed down my face, tears that were unstoppable. I tried to breathe through the pain, but it was excruciating. I reminded myself I lived through the King's Curse and I would live through this as well.

I fought for consciousness, pressing the glass firmer against my skin. If I fell into the deep abyss of sleep now, I wouldn't finish the job. I would have to start over and go through this again. I had to close my eyes though, the blinding blue was growing stronger, turning to a pure white that burned my retinas.

My arms were violently trembling and I wasn't even sure if my fingers and palms would be recognizable when this was finished. I lay on the cold dirt floor, flailing and fighting forces that felt much stronger than myself.

The last drop of iridescent liquid dropped from the glass into my bloodstream; there was reprieve. I threw the cylinder on the floor next to me, as soon as it contacted the rocky dirt it shattered into a million pieces of shrapnel, glistening in the candlelight.

The light finally extinguished, I lay there, too exhausted to move, too afraid to look at the damage done to my hands. The liquid spread out inside of me, infecting every blood vessel, pumping strongly from my toes to my heart to my head and back down again.

I breathed in preparation; gripping at the floor, digging my fingernails into the frozen ground, and feeling the first flicker of internal flame ignite in my blood. The flame spread, catching the rest of my bloodstream with a forest fire of pain rushing through my body and blinding me with torment.

Finding no rest, I flailed helplessly on the floor, cutting my arms and face with the broken glass littering the dirt next to me.

If someone would have asked me which pain was worse, the King's Curse or the initiation, I don't know if I could have said. Both were the equivalents of the eternal suffering belonging solely to the gates of hell. With the initiation, there was no one to help me. No one to share my agony with. No one to encourage me to fight through the overwhelming death and survive.

I remembered Avalon and his resolve to survive the King's Curse. It would be the same resolve he would fight Lucan with until the day he died. It was the resolve that gave him confidence in the back of the prisoner's truck, surrounded by Guard and without magic to heal his broken bones. It was the same resolve that would give him defiance even in the bottom of a prison cell, being tortured and beaten. Even then, he would not recall his magic. Even then he would stand for what was good. Even then he would fight for justice.

And that was what I needed to do. I needed to fight. Not just this excruciating torment, but the whole of the Monarchy. Avalon was enough to remind me that there was good left, there was an end that needed writing and it was left to me.

As the darkness clouded my mind, and the walls of unconsciousness closed in on me, I remembered Avalon and believed I would survive this. I had to.

My people had no one else to save them. I was the last of the Rebellion. There was no one, but me.

I was the next Oracle.

I woke up slowly. My head was pounding and my blood still felt uncomfortably hot, suffocating my lungs and slowing my heart rate. The snow had started again and was falling heavily on me, covering me with thick, ashy snowflakes.

I lay still for a moment longer, allowing my thoughts to gather completely and my senses to waken. The snow was unrelenting, but I was hot, so hot.

My eyes flew open and I sat up quickly, not on the dirt floor of the underground cellar but in the middle of a forest.... our forest.

Our forest that had been set on fire. Flames devoured the once breath-taking flowering trees, hungrily engulfing the delicate petals, leaving no evidence of their beauty behind.

I gasped, inhaling the ash I had mistaken for snow. As it fell down from the ruins of our dream-world it covered me in a thick paste of gray grime. I stood up, shaking out my hair, but the flames of the fire were destroying the forest too quickly for it to matter. The ash would continue to fall until there was nothing but scorched earth remaining in the celestial meeting place Kiran and I had fallen in love in.

I shouted his name, over the roar of the inferno, piercing the very depths of the magical world. But nothing came back. I knew he wasn't here.

He had brought me here to prove a point and nothing more. This was the end of anything we had.

I sunk back to the earth, pulling my knees to my chest and wrapping my arms around them. The glistening emerald of my engagement ring looked out of place in the middle of the destruction around me.

I held up my ring-finger, feeling violently ill, and then I fingered the necklace still dangling against my chest. How had I been so blinded by sparkling gifts and empty promises? How had I let this happen?

In this place, in the place built by Kiran, the architecture of a secret, enchanting world made only for us, I couldn't think about Amory, or Avalon or the lost. Watching the towering trees reduced to cinders and the wildflowers disintegrate into the raining ash I thought only of Kiran.

I had loved him deeply and wholly. And he was gone.

For the first time and the only time, I allowed myself to grieve not the lives lost today, but the love lost. I allowed myself to feel the pain of a heart ripped in two and the sickening separation of soul mates.

I let my head fall to my knees and wept, loudly and without

control. Above the roaring of the flames eating away all of the life in this place were my sobs; my throaty, raspy, raw cries of pain.

I stayed that way for what felt like hours, until the flames died down, leaving blackened tree stumps and the smell of sulfur burning my nostrils. I cried until there was nothing left, until there were no more tears left to be shed.

I grieved for Kiran completely. And when I finally left the now-barren wasteland that would be abandoned in the empty places of my subconscious, I left with a new resolve and a new dedication. I would have no more thoughts about a long lost love, or the soul mate who betrayed me.

I woke up into reality, on the cold dirt floor of the cellar. I stood, still weak, not having any idea if days had passed or only hours. I walked through the wreckage of the room and through the now softly lit hallway. I climbed the stone steps into the first light of morning.

The sun was rising in the east, painting the wide sky with pinks and soft purples, and just the hint of blue stretching beyond the horizon. The fresh snow from the night before left the air crisp and pure, the iciness brought cleansing in my charred lungs. It was going to be a beautiful day, one of those rare winter mornings when temperatures reach above freezing and the hope of a close spring was renewed.

I stared at the rising sun, feeling as though it were my kin. It was my turn to rise, my turn to shine. I pulled the engagement ring off of my finger and the necklace off of my neck, slipping the expensive ring onto the silver chain and then back over my head.

The jewels were not a reminder of a finished love or even of a forgotten life, they were tokens to fight by; the reminders of a vengeance left wanting and the war I would wage. They were the fuel I would light this fire with and then burn this Kingdom to the ground.

I would find Avalon and rescue him and the others. I would bring down the Monarchy. I would end the Kendrick line. I would destroy every last one of them. And I would start with finding my parents and rebuilding the Rebellion.

I had no idea how to find them or where to start, but it didn't matter. My mind had concrete clarity and I would do whatever it took to follow through, to carry on and finish the fight.

List of Resistance Teams
* Denotes the Team Leader

Brazil Team (Also known as the Rescued Team)

Ebanks Camera
Oscar Rodriguez
Ronan Hannigan
Jett Fisher

Omaha Team

*Avalon St. Andrews
Jericho Bentley
Titus Kelly
Xander Akin
Xavier Akin

Czech Republic Team

*Ryder Thompson
Fiona Thompson
Roxie Powers
Baxter Smith
Felipe Gonzalas
Trenton Chase

Australia Team

*Hamant Kumar
Christi Rogobete
Priya Fahir
Eshe Iyare
An Tang

Swiss Team

*Alina Pascut
Alexandre Ballamont

Hale Oliver
Ben Hamilton
Evie Santoz

Morocco Team

*Caden Halstead
Bex Costello
Kya Hasting
Lucy Barello

India Team

*Te Che
Pan Che
Grace Lewis
Naima Desai
Sunny Magar

South Africa Team

Abraham Patel
Henrik Van de Merwe
Jess Zuma
Mamello Mensah
Mandisa Mensah
Lenka Bello

About the Author

Rachel Higginson was born and raised in Nebraska, but spent her college years traveling the world. She married her high school sweetheart and spends her days raising their growing family. She is obsessed with bad reality TV and any and all Young Adult Fiction.

Hopeless Magic is her second book, and the second part in a four part saga, The Star-Crossed Series. Fearless Magic, the third installment of the series is now available.

Follow Rachel on her blog at:
www.rachel.higginson.com

Or on Twitter:
@mywritesdntbite

Or on her Facebook page:
Rachel Higginson

Keep Reading for an Excerpt from Fearless Magic, available now!

Acknowledgements

I am so grateful to get to write an acknowledgement section that I just might start back as far as I can remember and start thanking everyone I've ever met! Ok, maybe I won't. But there are so many people that have helped bring me to where I am today that I should probably start naming them!

First of all, this gift of writing that sometimes feels more like a miracle at the end of the day came from God alone and to Him I give the glory. He has had a plan since the beginning and I am so blessed to be invited along on this wild ride.

Thanks to my loving family, who have put up with my sleepless nights, and all of my "Not right nows…" and "In a little bits…." You've put up with a dirty house, dirty laundry and let's face it a dirty mommy, but you have supported me through it all and I thank you for that.

Thanks to my parents, who promised me from childhood I could do and be anything that I wanted. To my dad, who although might be disappointed I'm not a missionary in the jungles of Africa, would be proud to know I followed my dream. And to my mom who has spent endless hours babysitting, encouraging me, spreading the word about my books and even done my dishes and laundry a few times! Thank you for your support.

Thanks to Kylee who sat by me for hours and hours while I bounced ideas and thoughts off her. To Pat who let us exchange yard work for cover art. And to Carolynn for going through the first, very, very rough versions and donating her editing eye.

Thanks to Jenn Nunez who took me under her wing and walked me through this whole crazy process step by step, holding my hand and answering all of my millions and millions of questions!!

Finally, thanks to my amazing husband, Zach. Without him, I would never have taken the plunge and published, or continued to publish, or maybe even continued to write. He has been a constant source of encouragement, always helping me be better and pushing me to do more. Love you Zachary.

The old van rumbled to a stop in front of a faded, red sign declaring the entrance to the Inca Trail, the path that would lead to the ancient ruins of Machu Picchu. The trek would take four days of hiking, possibly longer since it was wet season and already the sky had opened up, emptying its stores of water upon the earth.

The trail was technically closed for maintenance during the month of February, but I would be taking it anyway. I was hoping the entire citadel would be less busy than usual, thanks to the consistent torrential down-pours that plagued the southern hemisphere in the winter months.

I took my bag from the short Peruvian man that had given me a ride from Lima to here. An old friend of Angelica's, he had driven the thirty hours with me in a much-appreciated silence. I handed him a stack of Nuevo Sol, the local currency, and turned my back on him.

Walking forward, I could feel the faint call of magic in the distance. They were out there. Somewhere. I had no idea where, or how to find them, but I could feel the faint calling of magic and the prickling of electricity igniting in my blood.

The path was well worn, and difficult to walk. The ancient stones were slippery in the relentless rain and the air thin with the altitude. But I was moved by the beauty of the Andes.

I had never seen a place so vividly and distinctly green. The deep greens of the trees blanketed the distant mountain sides in dark, flowing tones that stood drastically against the stone of the towering mountains. And the lighter, softer greens of grass stood out starkly in the landscape as if the two greens were not the same color at all. God's brush strokes had painted these mountains and valleys with the blessedness of variety, and I could feel my soul swell in awe of the creation surrounding me.

The sky had never felt so big from this vantage point, even under the thick canopy that housed the trail I walked. The rivers and streams tumbled down the mountain side in blue ribbons of moving water, weaving in and out of the thick forests. The raw beauty of such an organic environment reminded me that I was only a small piece to the elegant and divine puzzle that was this life. As small as I was in the middle of this magnanimous mountainside, so was my life in the scope of eternity. Yet, somehow, I found that comforting.

I walked for hours, deep into the wilderness that paved the

way to a once sacred escape for kings of old. Not that long ago, I would have been terrified to have had to take this journey alone. But now there was nothing, no fear, no anxiety. Just purpose.

I was beyond childish fears of the dark or being alone. I had reached beyond the naive immaturity that keeps one afraid of the unknown. When my grandfather died, something had broken inside of me. When they took my brother, the innocent part of my soul had died. When I watched my friends, my loved ones, be loaded into armored cars as prisoners, all of my fears had been faced. And when my heart had been ripped in two by the cruelty of betrayal, I had given up on emotions and feelings all together.

Alone on the trail, I tried to stay focused on revenge, on those loved ones I would vindicate, but my thoughts wondered unforgivably. I thought of him, that name I would not let myself speak out loud or even think. I thought of the man that had made me so blissfully happy and then betrayed those that I loved in the name of a selfish conquest.

The tears fell from my eyes hot with the stabbing pain of the memory of his betrayal. He had taken everything from me, everything. And then left me a shattered, and broken ghost of myself.

I stopped to catch my breath at the top of a slippery, steep, stone stairway and grasped at the necklace I had tucked underneath my rain jacket. The large stone of the engagement ring dug into my chest, a painful reminder of its existence, but one that I had come to treasure. As long as that ring stabbed at the place where my heart used to beat with desire for its giver, I would always be reminded of what he had done.

And now, alone on this trail, this journey to redemption, I would find others that had been wronged by him and his bloodline. I would rebuild the army of the Rebellion and we would fight against him and what he stood for. And we would not stop until there was nothing left of the Kendrick bloodline, until every last one of them was dead and buried.

I was soaked to the bone when the ancient city for Incan kings appeared in the distance. The rain had not let up for even a moment, but even through the fog and haze of the rain, the ruins, nestled against the steep cliffs, stood as a beacon for my weary legs. I had hiked the trail for days, fighting against the mud, the slippery stone and the overwhelming fatigue.

A few times, I had set up the small pop-up tent that fit easily into my backpack and slipped into the exhausted, dreamless sleep of the well-worn. I hadn't truly been able to sleep since before.... since before the battle and always I was woken in pools of cold sweat, screaming and lashing out. The nightmares kept the wild animals away and my magic kept my blood warm in the frozen temperatures once the sun had set.

The nightmares had plagued me since Avalon had been taken. Every time my eyes were closed the haunting torment of my subconscious attacked and I was always thankful just to be awake, gasping for air and clutching my throat, but awake.

At first I wondered if maybe they were Dream-Walks, that I was being tortured in a subconscious sleep-world without my knowledge. But always before, the Dream-Walk had been done consciously, and I was always capable of remembering the details when I awoke. These nightmares were fuzzy and disorienting and always, the particulars slipped away before I could put them together.

I breathed in relief, finally making my way past the modern structures set up as gift shops and ticket booths and to the doorway leading into the age-old city. It was very early in the morning and there was not a soul around. I treaded carefully through the stone passageway and onto the rough stone walkways that had stood the test of time.

I was alone. At this height, and with the ancient city sprawling down the mountainside at my feet, I had never felt more alone. I walked the stone pathways and up the hundreds of stone steps to the highest point of the Incan citadel.

I stood next to a wide square stone that was nearly taller than me and had some kind of pyramid built into the top of it and felt myself moved again. Machu Picchu was a religious experience, a moment in my life that my soul felt bigger than myself.

I stood with arms wide and chin tipped towards the sun rising in the east, over the pointed mountain peaks. I breathed the thin, crisp air finding a perspective bigger than myself, bigger than my problems. I stayed like that for a while, drinking in the sacredness surrounding me.

The Shape-Shifter colony was close, the magic had grown steadily stronger and I could feel the direction it was located in, clearly. I had been pressed with urgency until this moment at the height of an antiquated citadel that still stood, despite the modern world, as a gateway to the past. The hundreds of buildings made from chiseled stone, stairs that were worn with age and use, and religious structures for antiquated gods all but forgotten, shined as sobering reminders that Kingdoms rise and fall. I was just a small piece in the tides of change that dictated the currents of life. I had a part to play, but if I failed, someone else would rise. Injustice would not always be victor of this life.

The magic began to grow stronger, my blood igniting with the warning signs of an approaching magic. I dropped my arms, and opened my eyes, but I would not move. Whoever was out there would come to me.

A flash of black between two stone columns caught my attention. I had seen wild animals along the hike here, but the soft fur of an alpaca was nothing quite like the sleek black coat of a wild panther. I tilted my head, waiting for the man to turn back human.

"I was coming to you," I called out before the man made himself known. "You didn't have to meet me."

"You're confident that you could have found us?" he asked in his rich Jamaican accent, smugly confident that I would not have been able to.

Silas stepped from behind the stone archway, leading up to the sacred high place. His skin was as dark as the fur of his panther shape. He wore the same brown work pants and forest green sweater I had seen him in the night I first met him.

"I guess, we will never know," I replied, not willing to be humble, but not wanting to insult him either.

"So, you have come then. It has gone badly," Silas stated, and his words felt like a harsh accusation.

"Yes, but you knew that it would," I answered. We stood awkwardly far apart from each other. I had expected a warm greeting and a man thankful that I had come, but he eyed me suspiciously from a distance as if I were a threat.

"Still, I had hoped things would go.... differently," he looked passed me, at the surrounding mountains. His gray eyes clouded with sorrow, and his shoulders slumped in defeat.

"So did I," I surprised myself with morbid sarcasm.

"The old man?" Silas asked, ignoring my poor attempt at dark humor.

"Dead," I stated simply and then cleared my throat quickly to cover the emotion threatening to surface.

Silas took a step back, as if I had slapped him, before continuing, "And the boy?"

"Taken," I replied in the same way.

"And you?" his eyes flashed back to suspicion and then met me with new interest. "How is it that you are here?"

I was surprised by his question. "You are the one who told me to come," I lashed out angrily; how dare he give me cryptic instructions and then question my obedience.

"Did I tell you to take so many magics? You are radiating with stolen blood," his eyes turned from suspicion to hard distrust.

"Yes, I am. So, what?" I crossed my arms defensively. "Do you know what it was like when they came for my family? Were you there?" it was my turn to accuse, but I answered my own questions before he even opened his mouth to speak, "No, you were not. You were here, protected by your mountains and hidden from sight. My people were massacred. They were betrayed. My grandfather was murdered and my brother kidnapped. Do not question my stolen magics when I was fighting to save those that I love most," my voice broke, and a hot tear fell free from the prison of my eye and slipped without permission down my rain soaked cheek.

"And so you take other's magic without remorse?" he asked, disbelieving.

"I have remorse!" I screamed at the old man, my voice echoing off the mountains in a chorus of anger.

"No," he accused quietly. "No, you are an evil thing now. Unrecognizable and evil," his voice had dropped to a whisper, but I had no trouble hearing his accusations.

I knew that he was right.

"Will you help me?" I cut to the chase, unwilling to continue the hurtful small-talk.

"No, we will not help you," he said simply and with finality.

341

He turned from me, this conversation was over.

I watched him leave. I had come here for nothing. He would not help me and I had nowhere else to go. Worst of all, the last of my fears had been realized. I wasn't myself anymore. I wasn't a future Queen, or the next Oracle. I had slipped into an evil version of myself, the greatness that had once been whispered with my name would stay a hushed murmur that floated away with the wind. I wasn't recognizable anymore, Silas had said it.

I was evil. There was no more good left.

.GM

Made in the USA
San Bernardino, CA
10 April 2017